ZEN AND THE ART OF CANNIBALISM

A ZOMEDY

DANIEL YOUNGER

MUTANT PANDA

This is a work of fiction. The characters, incidents, and dialogue are drawn from the author's imagination and are not to be construed as real. Any resemblance to actual events or persons, living or dead, is entirely coincidental.

Cover illustration by Skot Lachance

Mutant Panda will kill you if you try to steal it. You've been warned. Find out more at mutant-panda.tumblr.com

Also by Daniel Younger:
Delirious: A Collection of Stories
The Wrath of Con: A Novel (Coming Soon)

Get in touch with Daniel:
danieljyounger@icloud.com
@YoungerDaniel
danielyounger.com

ISBN-10: 1511794070
ISBN-13: 978-1511794077

FOR STACEY REBERTZ

Who once said:
"Zombies are way done. Give me something new, and I'll
give you a cookie."

To which I replied:
"Well, I sure like cookies."

ZEN AND THE ART OF CANNIBALISM

A ZOMEDY

PART I
BAD MOON RISING

CHAPTER 1
EVIL UNLEASHED

The beast arrived in a Tasmanian Devil cyclone at the crossroads. It was a lonely stretch of coastal highway. The moon hung like a nibbled cheese wheel in the clouds, brambles shuddered in the breeze, and a low-hanging fog crept in from the coast. The huge black dog padded to the center of the road, surveying the intersection with glowing red eyes, and bayed at the moon with the sound of a thousand souls being shoved through a blender.

The dog grinned, wagging his huge tail. It was good to be back.

He was a little over four-hundred pounds, shaggy, looking somewhere between a wolf and a grizzly bear. His name was Seth, and he was a hellhound.

It had been seventy-six years since he'd last walked the realm of man. Last time, he collected the soul of a twenty-seven year old bluesman who'd traded it for fame and fortune. The irony, of course, was Bobby Johnson never asked for the fame to be in his lifetime, and it wasn't until long after Seth had chomped off the bluesman's head that fortune started rolling in.

And he might have even lived to see it, if he'd had the good sense to bring Seth a MilkBone. Sure, he was evil, but he wasn't *unreasonable*. Seth hated people with every ounce of his being, but a bargain was always interesting, and interest is a precious commodity among immortals.

Tonight was a different mission.

Tonight marked the first time in millennia that the beast was not topside on official hellhound business. That moon hanging in the sky was no ordinary moon, it was the Cerulean. A moon that only swung around every once and a while, and for good reason: the veil between here and the underworld was at its weakest, and certain creatures could pass freely if they had the juice to pull it off.

He'd been planning for centuries, staving his strength for this very moment. Now that he was here, the only thing the beast could think of was the next place he could get a snack.

The land surrounding the highway was all dairy pastures. A few miles down the way, a pack of uneasy Holsteins lowed at one another, as if to say: *Dude, moo! Dude... Mooo! There's a friggin' monster on its way over here... Moo... Moo... MOVE!!!*

Sadly, none of them got the message.

Seth padded over, shifting into his feeding form, which felt a lot like breaking wind after six hours of lovemaking. Or lovemaking after six hours of farting... Either way, it felt stupendous. He came up on his hind legs, his torso extending and his front legs turning into great claws. His hungry maw stretched into a pointed snout and his fur drew inward. If the cows had been nervous before, by now they were shaking in their udders.

"Hey guys," the beast rumbled like a diesel engine. "You know, you look like something... Oh right, *dinner*."

One-by-one, Seth chowed down until he was satisfied. His stomach grumbled ominously, but he didn't think much of it because everything he did was ominous. Five minutes later, the beast was barfing chunks of masticated livestock on the side of the highway.

"They have done some fucked up stuff to you guys since the last time I was here. You know, you used to be tasty."

The bloody piles of chewed up cattle did not respond, and when Seth thought about it, you really couldn't blame them.

"Ah, well. Let's go find a cemetery."

He slipped back into his dog-form and carried on along the shoulder of the highway, passing a sign that read: WELCOME TO OAK FALLS, THE HEART OF CARMEL.

A mile later, the beast found his cemetery.

It was a graveyard of bucolic charm: rows of tombstones running soft hills with a single mortuary building nestled in the center. The beast padded along the gravel under rusted gates and made his way to the crest of the hill, where he sat on his haunches and let off another vicious howl.

The wind picked up. The heavy oaks peppering the cemetery swayed and groaned. Lightning forked from the clouds and struck the ground as a roll of thunder rocketed through the air. Smoke billowed, grass burned, and another clap of thunder set it all in motion.

"Arise my pets!" Seth cried. "Arise, and feast upon the living."

Another bolt of lightning. More thunder.

"Arise! Shake the sleep of the dead and come forth, you stinky bags of flesh…"

Lightning. Thunder.

"Arise! Get your lazy butts out of the grave and do my bidding! Now is a season of evil… Hell will walk the earth. The Ancient Ones will return, but for now, arise! For I am seriously not kidding…"

Silence.

The graves lay still, the wind died down, and the clouds rolled off to look ominous in another district. The beast sighed, a little disappointed.

"Premature, huh?" he said. "Guess it really does happen to everybody."

CHAPTER 2
DON'T FEAR THE REEFER

Statistical fact: cops will never pull over a man in a sweet van if he's carrying forty pounds of sinsemilla buds. Another fact: ninety percent of all statistics are made up.

The Wizard's mind looped this mantra as he brought the ChevyVan over swells of coastal highway. The stereo crackled Clapton, and the V8 rumbled like a cougar humping a machine gun.

He was forty-three, bearded, tall and lanky; simultaneously resembling the philosopher Socrates and the Muppet Zeke.

Besides, he was only holding the pot for a friend—did that actually make a difference? Who knew. What he did know was that even if he did get caught, it wouldn't be him the cops were interested in. He was only the middle man. He didn't do the growing, and he didn't do the selling. He drove, plain and simple.

It was a two hour straight-shot between Big Sur where the Russian mobsters running the grow-op were camped, and Stanford where the wholesaler foot soldiers ran their market. To get twenty percent, all he had to do was drive from A to B without getting pulled over.

"Pull over," said Travis Schwartz. He was eighteen, a six-foot slab of muscle and crew cut, and was rarely seen without his football jacket. "I have to take piss."

"I told you to go before we left the Russians."

"I didn't have to go then."

"He gets pee-shy," said Hal Pearson, a shorter, brawnier version of Travis.

Wiz sighed. "Well, dude, what do you want from me? We're on a schedule here."

"Ugh, do you have like a cup or something?"

Wiz whipped around, pointing what he hoped was a threatening finger at Travis. "You're a free man, Trav. Liberty is important, and I'll be damned if I try and take that from you... But so help me god, if you relieve yourself in my bitching custom van, you can bet on your well-formed brow I will end you."

The linebacker bounced in his seat and affected the tone of a pleading grade-schooler. "But I have to go!"

"You are seriously harshing my roadbuzz," Wiz said. "Are you sure you couldn't just roll a joint instead?"

"Will that make me not have to pee?"

"No, but it'll take the edge off when I bitch-slap you to next Wednesday." He wasn't sure he could do that, but it sounded really cool, and Wiz hoped it would drive the message home that he really didn't like to stop when there was forty pounds of weed sitting in a secret compartment in the floor.

"But we're already smoking?" Hal said. He puffed the edge of a joint and the sticky spice of ganja filled the van. Wiz hit a button on the dash and the windows whirred open a crack. Smoke billowed onto the highway.

"Can you hold it to Oak Falls? I should stop for gas anyway."

"You sure it's a good idea to stop in town carrying this much heat?" Hal said, nodding to the compartment in the floor.

Wiz shrugged. "It's a safe spot. Sheriff and I have an arrangement. Besides, our cause it good fellas; noble, even.

Karma is on our sides, and when you've got good karma, you've got nothing to fear."

"How is selling forty pounds of pot *noble*?" Trav said, squeezing his legs together and bouncing in his seat while Hal passed the joint.

"Enlightenment," Wiz corrected. "Forty pounds of *enlightenment*, Trav. Pot is not the nefarious substance people want us to believe it is. It's a teacher herb. It's a gateway to joy and understanding and a greater acceptance of one's fellow-man... A gateway to awesome, if you will. And so, a noble cause."

Trav puffed the joint and croaked. "I guess—Hey, can we grab some munchies while we're there?"

"Yeah, screw Karma," said Hal. "I'm hungry."

Wiz grinned. In a world fraught with banality, you could always count on hunger to remind you you're alive.

He'd never been able to relate to the idea of building an adult life. "Doing something," as his friends put it. To Wiz, the only thing that really mattered was freedom. Life is a short ride, and to fight to make sense of it—to assign some greater *meaning* rather than to simply *be*—well, that was the path to suffering. The younger crowd understood this, which was why he always found himself riding with high school seniors or college kids on the burnout path.

Nevertheless, one thing was abundantly clear: you can't have freedom without a healthy stash of snacks.

He pressed a button on the dash and the glove compartment hissed open. A small caddy filled with beef jerky rolled out, and the Wizard tossed his cronies a packet each. They tore into them with the urgency of starving maroon victims.

Trav went to pass the joint to Wiz, still juggling the half-eaten jerky, and fumbled. "Oh, shit!"

"No harm, Travis," Wiz said, reaching under his bucket seat for the spliff. "It's just a—"

"Look out!"

Wiz came up to find a mass filling the headlights. It was a huge dog, shaggy black fur, eyes glowing red. He slammed his foot on the brake pedal.

The van lurched as the tires locked up, but they were going too fast, he'd seen the creature too late, and van began to skid...

You can't really spruce it up at this point, can you? They creamed it.

The front of the van crunched with a shotgun report, sending the dog flying a good twenty feet before bouncing off the shoulder with a deadly *thud*. Steam billowed up from a cracked radiator and the radio cut out.

"Did you guys see that?" Wiz said, panting to catch his breath. His heart jackhammered in his eardrums.

Groans came from the back of the van. Both of the linebackers had kissed ceiling and were nursing goose-eggs the size of grapefruits on their foreheads.

"Yeah," Trav sighed. "Sooner would've been better."

His jeans were wet and the acrid smell of urine mingled with the musty undertones of the van.

"I thought you could hold it," Wiz said.

"I *was* holding!"

"How is karma on our sides now?" Hal said.

"Because we're not the dog, idiot!"

Hal frowned. "Karma stinks."

"I think that's actually Travis," Wiz said.

He unlatched his seatbelt and crawled out of the van to survey the damage. The grill was dented inward, the right headlamp was shattered, the hood bent up at an angle no healthy hood would ever try, and a spiderweb crack crawled the windshield. It was, in a word, fucked.

"Fuck," Wiz sighed, running his fingers through his mangy hair.

The linebackers came out and followed his gaze across the damage.

"Shit, how big was that thing?"

"I believe the scientific term is *fucking huge*," Wiz said.

"That can't be right."

"He was being sarcastic."

"Well, excuuuse me!"

Before any of them could reply, a long wolf-cry came from the ditch where the dog had landed. The three turned just in time to see the creature leap out of the ditch, land on the highway, and glare glowing red eyes at them.

"Nice driving, ya doomed fucks!" it snarled. Then it took off into a farmer's field.

"I'm really glad I already pissed myself," Trav said, his voice trembling.

"Yeah, I'm thinking we should get out of here," Wiz said.

They climbed back into the van, all too dazed to comment on what they'd just witnessed. Wiz had been a full-time toker his whole life. He'd had visions, he'd thought he heard things, he'd definitely had his mind make up some interesting stuff when he wasn't expecting it... But a talking dog with glowing eyes? That was not ganja territory.

He shook his head and turned over the ignition. The engine coughed, choked, wheezed, chortled, and did everything but start running.

"What's wrong?" Trav said.

Wiz tried again, but the engine just wouldn't do it. "I think we wrecked it, fellas."

"What do we do now?" Hal said.

"We're only about a mile out. I think we can push it."

"Push it?" Trav said. "You want to push it?"

"Well, what else did you have in mind?"

Before Wiz could finish, Trav was already punching in the numbers of a tow truck on his iPhone. He held it to his ear to wait for the tone, but all he got was a no-service prompt.

"That's weird," he said. "Hal, you getting anything?"

Hal's face was buried in his phone too. He shook his head. "Full bars, but it's not dialing."

Wiz went to pull out his own phone, but before he could the red-and-blues of the unmistakeable fucked-over-ness that is the law lit up the rear view.

"Oh balls," he said.

Meanwhile in Stanford California, Max Reyes walked a column of red and blues toward a tan-colored duplex. The door was splintered inward. Two unmarked SUVs were parked at an angle, and about thirty people with jackets sporting yellow lettering that read DEA milled around the place. Three men, all in their twenties, were sitting on the curb with their heads in their hands while the investigating officer took a statement.

Max was thirty-nine, slim and Hispanic. He wore a neat suit and had his hair slicked back from a severe widow's peak. He walked over to the first guy holding a notebook, flashed his badge and said, "I do love the smell of drug bust in the morning."

The officer chuckled dryly. "More like bust bust."

"Huh?"

"Yeah, we come barreling in with automatics and raid material like we're hunting *Scarface*, and what we get is a few clowns, a bong and an eighth of an ounce. I'd call this bust a bust. You are?"

"Reyes," Max said, lighting a cigarette.

"So you're the jerkoff who got us all out of bed to arrest Cheech, Chong, and Bong over there, huh? Way to go, numbnuts."

He'd been working undercover with the guys currently getting cuffed for six months. They didn't look like much, but they were wholesalers moving large amounts of Red Leopard (a rare crossbreed of White Rhino and Afghani Kush) from a cartel of Russian growers located somewhere in Big Sur.

The Russians were dicks, but their unique blend of marijuana had effectively outsmoked the Mexican Cartel's Maui Wowi as the primo bud moving around the coast. They were big fish for an agent like Reyes to fry.

Max dragged his smoke and let the officer's snark slip past. You got a lot of lip from the uniforms when you went undercover.

"What tanked?"

"Your intel. It's bung. We did a sweep. The house is clean. No forty pounds of happy anywhere inside."

"You search the vehicles?"

"You're digging buddy," the officer chuckled, folding up his notepad. He slapped Reyes on the back. "Hey, don't sweat it. I got TiVo. But when I get home and the wife's looking for someone to blame for my absence... Just remember, you're my guy."

Reyes pulled his smoke down to the filter and stamped it out on the pavement. This was an egregious fuckup. All the intel he'd pulled over the past month had these guys unloading forty pounds of product tonight, but all he had was an empty nest and three guys who needed a shower. What had gone wrong? Had they gotten wise and sent him sniffing down a trail of misinformation? Max considered it, but these guys weren't smart enough for that. At any rate, it didn't matter now. His cover was blown. His case was also blown, and someone, somewhere had very seriously fucked the bulldog.

Now it was Max's problem.

He walked over to the three guys, flashed his badge at the investigating officer and lit another cigarette.

"Oh hey," the officer said. "It's Captain Fuckwad!"

Reyes rolled his eyes. "Mind if I have a word with them?"

"Well, getting more than two might be tricky with these space cadets, but go ahead. Knock yourself out," he chuckled and punched Max's arm. "I mean seriously, knock yourself out. I can't wait to hear the whirlwind of shit you get for this mess."

Max nodded. He sat on the curb next to the scrawny blonde guy in a Nirvana T-shirt.

"Badger," he said.

"Max," Badger replied.

Max tapped another cigarette out of his pack and handed it to him.

"Sooo," Badger said, taking the smoke and lighting. "This is awkward."

"Yeah, I'd say I'm sorry, but you know... Job."

"Right. Gooduns on the undercover persona though," Badger said. "I mean with a goatee that stupid, you could really convince anybody."

Max prodded self-consciously at his goatee, which indeed stupid-looking.

"So, am I getting any jail time for this?"

Max chuckled. His chuckle broke into a full-blown cackle and he punched Badger in the shoulder. "Only definitely. You don't have much, but I'm not leaving here without an arrest after the show we just put on."

Max watched as Badger squirmed with panic. "No," he said. "No, no, no way, man!"

"Yes, yes, yes, and yes way, Badger. You know what they say, you do the crime... Yada yada."

Badger let his head fall into his handcuffed hands. "That's not even what they say!"

Max shrugged and took a drag of his smoke. "Whatever."

Badger shot back up, hungry hope glimmering in his eyes. "Hey, wait a second... What if I like... Gave you information or something? Would that help?"

"Well that depends Badger," Reyes waved his hand across the scene in front of them. "What do you have to tell me?"

"What if... I like... Give you the Russians?"

"You are so going to prison. I know you've never met them."

Badger was scrambling now. "Okay fine! I don't know who they are but I do know who the driver is."

Reyes thought about it. "I'm listening."

"He's some dude called the Wizard."

"Thanks Badger," Reyes stood and pitched his smoke. "Don't drop the soap in county."

"I'm serious, man! His name is the Wizard and he lives up in Oak Falls. We were supposed to get our shipment tonight, but he bailed. I dunno what happened but —"

"Woah, easy buddy," Reyes chuckled. "You do know I was bluffing, right? You're going to go to county, get processed, and then they'll probably release you in twenty-four hours. You're fine."

"I am?"

But Reyes was already on his way back to his BMW. He had a two hour drive to make, and needed at least an hour of sleep before he found this Wizard guy.

When the agent was out of earshot, Badger nodded to his cohorts, Cheech and Bong.

"Cover me dudes."

They nodded back and Badger scuttled behind one of the SUVs. He stuffed his hands into his pocket, squirmed around a little, and came back with a cellphone. He made sure nobody was watching, then he dialed the number he was never, under any circumstances, *ever* supposed to dial.

He held it to his ear, taking a deep breath, and closed his eyes as the line picked up.

"We've got a problem."

"Well, well, well," the sheriff said. "What have we got here?"

He was forty-six, tall, lean, and mostly salt and pepper. He hitched up his slacks walked around the front of ChevyVan. He surveyed the damage and whistled through his teeth.

"That is one helluva fender-bender, fellas. Sure I couldn't put you down for some reckless driving and sweet van endangerment?"

The linebackers were both pale-faced and shivering in the back, but Wiz rolled his eyes. "Fuck off, Al."

The sheriff chuckled and tilted back his wide-brimmed hat. "Now, is that any way to talk to an officer of the law?"

"Can you tow us?"

"What's in it for me?"

"Well, I'll make sure not to show my friends here the baby photos of you trying to masturbate with a rubber ducky in the sink for starters, then maybe I'll order you a pizza... What did you have in mind?"

The thing Wiz knew that Trav and Hal didn't was that Sheriff Al Kowalski was his brother. Moreover, Al knew all about Wiz's clandestine occupation and the two had kept a truce for years. Wiz drove the pot, and Al turned a blind eye, so long as it never landed on the streets of Oak Falls.

Al squinted, put his hands on his hips and said, "You up to something?"

Wiz chuckled. "I'm always up to something."

Al removed his hat and sighed. "Well perhaps I'd better search your vehicle, just while we're here."

"Al…"

The sheriff gave him a smug expression, then sighed. He leaned in Wiz's window and grinned at the two linebackers. "Just fuggin' with you." Then to Wiz, "I'll grab the cable. Put it in neutral."

"Yeah, thanks," Wiz said. "Stupid head."

"Slacker."

"Fascist."

Brotherly bonds.

The mechanic's name was Lester Jones. He was thin, mostly bald, and had a face with wrinkles so deep they gave him the aspect of a melting wax figure. He was rubbing a veiny nose with a dirty rag and shaking his head at the damaged ChevyVan.

"Gonna cost you."

Wiz had never before had the pleasure, but Lester's reputation was spread through Oak Falls like herpes at a Christmas party. His diagnostic skills lay in the subtle art of replacing everything in the vehicle until the problem went away. One time, Lester had even managed to convince a tourist that replacing the seatbelts of his Prius may solve a transmission problem.

"How much?"

"Well, that busted headlamp, that's two-fifty. Bending out the grate's no problem. Another hundred even. Then there's the real damage. You got a cracked radiator, what looks to be a snapped belt, your oil hasn't been changed in about a month and there's a pretty fearsome urine stain in the backseat. I'd say you're looking at about five grand."

"Lester?" Wiz said.

"Yessir."

"You're trying to scam me, aren't you?"

Lester removed his Ford Motors ball cap and applied a new strip of grease to his bald head. "Yessir."

Wiz grinned. "How much, just to get her running?"

Lester blew his nose violently and shoved the rag in his overalls. "That urine stain will cause discoloration if you don't deal with it right away... Could be mighty bad for your brakes..."

"Lester!"

"Two grand."

"Two grand?"

"There's a surcharge on van repairs."

"What kind of surcharge?"

"I'm a sir, and I'm making a charge. Two grand. I'll have it ready for you tomorrow morning."

Wiz felt the wind fall out of his sails. He'd expected delays, but losing a whole day meant sitting on forty pounds of grass and who knew what kind of trouble from his associates. He rubbed his beard and sighed.

"I thought we could have it tonight."

The mechanic chuckled, wheezed, and hacked a phlegm ball out on the garage's oily floor. "You shittin' me? This is easily three hours of honest work, and twice that if it's my work. I don't know if you noticed, but I'm running a helluva fever and am presently seeing double. It'll have to be tomorrow."

The Wizard tried to think of a way to goose the mechanic to do it tonight. He could bribe him? Well, that would require money—something he wouldn't have until he got the delivery to Stanford. He could offer some bud for Lester's troubles, but that would likely earn him more shit than having the stash arrive late. He could threaten him? Well, how often had his threats *ever* worked on someone?

"Alright," Wiz said. "But I'll have to make the payment tomorrow night. I have a courier run of... Parsley to get upstate, and I won't be payed until I do it."

"You want to book credit?" Lester snorted. "Forget it. Take your sweet ride down to another mechanic. Oh wait, I'm the only one in town."

"I can write you a check, but it'll only bounce if you try to cash it."

The mechanic stroked his wrinkly jowls, staring off into oil stains as if he were consulting the gods of engine grease, then he brightened. "That'll do."

Wiz left the Texaco with an invoice for two grand he didn't have and walked over to a payphone. While he dropped quarters in the machine, he could feel trouble brewing on the horizon. The ringer throbbed as his mind came back to the giant dog with the glowing eyes.

"Nice driving, ya doomed fucks!" it said.

Somehow, Wiz got the feeling his troubles were only beginning.

CHAPTER 3
JUST A SMALL-TOWN WORLD

The township of Oak Falls lies in an oak forest near the mouth of the Carmel River. It is a sneeze away from Monterey, lying just north of the great Big Sur wilderness area on a partially man-made waterfall.

It got its start in the 1890s by a wheat farmer from Oklahoma who found the rich soil perfect for growing his crops. The settlement went unnamed until the early 1900s when textile weavers came to mine the coastal river for their wares, calling it Oak Falls in a fit of unprecedented creativity.

Industry blossomed, bringing millworkers and their families. The village doubled with the boom. Soon after (and by no small irony) came a growing trade in refining gunpowder from the leaves of local oaks. It was decided shortly thereafter that refining explosives in a milling town was, on the whole, a pretty bad call, and by the mid-1900s, most of the town had burned itself down.

It took decades for the village to recover. Life moved slow in Oak Falls until the completion of the coastal highway through Big Sur put it back on the map. Overnight, the town's blue-collar beginnings were swept quietly under the rug, making way for art galleries, cafes and trinket shops.

The Falls became a tourist haven, where passers-through could buy antiques, postcards, T-shirts and ball caps; up-and-coming artwork, handmade jewelry, homespun crafts, polyester textile knockoffs—even dud hand grenades—spending with the frenzy of a binging runway model at an all-you-can-eat taco bar. Kitsch became the lifeblood of the community.

Farmlands were subdivided; old mills gutted and reincarnated as thrifty condos, and soon the real estate market skyrocketed with young couples seeking to raise their children in a quaint little village rather than the city, bringing throngs of creaky retirees ready to simmer down and watch the grandkids grow before they shuffled off to the Great Shuffleboard in the Sky.

Again, the settlement grew. Soon the galleries and coffee shops outnumbered the gas stations and food markets, and thus became Oak Falls: tiny snow globe of the American Dream.

On any day of the week, you could find young families and old fogies shuffling the main drag, smiling and waving and generally not doing too much with themselves, as if tending an unspoken boredom. It seemed almost as if the entire town was preoccupied, quietly biding its time, waiting for something— *anything*—to happen.

And something was well on its way.

That night, fog rolled through sleepy streets. At three in the morning, every single dog in town started barking.

In the moments that followed, lights went on, slippers were thrown, curses shouted, and the sheriff's office answering machine filled up with a salvo of complaints. Threats were made, neighborly bonds strained, and up on Ivy Street, Geoffrey Miller, who lived next to the Oak Falls Kennel for the Canine Challenged, left a steaming dump on the hood of the company van.

Down at the boardwalk by the river, a crew of ducks took a break from their bobbing for bugs and erected a Slip-'n-Slide on the boardwalk using a tarp covering sidewalk artwork that the town had commissioned.

Up on Bay Hill, Minnie McGraff's thirty-two feline friends

all took turns doing a butt-skid across her brand new throw-rug, but they probably would have done that without supernatural provocation. Three of them escaped and took to the streets. Two of them were mashed by speeding cars. Two of them got back up. Nobody noticed.

At the Creaky Wheels Home for the Elderly, every man on the sixth floor woke up with an erection that could cut diamonds, and Earl Potvin, who'd been using the early rise to browse eBay encountered a pop-up for *Busty-AsianBabes.com*. The excitement proved too much for the old guy's ticker, and he flopped dead like a fish on the keyboard.

A half-hour after the cacophony began, it was over. The ducks went back to the water, the cats claimed ignorance, the rug was ruined, and all the dogs except the kennel hounds finally shut the fuck up.

As usual with dogs warning of a coming disaster, it went totally misconstrued; the lucky ones got an extra can of food, and most of them spent the night on the porch.

The next morning, the town arose, a little groggy, very grumpy, and completely baffled over what had happened.

Come seven, a coven of three was waiting at the entrance to Ava's Bakery and Cafe. It was a cute little coffee shop nestled off the main drag behind the town square. From here, Suzanne, Margy, and Ellie could survey the comings and goings on the town: gossiping, speculating, and generally judging the bejeezus out of everyone from a perch conveniently out of earshot from passers-by.

They were all mid-fifties, with gray hair streaming in ex-flower-child majesty. They wore yoga pants and woven shawls. Yoga mats hung from their shoulders like rocket launchers. Totebags stuffed with crystals, smudging sage, and tarot cards were at their feet.

"I just can't believe that Minnie would throw out that rug."

"Minnie's a nutter. Did you hear how many cats she's got?"

"Now, now ladies. Negativity. It's bad for your chakras.

Plus it gives you wrinkles," said Ellie. "We should be searching for the positive."

Margy blinked. "Such as?"

Just then, a red Volkswagen Beetle pulled up and coughed a huge plume of exhaust as the engine killed and Ava Elridge climbed out. She was thirty-eight, shapely, and had her hair up in a loose auburn bun.

"Morning ladies," she said, swinging her keyring like a talisman from the caffeine gods.

She unlocked the door and let the women into the dark interior of the cafe. Ava hit the lights and put the kettle on while the coven nestled into their usual gossiping perch.

"Did you hear about the disturbances?" Margy said.

"Disturbances? What happened, did the kennel hounds get out again?"

"Have we got news for you," Suzanne said. "The Riverwalk artwork was destroyed, every dog in town was barking like it was the end of the world—and the cat lady threw out a perfectly good rug!"

"Not only that," a voice came from behind as the bell over the doorjamb jingled. It was Franz MacFee, the local doctor. He was fifty-eight and had a sort of poor-guy's George Clooney look about him. "We had a fatality last night."

"No shit!" Margy whispered.

"Margy, language!" Ellie snapped.

"Who?" said Suzanne.

"Earl Potvin, heart attack." Franz made a face that Ava guessed was supposed to be somber, but it just looked sort of smug. He turned to her. "Hey Ava, could I get a—"

"Oh no!"

"—Coffee? What? Why?"

"No, no, no. You have got a lot of nerve showing up here, buster. You know that?"

Ava stalked back over to the counter and began pouring coffee into a styrofoam cup. Once upon a time, she and Franz had dated. Two weeks ago, they'd broken up.

"Ava, what? I'm just getting coffee…"

Ava slammed the cup on the table, sloshing dark roast all over the counter. "And I thought we agreed you wouldn't do that since… You know."

"Oh come on, you mean we really can't be mature about this?"

"I am being mature about it," Ava said. "And you can too, by getting your coffee at the Texaco like all the other sleaze bags."

The decision to split came from Ava's discovery that Franz had been two-timing her with a nurse from the Oak Falls General. The nurse was about half Franz's age, and for Ava (who was fast approaching forty) it had struck more than a bit of a nerve.

Franz went on the defensive. "I really don't see the point in calling each other names, Ava. I just wanted to check in, see if you were okay."

"Oh, well that's nice. I'm fine. Now can you please leave and never come back?"

"Hey, why the hostility?" Franz said. "I come in here, I try to check up on you and make a nice gesture and you call me names and try to kick me out?"

Ava pushed the coffee across the counter and wiped furiously at the spillage. "You want a nice gesture? Here!"—and here she gave him the finger—"No charge. Now take your coffee and please, whatever crazed notions of kindness possess you to come back, just don't."

Franz's face was going a bright shade of pink. "This is a little inappropriate."

"You wanna talk inappropriate, Franz? Try dating me while you're fucking Nurse Betty!"

"Her name is Pam."

"Whatever! The point is, you had a chance to be mature and decent and break it off with me before you took it up with her, but you didn't. You are therefore a sleaze bag and I would prefer it if you didn't come into my bakery anymore."

Franz's mouth opened, then closed, then repeated the process a few times.

"Fine, forget it." Franz whirled around and nearly dumped his coffee on the little man standing behind him.

He was a hair over five-foot, wearing a black suit and top hat. His features were exotic and he carried a long ebony cane, which he rapped against the floor, glaring at Franz, waiting for a response.

"Sorry," Franz said.

The air around the little man seemed to cyclone as he let out a rally of curses in a language nobody recognized. He chased the doctor out the door. The bell jangled, and he turned back to Ava.

"I've seen crusted dog semen with more charm than that fuckwad."

"You get used to it," Ava said. "Can I help you?"

"I would like to buy a bottle of rum."

Ava paused. "Uh, we're a bakery?"

He grinned. "Well, if I find one, you'll drink it with me?"

8 A.M. left the Gnarled Wood Tavern clear save for a handful of truckers dozing by the pool table. Even in the morning, the Wood's interior was like a carpeted cave—which, to Lanette Wilson's way of thinking, was exactly the impression any watering hole worth its weight in hops should give.

The floors were sticky. A crackling jukebox glowed from one of the bar's dark corners, and blue smoke hung in a perpetual cloud at about head height. The laws in California forbade smoking, but when it came to things at the Wood, the only law that mattered was Lanette's. She believed in high prices, low-ball liquor, and zero-tolerance for bullshit—and she enforced her rules with a well-oiled twelve-gauge she'd shoot into an empty beer keg any time things got rowdy.

She was wiping down the bar when Franz MacFee stumbled in with a dazed expression and slumped on a stool across from her. It may have been the light (something the

Wood didn't get a lot of) but for a second she could have sworn it looked like a trail of blue followed him.

"I think you supposed to stumble on the way out, Doctor Romeo."

MacFee smiled weakly. "Hey Lanette. Double scotch, please."

Lanette tossed her rag on the bar and cocked her hip, which was no easy feat for a seventy-three year old woman who had about two-hundred-and-twelve pounds of sister on her bones. "Ain't it a little early for a nightcap?"

Franz eyed the sign above the bar that read: *IT'S ALWAYS 5 O' CLOCK SOMEWHERE!*

The barkeep looked at it and shrugged. "Fair 'nuff."

This was their usual exchange. Every six weeks or so, the doc would come in, drink until he slurred, find the nearest woman who looked single, and lay the charm on them. Most nights he managed to take them home, cooing empty promises of brunch, expensive cars, and marathon lovemaking.

"I never understood if they meant 5 A.M., or 5 P.M. How you doing, Lanette?"

"They mean both. Busier than crabs on a toilet seat. Broke up six fights just last night. Somethin' in the air, I think."

"Summer fever," Franz said. He wasn't wrong. This weekend was the Oak Falls Palooza, the busiest day in all of the summer tourist wave. They'd close down the main drag tonight, and by Saturday the town would be crawling with tourists like fly larve on rotten meat, pouring their money into the town's coffers.

It was Lanette's favorite day to hate. Her tables would be full despite the cloud of smoke. She came back with the doctor's drink.

"So tell, why the early lunch, Franz? Ain't gonna find no tail but trucker until well after noon."

Franz tipped his glass. "Ah, lost a patient today."

One of the truckers by the pool table grumbled back to life. "Bummer," he said.

Lanette eyed the trucker and picked up her shotgun.

"Well, Doctor, death is a hard mothafuckin' fact of life we all deal with sometime."

Franz sloshed back his drink. "Just because it happens all the time doesn't make it any easier."

"Who was it?" Lanette started wiping down the bar again.

"Earl Potvin, heart attack."

Lanette dropped her rag, sighing. "Well, he had a fine fucking run, didn't he? It's not exactly like he was sprinting towards the great beyond."

"Lanette!"

"Relax, Franz. We all gonna be dead eventually."

"Oh, *death*," a voice came from behind. Lanette peered over the bar and found a man in a black top hat, holding a cane, grinning. "Death is a party. A delicious one. You're all just not invited yet."

"Yeah, and what makes you such the expert?" Franz said.

The man furrowed his brow. "I am Ghede, the Baron. Guardian of the underworld. Master of fornicating—you can bow if you wish."

"You're fucking loony, pal," Franz said.

Lanette pumped the shotgun. "Ever been dead guardian of the underworld before?"

The Ghede blinked and said, "Of course."

To this, Lanette wasn't sure what to say, so she fell back on some foolproof bar-speak. "So what'll it be, lord of the underworld?"

"I would like a bottle of rum," said the Baron. "And it's just *guardian*. I've a fuckfeast of a journey before I get to be lord."

"I kind of think he's already had a bottle," Franz said.

The Baron took his cane and put it under the doctor's chin. "You are a very unlikeable man. In my true form, I'd think you as little more than spooge on the bottom of my shoe."

Lanette knew she should be threatening to shoot this sonofabitch, but a strange daze fell over her like a warm blanket. Plus, she wouldn't mind seeing the doctor get in just one fight— he was a bit of a sleaze ball. "Bottle of rum, coming up."

Franz swatted the cane out of his face. "You don't know me. Besides, I'm not the one convinced he's a god."

Lanette shrugged and moved over to the liquor. The Baron lit a thin cigar.

"Ava thinks you are pathetic. Your groveling gives her pukey feelings and she's angry you fucked the slutty nurse. She also didn't mention it, but she thinks your shaft is short and bent like a gourd."

"Wow, and you're a mind reader too, huh Mister God?"

"Your insolence should have you stuck with winged monkeys fucking you for eternity. It's no wonder you are such a fuckface."

"Hey, fuck you, pal!"

Here, a crashing noise. When Lanette turned, she found the Ghede had produced a blade from his cane, and was currently holding it against Franz MacFee's throat on the floor.

"I would cut you now," the Baron said. "I would bleed you like a Glygabeast and ride your lifeless corpse. I would dance around and wear your scrotum as a party hat—I would do all of this, except I'm on a bit of a schedule."

Lanette fired three shells into the keg, spun back for the phone, and dialed the sheriff. As the ringer throbbed, she turned around, this time to put a shell into the back of the man with the sword if he didn't let Franz go.

But Franz was alone on the floor. The rum bottle and the Baron were gone.

Sheriff Al Kowalski's morning greeted him with a mountain of paperwork and a flaring ulcer. He put his sixth cup of coffee down the hatch and took a swig from a bottle of Pepto-Bismol.

Only a little after nine, and the slog was unending: He'd just finished the voicemails. The torrent of deviant behavior gave Al a feeling of impending doom. His town was going crazy. What's more, when you start thinking people are going crazy, it's a slippery slope to worrying it's *you* who's the crazy one.

Noise complaints. Vandalism. Public defecation at the local

kennel. Drunken disorderlies. One drunken orderly, and about a dozen different complaints of a big black dog roaming the streets.

"There's only one way to take this," he said to the steaming cup of heartburn on the table. "Throw it in the garbage."

He opened the first blank case file, and was just filling out the "Dump On Kennel Van" report when a Hispanic man with a stupid-looking goatee knocked on his open door.

"Sheriff Kowalski?" he said. "Max Reyes, DEA."

They shook hands. Al gave the agent his trademark whistle and said, "DEA? Aren't we a little far north for you guys?"

Reyes chuckled and sat in the chair facing the sheriff. "Mind if I smoke?"

"Well, that depends what you're smoking," Al said, immediately regretting it. What was he doing? Painting a sign on his face that read: *CORRUPT COP*?

Reyes fidgeted. "No, uh… I mean just tobacco."

"I was trying to be kidding," Al said. "Help yourself."

The two produced cigarettes with the alacrity of gunslingers drawing at dawn. Al pulled an ashtray out of his drawer and placed it on the desk.

"So what's the story?"

"I've been working undercover with some wholesalers up in Stanford the past few months, tracking down a cartel of Russian growers somewhere in Big Sur."

"So, I would have what to do with that, exactly?" Al said.

Reyes flicked into the ashtray and sighed. "Well, the wholesalers were supposed to get a shipment of forty pounds of product last night and they didn't show up. Oak Falls is about halfway between the two on the highway. It seemed like a good place to start."

Al smoked, thinking *it's the perfect place for you to start. Shit! Shit! Shit!* "That seems a mite like a leap, Agent."

The agent grinned. "My C.I. also told me the guy I was looking for was named the Wizard and he lived here."

Oh fuck, oh fuck, oh fuck. "Uhuh…"

"Al—can I call you Al?—I know you're brothers with the

Wizard. I assume you've had some kind of hand in his business, and I'm willing to let it go if you tell me where to find him."

Al latched onto the moment's righteous indignation. "That's absurd. I mean yes, he's my brother, but I've had nothing to do with his drug dealing. I mean… This is all news to me? Oh, fine. I maybe — sorta — stick my neck out for him once and a while."

Reyes butted out his smoke. "Well, it may very well get chopped off."

"My neck?"

"Your head."

"I said my neck."

"I tried to make it work."

The two lawmen sat in awkward silence for a moment, then Reyes stood.

"I'm taking your brother down, Al. You can help me or you can go down with him. But those are your choices, and if you do something stupid, if you obstruct or you get in my way, you will be very sorry you did. We clear?"

Al stared at the smoldering astray, his fingers steepled at his nose. "I think you'd better go."

"I was just on my way." And with that, the agent was gone.

Al sat for a good two minutes before he slowly let his head fall to the desk. This would be a problem. He tried to think of a witty comeback to the Agent's threat — Secret Agent Douche, perhaps — when the phone rang.

It was Lanette. Fight at the Wood.

CHAPTER 4
DEAD LIKE ME

Wiz was brewing a secret special dark roast from Vancouver, Canada when his roommate Noah Carpenter clomped down the stairs. Noah was thirty-three, shaggy-haired and athletic. He'd moved in with Wiz about a month after getting kicked out of the Bendy Legs Yoga Ashram.

His biggest problem? Noah had a temper, and tempers never wear well on teachers. Sure, a hard edge or a little ball-busting was fine if you were a personal trainer—but it was less suited to deep breathing and relaxation. Noah often talked of how he'd rather teach kung-fu or karate, but the money was in yoga, and even then it wasn't much without credentials. Thus his dream became a wish, and to supplement his income, he took a second job patrolling the town cemetery.

He shuffled into the kitchen, groaning and rubbing sleep horns from his head. He yawned, stretched his arms wide, and let out a glorious butt-rocket of a fart.

Noah tossed some granola in a bowl and eyed the Wizard. "You look tired."

Wiz got in late the night before. Thoughts of the busted van, no money, and the talking dog kept him wired. He tossed, turned, and watched hours slog by on his digital clock. He smoked a bowl, he snacked, but still slumber escaped him. Sleep was an albatross; the elusive white whale and he was Captain Ahab.

The business things he could handle, but the dog with the red eyes troubled him. He rolled over the possible explanations, and had come to the opinion that the dog was a cyborg sent back in time to end the world.

"I totaled the van last night," he said.

"No shit," Noah crunched his cereal. "You roll it?"

Again the dog filled Wiz's mind. "No, we hit something."

"What, like a deer?"

Wiz shook his head. "A dog. It was crazy. The thing was huge, and its eyes…" Could he seriously tell Noah about the Terminator dog? It was crazy. Too crazy to believe, and too weird to have happened. "Well… I just can't get them out of my head. Poor guy."

Noah shrugged. "Circle of life, man. Don't beat yourself up. It's fate. It was your fate to hit the dog, and it was the dog's fate to get hit by a sweet van. It's not like you went out of your way to run it over."

More like it traveled back in time to kill me in order to prevent a human-on-robot revolution in the future, Wiz thought. "I guess. Anyway, I'm picking up the van this morning. No idea how I'm going to pay for it, but— what about you, how was your night?"

Noah stole a cup of Wiz's coffee. "Equally crappy. Had to put out a fire at the cemetery."

"What happened, the dead start rising?" Wiz chuckled.

"No, it was a literal fire. I guess we had a flash storm and some lightning hit the grass. It was a nightmare."

"Gosh, the two of us must've been some real dicks in our past lives to get where we are, right?"

"Don't think so," Noah said. "Karma doesn't work like that."

"I thought that was exactly how karma worked."

"Well, they say that, but in my experience karma breaks-even more immediately. It's not some hokey spiritual thing, dude. It's consequence. It's not like you get a lifetime of hall passes only to come back as a pimple or something. We suffer the consequence of our actions, and there's no way of escaping it. That's karma."

Wiz chuckled. "Gee, how do we ever get ahead with odds like that?"

Noah bounced his eyebrows. "Maybe getting ahead's not the point."

"Desire is the root of all suffering, right?"

"Being broke is the root of all suffering. It's not the way it ought to be, but it is how it is."

Wiz shrugged. "It'll all work out. It's not the end of the world."

Noah propped himself up on the counter and sloshed back his coffee. "This is your problem man. You're always waiting for someone else to take care of you. What happens if you're on your own?"

"I'll think of something," Wiz chuckled. "I can be resourceful when I need to. Don't forget the time I made an apple into a bong when we went camping."

"I'm talking about money, Wiz. We need to get ahead. Both of us. We need a plan, or a scheme, or something."

"Noah, we're good people, we're not exactly schemers."

"Speak for yourself! You're currently sitting on forty pounds of pot, right? Why don't we skim some off the stash and sell it our own selves?"

Wiz gaped at him. "Dude, are you nuts? The Russians would have our balls if they found out."

"Who's gonna miss three pounds out of forty? They won't notice."

Wiz frowned. He didn't like the idea of stealing. "It just doesn't seem... You know, *honorable.*"

Noah chuckled. "Wiz, you're never going to get ahead thinking like that. We need to catch a break, and you've got a perfect opportunity right in front of you."

Wiz didn't know. "What about karma? What about consequences?"

"What about not being broke?" Noah said. "Besides, what's the worst that could happen?

Asher Cravington awoke on a cold metal slab with a dog the size of a Volkswagen licking his face. Something sticky was holding his eyes shut, but every lap of sandpaper tongue left a trail of doggy spit in its wake, and soon his eyes cracked open.

This was the the basement of the funeral home. The dog was a fucking monster.

The big dog licked again. "Hey, welcome back!"

Asher fumbled backward and crashed to the floor with a tray of embalming materials—a small tube pumping pink goo ran from a machine into his neck. He grabbed and pulled it from an incision in his neck with the sound of Velcro on vaseline.

"What's going on? What the fuck are you? How did I get here?" He rasped. The air was like razor-wire on his windpipe.

"Slow down, ace." The beast chuckled. "Relax. There's a sink over there, you should get yourself a drink. You've been dead a while."

Dead? It was four little letters, and all Ash needed to remember. The chest pains. The fainting spells. The doc telling you it's terminal lung cancer and you're pretty much fucked. Then the hospital, the chemo, the aches, pains, and finally the —well, you know—dying.

Mostly it was feelings of abandonment—on his deathbed of all places—that rang clearest in Ash's mind. Rage boiled up in him like battery acid. He was naked, he was dead, and most of all, he was pissed.

Asher climbed on legs filled with pins and needles. He shuffled stiffly to the sink—then he got a good look at himself in the mirror. He was bone-white. His eyes sank back so far in their sockets they bruised. A Y-shaped autopsy incision ran down his chest, and an artery dangled from his neck like a gruesome Christmas ornament.

He shuddered, ran the tap, and drank.

"So who are you?"

"I'm your new best friend, ace." The beast padded over, his huge tail wagging gleefully. "Your own, personal hellhound. The name's Seth, your faithful re-animator, at your service."

"How am I back?"

"The Cerulean Moon," Seth said. "Basically a time of the year when mystical mumbo-jumbo gets a little loopy and allows for bad stuff to transpire if you've got the juice. It's why I'm here, and it's why I brought you back. You're officially a zombie, ace. How do you feel?"

Asher thought about it, and eyed his reflection again. He couldn't smell. He didn't taste. Temperature didn't seem to bother him, despite the fact that he was buck-ass nude.

"I don't," he said.

The beast grinned. "Perfect. All as it should be. So, I've got this plan to unleash the forces of darkness and destroy the word—you in?"

Seth kept talking as if zombification, being evil, and wanting to destroy humanity were nothing more than deciding what to have for breakfast. For Ash, it didn't seem so glib. Sure, he was back from the dead. But evil? He didn't feel evil.

"Why would I want to do that?"

"Because you're a soulless instrument of the forces of darkness now. You know what undead is? Undead is power. It's freedom, and it's you, amigo. The sooner you can accept it, the sooner we can do some nasty."

"You might want to rephrase that last part," Ash said. "You mean I really don't have a soul? What happened to it?"

"All in due time ace. But how'd you like to be king?"

"King?"

Seth cocked his head, "Well, zombie king... But king's king, right?"

"King of who?" Ash said. "And how exactly do you plan to overthrow the human race with one zombie?"

The dog grinned again. "We can talk about it later, but hey... You're a zombie! How cool is that? You can run around and eat all the flesh and brains your little unbeating heart desires."

Ash rubbed the back of his head. The longer he was up, the easier his movements came. The anger he felt earlier continued to growl in his belly, and before too long, he'd reconciled any issues he had with being evil. Evil meant revenge. It meant making other people suffer the way you suffered. It meant being able to cut in line at the theatre—maybe evil wasn't so bad.

"When do we start?" he said.

The beast shrugged. "The real fun starts tomorrow. Meantime, how about a snack? You must be famished."

Asher realized the grumbling in his stomach was not just the byproduct of rage. It gnawed at him, like when you drink too much coffee and skip your breakfast. It was hunger.

"I could eat," he said.

"Swell. Grab that hammer over there," said the beast.

The Coven were all flicking tarot when their daily gab session actually reached the ethereal. It started with everyone pulling their morning dream journal from their totes. From here, they'd share their most recent entry: Ellie dreamed of golden mansions. Margy dreamed of boning Burt Reynolds, but it was Suzanne's dream that was the one out of place.

"Tell us!" said Margy.

"Well," Suzanne said, taking on the hushed tone of an escort offering a blow job. "It was about a dog."

"A dog?"

"A shaggy black dog." Suzanne nodded. "It was huge! And it had these glowing eyes... I was in an apartment—or a house —somewhere. And I'd go from room to room, and every time, this thing was at the window. Big glowing eyes, panting... Then I realized I was naked and woke up."

"Holy shitballs," Margy said.

"Margy, language!" Ellie snapped.

"I know, but that's a crazy dream!"

The three looked at each other with a knowing grin.

"Book it," they said in unison. Then Ellie withdrew the

most prized possession of the mystic totes: *The Abridged Encyclopedia of Dreams for Divas, Vol. II*

After picking up the recovered ChevyVan, Wiz made a pit stop at Ava's Bakery and Cafe to steel himself with caffeine for the trip to Stanford. He'd had two mugs at home to offset the three bong rips he'd taken upon waking. Then he'd had an exchange with Lester that put him in a mood, so he smoothed that over with a hit from his smokeless pipe.

The journey to Stanford didn't require a great deal of alertness—it was a straight-shot down the highway, with a nice view and wide lanes to glide over. The problem was if Wiz did it without caffeine, the two-hour trip would seem like four. Not to mention the already awkward paranoid exchanges with the wholesalers would be even more awkward.

He needed to cut the buzz. He climbed out of his patched-up purple steed and headed through the door.

The cafe was cool, all natural light, and heavy with the aroma of brewing beans and pastries. The wood floor creaked lightly under Wiz's feet, and he made his way past the coven thinking: *This is a good place. I should come to this place more often. It has everything you need. Coffee, snacks, low-lighting...*

Then he realized he was still completely baked.

"Hey Wiz," Ava Elridge said, coming out of the back room with a tray of doughnuts. She had a flour-dusted apron over a tight pair of jeans and a low cut blouse. Wiz's heart began beating faster, and the swift ecstasy of a different drug hit his system: desire.

Wiz had had a crush on Ava ever since he moved to town. The second he learned she and the doctor had split up, he'd made a point of coming in for visits in a hope she'd eventually catch on to his ninja-courting skills and ask him to dinner. So far, it had been going splendidly.

Play it cool, Wiz. Play it cool, he thought.

"Ava, heyy..." Damn, he'd gone wrong with that inflection. Why did he try and be all smooth and aloof all of a sudden? All he had to do was act natural. *I am an irredeemable tool,* he shrugged and tried to recover. "How's life?"

"Oh, same old," she said. "Although I'm thinking of taking up murder, so that's new."

Wiz blinked. "Huh?"

Ava set the doughnuts down and started picking at one. "Franz is still badgering me."

Man, he even liked the way she ate... That was not something you found in a partner everyday. If they ever got together, there would be the most delicious feasts every night. They'd cozy up by the fireplace in the great living room at his place. They'd go for picnics. They'd...

"I'd love to," he said. *Dammit! Mayday!!! We are flying without fuel, people...*

"Huh?"

And a foothold! Conversation not obliterated by mass bakeage. "I mean, that blows. You should just hire a hitman. Less mess."

"More money," Ava bounced her brow. "Coffee?"

"Please."

Ava went to work behind the register. "So any plans for our much-famed Palooza?"

"Oh you know, some *Hobo Trashcan*, some Pizza Shack, then me and Noah are going to check out the moon."

"Sounds like a fun weekend," she said.

No way. No way! She was beautiful. She was single. She was interested in what he was up to tonight. Noah was right, in all aspects of his life, Wiz never failed to not do anything. He had to try, didn't he?

"Oh, it'll be grand. You should come."

Ava came back with his coffee and a strange grin on her face. Not shock. Not confusion. Just something different. He gave her money for the coffee and she flicked open the register. She was actually considering it. This was good. This was hopeful. This was—

"I actually have a date," she said.

—Oh, dammit!

"Aha! Here it is," said Ellie. "The black dog is a harbinger of dark times ahead. Questions of — uh-oh."

"Uh-oh what?" Suzanne said.

"Yeah, read it!" cried Margy.

"Questions of identity. Binge-eating salty foods. Forbidden longings of the loin. Low blood-sugar. Fainting Spells. Thoughts of suicide. And... Bunnies..."

"Bunnies?!"

"That's what it says."

"But raincheck?" Ava said. She handed Wiz his change and found him pale-faced and apparently catatonic. He stood there, dazed, as the coven went on about their dreams, just staring at the change.

"Wiz?"

He snapped out of it, pocketed the coins, took his coffee and said, "Thanks."

Then he rushed out of the bakery.

Well, that was weird, Ava thought. *He usually stays and chats.* She wasn't sure, but he seemed a little more stoned than usual. That was probably what was going on. She knew he was a bit of a burnout and always kind of reeked like weed, but ever since he'd first walked into her bakery three years ago, Ava had had a bit of a crush on Wiz. She just didn't know he felt the same until today. Sure, he was probably a drug dealer or something, but when the heart wants...

When Wiz crawled back in the van, he slid through to the back and punched the keypad lock on the secret compartment in the floor. Okay, so the trying in the love life department didn't work so well. At least he'd tried, right? Well, sort of... But there had been effort. Didn't that count for something? Effort was a sign of *something* — wasn't it?

"Yup," he said. "*Huge* tool."

He pinched a bud out of the sample brick and shoved it in

his stick-shift bong. He lit up, furrowed his brow, and exhaled a huge plume of smoke. He looked at the remaining forty bricks, thinking he was never going to get ahead if he didn't do something drastic—which in his case, would be anything at all.

CHAPTER 5
TOUCH THE DEAD GUY

Gus B. Kiltson — Digger to his friends — was a seriously crappy mortician. His rap sheet for bad undertaking was longest in the county. Countless cases of sloppy craftsmanship — the most frequent of which was letting the embalming machine run while he ate lunch upstairs.

Usually, no one was the wiser, but every so often, the pump would run a little long and the deceased would wind up a little, well... exploded.

It was all on file. But Digger had figured out long ago that nobody read those files.

Besides, what wasn't on record — perhaps the biggest peccadillo in the crypt keeper's repertoire — was still secret. That's how he planned to keep it. Digger had what he liked to think was a *special* relationship with his clients.

When the patient (he called them all patients) was scrubbed clean, Digger would give them one final hump to the great beyond. Sure, it was necrophilia, but what was so *wrong* with that? How many people on their deathbeds wished to be laid one last time? He gave them that. It was his calling; his duty; his purpose...

He was also a barking loon.

And currently, he was halfway through a dogeared copy of *The Silence of the Lambs*, munching ham and cheese, while his most recent patient filled with pink goo.

Dr. Lecter was explaining the pairing of brains and fava beans when a loud crash thundered up from the basement.

In another tale, it might be justice, coming to carry Digger off to a padded cell where he could conquer the madness and redeem himself, but this is not that kind of story.

No, fair reader, because in just a few pages, someone is going to bash the crypt keeper's brains in with a hammer.

It really wasn't going to be Digger's night.

Another crash set him in action, moving from lunch table to security room, where he toggled a black and white display from room to room searching for the source. Everything appeared to be as he'd left it.

He went to the hallway and hit the lights, but the environmentally friendly generators running the place had shifted to snooze-mode about an hour ago.

"Great," he grumbled. "*Spooky.*"

He loped to his locker and collected his chrome flashlight and off-the-books Glock 9mm. Then, he descended the darkened stairs in search of the problem.

He suspected a gang of kids: hell-spawn from town, here to creep each other out over a game of Touch The Dead Guy.

Touch The Dead Guy was pretty simple in concept: Break into a funeral home. Find a dead guy. Run up to the slab and touch him. Laugh. Cry. Vomit. Leave. Drink, and forget it ever happened.

Such savagery, coupled with the influence of Doctor Lecter, ignited murderous rage in his belly—or perhaps it was just the ham and cheese.

How could anyone treat his loves like that? Dying was *poetry*. Fucking was poetry. Putting the two together might stir up some controversy, but playing Touch The Dead Guy was *not* poetry—not by a long shot.

It was simple: he'd catch the kids, finally dip his toe in the murder pool, and pop their bodies in the incinerator. That would teach them. It would be his graduation into infamy, just like all his bloodthirsty heroes.

"I'm coming to get you, kiddies!" he bellowed to the hall leading to the owner's office and the embalming room.

The hall didn't seem to give a shit. It lay dark, silent, an exit sign making a spotlight over the back entrance.

Gripping the gun with sweaty palms, Digger padded down the hall.

"Heeere's Digger!" he called, really wishing he had an axe.

More silence.

He made his way to the embalming room. Four corpses lay on Digger's slabs waiting to be dressed and manicured. The fifth, another notch on the belt of lung cancer named Asher Cravington, was missing. Digger's tools were scattered around his slab—the embalming pump still oozing on the tile floor.

"Well, that's unusual," he said

Then, a sound like paws scraping linoleum. A ringing sound came from his boss's office.

Digger whipped around. He moved, silent as his trade to the door and pressed his ear against it. The only thing he could hear was his heartbeat quickening. He waited, then took a deep breath and flung the door open.

Moonlight filtered in through shuttered windows, describing the silhouette of office banality. A foul odor filled his nostrils.

Gus let the light fall over the desk and found an old clerk's bell. That explained the sound—now, what about the smell? He scanned further.

Then a sinking feeling fell upon him. A long smear of embalming fluid painted the desk and carpet. Next to it was a steaming turd the size of a land mine.

"Oh, for fuck's sake!"

Behind him, the door swung shut, plunging the room into darkness. He wheeled around just in time to catch the shape of a humungous dog-like creature on its hind legs, towering over him—then the gleam of metal from his periphery.

Asher Cravington lunged from the shadows, swinging the bone hammer in a vicious haymaker that terminated in the back of Gus's skull.

Then it was red. Then it was white. Then Digger was gone.

CHAPTER 6
SOMETHING WICKED

"Okay, run me through it one more time." Al Kowalski leaned against the bar at the Gnarled Wood, underlining the words BAT SHIT on his yellow legal pad. He was trying to follow standard cop procedure here, but the din of the bar, the stress of the morning and the anxiety over the DEA dickwad sniffing around made him feel like ordering a beer. No wonder Lanette did such good business—it was as if the barkeep had a spell over her establishment that made people booze-hungry. Al felt his grip over his professionalism slipping.

Lanette sighed and wiped the bar in newfound frenzy. "We been over this, Al. Guy comes in, buys a bottle of rum, and the next thing I know he's got Franz on the floor with a samurai sword."

"A samurai sword?"

"A samurai sword," Franz slurred over the top of his glass.

Al made a note. "And you say the guy verbally harassed you?"

"Harass is an understatement," the Doc belched. "That little fucker was sadistic."

Al tried to shake the weirdness out of his head. "Far be it from me to tell you how to run your business, but Lanette? Why would you let a guy with a sword into the bar in the first place?"

Franz intercepted. "He had it concealed in a cane."

Al sighed. This was the kind of report he expected to get from bored teenagers looking to prank him. It was not the kind of thing he'd ever had to consider taking seriously. What was going on in his town? Al's bad day was slowly growing into a day from hell.

"Can you describe him?"

Lanette tossed her rag on the bar and lit a Benson & Hedges ultra-thin. "Oh, you know, short, dark, top hat, kinda sexy, armed with a mothafuckin' samurai sword? Kinda hard to miss."

Al folded up his legal pad. "Well, I think that's it. I'll file the report and submit his description to all the local dispatches. We'll get him if he hasn't left town by now. Meantime, sit tight."

"I don't mean to be a dick, Sheriff," Franz said. "But if I run into this guy again, I'm more than prepared to take care of him myself."

Franz MacFee didn't need to mean to be a dick—he *was* a dick. He was the town dick. You couldn't play playboy in a small town without earning a reputation, and the doctor's was cemented in a growing posse of women he'd used who now considered him scum. Al's opinion was similar.

"That's not the greatest idea, Doc. If the guy's got a sword, odds are he can use it. Not to mention the legal can of worms you'd be opening."

"Oh, I've got a good lawyer," Franz said.

"Just the same. Have some coffee. Sober up."

Franz slapped the bar. Drunken fury burned in his eyes. "That creepy little fuckweasel tried to kill me! I'm not going to do nothing."

Al rubbed his neck. "I could put you in jail?"

"I'll have a coffee."

A few minutes later, Al slipped through the tavern's doors back into the light of the real world. This day kept getting crazier. Hundreds of complaints from the locals, a nosy DEA agent looking for his brother, and now a crazed tourist with a samurai sword stalking the streets and the town doctor threatening to go vigilante.

Al drove the main drag to the intersection for the highway. He hung a left and brought the cruiser up the steep hill surrounding the bay at the foot of the falls. He pulled into the Kennel's lot next to the second of two gas stations in town.

Mack Gaffey, resident veterinarian and owner of Oak Falls Kennel for the Canine Challenged came to greet him. He was a tall, painfully thin man with a tuft of wiry gray hair sticking out in horns on his head and a pair of thick-rimmed glasses.

"Sheriff, glad you could make it." They shook hands.

"Alright Mack," Al said. "So you've had yourself some vandalism, huh?"

Mack nodded and lead him around his white GMC. On hood of the van was a fogged-up ZipLock bag. "Some sicko took a dump on my van."

Mack held up the bag so Al could see the giant, steaming turd inside. "It's human shit, Al. I did the tests this morning."

The sheriff frowned and started wiping the hand he shook Mack's with against his pants. "Well, this stinks."

"You should smell it out of the bag, Sheriff."

"I'll take your word for it. Mack, have you been getting shit from the neighbors about the dogs?"

Mack sighed and flopped the bagged turd back on the van. "Sure, but this is a bit literal, don't you think?"

"We received over twenty noise complaints last night," Al said. "All over dogs barking. I'm thinking if your neighbors were already threatening you about the dogs, it's likely one of them just snapped."

"Well, I guess there's nothing we can do about it. I just wanted to file the report."

"Well, I think that's all I need, Mack. I'll let you get back to it."

"Appreciate your time, Sheriff," Mack said.

Al slipped back in the cruiser, lit a smoke, and made it official: Today was hell-day. It couldn't possibly get any worse. Could it?

Awkward conversations. They're the heart of the drug trade. The driving force that keeps criminals out of jail is paranoia. You can think you know people, but the truth is, you never know who they're talking to. The life of an outlaw: Around every corner lies a cop. In every basement waits a bust. Every friend is the guy who sells you out to keep his own ass out of jail. Sure, it was rare, but you just never knew.

The result was a series of shorthand and euphemisms so obscure even the pros often weren't sure what they were talking about. Sales became pickups. Pot, ganja, bud, or weed became lettuce, green, happy, herb, smoke… the list went on, and changed from dealer to dealer.

Wiz sat on a tattered couch in the basement of Badger's apartment. The room was fashioned in the stoner-minimalist motif: The windows covered with long black curtains, a dusty lava lamp in corner. A shag carpet grew unknown specimens of mould under a weathered-looking coffee table.

"What happened to your door?" Wiz said.

"Uh… Well… You know, I locked myself out—and I forgot my phone inside, so I kinda had to, you know, bust it in…" Badger said.

Wiz was impressed. Badger wasn't a wimp, but he was pretty scrawny. Visions of the greasy blonde guy throwing himself against the door until it burst open filled Wiz's mind, and he suppressed the urge to giggle. Clearly, the effects of the bowl he'd smoked before hitting the road were still going strong.

"You been working out, Badge?" Wiz said.

"Oh, you know… Pushups, sit-ups… Stuff," Badger trailed off. "Anyway, you're here."

"Seems like," Wiz said.

Badger lit a cigarette and started twisting it while he tapped against the edge of his ashtray, pensively. "You got the product?"

"Yup. You got the check?"

"Upstairs in a wallet-box. We'll move the skunk and lock it up down here in a minute. You sure you're not carrying heat?"

"The rabbit's free of tails, Badger. Don't worry. I was super stealth and took the slow-lanes. The pigs are sleeping in the pen and we're free to do our thing."

Roughly translated, this said:

"You got the pot?"

"Yup. You got the money?"

"Yup. Cops follow you?"

"Nope. I was extremely stealthy on my way over and the cops never saw me. We can unload whenever you're ready."

Badger smoked, nodding slowly, as if to an unheard beat. "Cool. Sweet. Let's do this."

He stood and moved over to the stairs. Wiz followed. They came out in the kitchen and slipped through the back door to where Wiz's van was parked.

"What happened to your van?" Badger said.

"I uh… You know… Accidentally ran over a porcupine."

Badger blinked, staring at the van as confusion blossomed on his brow. "Dude… it really fucked up your van."

"You should see the porcupine," Wiz said. "We doing this?"

Badger took three quick breaths and surveyed the area. When he was sure there wasn't a cadre of DEA agents with riot guns and hungry dogs waiting behind the neighbor's fence, he nodded. "Let's go."

Wiz threw open the side door to the van and punched the numbers on the keypad. The secret compartment slid open, and the skunky aroma of the stash wafted out. He climbed in and produced a large black duffel bag filled with the bricks of Red Leopard from the compartment.

This was it. Moment of truth. He was going to hand the duffel off to Badger, and if anyone would notice the three bricks he'd swiped off the top, it'd be now. Wiz's heart began beating double-time.

Badger took the bag, slung it over his shoulder, and swiveled his head looking for cops. Wiz knew the feeling. Many times, he felt as if the act of just possessing a large quantity of herb was enough to tip the Thought Police off to what you were up to.

He power-walked it back into the house. Wiz followed. Every time Badger shifted the weight of the duffel on his shoulder, Wiz was sure he was about to get busted.

Play it cool… Play it cool…

They moved back into the basement. Badger pulled open the duffel and began stacking the vacuum-sealed bricks into a large safe under the staircase. Uncertainty played up Wiz's spine like an electric keyboard.

"Do you uh…" he said. "You sure you don't want to weigh it?"

Badger sighed. "You're seriously not working with the cops?"

"What?! No!" Where the shit had that come? Jeez, and Wiz thought *he* was paranoid. "I just thought—why did you think I was working with the cops?"

Badger continued piling the bricks into the safe. "Well, they tried to bust us last night and when you didn't show up… I guess I just kinda figured."

Wiz chuckled. "Dude, Badger. You really do think too much. I'm five-oh-free, good buddy."

"Oh… Uh, good," Badger said, thinking *probably better not to tell him you sold him out.* "Anyway, it's all good. I don't need to weigh it, I trust you. Let me get your dough."

Wiz felt a twinge of guilt as Badger scurried back up the stairs to get him his money. Trust, huh? Trust is a scarce luxury in this business—and the first time he actually had it, he was using it to his advantage.

I am so seriously boned, he thought.

As raw meat went, Asher Cravington thought brains were pretty good. Fatty, salty, chewy, but easy to munch on. Ash had never considered cannibalism before, but when the gravedigger's skull cracked open, it was as if a force washed over the zombie king, leaving only a primal hunger for brains in its wake.

Before he realized it, he was digging his hand into the gooey hole in the back of the mortician's head. A swift jolt of electric ecstasy shuddered through his body. A blinding light filled his head and he nearly doubled over. It was like a 100 proof shot of liquor.

Now he was scooping the last of Digger's skull and licking his fingers as if he'd just polished off a bucket of fried chicken.

"So, that's cannibalism, huh?"

Seth in his eating form stood over eight feet tall, humanoid, with razor-sharp claws and a great snarling maw of teeth. The head of the dog, the body of a human, only with the texture of a drowned rat. He snatched up the gravedigger's corpse with one claw and plopped it into his mouth like a cocktail shrimp.

"Pretty much," he said. He belched. "How do you feel?"

Asher swiped a great streamer of brain goo from his chin. A new undead energy surged through his body—he felt like a million bucks. "I feel like a million bucks!"

The dog grinned. "So, now you get the whole eat-the-brains-of-the-living angle, don't you?"

Ash nodded. It was like ten cups of coffee mainlined to the system. He felt like doing pushups. He felt like going for a run. He couldn't remember the last time—even when he was alive —that he felt better than this.

"They taste pretty good, too."

The two headed back to the embalming room. For the first time, Ash noticed the woman laying on the slab next to his. She was about fifty-three, bone-white and curvy. Her breasts pointed toward the ceiling. Ash looked at her, wondering what her name was, and whether she'd be waking up as a zombie soon. A long-forgotten urge worked up from his groin.

"So, since we're talking about it, you don't, you know, feel anything different, do you ace?"

"I feel supercharged," Ash said, unable to break his gaze from the attractive cadaver. "What do you mean?"

"I mean, you don't happen to be thinking or feeling things that are decidedly *not*-Asher-like, do you?" The big dog wagged his huge tail and nodded at the woman's body. "Pretty cute, right?"

Then Asher realized what he was feeling. He looked down

and found his unit at ardent attention, throbbing with embalming fluid. He stared in disbelief for a moment, then struggled to cover himself with his hands.

Seth chuckled. "You're horny for dead people!"

Ash felt the urge to blush, but found no circulation to pull it off. "...Only a little? Okay, that's new."

The big dog rolled on the floor, breaking out in an earth-rattling cackle. "The guy you ate was a necrophile!"

"What?" Ash said. "I mean... Ew! Why didn't you tell me before?"

The dog gave the zombie a knowing grin. "Would it really have made a difference?"

Ash thought about it. "Good point. So why am I suddenly horny for dead people?"

"You are what you eat, ace."

"What?"

"Well, let's just say that anyone you eat... You sorta-kinda absorb their personality traits for a while. You don't become them, exactly. But you might find yourself developing tendencies after a snack."

Ash decided he needed to find some clothes. They headed to the room where bodies were dressed before hitting the casket. Inside was a closet full of donation suits and dresses from local thrift shops.

The dog went on. "It goes without saying there are some types of people you just shouldn't eat. No drunks, no kids, and whatever you do, don't eat a vegan. Otherwise, go to town!"

"I'm actually kind of full," Ash patted his belly, then found a moth-eaten black suit that fit.

"No, I mean get your clothes on and go to town." The beast used one of his claws to pick a piece of Digger from his teeth, then shrunk back to dog size. "I have a couple of errands to run. Take a tour, decide what place you like, raise a little hell."

"You mean I'm on my own? What about being king?"

"A good king works well alone," Seth said. "You're a part of something now, ace. And it's much, much bigger than just zombies."

"What do you mean?"

The beast shrugged. "You want to have a good apocalypse, you've got to open the gates of hell. So I've got some things to do to make sure that happens."

"What about the other zombies?" The idea of being brought back from the dead, killing in cold blood, cannibalism, and being left to his own devices so soon made him dizzy.

"It's kind of a gradual thing. They'll start rising tonight. Tomorrow the Cerulean is at its peak, so the rest will be with you by nightfall. And I'll be back then, too."

"What am I supposed to do?" Ash said.

"Go to town," the beast said. Then he walked off, turning into a cloud of black smoke and slipping under the door.

Ash sighed. "Great, what am I supposed to do, walk?"

CHAPTER 7
WHITE RUSSIAN

Boris Vloydeskvi rolled into town driving an Eldorado that was more patchwork than paint job. He was fifty-eight, wore Hawaiian shirts, Day-Glo shorts, and a neon-orange stocking hat. He smoked a thin cigar and reeked of cabbage. On the passenger's seat lay three fake IDs, a bottle of nasal spray, a fifth of vodka, and soup packed to-go for dinner.

He didn't like pansy smuggler the Wizard.

Boris only wanted a drink and wife's sweet handjob before Larry King. Instead, the boss sent him up to shit-speck town where poopstick lived. One of the wholesalers in Stanford had called last night, saying that the DEA had raided them and that poopstick Wizard hadn't shown up when he was supposed to. The boss mulled it over, and after some deliberation with his advisors, it was decided poopstick Wizard was traitor swine and ought to be removed from the picture. The only thing that made Boris happy about any of this was that he'd finally get to do some killing.

The Eldorado chugged down the main drag and pulled into the Rooms-R-Us by the Texaco. Boris checked in on the west side of the building so he could get a good view of the town's comings and goings through binoculars.

He threw his duffel on the bed and unloaded his sniper rifle, his Desert Eagle .50, a fourteen-inch hunting knife, and thermos filled with milk and Kahlua.

He placed a thermos next to the fifth of vodka on the bar. Boris didn't really want to be a gangster, he wanted to make vodka from his own potatoes. This was his second batch, and it was much better than the first, which tasted like sweat from the gonads of a bull with venereal disease. It did the trick, though.

He produced a map of the county and the slim Oak Falls phone book and placed them on the writing desk next to a lozenge-shaped reading lamp. He moved back to the bar, fetched a glass wrapped in plastic, and poured out four fingers of vodka to the Kahlua and cream mixture. He stirred with his finger and sipped while he padded back to the writing desk. He unfolded the map and opened the phone book.

Boris gulped his drink and lit a cigar. "So, poopstick Wizard is not listed in phone book," he said. "Under *T* or *W*."

He sighed and stared at the map until his stomach grumbled. He scanned the businesses section of the phone book for Russian cuisine, but found nothing. He slouched on the bed, picked up the phone and dialed room service.

"Rooms-R-Us, how can I help you?"

"This is two-seven-tree. I have question."

"Go ahead sir."

"Where do I find guy named the Wizard?" Boris said. Hey, it was a small-town. You never know.

The operator sighed. "No, I do not know where you can find a wizard, sir. Did you try the phone book? Now did you have a serious question for me? Or would now be a good time to send the tooth fairy to your room, *sir*?"

Boris was confused. He'd spent a lot of his life feeling this way, so it didn't really bother him, but clearly this room-service guy had misunderstood.

"I need to use microwave."

Like many of the near-forties women of Oak Falls, Ava Elridge was a victim of divorce. She came here with Pete, an insurance broker from Texas, a year after they'd married in San Francisco. Pete was hardworking, successful, and looked fantastic in a suit. She'd fallen for his light brand of Southern charm in a night. Ava, then putting herself through night courses in business at SFU, found herself falling quickly in love.

A few months later she'd moved in, and a month after that she'd cut her classes and gotten engaged. They married in Carmel, and while staying at a B&B in Oak Falls on their honeymoon road trip, Pete suggested a small town like this was a good spot to settle. The quiet streets and considerate neighbors would make the perfect place to raise a kid. Ava wasn't even pregnant.

So they moved. They got a three bedroom house in a blooming subdivision. Ava's plans to start a bakery went on hold. Pete's dashing suit was hung up in favor of a pair of Levis and T-shirts.

After two years of honeymoon bliss, an autumn chill descended upon the couple. The sex became less and less frequent. The conversations fizzled. Pete began working longer and longer hours and took even longer stints at the bar. Still, every night he expected dinner ready at 8 P.M., and would slip away to his office or the bar as soon as the plates were cleared. He didn't even kiss her hello anymore.

Ava, raised by a happily married mom and dad, decided after some consideration that cooking an inattentive jerk's food six nights a week with sex on Wednesdays was not the adventure she'd signed up for. Then, as if the pie needed a cherry, life decided to throw a kibosh on the couple's fertility, and not long after that, she woke up to Pete packing his bags.

"Business trip," he said. "I'll be back in a couple of days."

"At three in the morning?" Ava said.

"Okay, fine. I think I want a divorce."

Ava sighed and pulled the pillow over her head. "Okay."

Pete kissed the pillow and grabbed his bags, then he headed

through the door with a one-way ticket to Austin in his hand. Ava never saw him again, but every month an alimony check would show up in the mail. She saved until she had enough for a down payment on a main drag storefront, then opened up her bakery, serving locals with a smile and grace.

Maybe divorce wasn't so bad after all. She'd learned a valuable lesson: only tools rush in. She also had the bakery she'd always wanted. Sure, it wasn't a trendy neighborhood in San Francisco, but the rent was way cheaper. She could manage. It was real. It was hers. A living dream. People always called divorcees victims, but for Ava it had been the best thing to ever happen to her.

Still, it had left something behind. An empty feeling. A gnawing sensation that gripped her insides randomly over the weeks and months. Loneliness circled like a vulture. She tried to fill the space with a series of meaningless flings and vapid relationships with underwhelming men. That was how she ended up with Franz.

Now, sweeping the bakery, waiting for the clock to hit five, Ava was beginning to wonder if she didn't have a problem with selecting her mates. Only tools rush in, and yet somehow, within only three minutes of meeting the mysterious stranger in the top hat, Ava had agreed to go on a date.

Why? Who *was* this guy? She knew better. She'd made her resolve to stop making the same mistake over and over, dating the same guy in a different package—but something had come over her. He walked in, and she found herself fantasizing about taking him to bed almost instantly. He wasn't even her type, but that didn't seem to matter. He came in, asked for booze, and she was poleaxed with desire.

The phone rang, startling her out of rumination. The clock on the wall said it was five-to-five.

"Ava's Bakery and Cafe," she said. "We're closing up…"

Heavy breathing came over the line, followed by Franz MacFee's voice. "Ava, baby, come back to me!"

"You dumped me, Franz. Remember?" What was with this

guy? Hadn't she made herself perfectly clear this morning?

"I did not!"

"Well, you did the hard part when you cheated on me—"

"There's a dirty joke…"

"—I just made it official. Are you seriously drunk enough to think you can call me after today?"

"You," Franz slurred. "Yooouu… Youuuu… Well, I dunno. I guess I just feel bad."

"You *should* feel bad, Franz. That's what normal people tend to do when they do bad things."

"Look, I made a mistake," Franz's voice was thick, like he'd recently been crying. Ava could nearly smell the booze through the receiver. "You want me to break it off with Pam? Done. You want me to walk over hot coals? Done. You want me to wear the Morph suit again—"

"That was your idea. And it was insanely creepy. You're drunk, Franz. Sleep it off. Wouldn't want you to be hungover in the E.R."

"Ava, I miss you!" Franz cried. "I miss your smell and your hair and that thing you do with your tongue when you—"

"Eat a dick, Franz! You had your chance and you blew it. I've moved on, and you really need to do the same. You're turning into kind of a stalker."

"Hey!"

"And furthermore," Ava snapped. "What would your new nurse girlfriend think if I tell her what you just said to me? Pull it together."

"Ava, who was that guy today?"

"What guy?"

"The GUY," Franz moaned. "THE guy. The guy with the stupid hat. Who is he?"

"Oh, him," Ava said. "He's my new boyfriend. Pretty dapper, right?"

"Ava, if you're just trying to make a point or get me angry, don't go out with him. He tried to cut my throat with a samurai sword today. He's dange-er-rous…"

"Well now I'm *definitely* going out with him. Goodnight Franz. Don't call back." Ava slammed the phone in the receiver as the bell above the doorjamb jingled, and the little man in the top hat—the man who called himself Saturday—appeared.

The funny part was, Ava couldn't remember him introducing himself.

When he arrived in town, Asher was expecting panic, blood-curdling screams, and throngs of horrified locals piling over each other to get into hiding. He wanted car crashes from terror-stricken drivers, gunfire from police officers; mass hysteria, explosions, denial, and hopeless defeat gripping the town by its very soul—he wanted blood to run the streets.

What he got was packs of tourists, all either too busy flicking away at their phones or surveying the best place along the main drag to catch a bite. He got a warm summer breeze and the jovial murmur of hundreds of people milling through life—totally oblivious to everything that didn't relate to their travel itineraries. They milled along the sidewalk, looking but not really seeing; hearing but not really listening; breathing, but not really living.

Not a single person seemed to catch onto his undead-ness.

In fact, it seemed to Ash, awash in the flood of aloof pedestrians, that the world had changed. He had only been dead for a couple of days, but it had taken an entire life to realize it: Nobody was awake anymore. Here he was, soon-to-be-king of the undead, walking among the living, and everybody seemed more zombie than he did. Had he been like this? Was the whole world like this?

Moving around, using only the base senses to keep from bumping into one another, mindlessly consuming whatever shopkeepers or advertisements told them to—just going through the motions. Was that life? Was that *his* life? Was that everything he had been?

Maybe he was wrong. He turned and looked at his reflection in the shop mirror. He'd wrapped a handkerchief around the wound on his neck and had cleaned the bits of gravedigger out of his grin, thinking calling too much attention to the fact that he was a zombie might result in getting his head smashed-in. Now he was beginning to regret it.

Still, he looked dead, didn't he? Why was nobody noticing? He was going to need to do something drastic here. He needed to do what the dog had said: raise a little hell, get the townspeople riled up and well-marinated in fear for the impending apocalypse. He removed his makeshift bandage, found the first guy with his nose buried in his phone, and marched directly at him. The man didn't look up. He just kept walking. Only when he finally collided with Ash did he break his gaze from the device and look at the zombie king.

He blinked a few times, mouth hanging open. *Finally,* Ash thought. Now the terror would begin. Now he could have his moment. Now the town would fall into irreparable pandemonium—

"Sorry," the man said. Then he carried on with his day.

"Motherfucker!" Ash cried.

A woman across the street shushed him, gesturing reproachfully at the two children by her side. He tried dangling his artery at her, but she just rolled her eyes—the world-weary mother who'd seen it all.

This was going to take serious action. If Ash wanted to scare this town into chaos, he was going to have to go big. Much bigger than a zombie cakewalk down the boulevard. He needed a plan.

After passing the town hall, which was flanked by a sandwich board advertising the annual council meeting Sunday morning, he headed through a subdivision hugging the main drag. What the hell was wrong with people?! He was a friggin' zombie and nobody would even take him seriously.

Up ahead, a kid was beating the shit out of something by the curb with a piece of rebar. He was about nine years old, pudgy, and had a ring of soda stain around his lips. He wore a *Transformers* T-shirt and cargo shorts, with a red bandanna tied around his head like preteen Rambo. His victim was an empty Dr. Pepper bottle.

"Hey kid, you live around here?"

The kid, who Ash was thinking of as Rambo Jr., stopped pummeling the soda for only a second. He eyed Ash suspiciously, then resumed smacking. "I'm not supposed to talk to strangers."

"Smart kid," Ash said. "Listen. I'm a little hurt, and I'm looking for a phone. I'll talk to your parents if you just point the way."

He took a step towards Rambo Jr., who rested the rebar against his shoulder and stepped back.

"What's wrong with your neck?"

"I told you, I'm hurt. Now... Your parents?"

But the kid wasn't buying it. "You look dead..."

"Well, funny thing about that—"

"ZOMBIE!!!" Rambo Jr. shrieked. He gripped the length of rebar and started swinging.

The metal connected with Asher at about hip height, letting off a wet-sounding *thunk*. The force of the blow doubled him over.

"Ow," he said.

Another blow came to his ribs. Bones crackled.

"Die, you undead fart gobbler! Die!!!"

Smack.

"Stop it!"

"Aaaahhrrrrggggh!" the kid wailed. He moved the rebar in a jabbing motion and caught Ash in the stomach.

"I'm not kidding, you little shit. Cut this out before I—"

Smack! *Thunk!*

"Kid... I'm warning you—"

Smack, crackle, *thunk*.

Oh, fuck it. Humanity was doomed anyway. He might as well help them get it over with. Rambo Jr. brought the rebar in a great overhead swing, delivering what was to be the death-blow to the side of Asher's head.

Instead, Ash caught the rebar. Bones crackled as his hand made a fist. He grinned a wide, bloody grin.

"My turn."

CHAPTER 8
MUSING MOZZARELLA

"Okay, my turn," Wiz said, grabbing the controller from Trav and entering the game. It was him and Noah against a swarm of pirates cursed by Aztec gold. They were armed with only machetes and backed into a corner. The stakes were a chest of gold back on their ship, the *Airbud*; the lives of their crew, and as usual with video games, the odds were ruthlessly stacked against them.

"Get the captain," Noah said.

"I'm trying," Wiz said, punching the buttons on his controller with stoned fury.

They were sitting in the great room under a haze of smoke. Wiz was in his armchair. Hal, Travis, and Noah were on the couch. The four musketeers of pot—emphasis on the *musk*—were banded together for their first-ever caper. The air was heavy with the scent of dank nugs, incense, and crackling cedar from the stove in the middle of the room.

The pirate horde grew closer.

Noah punched the buttons and withdrew a grenade—*Dead Seas* was great fun, but held about as much historical fidelity as a colander holds water.

"Where did you get that?" Trav said from the couch.

"Found it on the poop deck."

Hal giggled. "Why do they call it that?"

"Because it's where the seafarers poop," Wiz said.

The entire living room burst into laughter. The pirate horde closed in and tore Wiz and Noah's avatars to gory bits. They shut off the game.

"So, we kinda need a plan here," Noah said.

"Can someone tell me why Wiz took three pounds from the Russians?" Trav said.

"It does kinda seem like a bad move," said Hal.

Noah finished rolling a joint and lit up. "He took a stab at asking Ava out."

"You dog!" Hal said.

Wiz flinched. The combination of six bong hits, depression over getting shot down by Ava, and the recurring mention of dogs whenever he was around was beginning to wear on him. "Can we go back to the plan thing?"

"What'd she say?" Hal said.

"Doesn't matter," Wiz said.

"She shot him down," Noah said.

"Why would she do that?" Travis croaked, passing the joint back to Noah.

"It doesn't matter," Wiz said.

"She already had a date," Noah replied, then passed the joint to Hal.

"With who?"

"It doesn't matter!" Wiz cried. "Now can we get back to the point?"

"What about the Russians?" said Trav.

"Yeah," said Hal. "If they find out that we stole from them, we're all dead."

"They won't find out," Noah croaked and passed the joint to the worried linebacker.

"Well, that's optimistic." Travis frowned and folded his arms over his chest.

"No, Noah's right." Wiz steepled his fingers under his nose

and took a great sigh. "Badger didn't weigh it when I made the drop. There's no way they'd know."

"Which leaves us out of danger, but still in need of a plan," Noah said.

"How are we supposed to move product?" Trav groaned. He took the joint from Hal and toked a few times. "I mean, it's summer. We can't sell it to the school kids."

"Not to mention it's tourist season," Hal added. "Wiz, I know you and the sheriff are cool, but he'll be crawling all over the town making sure the Palooza is under control."

"Look, the point here is not what's stopping us," Wiz said. He took the joint from Travis and started puffing like a steam engine. "The point is we need to get rid of this stuff as soon as possible. What's everyone doing this weekend?"

"I work," Noah said. "Prospects aside, I'm the only one here with an actual full-time job, and I'd rather not lose it."

Smoke climbed up around the Wizard. A buzz began to wash over his head. They were looking at this all wrong — seeing what wouldn't work was not the same thing as figuring out what *would*. If they were going to get this done, they were going to have to figure out a way to use their limitations to their advantage...

"Holy fuck," he said. "I think I'm having an idea here."

"What?" said the three musketeers.

Wiz started nodding, as if to the rhythm of the idea forming... "And now I'm having a plan. It's simple!"

"What?!" said the musketeers.

"The Palooza," Wiz said. "We sell it to the tourists, the locals, everybody. Who wouldn't like a little herb to dial their vacation up to eleven?"

"What does that even mean?"

"Noah runs his rounds at the cemetery. Trav and Hal split up and make some new friends. I talk to the grown-ups looking to bake. We lose the drugs, one of us keeps an eye out for the sheriff, then at the end of the day, I'll pick everyone up. We'll go to the bar, have some shots, and celebrate."

The three nodded slowly.

"What if we get caught?" Trav said.

"I'll give myself for the greater good. Tell the sheriff it was my idea. If anything bad happens, I want you to blame it all on me."

Hal nodded. Noah took the joint from Wiz and said, "That's a plan."

"Now what?" Trav said.

Wiz felt his stomach rumble and raised a finger to mark his point.

"Now, my friends, we go for pizza."

The Baron put the bottle of rum on the counter next to the register, adjusted his top hat and said, "I do enjoy a woman who cusses."

Ava sighed, hanging her apron on the door to the back of the cafe. "You heard that, huh?"

"I hear a lot of things," he shrugged. "Don't take it personally. Everything I hear from you sounds delicious."

Ava didn't know what to make of this. She'd heard guys give a commentary of the baggage of relationships-past before… But about the last adjective she'd ever expect to hear describing it was *delicious*.

"Thanks, but I'd rather not be eaten," she said. "So you found your rum."

"I rarely don't get what I want."

Now that she *had* heard before.

"So, what kind of parents name their kid Saturday? Hippies?"

The Baron frowned. "Hippies? I don't understand."

Smooth, she thought. *Yeah, make fun of his parents for his bizarre name right off the bat. Good move, Ava.*

"Never mind."

Saturday took off his hat and rested it next to the rum bottle. "Long ago, I was given the sixth day by the Creator. He said it was to be called Saturday, and it should be mine. I accepted the gift, and took the name as a moniker because people kept asking me who I was. Do you have any glasses?"

"I've got mugs," she said. "You got a problem with that?"

"Mugs would be fine. Do you have any chili powder?"

"Sure, I use it in pastries."

"Some of that too, if you don't mind."

Ava smiled her best first-date smile. "Be right back."

She slipped into the back room of the bakery and leaned against the door. Her pulse was skipping in her throat. Just like this morning, for no reason she could figure, the man had the same intoxicating effect on her. Then, another, almost alien voice slipped into her thought-stream.

He's safe, Ava. You should do him.

Right away she recognized it. It was her first date monologue: a running commentary on whatever was going on when she was on a date with a new guy. She moved over to the storage rack where she kept the mugs. It was also the voice that usually got her in trouble.

"Yeah, well it's not like you've got the best track record with this sort of thing," she whispered.

Okay, fair deal. But maybe I'm right this time —

"Or wrong. Again."

Hey, you never seemed to have a problem with 'wrong' before Franz, honey bean.

"I don't want to think about Franz." Ava moved over to the spice rack, found the chili pepper and stuffed the bag in one of the mugs. She wrung her hands through her hair. "What did I get myself into?! This guy could be a murderer or crazy or not even a good kisser!"

Or, he could be really sexy and you want to find out about argument number three. Like I said, Ava. Go for it. What have you got to lose?

"Only living," she sighed, and before her inner voice could respond, she slipped back through the door.

On the other side, the Baron was leaning over the counter, smoking a skinny black cigar, flicking ash into her tip jar.

Okay, he kind of is an asshole.

"Saturday, what the fuck are you doing?"

The Baron looked confused. "I'm smoking?"

"Well, I can see that. You *do* know you're ashing into my tip jar, don't you?"

Saturday shook his head. "What's a tip jar?"

Ava frowned, placing a hand on her very, very pissed-off hip. "It's the thing you're flicking your ashes into. Now could you stop? Normally people put money in there. You know, a gratuity?"

The Baron licked his thumb and index finger, then pinched out the cigar. A tiny smoldering cherry fell into the tip jar. "Well, if you want a gratuity you'll need to come over here and I'll give you one."

Okay. I was completely wrong. Sorry!

"What the fuck is the matter with you? You can't just treat people like this—"

Ava had a good argument here, she was sure of it. But before she could unleash it on this vertically challenged, top-hatted dick brigade, he was over the bar and upon her. A tongue slipped into her mouth, and before Ava could tell what was really happening—and if she could, it would make her very, very unhappy—she kissed him back.

I told you so, said her first-date commentary.

CHAPTER 9
WHAT YOU DON'T KNOW CAN TOTALLY KILL YOUR NEPHEW

Amy paced the length of her aunt and uncle's living room while a slasher flick played on the TV. A woman in a skimpy outfit ran through a lawn full of conveniently placed sprinklers, shrieking. Behind her, a sinister figure carrying a meat cleaver stalked slowly, methodically—there might as well be a print on her water-logged shirt reading: DOOMED.

Yeah, Amy thought. *You think you've got it rough. I'll bet my college tuition you wouldn't trade places with me if you even had free will.*

She was twenty-three, blonde with a cheerleading-toned physique (pretty much the only reason she'd signed up for the varsity cheer squad to begin with) and eyebrows set in a perpetual look of incredulity. It was a little after sundown. A cool breeze poked the curtains through open windows around the house. Another postcard-worthy evening in Oak Falls. Only one thing was not so perfect: It was long past curfew, and Todd, her most recent charge of the babysitting trade, was missing.

Here are the rules for five-star babysitting of the Craig's List high order:

1. Be firm, but willing to compromise; a half-hour of G.I
   Joe or Pokémon after bedtime in exchange for a couple
   hours of peace and quiet is more priceless than Van
   Gogh. Compromise. If you give them something they
   want, they'll end up tucked in before the boyfriend sends
   you a sext message.
2. If compromise isn't an option, go for Valium—or at least
   Xanax. Most moms keep it in the medicine cabinet. And if
   you mix it with milk, you'll still be good for happy hour.
3. When all else fails, go for broke: cry. Crying, for a nine-
   year-old, is tantamount to getting whacked with a
   wooden spoon until cookies give you PTSD.

But the biggest rule, the one that breaking will definitely
earn you a pink slip; the one you'd have to be a supreme
knucklehead or complete noob to break—the one thing in all of
the sitting profession that is the golden rule: Do not lose the
kid. That's kind of the big one.

In hindsight, she should have seen it coming. To start with,
Todd was creepy. He knew far more about what lay in the land
of halter top than any nine-year-old should. How many times
had the little perv *accidentally* dropped a spoonful of mac and
cheese in a ploy to catch a glimpse at Amy's cleavage as she
cleaned it up? Furthermore, he was gross. She couldn't get him
to bathe. He refused to wear anything other than a *Transformers*
T-shirt and god only knew where he found that handkerchief.

Sneaky little fuck. It was coming up on 9 P.M., Todd still
hadn't come home, and Amy, for all her five-star ratings on the
web as temporary guardian, slinger of milk, grilled-cheese
dominatrix and tuck-in queen of the West Coast, was totally
and irrevocably fucked.

"Goddamnit!" she kicked the side of the coffee table while
the blonde on TV screeched and tumbled to the ground, her
grisly death loping after her.

Before Amy could catch the foreshadowing, however, the
front door slipped open. *Finally,* she thought. Now, she'd

unleash the wrath of worried babysitter on the little brat: full-on, tears-threatening-to-spill guilt trip. "People care about you, Todd," she'd say. "And when you don't come home before dark, it makes everybody so scared. I almost called your parents—you wouldn't want that, would you?"

She rushed over to the door, threw it open and said, "Todd!"

"Nope," a man's arms closed around her. She felt hands on her ass, stubbly cheeks scratch her face, and slammed into a wall of whiskey breath. Lips connected with hers, a tongue slipped in her mouth, and she decided that this was not Todd. Not unless he'd aged about twelve years in the time he'd been gone.

"What's up, babe?" This was Mario, her boy-toy. A gardener who wore a leather jacket, Doc Martins, and his hair like Jesus.

Amy ripped away, wound up, and slapped Mario so hard his eyes fluttered like tumblers on a slot machine. "Where have you been? Asshole. You were supposed to be here like an hour ago."

"Surprise visit from my good buddy Jack." The gardener grinned, raising a fifth of whiskey and slumping against the doorframe.

Amy snatched the bottle and took three belts. The whiskey took the edge off almost instantly—sandpaper for all life's woes. "I lost the kid."

"He's a kid, babe. Kids do that." He grinned again and moved in for another attempt at a kiss.

Amy sidestepped and he nearly tumbled into the entrance. "Not the time, Romeo."

"Mario."

"This is serious!" Amy said. "This isn't my car keys or my virginity I lost—it's a whole friggin' kid."

"Kids stay out late. He's probably just torturing a dog or something. Now will you relax? It'll be fine babe, Mario's here."

"Uh, hello? Asshat? I'm worrying here. You know… Being responsible?"

Mario chuckled, eyeing the bottle hanging in the hand she'd been waving around to mark her point. "Sure, I can see that."

She brandished the bottle, threateningly. "Not the time to be a smartass, Mario. A little comforting here?"

Why she bothered with this idiot had been the single greatest mystery of her summer vacation. But then, that was sort of the answer too: Mario was a bona fide summer fling. While Aunt Maude and Uncle Terry were off vacationing in Canada (another of life's mysteries), she took care of the kid between bouts of drunken, peel-paint-off-the-walls sex with Mario. It was a good arrangement—now she could feel it all slipping from her control.

And Mario, stud though he was, had a capacity for empathy that was on par with a bug's for literacy. Sure, he was a stud. Sure, he was a good screw. But in every other facet of being a functioning human being, he was a royal fucking dingus.

"I'm so fired."

"Hey," the gardener hushed. "It will be fine. Todd will be back in like three minutes. It's okay—"

But it *wasn't* okay. She could feel it. Her babysitting radar was coming up with danger on the horizon. *Oh my god, what if he's been kidnapped? What if he's dead? Oh god. Oh, no. Not an option, Amy. Pull it together…*

"I'm calling the sheriff."

She wheeled around for the phone and Mario came in and closed the door.

"Good plan, and after that, how about some more booze and a little nookie while we wait?"

This time, she nearly knocked him out cold.

Al Kowalski pulled the cruiser into the lot in front of the Superior Grill diner and killed the engine. He pulled his fingers through his close-cropped head of salt and pepper and lit a smoke. The nicotine buzzed in his temples and his chest felt like a ten-ton truck was sitting on it.

By city standards, it wasn't much. But Al wasn't equipped to handle a crime-wave. And why should he be? Nothing happened here. That was his reason for moving to the sticks to begin with: short workdays and the quiet life. Now, he was coming up on the twelfth hour of his day and had decidedly quit the whole quitting smoking thing. Something had to give in order to preserve his sanity—a virtue it seemed was in short supply around Oak Falls.

Al smoked his Camel to the filter and tossed the butt out the window (He'd had the ashtray removed from the cruiser years ago to help him quit). He collected his badge, his wide brimmed hat, and a large, stainless steel thermos from the passenger's seat, then unlatched the door and ambled up to the Soup.

The Soup's interior was decked-out in vintage diner quaintage—red vinyl booths with lacquered tables, bright colors, a long counter-bar running the wall by the door, and black and white tiles on every other surface.

The idea behind the restaurant's decor was to make the place appear as if it could be any diner in any small town across America—the effect looked more like every diner in every small town in America had barfed it up. Kitsch.

Jenny was at the till behind the counter. The sheriff walked in and tossed his hat on the bar, then he took a stool. Jenny came over from the register.

"Hey babe." She kissed his forehead. "How was your day?" She brought him a coffee and leaned across the bar.

"Crazy," he said. "We're moving. Tonight. Pack your things."

Jenny chuckled and went back to the register to grab her purse. "And will this be before or after you quit smoking?"

Smooth, thought the sheriff.

"What?" he said. "It really *was* a crazy day. You know my policy when it comes to smoking and crazy days. It's not like this whole thing is easy on me —"

"I know, I know," Jenny said, sliding over the bar on her butt. "Heroin is easier to quit... *yada yada*." —she walked into his arms and put her head against his chest, sighing—"But honey, you smell."

Al shrugged and started hip-checking her to the door.

"One of these days," he said. "I promise."

"Don't promise me stuff you and I *both* know you won't keep—it's dishonest," she said, giving him a little jab. She *had* just finished *her* shift too, after all. "Now, what would the little lawman living inside of you say about that?"

Al rubbed her shoulders and sighed.

"He'd say, are we ready to go now?"

Jenny looked around the diner, which was empty and completely shut-down, save for the light at the entrance.

"Yeah," she said. "Lie to me more, Sheriff. I'm game."

She flipped the switch and turned the sign in the window.

"In fact, I believe I sense a primetime TV drama in our futures."

"Oh, that'll end well," Al said.

He opened the door for her and she walked under his arm, then stopped.

"Shit," she said. "We're out of cream at home—I'll just pop back in and grab some before we—"

Al held up the big thermos and smiled.

"Put out an APB."

Jenny smiled and walked into his arms again, covering him with kisses.

Then, she pulled away, fished her keys out of her purse, and locked the door.

"Hun, that doesn't make *any* sense, whatsoever," she said. "Even I, a homely waitress, know enough to know this."

They got into the cruiser. Al started the engine and looked into his wife's eyes.

"You are *not* homely. You, my love, are gorgeous—but this whole town is beginning to not make sense. I swear."

Jenny smiled and looked out the window while he drove.

"The horror! I'll call the papers."

"Hey, I mean it." Al play-punched her shoulder. She narrowed her eyes at him, threateningly. He watched the road and went on.

"Noise complaints, domestic disputes, destroyed property, angry shopkeepers, apparently some guy with a samurai sword... Vandalism... Oh, *and* I haven't even made love to my wife yet!"

She slapped away his hand.

"Perv," she chuckled. "So, what d'you reckon, Sheriff—end of the world?"

He grabbed her hand and kissed it while he brought them into the driveway.

"You know, you just might be right," he said.

"Ah," she sighed, unlatching her seat belt. "So, pizza for dinner then?"

The sheriff nodded gravely. "And morning sex."

But before Jenny could reply, Al's phone rang for the zillionth time that day.

It was rumored through town that beneath her hefty figure, Lanette Wilson moved with the parts of a cyborg. The runner up to this small-town myth was she'd earned her longevity beating Death in a hand of snooker. How else could it be that despite her being owner, proprietor, and soul barkeep, the Gnarled Wood never closed? The truth was, Lanette—who was either eighty or three-hundred—had simply grown too old for sleep.

It was 10 P.M., and rather than the last wave of Friday regulars capping off the workweek with a pint, the Wood was bumping. Opening night of Palooza found the tavern stuffed with tourists in every nook and cranny. The jukebox thumped. Stools creaked. Pint glasses jangled, and the collective murmur of the patrons buzzed beneath a haze of cigarette smoke.

Lanette wiped the bar while three men, all four-pulls over the line, shot the bull, mourning their recently expired Sunday poker buddy Earl Potvin.

"Damn shame," Lenny Taltree, a wrinkled beanbag of a man, frowned into his pint.

"No kidding," Hunt grumbled. He was all beer gut and day-old stubble with a bald spot so clean you could use it as a dry-erase board. "Where are we supposed to play poker now?"

"Maybe he put it in the will?" Miles suggested. He was tall, scraggly-haired, and bearded.

"How would that help?" Lenny sighed. "It's not like he owned the damn place. The home wouldn't bite."

Miles thought about it. "We could play here?"

"Like hell you could," Lanette snapped. "You'd have better odds taking your game to the great beyond—which is exactly where I'll send you wrinkly fucks if you bring your cards in here."

"Come on Lanette," Hunt pleaded. "What's the big deal?"

The barkeep threw her rag against the bar and pushed her wire-rimmed glasses up her nose. "The big deal is y'all come in and play your cards and don't order a goddamned drop for hours. Shit's bad for business."

"We could order food?" Miles said.

"And I'd have to cook it. I'm a bartender, Miles. Not a cook. And I ain't about to start just so you can play cards."

Hunt's frown deepened. "But—"

"But nothin'. Now, y'all want another round, or should I introduce you to my friend Betsy?"

Miles didn't get it. "Who's Betsy?"

Hunt rubbed the bridge of his nose. "Her shotgun."

Lanette raised an eyebrow. "Well?"

"Okay," Lenny said on behalf of the gang. "We'll have another."

Lanette collected their pints and moved over to the tap as a good-looking blonde guy in his thirties, fresh off the college bus came up to the bar. "Hey, can I get three Jägerbombs?"

"Fifty bucks," Lanette said.

The old guys gave each other a knowing grin. Lanette always charged double to newcomers.

"Fifty?!"

Lanette finished pouring the draft and slid the pints down the bar, *Cocktail* style. "You wanna bitch or you wanna drink?"

Jägerbombs sighed. "How about tequila?"

Back at his table, his date wooed like a mashed cat. Lanette eyed her warily. Her bullshit meter had redlined earlier today when she'd gone to mop up the bathroom and found another couple fucking on the sink. She'd chased them out of the bar with their jeans around their ankles. Since then, the craziness hadn't improved. "I can't believe I'm about to say this, but what do you think you need that for? Look at her. You don't need no liquid panty remover to get her in the rack. Grow a pair and take her home already."

"We'll be out of your hair after this round, I promise."

"Yeah, and I'll fuck Morgan Freeman in the back of a Pinto. Promises are cheap." Lanette sighed. "Tell you what. I'll give you this one, but I better not catch you two boning in the bathroom. You got it?"

"I got it," Jägerbombs nodded enthusiastically as someone popped a quarter in the jukebox and James Brown came screeching over the bar, telling everyone he felt good and knew that he would. As if on cue, every chair in the Wood scratched the floor as patrons paired up and started moving to the sax solo. Lanette poured the shots and took the guy's money.

Lenny beamed at his comrades. "Damn, look at those kids move."

Hunt sighed. "I'd kill to be young again."

"Put something special in the drinks tonight, Lanette?" Miles said. "I've never seen so many horny kids in one space."

"Lucky spuds," Lenny said, looking at the gyrating crowd wistfully.

But it wasn't just the kids feeling the itch tonight. Lenny, Miles, and Hunt were all sporting hardons below the bar. Even Lanette felt like she could go for a few rounds with some kinda stud in the bathroom.

"Somethin' in the air," she said. "Been like this ever since last night."

And to mark that point, the jukebox switched over to "I Put a Spell on You".

The lights around the bar flickered, and the door flew open. It was the little mofo with the samurai sword in his cane, pouring through the entrance like midnight. On his arm was a sheep-fuckingly drunk Ava Elridge.

Somethin' in the air indeed.

CHAPTER 10
SOMETHIN' IN THE AIR

"AW, HELL-NO!" Lanette Wilson screeched, firing another round from the shotgun into the empty keg beside her, but she was drowned out by Screamin' Jay Hawkins growling through the jukebox.

The Wood was crawling with a salvo of drinkers under a haze of cigarette smoke, guzzling the discount shots Lanette had been tumbling all night—including her signature drink, the Peruvian Dogfucker.

"And fuck yo-self if you needa know what's in it," she'd say. Some things are sacred, and the ingredients of a signature shooter was sure as shit one of 'em.

Since the little man in the hat had arrived with Ava, the mood in the bar had shifted to full-on slosh fest. The jukebox rattled, glassware shimmered, and a space cleared in the middle of the bar for dancing.

Lanette did not care for dancing in her bar. People are unpredictable when they drink. One minute they're your best friend and the next they want to put your eye out with a cocktail sword because you're not as drunk as them. Throw in some bump-'n-grind and you've got a three-minute recipe for flying fists of jealousy when the wrong guy hooks up with the wrong gal in front of the spouse they walked in with.

The Baron didn't understand any of this, although he heard Lanette Wilson's thoughts like a radio broadcast in his head. He hadn't been out of his prison in what, a thousand years? A million? Didn't matter. He was out now, and soon enough he'd be free.

To do what? Didn't matter. Maybe a nice, long vacation in the Caribbean, with all of the rum, spice, tobacco and topless concubines he could handle.

And for now, he'd take another drink. The woman looked ravishing in her little black dress. She was delicious, and every ounce sex appeal: the dress accentuating her curves; her long locks like an auburn river cascading her neck. Even to a god of sex, Ava was quite the slice.

The music throbbed. She moved her hips. Slow, at first, ringing her hands through her voluminous hair; drunk on music, booze, dancing—drunk on everything.

The Baron saw his moment, grabbed her by the waist, and pulled her in. Together they moved and Ava nuzzled his neck, cocking his hat back on his smooth, waxed-chestnut head.

He kept a hand around her waist while he took off his hat and put it on her. She laughed, and he pulled her in for a kiss.

Ava melted like butter on a skillet and slipped the god a little tongue, which pleased him, and he pulled her closer.

The lights began to flicker again. The jukebox wailed. Music filled the bar with a rattle and boom not even the holiest of jukes can deliver. The lights stayed low and the crowd on the dance floor pulsed with the rhythm. Arms draped over shoulders. Skirts hiked up. Lipstick smeared on collars, and every man popped a tent.

The Baron was good with two things: sex, and death. And what was sex anyway—what was orgasm but what the French (those cunning linguists of the language of love) referred to as a Little Death? What was life but a ticking clock toward the grave, and how did life start but with an unfettered hump toward morning? Energy surged through the air, through the floor, through the patrons of The Gnarled Wood, through him. The Baron writhed with the energy like sizzling bacon.

"I want to tear that dress off and lick your downstairs," he growled in Ava's ear.

"'Kay." Ava was blackout drunk, and would have said the same if you'd asked her to give a handjob to a walrus.

The Baron considered this. "I want to taste salt on your lips, and I don't meant the ones on your face."

"Not a problem," she slurred.

That was interesting, usually he got whacked with a sheepskin of wine for that. He'd try one more. "I want you in the bottom."

"Not on your life, mister."

Back at the bar, Lanette scrambled for some sense of order. At this rate, there'd be an orgy in a couple of minutes. She pumped the shotgun and let off another blast, but it went lost in the thump of the jukebox. She tried again and hollered.

"That's it, we closed mothafuckas! Anybody shy of a trucker hat and a long drive home, go on and two-step yo ass outta here or I'll stick you fullah lead."

The Baron pulled away from Ava.

"Let us go and tangle the sheets in sweaty abandon."

"Only if you brush your teeth before you kiss me again," she said. "My lips are burning from the chili powder."

While the Baron brushed his teeth, Ava slipped out of her dress and under the covers. The lights were out and he moved like a shadow, naked save for his top hat, over to the bed. Ava threw the covers back.

"Ravage me," she said.

The Baron grinned. In the moonlight filtering in through the curtains, his teeth looked sharpened to points. The moonlight reflected out of his eyes in a soft blue glow and he climbed on top of her.

Then, Ava closed her eyes and felt his skin against hers.

Felt his breath heavy on her neck, and then he was kissing her again. She arched her back and opened her legs, and he entered her.

Then it was bliss. A million movements, tiny adjustments and shuddering volts of electric pleasure rocketing through their bodies. It was like releasing a valve. All the tension broke with a screaming siren of pure ecstasy.

She felt his tongue in her mouth, on her lips, tickle her earlobe and lick the sweat from her neck.

Then she felt sharp teeth and hot breath against her neck. She writhed and groaned under the top-hatted man.

When her blood hit his tongue, the Baron knew everything. He knew regrets, longings, dreams and nightmares. He felt what she felt, discovering the vacant room waiting for a love — a true, undeniable bond and intimacy which Ava deserved and had never had. He remembered everything she remembered, and as death plays life before one's eyes for the swan song—as Ava met her climax—he got the whole show, from first birthday all the way to the first moment of heartbreak.

But this woman was strong. He could feel it. For all life's unkind blows, she hadn't given up—wouldn't give up—on the dream. She believed it, so he believed it.

He found the meaning of life at the curve of her hip, the explanation of all tragedy in the small of her back, the tiniest of all life's pleasures at the nape of her neck and the song of reason in the smell of her hair.

He found what all men find at their most vulnerable, naked, next to her, breathing heavy, all the energy drained from him. That, and the Baron had also unlocked every fact about the town Ava had ever put in her mind.

He knew street names and addresses, townspeople, SUV models, phone numbers, and exactly how many calories were in a Snickers bar (something even he had a hard time believing). He knew which person drank decaf and how many preferred doughnuts to bagels with their morning brew. He knew what she knew, and had found exactly what he was looking for—what this whole courtship had really been about: he knew how to find the one who would free him, once and for all.

Life: What a party, what a hangover.

Ava awoke to the world spinning above her and the bed beside her empty. She looked at the clock on her nightstand, but the numbers were too fuzzy to read. She sat up, and immediately suffered what felt like a full-speed collision with an icepick to her forehead. Nausea rose, her insides twisting like pretzels, and she rolled off the covers and scrambled for the toilet as what looked like the contents of an entire bar shot out of her in a putrid comet.

There were no thoughts; no words to describe the malaise that gripped her like an iron fist, squeezing every drop of booze from her until all she ralphed was a streamer of bile. Her head throbbed. Her vision spotted. She tried to gasp for breath, then the process repeated itself until she was sure she would never breath again.

Then, a reprieve. "Uuggghh," she grumbled, grabbing a piece of toilet paper to wipe away the trail from her ride on the vomit comet. Then, the smell caught her and she was back again. This was it. This was death. Her hand caught the flusher and she slumped on the cool tile floor.

Time passed.

Eventually she worked up the energy to crawl back to bed. As she crawled back under the covers, she felt like she'd reopened the scar that held her college years. No adult drank like this. No adult found themselves painting the toilet with a multicolored liquor fusillade after taking a strange guy to bed only hours after meeting him. Was she having a midlife crisis? And where the hell *was* Saturday, anyway? She *had* gone to bed with him, hadn't she? Now a different feeling crept into her stomach: rejection.

We've all felt it, and we all know it. But for all our familiarity, when rejection strikes it still smarts like a spiteful harpy. Questions began circling like a sea of buzzards in her mind. Did she do something wrong? Say something off-putting? Was she out of practice? Or was he, like that stupid book said, just not that into her? Was she not hot enough?

Stop the truck right there, of course she was hot enough. She was sex on a pogo stick, she was sultry on a bearskin rug... And *he* was just a complete douche nozzle.

Bingo, honey bean, said her inner voice.

"Oh, shut up. You weren't any help in stopping this misadventure."

Hey, no fair. You drowned me.

"Well, if you weren't so persnickety I wouldn't want to so much."

Fair deal. But still, a modicum of judgement...

"You're supposed to be the one guiding me, remember?"

Hey, nobody ever said it had to be in the right direction, did they? I just told you what I thought.

"Well, hate to be the bearer of bad news, inner voice, but you have total shit for brains."

Be that way. Just remember that saying that technically means it applies to you as well.

"Uggh!" Ava grabbed her hair and tugged.

Not to mention, talking to yourself? Never a good sign.

Ava sat up and snatched her phone off the nightstand. "That's it."

It was time for drastic measures. It was time to find the number she'd been thinking of calling since this morning. It was time to do something about this skull-fucker of a hangover before she drove herself crazy wheeling over what she'd done to get rejected by a guy in a fucking top hat.

So... What exactly are we doing here?

"Something I should have done to begin with." Ava found the number and dialed.

Oh, come on. I thought we agreed!

"Too late," Ava sing-songed as the line began to ring.

Fine. But this is a seriously crap idea.

"This was a great idea," Hal said through a mouthful of pepperoni and cheese. They were sitting around a picnic table slathered with random quotes in psychedelic Sharpie ink at the Pizza Shack — Oak Falls' only pizza canteen. The Pizza Shack was aptly named because they did, indeed, serve pizza, and because it was, indeed, a shack. Well, more like a log-house with a six foot neon pizza slice hanging out front. Inside the shack was moody, with the radio tuned to classic rock, about a handful tables the staff encouraged customers to write on wedged in the middle, a bar-top counter, and a battered old pin ball machine by the window.

It was like a seedy bar in an action movie if the bar only served pizza and the action heroes were — well, stoned. A scribble on the table nearest Wiz said: BELIEVE, in large, curly handwriting.

"I don't believe it," Noah said. "You're saying it said *nice driving, ya doomed fucks!*? I need to smoke what you guys are smoking."

"You are smoking what we're smoking," Hal said.

"I'm serious dude, that's what happened." Wiz had really been banking on Noah believing. Of all the people he knew, Noah was the one who believed in spirituality — what was more spiritual than an unkillable talking animal?

"It's true," Trav said.

"We all saw it," added Hal.

"Well… Come on, really? You guys were all stoned and probably just heard a voice on the radio and thought it was the dog."

"I'm telling you man. It was real. It was like the Terminator." Wiz snapped cords of cheese from another slice of pizza and took a huge bite.

Confusion blossomed on Noah's face. "Huh?"

Okay, Wiz thought. *Terminator dog really is a stretch.* "Forget it."

"So we were saying," Travis interrupted. "Jason Vorhees. Demon serial killer, or zombie?"

"Definitely zombie," said Noah, happy to change the subject. "He's clearly a reanimated corpse."

"True," Wiz said. "But he drowned when he was a kid, right? So even if he was a zombie, how'd he get so big?"

"I dunno, magic zombie?"

Hal scoffed, spewing crumbs and cheese everywhere. "That's stupid."

Wiz grinned. "But it does raise an important question, fellas. You're in a zombie movie—who do you be?"

"Easy, I'd be the unlikely badass who saves the day," said Hal.

"I'd be the first to get the fuck out of dodge," Trav said. "I never understood why nobody ever tries that."

"They *do* try it, it just never works."

"Okay, fine. Sidekick."

"I'd be the guy who consoles the beautiful woman who just had to brain her infected husband with an egg beater," Noah said. "I hear you can get serious points being the consoling guy."

"Well, that leaves us with the first to die," Wiz shrugged. "Guess that's me."

"Yeah," the three chimed in unison.

Good friends. They always bust your balls. It was moments like these that made Wiz glad he could let the night go on as long as he wanted: no work in the morning, no responsibilities. How grown-ups managed to keep a social life was beyond him.

Across the table, Noah yawned. "Man, I'm beat. I think I'm gonna have to pack it in early,"—then to Wiz—"you mind if we do the moon thing tomorrow instead?"

"Sure," Wiz said, thinking: *I think I've made my point.* "It's just the moon. It's not the end of the world."

Just then, something smacked against the window across the Pizza Shack. They all turned to find a pale man in his sixties wearing a ragged suit, his hand sliding down the window as he let out a sort of extended groan.

"Tourist," Trav chuckled.

"Should we help him home?" said Wiz.

"Don't bother," said Noah. "He's just a drunk looking for attention. Ignore him."

"Fuck!" said the man through the glass.

"Angry drunk," observed Travis.

"What's up with his neck?" said Hal.

Wiz turned and grabbed his keys off the table. "Noah, it's the right thing to do. The van's right outside. I'll be like five minutes…" But when he turned back, the man staggered off. "Or not?"

"Hey, mind if we crash at your place?" Trav said. "I said I was crashing at Hal's."

"And I said I was crashing at Trav's."

"So we're kind of out a place to stay. How about some *Hobo Trashcan* and another doobie?"

"Now *that* is an idea," Wiz said. But before he could continue, his phone started ringing in his pocket.

CHAPTER 11
HELLO, KITTY.

He had no idea what he was doing. Actually, Wiz had spent a huge amount of life not really knowing what he was doing. He subscribed to the philosophy that life was more or less completely out of his control, and the easiest way to cope was to smoke shitloads of weed and go with it. It had never failed before. But now things were different. Now, he was doing things, and he had absolutely no idea how to do them. In fact, all of his experiences over the past twenty-four hours were completely new to him—and for the first time in his life, the pot wasn't helping.

So, when he found himself under a cloud of it, next to Ava Elridge on the couch in her living room, a fire burning under the mantel across from the coffee table, the weight of his actions began to dog-pile his psyche. He was bugging out—and even *that* he didn't know how to manage.

"So, that conversation we were busy not having?" Ava said.

"Sorry," he said, snapping out of it. "I'm kind of new at this."

"New at it?"

"I mean I'm out of practice." He took a great sigh and handed her the joint.

"You're out of practice with smoking pot? I find that hard to believe."

"Woah, hey! Way to bring the snark to the party."

She puffed three times and took a deep breath. "Sorry. I'm in a mood."

"Mood?" Gosh, he really was out of practice. How was he suddenly incapable of conversation? He'd had dozens of these, hadn't he? Was he that stoned? Since when did *that* make any difference?

"Bad date. And Franz keeps bothering me. And I'm somewhere between either drunk or hungover and I'm pretty sure I have a tendency for self-sabotage."

"Sabotage?"

Ava sighed and brushed her hair back. "I just keep picking the wrong guys."

"Wrong guys?"

"Yeah," she toked again and passed the joint back. "If they've got an edge or a cheeky grin or a leather jacket I suddenly lose all sense of not being an idiot and go for them. Then the spotlight falls on the douche within and I get my emotional ass kicked. But for some reason I just keep doing it."

"The douche within?"

"With a top hat and everything. I seriously don't get myself. And I don't get *him*. We had a lot of drinks. We danced. We were having fun. Then I take him back here, he has his way with me and poof! He vanishes."

Things were moving way to fast to process. "He literally vanished?"

"Well, it might have been figuratively. I passed out for a while. Either way, he's a dick. And Franz is a dick. And my other ex is a total dick, too. Every guy I date turns out to be the wrong guy."

"Hence the self-sabotage," Wiz said.

"Exactly. So then there's you. Not to jump into it or anything, but you're a nice guy. We get along. You don't give off that total douche bag vibe and we're having fun. Are you the right kind?"

Me? Well, obviously not, he thought. *I'm a professional slacker. I haven't had anything resembling a relationship since college. I have absolutely no idea what a date looks like, and I've recently stolen three pounds of pot from a gang of Russian mobsters. I'm definitely the wrong kind of guy.*

"I have to go for a smoke," he said.

"I'll make some food," Ava said.

Wiz stepped out into the night. The air was crisp and the sky was clear. A nearly-full moon lit up Ava's backyard. He walked along the deck and lit a cigarette.

A screech came from above. Wiz looked up and found a bird lolling back and forth on the updraft, swinging closer and closer to the lawn. He watched as the bird landed like a falling leaf. It was big. It wasn't just any bird either, it was a bald eagle.

The eagle ruffled its feathers, bounced its head and cawed directly in his direction. "Woah," Wiz said. What a beautiful, majestic beast. It was no wonder the forefathers decided to use this bird as a national emblem—it was a fucking winged badass. Almost immediately, thoughts of the flag turned into thoughts of money, which turned into thoughts of capitalism, which turned into thoughts of THE SYSTEM, which turned into a sour-tasting spot of disdain at the back of his throat.

Irony, man. A nation built upon the concept of freedom that's also bound by a class/economic structure that requires the exact opposite. No wonder everybody's so agitated. We're a national oxymoron.

Shadows moved around the fringes of the yard. Three feline figures crept toward the eagle, and before the feathery creature could realize what was happening, they were upon it. Screeches came first. Feathers flew. A yowling frenzy came from the writhing lump of cat on top of the bird, followed by another scuffle.

A crunching noise, and then the sound of teeth tearing flesh.

"Holy fuck," Wiz said.

The cats stopped and turned in unison. A gray Siamese with a tire print running up its back, its tail kinked at a right angle; a fat orange tabby with its head sitting crooked on a battered looking body; and a token black cat with a gory eyeball, all swathed in blood and feathers.

"Holy fuck! Zombie cats!"

The cats let off a series of blood-curdling yowls as they shambled slowly toward the steps of the deck. Wiz didn't need to see any more. He wagged the disbelief from his head and spun to grab the door.

The knob didn't turn. Shit, he'd locked it from the inside.

"Ava!" He knocked, but Ava was busy moving around the kitchen. He slapped against the door again, feeling the space behind him closing off. Death was prowling closer...

Oh fuck, oh fuck, oh fuck!

Noah Carpenter dreamed. In the dream, he is sexing a cute yogini named Christy back at the Bendy Legs Yoga Ashram in Portland. It's just getting to the good part when the door crashes in and a gang of monks lead by a man in a top hat fill the doorway in silhouette.

"Fornication," the little man says, pointing a craggy finger. "Forbidden indulgence numero uno!"—then to the monks—"Sic him, boys!"

The monks tumble in. Christy shrieks, and Noah tumbles out of the bunk. He runs across the room and smashes through the window, only rather than falling, he finds himself in the wide, high-ceiling study of Sister Lady Margo Stzu-Li: the slim, sharp-featured Asian lady who owns Bendy Legs. The room is dark, save for a lone candle licking light around the room. There's a bathtub where the desk should be, and Lady Margo suds herself with a 100% organic cotton loofah.

"Noah, you've been very naughty. What are we going to do with you?"

"Lady Margo, I can explain—"

"No need." She turns, revealing her rotted eyeballs drooling into the bathwater. Now Noah realizes the loofa is scraping off huge chunks of her skin. She rises from the water, flayed skin dangling off her body like a peeled banana. The candle goes out.

Noah closes his eyes and finds himself at the start of a long hallway. Heavy wooden doors flank both sides, and an exit sign glows at the end of hall. He makes a break for it.

Every time he passes a door, it flings open. Wiz crawls out of the first, his head mashed-in. Pieces of brain drip onto the floor. "First one to die, Noah."

He vaults over his undead friend and the next door flies open. Trav and Hal spill out, one missing an arm, the other missing a leg, and neither with any skin on their face. "Noah... Let's play some *Hobo Trashcan*. We can eat you after!"

They reach out but he brushes past. The next door explodes open, and behind it is Noah's three-hundred pound Aunt Susan. "NOAH!!!" she screeches. "Come and give your auntie a kiss."

He reaches the end. The door under the exit sign is locked. Above him he finds the little man in the hat sitting on the sign, cackling like he's just huffed a tank of laughing gas. "Your fate is sealed, Carpenter!"

Noah pounds the door until blood runs from his fists. The whole gang of his undead past closes in on him, biting into the flesh on his back and arms, his thighs—and yes, even his butt cheek. Still he keeps pounding until the little man produces a samurai sword and brings it down on his head.

Noah shot upright in bed with the knocking in his dream replaced with actual knocking on the actual door. He sighed, rubbing sleep from his eyes. He flipped the blanket off and stepped into his jeans.

"One minute!"

Down the stairs, past the kitchen and through the living room. Hal and Travis sat in front of a long timed-out round of *Hobo Trashcan*, a pooched bong next to an ashtray filled with roaches on the coffee table.

Knock, knock, knock, knock knock, knock knock... Knock—

"One minute!!"—then to Hal and Travis—"Tell me you guys didn't order another pizza."

He hurdled over the linebackers' outstretched legs and flung open the door. The smell of cabbage was the first thing that hit him. On the other side was a scraggly-looking man in his fifties wearing Day-Glo shorts, a red stocking cap and an unamused expression.

"I'm guessing you're not delivering pizza…"

The man moved with incredible speed. Noah caught the gleam of metal and the first blow struck him across the bridge of the nose with an excruciating crunch. He hit the floor and the wind knocked out of him. Water filled his eyes and hot blood spewed over his chin.

The second blow caught him just above the eye. The back of his head cracked off the floor. Pain radiated through his whole body like a strobe light. The man raised, wiping his mouth with the back of his forearm.

"Where is poopstick Wizard?"

Wham! Crunch. Thunk.

"He—"

The world began to flicker. Noah tried to catch his breath, but the man laid three furious kicks to his ribs and something inside that definitely wasn't supposed to pop, popped. Air and blood wheezed out of him. The last thing he heard was scrambling from back in the living room, then Noah was out.

Past the surface, Ava thought that Wiz was a pretty decent guy. He was kind, funny—cute in a sort of shaggy dog way. To be honest, it took her by surprise. She'd been expecting a lazy burnout who could hardly string a sentence together, and the way he was spouting off rapid-fire commentary on the pack of undead felines in her backyard might be wacky, but it was certainly articulate.

"You want a doughnut?" she said.

Wiz sighed and pulled his hands through his hair, bewildered. "Can we go back to the part where you've got a pack of fucking zombie cats in your backyard?"

Ava shrugged. "I really doubt they were zombie cats."

"Ava, they tore apart a friggin' eagle. Not exactly your garden variety feline behavior…"

"Well they probably had rabies or something? I mean, there are plenty of explanations for cats attacking birds before we jump straight to the purring dead."

"Look, I know it sounds crazy, but I *saw* them, Ava." Wiz picked the joint out of the ashtray, lit it, and puffed until he broke into a coughing fit. "And they definitely did *not* have rabies. Something is going on. I don't know what that something is, but I am definitely sure that *something* is going on, and that something explains the cats."

"So, what? Radiation? Fallen satellite? Cannibal-rage-virus?"

"I don't know," Wiz said. "But what I do know is those cats weren't just hungry — they were all mangled and dead-looking."

He passed the joint to Ava. She took it with a patient expression and said, "Well, maybe you saw that... Or maybe it's, you know, something *else*?"

"What do you mean?"

Wiz was cute, but this wild paranoia that the dead were rising had the marks of a closet conspiracy nut all over. "Well, you know... We *have* been smoking pot here. You were baked. It was dark. You probably saw the cats attack the bird and your mind just filled in the rest."

"Ava, I've been stoned before," Wiz said. "Actually, I've been been stoned for most of my life. But I know what I saw. Those cats were all zombified and tore the bird to bits and I'm sure it all has something to do with this talking dog I ran over."

Here Ava couldn't help herself. She burst out laughing and handed the joint back. "Okay, now you're just making things complicated."

"I'm not trying to!" he said. "I'm just saying what I saw. Honestly, I like to keep it simple. But I know what I saw and I'm not making it up to impress you or something, believe me."

Now, how had he known she was thinking he was just trying to impress her? Were her thoughts on broadcast here or something? Oh crap, did that mean he also knew that she found him cute and had already thought about kissing him at least two times? Or was she just really, really stoned?

"I'm just saying," she said. "Maybe you just smoked a little too much — "

"What? No way! Thomas Jefferson was a pot farmer, and

therefore a routine toker and he was the president. Same with George Washington. Ben Franklin smoked pot; he invented the fucking lightning rod! The Beatles, Lenny Bruce, Bill Clinton... All stoned and all successful. Smoking pot is not my problem. My problem is crazy shit keeps happening to me and nobody will believe it."

"Woah, speech much?" Ava chuckled. She enjoyed nothing more than busting his chops, but secretly Wiz's rants were the thing she liked the most about him.

"I'm sorry," he sighed. "I'm not good with brevity."

Ava moved over on the couch. She squeezed his arm. "Wiz, I believe you... But it's just a little, you know, *out there*, is all. Now..." she released him and stood. "You want a doughnut?"

"Yes —" Wiz said. But before he could continue, a tinny version of Bob Dylan's "Mr. Tambourine Man" came from his pocket.

Wiz furrowed his brow, then dug into his pocket and produced a cell phone.

"Hello?" He paused, listening. His eyes went wide. "What happened?"

"He just came in and started hitting him," Trav said.

Wiz bounded through the entrance and found Noah laying on the couch. Blood caked his face. His left eye was swollen shut and his nose was bent sideways. He was unconscious. Hal was hunched at his side.

Wiz crouched beside his beaten friend and sighed. "Did he say anything?"

"No," Trav replied. "He's been out cold since it happened. He's still breathing though."

"I mean the Russian," Wiz said. "Did the Russian say anything?"

Hal frowned, crossing his arms as he leaned back in his chair. "No, the fucker just came in and started hitting."

This was bad. Seriously bad. The Russians had figured out they'd stolen the pot, and now they were here to make someone pay. Noah's beating was just a memo: They were fucked.

"We are so, *so* fucked," he said. How? How could they possibly know? It didn't matter now. None of his plans mattered now. Things were going way too out of control. "I'm calling the sheriff."

"The sheriff?!" Trav said. "How do you plan to explain this to him?"

Hal crossed his beefy arms. "He'll definitely bust us if he finds out about the pot—"

"Guys, priorities!" Wiz snapped. He started pacing the length of the room. "If the Russians are in town we need to tell someone."

"Staying out of jail is a pretty big priority, Wiz."

"Why don't we just give them the pot back?"

Wiz wheeled around. "How would that make it any better?"

From the couch, Noah let out a long, wet-sounding breath.

"Fuck!" Wiz said.

"I know that sound," Hal said, the experienced linebacker coming out in the time of crisis. "That's a broken rib."

"What do we do?" Trav said.

CHAPTER 12
AWAKENING

1 A.M. The hospital was a ghost town with a handful of orderlies stalking the corridors, zombified by lack of sleep. Wiz, Trav, and Hal sat outside the emergency room where Franz MacFee was working on Noah.

"You guys get home before the sheriff shows up," Wiz said. "I'll tell him Noah mouthed off to the wrong trucker on his way past the Wood and I found him like this."

"What if he doesn't buy it?" Trav said.

"I'll figure it out as I go."

"What if he asks Lanette and finds out you're lying?" Hal added.

Wiz stood and raked his hands through his hair. "Then I'll make something up. Now get out of here."

"What about Noah?"

"I'll call you as soon as I know anything. Now, please, guys. I can't cover for the three of us. Go."

The linebackers exchanged worried glances, then shuffled off down the hall. Wiz collapsed in the chair by the door. He felt heavy. Exhaustion jangled his nerves, putting him in a state of half sleep, half heart palpitations. The light in the hall seemed to fade, and before he could stop it he was nodding off...

The emergency room door slammed open and Franz MacFee came out with a troubled expression. He slumped in the chair beside the Wizard and said, "Got any weed?"

"Seriously? That's what you lead with?"

"What?"

"Not exactly the time, Franz." Now Wiz felt like he'd guzzled four cups of coffee, then he remembered he actually had guzzled four cups of coffee right before he phoned Al. "Seriously. How can you even think about smoking up when Noah's—"

"Relax," Franz said. "He's stable. Sure, he's got a busted rib and his nose looks like blood pudding, but he'll live."

Wiz let out a relieved sigh and melted into the uncomfortable chair. "You're sure he didn't puncture a lung or something?"

"Actually, he's lucky. The chunk of rib just missed. We'll need to keep him overnight to make sure he doesn't croak on account of something I missed, but I figure we'll have him back to you in the morning."

"Something you missed?! What do you mean something you missed?"

The doctor chuckled. "Joke, Wiz. Joke. I may be about a quarter in the bag, but you know me. Genius surgeon. You should go home, get some rest."

"Can't," Wiz said. "I'm waiting for the sheriff."

"Oh, well in that case," Franz leaned in and affected a conspiratorial tone. "Have you got any weed? I feel a hangover coming on and could really use the edge off."

Wiz eyed him balefully. "I'm going for a walk."

Okay, eating the kid had been a bad move. Ash's mind was wrought between thoughts of boning dead people and thoughts of building forts. He wanted to play with monster trucks and firecrackers and paintball guns. He wanted to shag corpses and wash them and shag them again. He wanted to shag corpses on top of monster trucks while setting off firecrackers, all under an enormous fort. He wanted to see boobs. As many boobs as possible — preferably dead ones if he had the option.

Pretty strange place to be, Ash's brain.

"Dumb fucking dog," he said in what surprised him to be the tone of a nine-year old. "Why didn't he tell me?!"

Of course, the dog *had* told him. The effects of the gravedigger's brains were mixing with the effects of the kid brains — something he hadn't been expecting. Really, he'd only taken a nibble. It wasn't like he'd done the same kind of damage on Todd he'd done on Digger, but it didn't seem like the amount of brains he ate made any difference. How was he supposed to terrorize a town in this state?

He stalked down the gravel path into the cemetery. When he thought about it, it didn't seem to make much difference. He could walk among them, the legitimate living dead, and all he got was a handful of eye-rolls. They thought he was crazy, or a zombie uber-fan dressed up for shits and giggles.

Defeated, he trudged up the steps toward the mortuary. He needed a plan. Moreover, he needed someone to work out a plan with — where the shit was the talking dog now?

He reached for the knob when the door flung open and a slim, pale-as-death arm caught him by the chest and dragged him inside.

Wiz wandered the corridors of the hospital with his hands in his pockets. Guilt clouded his mind. He rounded a bend and came up on a hall filled with gurneys, medical equipment with lots of tubes, and all manner of unbleeping bleeping technology for heart stuff. The light behind him shut off. Darkness threatened to swallow him. On he went. He reached an intersection and found a corkboard with advertisements supporting ORGAN DONATION!!! a little too enthusiastically in bold letters. Wiz sighed the sigh of a very tired, very guilty man.

From the unlit hallway leading to the morgue came scuttling noises. He frowned, taking a step into the blackness. Rats? Something moved across the floor. The sound crept closer, and from the shadows came a dismembered hand, walking on its fingers like the Thing from *The Addams Family*, a trail of gore in its wake.

"What the hell?"

The hand paused, as if it were sizing him up, then scuttled back into shadows. Wiz blinked. Disbelief sang like a chorus in his mind. Seeing things? Was he that stressed? He waited a moment as the scuttling trailed off, then decided to follow when a hand grabbed him by the shoulder and spun him around.

"Do you have any idea the world of shit you're in?"

"Holy fuckballs! Jeez, Al. When did you get so sneaky?"

The sheriff shoved Wiz against the wall. His lip tightened as his eyes lit up in full-blown sibling fury. "About the same time you became such a moron. The Russians!? In my town?!"

"I thought you should know?"

Al removed his hand and rubbed the bridge of his nose. "We had a deal, Wiz. I turn a blind eye, and *you* don't let the product hit our town."

"Wh—"

"Now there's a fucking miscreant running around wreaking havoc!"

"It wasn't—"

"Do you know who showed up in my office this morning? A DEA agent, looking for you."

"Me?"

"You. And if that's not enough, I'm in the middle of a goddamned crime wave and a kid's gone missing."

Wiz bowed his head, letting it all sink in. "Fuck."

"I'll say!"

Still, if what he *thought* was going on was actually going on, he needed to warn the sheriff. "Al, look. I'm really sorry, but I don't how this happened. Something's going on."

"I just finished telling you what's going on!"

"No, I mean something strange. I don't know how, and I know it sounds crazy, but I think the dead are coming back to life and—"

But the sheriff grabbed Wiz by the front of his shirt and slammed him against the wall again with a wrath Wiz had never seen before.

"Listen to me. I don't know what kind of shit you pulled, but this is so not the time for games, Wiz. The DEA! You keep this up and I won't be able to protect you. Do you understand me? Find a safe place and stay there until I get this Russian guy off the streets."

Safe place? The only place he had was where he lived, and the Russians already knew that. "Dude, where am I supposed to go?"

"Figure it out, idiot." With that, the sheriff released him and stalked off.

Two floors below, Earl Potvin awoke in a brightly lit room. He was lying face-up on a gurney, and something itched around his big toe. He sat up and scanned the room. There were more gurneys behind him. The wall of slabs with busted open doors unsettled him—but at least he knew where he was. The hospital. Accidentally relocated to the morgue. *Stupid nurses left me for dead before I actually kicked it.*

He stopped to scratch his toe and came back with a body tag. His name was on it. But no, it couldn't be—could it?

Earl looked down and found a puckering pink incision running along his chest. The wound wasn't healing. The flesh looked—well—dead.

Behind him came a sound like eating soup through a snorkel and a chorus of groans. He turned and found ten, pasty-looking naked people tearing pieces off what appeared to be the coroner. A tattered piece of uniform, stained almost purple with blood, flew through the air. They were trying to smash the guy's head in.

"What the hell are you doing?" Earl shouted, scrambling, but his legs gave out and he flopped to the floor where he got an even gruesomer view of the coroner as the skull finally went like a crunching coconut.

Brains started flying. One of the cannibals looked toward Earl, picked up a piece of coroner, and said, "Sorry, here."

He tossed a chunk of fresh brains.

Earl was disgusted, but all the same snatched the meat from the air and gobbled it down. "Hot damn, that's not bad!"

One of the women of the group, a blonde in her mid-twenties, looked up from the corpse with a bloodied grin. "We're fucking zombies, how cool is that?"

"Yeah! Braaaaiiiins!" said the guy who tossed Earl the chunk of melon.

"Braaaiiiins! Braaaiiiiins! Braaaaiiiins..." they all groaned, then giggled. (They were still trying it on.)

Earl crawled over—the strength returning to his legs with every chew of the coroner's noggin—and reached into the skull for another chunk of the good stuff. He licked his fingers.

"Brains, huh? Pretty good."

Another woman—a brunette in her fifties with a hole in her cheek from a Chihuahua attack which had ended on an upturned garden hoe— was bothered. She pouted and wiped a great glob of coroner from her chin.

"Great, now what do we do?"

"I dunno, I guess we just keep doing it."

"I don't want to keep doing it. I'm full. Besides, I need to lose five pounds."

"You're dead, toots. You think it matters anymore?"

"This is why zombies have such a bad rap," the blonde said. "They have a *serious* image problem."

"Says the chick who chokes to death on her own vomit after eating a whole Chinese buffet."

"Says the girl with a hole in her face from a stupid little dog!"

"Zombie bitch!"

"Undead skank!"

"Dog-loving corpse-whore!" The blonde had been called a skank before and had forged her comebacks sharper than Damascus steel.

Earl stood up and belched as if he'd just conquered a

Thanksgiving turkey. "Will you all just shut up?!"

The group fell silent, wiping man bits from their faces.

"There are probably more of us. If we're all zombies, then there's got to be more. I say we go up to the cemetery and find out."

"Can we get soda on the way?"

Nothing washes down brains better than a can of Coca Cola and a little shameless product placement. (Hey, the undead *do* have an image problem.)

"Soda and cemeteries! Soda and cemeteries!" they chanted.

"And braaaaaaaiiiiiiiiiins!"

"Hey Bernie, you're getting pretty good at that."

"Okay, you try."

"Braaa—" the zombie belched, "—aiiinsss."

Earl heaved the coroner's body out of the way. They headed off for the cemetery, each trying furiously to perfect their own, unique and personal call for brains like an undead choir, out of tune.

"Braaaaiiiiins!"

"Braaiiiiiiiiinns!"

"Braaaaaaaaaaains!"

"Bray-uns."

"That was just awful."

...Away into the night.

For some, sleep comes easily. For others, it's climbing a greased pole. Mack tossed and turned in the moonlight. He watched the hours tick by on his alarm clock. He listened to the kennel dogs go through their nightly barking ritual. He thought about sleeping. He tried to stop thinking. He started thinking about how hard it was to stop thinking and rolled onto his back with a sigh. Sleep was miles away.

He'd been an insomniac for as long as he could remember, never managing to hit that delicious sweet-spot of tuckered out fading that unaddled folks so often could use five minutes more of. He'd even come to terms with it, but for some reason, anxiety had decided to be his bedside companion for the night.

After a while he gave up. He stalked off to the bathroom for a cup of water, then opened the medicine cabinet and popped an Ativan. Another swig from the tap and he headed back to bed.

He was just beginning to drift off when something rapped against the window. He opened his eyes and found the huge shape of a doglike creature with glowing red eyes, a maw of hungry teeth, and deadly claws hanging off the windowsill.

"First thing's first," it said. "Got any MilkBones?"

PART II
HELL UNEARTHED

CHAPTER 13
HANGOVER, CALIFORNIA

Saturday morning hit the people of Oak Falls like a swinging sack of hangover bricks. Pillows were beaten, slippers were thrown, dogs were exiled to the porch, and heads pounded in agony. Sun shone through windows, covers were tossed, Advil, Gravol, and Alka Selters were guzzled. Coffee started brewing.

As morning plodded on, hazy snapshots of the night before materialized: Fourteen martinis and shoeless dancing on a table. Confetti at one point. People sneaking off to shag on the bathroom sink—some of which with another person's mate. Arguments, fights, breakups, and groveling...

It stood to reason that this day should simply be a write-off; erased from the calendar so that everyone could move on and forget it all happened. But then, the same has been said of Mondays, and we all know how that turned out. Some stores opened grumpily on time, others were late, and some didn't open at all.

Down at the Gnarled Wood Tavern, Lanette was busy installing a new sign above the bar that read: NO DANCING ON THE TABLES. The electric drill roused one of the truckers halfway between drinking and dozing at the bar.

"Well, whatchu think?" Lanette said.

The trucker grumbled and lowered his hat. "Frankly, I like it when the gals dance on the tables," he said. "Improves the point-of-view, you know?"

"Well, it ain't like she gonna fall off the table and onto your dick." The barkeep slammed the drill against the bar and the rest of the truckers snorted to life. "What d'you say fellas? Bloody Mary? First one to pick up a broom gets his on the house."

The ladies of the coven started their mornings with bath salts, tinctures, mineral water, and prayers to Dionysus for speedy recovery. Later, a little power-walking around the football field, some yoga, some quinoa, and the day was back to normal —well, almost.

Suzanne, Ellie and Margy all stood in front of Ava's Bakery and Cafe, where the sign in the window stayed adamantly fixed on CLOSED.

"I can't remember the last time Ava hasn't opened," Suzanne said.

"Looks like we weren't the only ones who had a rough night, ladies," said Ellie, massaging a headache from her temples.

Margy was bent over, ralphing up the tinctures and mineral water she'd had earlier. "Dionysus is such a bitch."

"Margy!"

"What? Uuughh—" *Splatter, splatter.*

"Let's try the Soup. Margy needs fries, pronto."

What Franz MacFee needed was a good huff of oxygen to cut the hangover. He piloted his Prius down the main drag as his head pounded with root-canal-level torment. He decided to make a pit stop at Ava's for a coffee. Sure, she'd told him not to visit, but honestly this time wasn't personal. Sure, he could go to the Texaco like all the other sleaze bags, but their coffee tasted like ass and he didn't consider himself on the same level of sleaze as the truck stop Charlies... Or whatever their names were. (Tidbit: all truckers at the Texaco had the same name.)

He threw it in park and heaved himself out of the Prius. Blearily, he stalked over to the door and tried, but it was locked.

"Weird." Ava never missed a workday. Especially in tourist season. He noticed the rest of the main drag was deserted, which was also weird, since there were hundreds of out-of-towners in for the Palooza. In fact, this was the first official day of the Palooza—streamers, balloons, and welcome signs hung from every streetlamp—yet there was nobody out. That's when the shrubs in town square began to snore.

The town square wasn't really much of a square. It was a stop sign-shaped, cobbled stone bed of flowers, shrubs, and a far too often replanted ancient oak tree that approximated the town mascot. The snores came again and Franz went over to investigate.

A black wingtip shoe poked out from the shrub. Next to it was the ivory length of the cane that held a samurai sword. It was the little guy with the top hat, passed out with his back slumped against the tree. In his hand was a half-empty bottle of hot sauce.

Franz grinned. His mind switched gears from hangover curing to revenge. "Well, Oddjob," he said. "Haven't you made my day."

"Tell me again why I have a beaten up Noah on my futon?" Ava said. She indeed had a beaten-up Noah resting on her couch, bandages and gauze over his nose, an icepack on his brow.

Wiz, Hal, and Travis sat around him, cups of coffee and homemade croissants steaming on the table. Ava stood with her hands on her hips, her brow expressing a pressing need for answers.

"I got beaten up," Noah said, sounding like he had the worst head cold in history.

"Well, duh."

"We needed a place to hide out," Wiz said. "Sorry for the short notice."

"Don't worry about it," Ava said. "But some insight as to why the hiding out would be nice?"

The four musketeers all stared at their plates sheepishly.

"These croissants are excellent," offered Travis.

"Yeah, delicious," added Hal.

"Guys!"

Wiz stood. "Okay, sorry. You're right. If you're kind enough to grant us a hideout you should really know why we're hiding." — He paused, collected his thoughts, and dove in — "Last night, a guy who wants something from us decided to lay the beats on Noah."

Ava raised her chin, questioning. "Wants something what?"

The guys all stared at their plates again.

"Guys!"

"Okay, fine!" Wiz said. He rubbed his eyes and sighed again. "We maybe — sorta — kinda — "

"Wiz…"

" — Stole three pounds of pot from a gang of Russian drug farmers?"

"You did what?!"

"We stole three pounds of pot from a gang of — "

Ava wagged her head and began pacing. "Rhetorical!"

"Right."

"We need a plan," Noah said.

"I told you the plan. We hide out here while the sheriff deals with the Russian."

Noah propped himself up on the couch, wincing as he adjusted the icepack. "No, I'm mean like a plan to get rid of the pot."

"Selling weed while there's a DEA agent in town," Wiz said, wagging his head. "Noah, are you high?"

Noah shrugged. "A little. Those painkillers the doc gave me are kinda fun."

"So you guys are fugitives from the DEA, too?" Ava said.

"Which is exactly why getting rid of the pot is a high priority," Noah said, as if that explained it all.

"But we're stuck here?" Wiz said. He couldn't believe that even after such a vicious attack from the Russian, Noah was already back to scheming.

"No," his roommate corrected. "You're stuck here. The Russian was after you, I got that much through the beating. The DEA guy's only looking for you, too. Right?"

"Wh—"

"Neither of them is looking for a couple of high school linebackers," Noah said, looking at Hal and Trav as they dropped their pastries in unison.

"Us?" Hal said.

"I agree, us?" said Trav.

"You," Noah said. "Nobody will ever suspect the two of you being the pot kingpins of Oak Falls. I'll swing by the house on my way to work, get you guys the weed, and you get hustling."

"You're going to work?" Wiz said. "Are you sure you're—"

Noah waved him off. "Franz said I'm fine. A little bruised maybe, but if the doctor says I'm good to work, I'm going to work. You stay here, try not to drive Ava nuts, and Trav and Hal will meet me at the cemetery tonight. We all come back here, split up the money, and everything will be peachy."

"That's actually not a bad plan," Ava said.

"There's something else," Wiz said. "Guys, I saw something last night at the hospital. It's crazy, but I think something weird's going on."

Ava sighed and sat on the corner of the sofa. "You're not talking about zombie cats again, are you?"

"Actually, I think it gets worse."

Max Reyes awoke in his room at the Rooms-R-Us feeling like he'd spent the night licking tinfoil. He'd been up until three, chain-smoking, going over his notes from the past three months. He'd also brought a whiteboard with a cluster diagram of all his facts surrounding two words circled in red dry-erase: THE WIZARD?

The sheriff was stonewalling him. He'd really expected his threats to land heavier on the local lawman, but Max was beginning to suspect he wasn't nearly as threatening as he needed to be. He'd watched back-to-back Clint Eastwood movies on the motel TV, trying to get some insight into being scarier, but he could only really relate to the *good* in *The Good, The Bad, and The Ugly.*

He played around with the coffee maker that looked like it had been imported from the 1950s, got something dark and sludgy coming through the percolator, and said, "Go ahead punk, make my coffee."

He dumped the contents in a styrofoam cup and moved over to the window, where he parted the blinds and met a day so bright he wanted to punch it. In the parking lot was a rusty Eldorado. Max's cop spidey-sense started tingling. He whipped out his phone, took a sip of the coffee sludge, then spat it out on the rug.

"Would it kill these people to adopt a Starbucks?" He punched the numbers for his contact back at headquarters and waited.

"Howdy pumpkin," a man's voice came through the receiver. "How's life in the sticks?" This was the Queen, a chief technical officer back in Arlington who also happened to be a flaming homosexual with a predilection for fine dining, fine shoes, and even finer suits. The Queen offset this with a 400-pound bench press and a well-groomed mustache.

"More thrilling every minute. Can you run a vehicle ID for me?"

"Depends, sugar. What's in it for me?"

"I'll, uh…" Max had really been going for more of an I.O.U. arrangement. "Get you a coffee?"

"Not good enough, handsome. P.S., have you shaved off that horrendous goatee yet?"

"Not yet," Max said. "Dinner then?"

"You call yourself a dealmaker? Do better."

Across the catwalk running the horseshoe motel, the door to room 273 opened and a man in his late fifties wearing a red stocking cap made his way down the steps and over to the Cadillac.

"Your highness, sorry for the short-windedness, but what *can* I do for you?"

The Queen considered. "Well, there is this pair of boots on eBay I've been eyeing. Snakeskin. 'Bout a five-inch heel. Sex on a pogo-stick—"

"You want me to buy you shoes?"

"Boots, Max. Boots. Shall I send you the link, my little love monkey?"

Max could go about a year before he heard the Queen call him a *love monkey* again. "Done. I see the perp now. If I get you a visual, can you ID him?"

"Honey, you buy me those boots and I'll get you a mug shot."

Max angled his phone at the door as the guy came back up the stairs with two bottles of Kahlua and snapped a photo. "Sending it to you now."

The Russian made the trip from the room to the car three times, then climbed in and peeled off around the bend.

"Aha," the Queen said. "Boris Volydeskvi. Fifty-eight, and well preserved by the vodka if you ask me. You've got yourself a Russian, honey. You want me to call you some backup?"

"They'll take too long. I've got it from here. Send me the link for your shoes and I'll get them for you. Thanks."

"Boots, Max! Boots. You're not gonna do something stupid, are you?"

"Gotta go," Max said. He hung up, grabbed his gun from the desk, and slipped through the door.

The door was unlocked. *Amateur,* Max thought. He slipped inside.

Bottles were everywhere. On the desk, the sofa, the nightstand, even the windowsill. In the tub, three fresh bottles of vodka were nestled in ice next to the Kahlua. Max moved back into the main room, his firearm in traditional action-cop position. There was a map of the town over the desk with pins and a length of string describing some pattern. He moved closer, then felt his stomach drop into a parallel universe.

The string was in the shape of a happy face.

"Oh, fuck."

The door flew open. Reyes wheeled around just in time to catch a tire iron to the back of his head. He crumpled to the floor.

"Dumb fucking police detective," Boris said. "Falls for oldest trick in book."

CHAPTER 14
DON'T EAT THE DUMBFUCKS

Little is known about the love lives of the undead. Really, past the brain-eating, reanimated corpse angle, not much is said for the zombie's perspective. So they ate brains—big deal! Sure, they were corpses—so what? Indeed, there was the smell, but whose fault was that?

At first glance they were brain-hungry cannibals, (Mmm, brains. Maybe with a little cilantro or a garlic rub—mashed potatoes and brainsloaf—brains pot pie—penne a la brains…) but in reality, zombies were not the mindless man-eaters or virus-addled lunatics jonesing for human flesh depicted in the movies. Just like everything in life—or rather, *unlife*—things were more complicated. Zombies were, until very recently, people. And with that came wants, desires, longings. Needs.

Asher had been troubled by the zombie loneliness until Brenda, the attractive corpse he'd met in a less animated state earlier, pulled him into the cemetery, threw him down on a slab and shagged him silly.

And so, they found it in each other: their wants allayed, their needs quenched, their desires fulfilled. Loneliness drifted off like a tiny raincloud to pour on someone else's zombie parade. And although it was a little awkward like all first times, while there lacked a movie luster (and yes, lubrication), they enjoyed each other until Brenda melted in a pool of post-coital bliss in the zombie king's arms.

Brenda had awoken shortly after Ash and the dog left the cemetery. She'd wandered around, a little disoriented. Then she found the gravedigger's blood-caked pistol with a tiny cherry tomato of brains left behind. Before she could think, she swallowed the grey-matter morsel and felt the warmth of life wash over her.

We know the drill from here. When it comes to zombies, you really are what you eat—which is why it's so important to read the label. *May contain traces of necrophilia, nymphomania and wannabe-serial-killer extract*, Digger's might have read if people were more often packaged.

A few minutes later, an unmatched horniness fell upon the zombie-ette, and when Ash had come up the driveway, she just couldn't help herself. When they finished, Ash explained the brain-eating thing, the soulless thing, and even had a go at explaining the giant evil talking dog—but that only got a laugh from Brenda.

"A talking dog?"

"Well, come on," Ash replied, still a little out of breath. "The jump from *you're a zombie now* isn't really that far…"

Brenda shook her head. "You're fucking with me?"

"Nope," came a low, gravelly voice from down the hall. The beast came in wagging his tail. "Well, haven't you two just hit it off. Hiya, toots. I'm Seth, the hellhound."

"I'm Brenda."

Seth woofed. "Would you get a load of those pagodas?" he said. "I mean, *woof*."

Brenda scrambled to cover her breasts. "Excuse me?"

"I said you've got a pretty nice rack of lamb for a dead chick. Did the great king Asher fill you in on the skinny?"

Brenda nodded. "If you're dead, you wake up… Blah blah

blah, soulless freak... Blah blah, murder the town... Blah blah you are what you eat, and blah. Don't bite a nine-year-old."

"Hey, she learns pretty quick," Seth said, streamers of doggy drool hanging from his jaws. "Unlike you, little Asher."

Ash was wearing a sheet from one of the slabs over his head and was making wooing sounds. The sheet ghost cocked its head, as if it were doing a trig problem. "I don't get it. I'm not small at all!"

"Well," Brenda chuckled.

"I'm *not* small!"

She sighed. "He's been on-and-off like this all day."

Seth nodded. "He needs to munch some grown-up brains to push the kid tendencies back to normal man-level."

"Hey!" Ash said.

Just then, the door at the back of the embalming room flew open and a pile of zombies lead by a stocky man in his mid-sixties with a thick grey mustache came through. He was flanked by an Asian woman in her late thirties who had clearly died in a car accident—although it didn't seem to be bothering her now.

"Uh, hi!" she said. "Are you guys zombies too?"

The man frowned at her. "Carly, of course they're zombies. This is the mortuary, remember?"

"New recruits!" Seth said. "Come on in, welcome!"

The beast turned back to Ash and Brenda and said, "Not that I'm complaining, but you might wanna find some clothes now that we've got company."

"Oh!" Brenda flung herself behind one of the slabs.

Dead Earl chuckled. "So, what's the story here?"

Al Kowalski sat in front of a mountain of paperwork that could crush him if there was an earthquake, but all he could think of was how he'd explain himself to Jenny if the Drug Enforcement Ass-bag decided to take him down with his brother. What would she think? How had he let himself slip so far? One little favor for his slacker brother and it would be his undoing.

He massaged his temples. A stress headache worried away behind his eyeballs. Coffee steamed next to a burning cigarette in his ashtray. He tried to will himself to focus, grabbed the pen and the first noise complaint to file, and started writing.

Beep-beep, chirped the office phone. Al's secretary Darleen came over the line.

"Sheriff? I have the mayor on line one for you."

"Ugh." Al slammed the pen on the case file. "Can you take a message?"

"Don't think so. He's really pushy."

"Well—"

"Actually he's kind of a dick."

"You're right. Put him through." The line blipped as Darleen made the transfer. "Mayor Peters! What can I do for you this morning?"

"You know exactly what, Al," The mayor huffed. "The council meeting is tomorrow morning and security must be perfect. What's your plan?"

Al sighed, pinched the bridge of his nose. "Oh you know, I was thinking bazookas. A couple F-18s. Hell, I may even call the National Guard if things get wild enough."

"Damnit, Al! You know I don't approve of sarcasm." It could be as little as a local walking their dog without the leash, but Mayor Peters could always find the calamity.

"Mayor, we're a low-budget police force as it stands. Deputy Slaesburg is on leave until January. It is literally just me and Darleen here. Now, I've got about a hundred noise complaints, half as many domestic disputes to write, a crazed man running amok with a samurai sword and even a local kid gone missing. So, when I say I'll do what I can, mister Mayor, I assure you, it'll be the very best in police-work. Seriously, I might even show up with a gun and stuff."

"Sheriff, the council meeting is essential!" The mayor shrilled. "We're discussing the building of the new Whole Foods and a lot of locals are miffed enough already—you do understand what's at stake here…"

Just then, the door to the office slammed open, and Mack Gaffey bounded in, wide-eyed, sweaty, and considerably out of his fucking mind.

"GIANT. TALKING. DOG. It ate the fucking cat lady! Where's the sheriff? Al!? Get me the motherfucking sheriff, Darleen. Nefarious shit is afoot. SHERIFF??? AL??? AAAAAL!!!"

What the fuck? "Gotta go, Mayor."

"Sheriff—"

Al slammed the receiver and marched into the reception area. Without a word, he grabbed the vet by the shoulders, marched him back down the hall into one of the interrogation rooms, pushed Mack into a chair and said, "Calm down."

"Don't tell me to calm down," Mack reeled around as Al took a seat on the table, mad-principal-style. "I gave a fleabath to a fucking monster last night. I'd say that's some prime fucking real estate for panic, Sheriff!"

"Mack…"

"With glowing eyes and talons and everything. I'll calm down when I'm dead and ready."

Al rubbed his eyes with the palms of his hands. "Mack, are you using again?"

"Oh for fuck's sake. No! I haven't touched the Special-K for over five years, man."

Years ago, Al had taken Mack in nearly every Friday, rolling on large quantities of ketamine, talking about alien abduction conspiracies. He'd helped the vet get clean but… "We all make slips, Mack. I'm not judging—"

"And I'm not using! I'm not using, and I was accosted by a large, speaking animal last night."

"Okay," Al said. "Alright," he added. "Fine."

He produced a set of handcuffs and slapped them over Mack's wrists.

"Oh, what? You're arresting me?"

"I'm giving you time to think. You need to get a hold of yourself, Mack. Until you do that, you're staying here."

The vet wagged his head, betrayal burned in his gaze.
"What the f—"

Forty minutes after she'd woken up, Amy had taken to the
streets looking for Todd. The sheriff had told her not to worry.
Small towns weren't the kind of place kids went missing for
long, and he'd make sure finding Todd was at the top of his
priority list. He'd been calm, comforting, assuring... But Amy
had spent enough time in Oak Falls over the years to know
that small town folk were always that way: Friendly, congenial,
and totally useless. Sure, having the law looking out for Todd
was a step in the right direction, but sometimes you just have
to do things yourself.

She was responsible for him, after all. Todd was her charge.
She couldn't just sit idly waiting for him to turn up. She'd
driven the main drag about forty times, brainstorming all the
possible hangouts a kid gone wild might end up. The arcade,
the candy store, the park—all empty. Shit like this wasn't
supposed to happen in small towns. Wasn't the entire reason
people moved so far from civilization to avoid danger? To
thwart kidnappings and disappearances? If this had happened
in the city, she'd have put out the amber alert and Todd would
already be back at home, drinking chocolate milk and nursing
a welt from the wooden spoon of discipline.

She pulled the Volvo up across the river and headed in the
direction of the high school. The only place left to look was the
baseball diamond, and if Todd wasn't there—well—he had to
be there. She'd looked everywhere else. The field across the
street was empty. No kids playing ball. No Todd.

It was here Amy realized her life was probably over.
Goodbye, kid-sitting career—and that was just the tip of the
berg. Maude and Terry would kill her for this.

Blip-blip! Text message. MARIO: KID JUST GOT
HOME. MAKING HIM TAKE SHOWER.

"Thank fucking god!" she cried. Relief washed over her like
a cold shower after a Booty Bootcamp session.

She slowed the car and sent her thumbs flying on her phone: THANK FUCKING GOD!!!

Blip-blip! MARIO: YEAH... SHE'S STILL OUT LOOKING FOR THE STUPID KID. STILL ON FOR THIS WEEKEND? CAN'T WAIT TO SHOW YOU MR. MONKEY. XXX

"Mr. Monkey?" Something wasn't right here... And hold the fucking horn a minute—who was he texting? Who the fuck was he seeing this weekend? Sure, they'd never declared exclusivity—but when you've granted a guy access to your poop-chute, it kinda went without saying, didn't it?

Rage bubbled up in her like boiling tar. He was cheating on her. Her! Him!? Who with?! What a total—

"Motherfucker!" she yelled at the dash, flinging her phone onto the passenger's seat.

The dashboard babbled top-40 back at her.

She wanted to speed. She wanted a field of cute little bunny rabbits and a lawnmower to puree them with. She wanted to find whatever bimbo Mario was two-timing her with and put her head through a windshield. She wanted to jerk the gardener off with an angle grinder. "Mr. Monkey?!?! But I gave him the ass!"

Blip-blip! Never has a ringtone been so irritating. Furious, she snatched the phone off the seat, swiped to unlock, looked at the phone, then back at the road, then back at the phone. Then she moved as if someone had dropped a scorpion down her top.

It was a picture message of Mario's engorged unit. And yes, the gardener had dressed it up like one of those clapping monkeys. She totally lost it.

Curses, threats, and wishes for gonorrhea frothed out of her at the harshly-lit closeup. Complete fucking fuckwit! That fucking fucktard! You'd think if you're going to take such a compromising photo, you'd really take more care in where you sent it. Unless this was the idiot's idea of an apology. While she considered, Amy couldn't take her eyes off the phone. The car kept moving. Her hands started shaking.

Apology? No, Mario was a major fuckwad, but even a booger-eater would know not to fuck another woman and apologize with porno. He was *really* stupid, and had no idea who he was texting. Lucky guess? He'd broken into the family liquor cabinet and drained it.

Piece of shit, she thought. *Motherfucker. Asshole. Raging asshole. Fart-burning, tree humping brainless toad-shagger of a man. Dick! Moron!! Two-timing sack of pig spunk!!!* She rounded the bend and hit the gas, still unable to look away from the picture.

Something thumped hard against the front of the car and a man wearing a football jacket somersaulted into her windshield, sending spiderwebs through the glass. Amy braked with a slow-motion "Oh fuck!"

The guy tumbled backward off the hood and rolled along the pavement. The Volvo lurched. The seatbelt cut into her shoulder. The radio throbbed, but she couldn't make out what was playing past the buzzing in her ears. She peered over the wheel at the linebacker lying prone on the street.

Then the airbag went off, and Amy started to cry.

CHAPTER 15
SNACK-TIME OF THE DEAD

"So," the beast said. "Now that we're all together, I guess I should tell you the plan." The undead stood in a horseshoe around Seth, ten strong.

"I thought we were the plan," said Dimitri, an ex-school teacher who'd kissed a telephone pole doing ninety, late for book club. His face forever a misshapen pancake.

"Yeah," said Carly. "I mean... The dead are walking. It's apocalypse-now. We go to town, kill everybody and eat their brains."

"Braaaiiiinns!" chanted the undead.

"Heh, good start my friends, but I'd like to point out there's only ten of you."

"Not much of an army," said Ash.

"Like an Army of Darkness," said Silas, twenty-two, accomplished suicidal. He'd downed a bottle of sleeping pills and woken up a little green for it. "I love that movie!"

Considering he was a beast of the underworld less than twenty-four hours away from world domination, Seth was not having a good afternoon. The undead were supposed to be brain-dead, but when he'd raised them he thought: *Well, that's boring,* and decided to give them their personalities from life.

Now he was beginning to regret that decision: there was a reason zombies didn't talk or think. They were much easier to get to do your bidding without it.

"Don't be ridiculous," said Andy, forty-one and pudgy. Heart attack on the toilet seat, better known as death like Elvis. "That was just a movie."

"So?"

"So, this is real life, kiddo," tutted Nancy, thirty-nine and an ex-advertising consultant (she was the one who'd suggested the soda angle back at the morgue). "Numbers are kind of a big deal."

Christine (death by Chihuahua); Carrie (freak paraffin wax crafting accident); Bernie (radio guy with a drinking problem and subsequent liver failure); Jerome (deer hunting mixup), and Christine (who'd just dropped dead for plot conveniences) all nodded in unison.

"And we'll get to that in a minute," Seth said. "You're all a part of a bigger picture, gang. A distraction from the real action, actually. A handful of zombies is a handful of zombies, but this town has a better secret."

"What?" said the zombies.

"Well, it's a little hard to believe, but being as you're all dead, just go with it. The town was built on top of a very old portal thing that links the human world to the underworld. What lies below is the stuff that every nightmare is made of. I want to open the gate and let the hell flood forth."

"So why us?" said Brenda.

"Because you're distracting, toots. Everybody in town will be looking at you, while the real threat is barreling at six hundred and sixty-six miles toward them from behind. Now, can I tell you the legend?"

"This is boooring," said Silas.

"Pipe down, emo-tard. We need to know this stuff," said Carly.

"But what about brains?"

"Braaaaaiiiins!!" went the gang.

Seth resisted the urge to remove both of their heads just so he could get this over with. "The legend goes, the portal can only be opened at the height of the Cerulean Moon—"

"Which is tonight," Ash added.

"—And it requires a creature of pure evil to sacrifice themselves as a token of faith to the underworld that we really mean business. Now, I can't exactly do that myself since I'm immortal. So I figured one of you would be willing. Whadduya say, gang? Unholy sacrifice. Any takers?"

The undead all fidgeted, solemnly.

"But I don't want to die," said Christine. "I mean… Not again."

"Oh come on," the beast groaned. "It'll be great! Whoever plays the sacrifice card will be the end-times mascot for all eternity. Do you have any idea what kind of frequent-evil-flyer miles you'd get out of that? It's a gift."

The zombies all looked to one and other, then together said, "Nah."

"Besides, how would the nine of us remaining stand a chance against the townspeople?" said Earl.

"Good question, big guy. You guys are just the preview. The rest of the dead will be rising this evening. There you go. You've got an army. Are you guys sure about the sacrifice thing?"

"Well, I just got back."

"…Don't want to miss the Superbowl."

"What fun is waking up to die again?"

"What about eating people?"

"Screw sacrifice, I'm hungry!"

"Braaaaiiins!!!" they chimed together. "Braaaaaiiiiiinnnnnsss!!!"

"Shut the fuck up!" Seth howled. He shifted into his monster form and loomed over them. "Now, the plan is to end the world, and to do that I need one of you mooks to punch their ticket, and I'm losing my patience with the brains thing! You guys aren't even good at it!"

Silence.

"Now," the beast went on. "There's also another matter. Apparently there's someone in town who can fuck this whole thing up if they keep living. Something about red hair and a good ass…"

"Huh, that sounds like Ava," said Nancy. In life, she'd helped the baker brand her business. It was her idea to hang the cupcake off the A. (Hey, some consultants are better off dead.)

Seth reeled around and lay a claw against the ex-ad exec's neck.

"Tell me what you know, corpsie."

Max Reyes didn't know how he let this happen. He was propped on a chair in Volydeskvi's motel room, his arms tied behind his back with a length of braided nylon, his head throbbing like a rave of pain fairies were moshing on the back of it. The Russian moved around the room with a glass of vodka, cream and Kahlua in one hand, and his cell phone in the other.

"No, I say… I go to house, but poopstick Wizard wasn't there. So I break roommate's nose."

"*V'what did poopstick's roommate say?*" a voice croaked over the line like a bullfrog.

Boris sighed. "V'well. You know. Sort of like 'Aarrrrghhh'. Very hard to understand. His nose was broken."

What a complete shithead. Only a novice would chat with his boss in front of a DEA agent. It was obvious the voice on the phone was Olaf, the big Vloydeskvi. Then again, Max suspected this was a pretty good indicator that the Russian planned to kill him. However, Boris's novice card did play to Reyes's favor—he'd spent six weeks training to free himself from virtually every knot known to man, and Boris had tied the rope right between his hands.

So, now would probably be a good time to start using those skills. He began working at the knot. He continued to play unconscious. He listened.

"*Tell me your plan.*"

"V'well, I will go back to poopstick's house when he is home. Then, I will put bullet between his eyes."

Double not good. If the Russian was planning to kill the

Wizard, then it meant Reyes would certainly be the warmup round. Max wasn't big on the idea of dying and losing his only suspect. He found the head of the knot and started pushing with one hand, worrying at the coil with the other.

"Good, Boris. But before you do it, make sure to torture him."

The Russian nodded happily. "Knife or blowtorch?"

"Neither. I mean torture with psychology. Poopstick must lose everything he loves before he dies. Traitor scum does not deserve an easy death."

The knot began to give. Max twisted it, but it stuck to itself like a tightened shoelace.

"Do I kill roommate? Lover? Mother? ...Pet cat?"

A pause as the Big Vloydeskvi brainstormed. *"Steal his van. Poopstick loves his ugly van painted Barney the Dinosaur. Wait a day, then come back and finish him off. Make sure to kill sneaky cop, too."*

Fuck! Really, definitely not good. Reyes attacked the knot with newfound ambition.

"Okay boss. *Polka.*"

Boris turned, sloshing his drink.

Reyes slipped the rope and came at the Russian in a low tackle. The two crashed backward into the desk. Glass shattered as empty bottles hit the floor. Max wheeled a vicious haymaker, but the Russian grabbed the lamp off the desk and swung it like a baseball bat, catching the agent under the chin. Max staggered. Stars spotted his vision. He wagged his head and went for another punch, but Boris saw it coming.

The Russian grabbed Max by the shoulders and threw him against the wall. Then he punched Max in the solar plexus until the agent saw blue. He reeled back for another when Max slammed his heel down on the Russian's toe.

Boris howled and lunged, swinging furiously.

Max somersaulted over the bed, snatched the blanket off the bed and tossed it over Boris. He grabbed the chair and smashed it over the Russian. Bits of wood rained over the room. The Russian struggled under the blanket, his hand finding the bedpost and he dragged himself off the floor.

Reyes moved for another tackle just as the Russian freed himself from the blanket and sidestepped the agent, grabbing him in midair and hurling him onto the bed. Max spun to recover. The Russian leapt on top of him, grabbed the alarm clock off the nightstand, and mashed it against Max's skull.

Chhrrrr—cuckoo, cuckoo! went the alarm clock. Boris brought it down on the back of Max's head again.

Chhrrr—Another beautiful day in coastal California... said the radio. Blood trickled down the side of Reyes's head. Pieces of plastic flew through the air.

The Russian brought it down again.

Chhrrr... All you need is love... went the Beatles. Boris continued to mash the clock against Max's head in time with the rhythm. Max howled. Bigger and bigger chunks of the alarm clock sailed with every blow.

Reyes could just make out the shape of a full fifth of vodka on the nightstand. He struggled under the Russian and reached...

Mash, mash, mash. Blood ran into his eyelashes. He stretched as far as he could. His fingers found purchase. The Russian brought what was left of the clock up for another blow and Reyes grabbed the bottle, twisted, and walloped him.

The Russian yelped and flopped backward off the bed, unconscious. Max dragged himself off the mattress, tripping on the sheets, and tumbled toward the door. He stood, his breath coming in choppy bursts. He found his cellphone on the decimated writing desk. The air in the room was heavy, and he staggered out to the catwalk outside the unit while he keyed the numbers for the sheriff.

"Kowalski."

"Shut up and listen," Reyes said. "I have a suspect in prime need of a jail cell and we need to get him there pronto."

"Wh—"

"Didn't I say *listen*?" Reyes snapped. He found his crumpled pack of cigarettes, fished one out, and lit. "Now, how soon can you—"

Footfalls behind him. A car door opening. An engine starting. Tires screeching. Reyes turned just in time to see the Eldorado peeling off.

"Fuck!"

When Amy met Travis, she had tears streaming down her face. Her makeup bad been augmented by the air bag to the look of a sad, battered clown. Her outfit wasn't even color-coordinated... She was, in short, a mess. Definitely no state to meet a hunky guy.

When Travis met Amy, he was tumbling through the air. He was rolling across pavement, scraping his knees and getting a good whack to the head on the way. He was, in short, getting hit by a fucking Volvo, and also a mess.

Now, the two had recovered and were sitting in the Noble Bean, one of Oak Falls' ubiquitous cafes. They were sipping lattes as Amy finished her long-winded telling of the thing with her gardener beau. Honestly, Amy had started thinking of it as sort of a pity date. But over the course of the conversation, she'd been surprised to find the linebacker amicable, charming, funny where he needed to be, and most importantly a good listener.

"I just don't get it. I mean, look at me! I'm a scrumptious slice of cheerleader pie. What is his deal? I gave him everything he wanted."

"Uhuh," Travis said. He'd been trying very hard for the past twenty minutes not to show that his hip hurt like hell, and had been responding to most of her remarks this way.

"You don't get it, any perversion that filled that turd-muncher's mind, I went with it, and still somehow I couldn't keep his attention."

"Maybe he got bored?"

"How?"

Travis shrugged. "Guys get bored when they're given everything."

Amy wagged her head like a dog clearing water from its ears. "That's... stupid."

"Yeah, well. It *is* stupid, but guys have this thing where they need to feel like they've earned something before they can enjoy it."

"That's ridiculous. Why would you not want what you want if you're getting it on a silver, well-chested platter?"

Trav waved as if it were understood, then immediately realized how intellectual it looked and tried to pawn off the gesture as if he was adjusting his hair, which was buzz-cut. "It's the chase. Men are obsessed with the chase. All we want is to feel like we want something and that somehow, getting it is insanely hard. That's what we're after."

"That is like... The most idiotic thing I've heard since the last time I talked to him."

"I know, but what can I say? It's a cultural standard. We're raised believing that the only things worth having are the things we fight to get. Without achievement, it's impossible to feel like a man."

"But, everyone struggles. That's not a manly thing?"

Trav chuckled. "I didn't say I believed it, it's just a stereotype."

Amy pursed her lips, giving the linebacker a curious expression. "You are way smarter than you let on, you know that?"

Trav did. He was loathe to admit it, but in addition to being an all-star linebacker, he was also graduating from Oak Falls with a full academic scholarship. He spent most of his time fighting intellectual urges in order to keep up his linebacker exterior. His friends at school were simple, sure. But he still enjoyed the camaraderie. It was refreshing to be able to talk this way with a person.

"A little," he said.

"I'm so pissed," Amy said. "All I wanted was a nice summer fling while I'm stuck in Oak Falls for summer. I did not sign up for this drama."

"Really?"

"Really."

Trav resisted a wince as the pain in his hip flared up again.

"You don't think… I mean, you're not worried that that'll make you seem… Well, you know, slutty?"

Amy nearly snorted her macchiato. "No. Why would I think that? And P.S., why is it that every time a guy hooks up with a zillion girls he's a champion, but if a girl does it she's a slut, anyway? Double standard much?"

Trav grinned. He couldn't help himself. Sure, the circumstances were weird. Sure, she was still technically seeing someone and had hit him with her car—but he really liked Amy. He didn't know how to explain it, but he knew. "Double standard?"

"Fuck double standards," Amy sighed.

"I agree. And I think revenge is in order," Travis tried to affect his best smooth pickup line delivery. Confident, but not conceited. "So… You wanna make out?"

Hey, give him a break. He was only eighteen.

Amy gave him a full once-over. "You wanna make out? With me? Here?"

"Well, no. You've got a car, right? How about there?"

Amy considered it. At home was a guy who she'd love nothing more than to run over with a wood-chipper. Here was a guy who could actually hold a conversation with her, was good-looking, and didn't seem to be intimidated by her. It was a rare brew, and considering she wanted a summer fling…

"We could smoke a joint?" he said.

"At last," she said. "The romantic evening I've been waiting for."

CHAPTER 16
MIXED MESSAGES

"No," Wiz said. "No more joints." They sat at the breakfast table in Ava's kitchen, mugs of coffee steaming in the afternoon light. Noah had left with linebackers to hook them up with the pot. Trav was headed to the high school to sell to his gym teacher, and Hal said he'd call all his friends to see who wanted to blaze. Wiz stayed at Ava's, worrying about his friends, the Russian, and of course, the growing number of strange things that nobody except him seemed to believe.

He felt agitated, like there was a nagging itch in under his skin to do something—anything. For the first time in his life, his slacker philosophy betrayed him. He needed action. He had to figure out what was going on, and then figure out what to do about it. Of course, the first time in over a decade that he experienced motivation would hit when he was under proverbial house arrest.

Ava chuckled and slipped a bagel across the table to him. "Jeez, I really never thought I'd hear you say that."

This had been the most time they'd ever spent together. Wiz knew he should be doing something about that, but he couldn't get his mind off what he was pretty sure was the apocalypse.

"I've spent way too long living in a womb of reefer. How many years have I lost, just letting things pass me by while I blaze the trail of munchies and video games?"

Ava shrugged. "It's not so bad. Life moves fast whether you're stoned or not, Wiz. Didn't you say you liked to keep things simple?"

"I do. But things got complicated anyway." Complicated? Now there was an understatement on par with calling the K2 climb a jaunty hike.

"You're stressed," Ava said. She grabbed his hand, gave it a squeeze. "Everything will be okay. You want a massage? I give great massages…"

Wiz shook his head. "I've just never done anything. I've sat around a whole lot thinking good things will fall in my lap. Now I've got the opposite."

Ava's gaze upon her coffee. "It's not all bad, is it?"

"No," Wiz rubbed his eyes and let out a huge sigh. "I just want my old life back."

"I thought you just finished saying your old life was the problem."

"I am. It is. I don't know. I guess I'm starting to think my entire way of life has been a colossal mistake." — And here he started nodding to himself — "I need to be more proactive."

Ava bit her lip. She could feel her heartbeat speeding in her chest. She thought, *he's gonna do it. He's gonna make a move…*

Meanwhile, Wiz was staring into the blackness of his coffee, thinking: *I am such a loser.* "Ava —"

"Wiz?" Hope sang through her ribcage. She'd been thinking of today as a sort of date — or at least an opportunity for the two of them to hit it off. She'd been trying to flirt with him all afternoon. Now, it looked like her efforts were finally sinking in.

"I think I need to go," he said.

"What? Why? What about the Russian? What about the sheriff? The DEA? What about hiding out?"

Wiz frowned. "I know, it's probably a dumb move, but there

are things I need to figure out, and I need to do it now. I've spent too much time sitting on my ass. It's time to be proactive."

Hurt replaced the hope she felt. Ava stared at him a full minute, waiting for him to wake the fuck up, and when he didn't, she said, "You know what? I think you're right."

Wiz stared out the window, looking as if he were about to change his mind. "I'll be back in like an hour, okay?"

And here, Ava lost her temper. "Do you seriously have no radar for subtext? You complete romantically-challenged nitwit! No, you can't come back."

Romantic? *Romantic?* Wiz was flummoxed. The whole day, he'd been thinking of himself as a burden: the hopeless burnout, so useless that Ava had let him and his goofball friends crash her living room out of pity. He thought *he* was the one who had the crush, that she'd never even think to think about thinking of him in the same way... Romantic? He'd misread all the signals — he really was a nitwit.

"Ava, wait... I — "

"I'm tired Wiz. You want to go on about the fucking end of the world? Fine! Go home and do it there."

Shit. Shit! Shit!!! He'd completely screwed the pooch. "Ava — "

"Go," she said. "Just go."

The Baron awoke tied to a hospital gurney. Franz MacFee stood beating him with a tennis racket, chanting, "Serves you right, motherfucker! Take that! Take that!"

"Release me," said the Baron. "You can't hurt me, and you're wasting my time, you goat-humping buffoon."

Franz roared, swinging the racket. "Fuck you, you diminutive little twerp! You stole my girlfriend! Taste my pain!"

Thump, thump, thump. Whack, whack, whack.

The Baron rolled his eyes. "Stop it. I told you, you can't hurt me."

"We'll see!" The doctor's face was bright pink. A vein was popping out of his forehead.

"Besides, Ava isn't yours. You're just a sad little man with a bent little dick who can't move on. You would do well to be gored by a pack of wild Furybeasts, or perhaps humped to death by a Shmegmatile. Now, release me—or I'll be forced to run you through with my sword and kick you in the balls… Just because."

Franz cackled. "Oh, I think you'll stay where you are!"

Thump, thump, thump. Whack, whack, whack.

They were in one of the old intensive care wards on the third floor—a wing of the hospital that had spent the last five years in a state of perpetual renovation—deserted. They wouldn't be bothered here, which was exactly what Franz wanted.

"Are you done?" the Baron said with a bored expression.

"No!" Franz shouted, swinging the racket.

Thump, thump, thump. Whack, whack, whack.

"What about now?"

"Still no!"

The Baron sighed. "This is growing tiresome."

Franz screeched and cracked the handle of the racket off the guardian of the underworld's forehead, which only prompted giddy laughter.

"Pleease! Stop! It tickles!"

"No!"

Thump, whack, thwack!

The Ghede roared with laughter. "Oh, a little to the left! The left!!!"

Franz thumped, whacked, and thwacked until he was blue in the face and sweat glistened on his brow. He finally gave up, panting, seething. "I really can't hurt you, huh?"

"Do you have big hairy dicks in your ears? I told you, you weak-minded fuckstick, I'm a god! Now, let me the fuck go!"

"Fuck!' Franz cried, tossing the racket across the room. "Fuck, fuck, fuck!!!"

"Fuck indeed, doctor."

"Shut the fuck up, you crazy fuck!" Franz wheeled around and started pacing. "There's no such thing as gods. You are just a few too many monkeys short of the barrel…"

The Baron erupted in another bout of wild cackling. "Why is it so hard to believe?"

"I'm a doctor!" Franz said. "In my profession we don't operate on belief. We operate on terms and proof. And *you* are a textbook loony toon."

"Go chug a flagon of monkey jizz, you asinine mortal. I'm big in the Caribbean."

"Oh, he's a voodoo god, is he?" Franz chuckled with a questioning brow.

"Bingo, fucktard. Do you believe now?"

Franz considered. "Nope. Creative, yes, but you're still bonkers."

The Baron snorted and horked a great loogie that fell just short of Franz. "There's no time for this. Your town is in danger, Doctor. Darkness has opened its jaws and will swallow it whole. A beast prowls your streets, in search of the sacrifice, and even now, as we speak, the dead rise from their graves. Khali's six-handed tugjob, you festering fuckball. It's the apocalypse — can't you smell it?"

Franz sighed, leaning against an ancient heart-rate monitor, looking out the window as the sun began to set, casting a blood-orange corona on the horizon. "Yeah, really not helping with the whole 'bonkers' verdict, Mr. Peanut."

He spun, winding up to coldcock the Baron square in the jaw, but the bed was empty. The bonds that had restrained him hung on the bed like lifeless leather tentacles. The sheets were unstirred. The air hadn't moved. There hadn't even been a sound; not a sharp breath nor a grunt or shuffle — but the Baron was gone.

"Dammit!" Franz sighed. "I wish he'd quit doing that!"

The doctor grabbed his stethoscope and flung open the door to the abandoned room. He trudged down the hall in search of the lunatic with the sword who thought he was a voodoo god.

When the door to the ward clicked shut, the Baron slipped out from under the bed. Boy, he could use a drink. But it was good he wasn't drunk for that. One wrong move, and he'd be stuck in the springs of the mattress. It was all about concentration: he pictured himself under the bed and there he was.

Had he not been specific? Well, the Ghede didn't bother himself with the mechanics of it. As far as he was concerned, he was a god, and gods just got what they wanted. Poof! Magic. It was kind of a given for a guy who'd seen the world before there were people to live on it. Whatever it was, he got what he wanted.

Rum. The guardian of the underworld was in desperate need of rum—and chili powder. He stood and grabbed the shadow from under the bed as if it were a throw rug, then stepped inside.

The supernatural always happens just out-of-frame; just a little left-of-center. If it's seen at all, it's from the corner of an eye: the shadow of a man in a hallway; a catlike shade scuttling along the floor... The list is big. Real big. You never really *see* something weird, even when you're sure you saw it happen. That's why it's the supernatural—because whatever it is, that shit is just not natural.

Thus the Baron moved, carrying the shadow like a cape as he crawled the floor, bringing himself to the room's window, which unlatched, letting in a gust of evening air. The shadow crawled—just out of frame; from the corner of an eye—up the wall and over the sill.

It crept outside, then down the wall of the hospital, snaking in tight with an eavestrough like an oilslick on the concrete, far more bull-headed than any trick of the light. Down it went, sliding off the building and cuddling into the lawn below.

Not a single person saw it.

Boris Vloydeskvi stood in front of the Wizard's house, staring down the barrel of a problem. He was supposed to steal the poopstick's van, but instead he was looking at a rusted neon orange Civic. Boris didn't like problems. The scuffle with the idiot cop had left him bruised. His back ached. His head pounded, and he was in serious need of another fifth of vodka. It was indeed a car, but it was not the one Boris had come to steal.

Boris hated problems.

He was the killing guy. When things got out-of-hand, you called in Boris and he tied off the loose ends. He was the exterminator. He was not a chaperone, and he did not enjoy anything that didn't involve the death of someone.

"I see poopstick has taken Barney the Dinosaur van out for drive," he observed.

Could he try back later? No, he'd come here on foot. He wasn't going to leave unless it was while driving someone else's vehicle. Besides, how much could it matter? Sure, boss had wanted to damage poopstick Wizard with psychology—but what difference did it make when he was dead? A car was a car, and so Boris saw the Civic with an almost supernatural glow—here a problem, and there a solution.

Once he killed the poopstick, Boss would never know the difference. "Did he suffer?" Boss would say. "Yes," Boris would answer—and he'd be sure to make the Wizard suffer. It was simple borscht.

He padded over to the Civic and tried the doors. Nothing. He tried the hatchback. Nothing. He tried the hood, then realized how pointless that was and sighed.

"Fuck it."

He produced a handkerchief from his back pocket, wrapped it around his hand, and shattered the driver's-side window. He popped the lock and climbed in, brushing kernels of safety glass from the seat. He fished out his pocket knife, flipped it open, and started working out a hunk of the steering column where the key would fit.

He pried, jostled, kicked, heaved, and finally went ape on the steering column before it popped off, sailing directly into Boris's forehead. He blinked, wagging his already well-battered noggin.

"Fucking Hondas," he grumbled.

He cut the two wires specifically designed to prevent

criminals from getting stuck with your car in park while the alarm goes off, crossed them, and just like in the movies, the engine fired up. Boris grinned, lighting a cigar. He loved any time real life worked the way it did in movies. Hot wiring cars wasn't just part of the gig for him—it was part of the fun.

He surveyed the car's interior, changed the mirrors, adjusted the seat, messed with the A/C, knotted the seatbelt twice, and generally fucked up anything and everything that Noah might have cherished about it. Then, he ashed on the floor and puttered the hatchback out of the driveway, completely unaware that there was a pound and a half of his family's pot hidden in the fold-out trunk.

CHAPTER 17
THE BUZZ HARSHENS

Dusk. Wiz got home, heartsick and completely out of his depth. How could he be so stupid? How could he have missed the signals? She'd offered him a frigging massage and it sailed right past him. Stupid! Now he'd fucked it all up. Ava was angry at him, the Russians wanted him dead, and he was pretty sure the world was ending. Wiz felt his life swirling down the drain.

He slumped in his chair and woke up his computer. Might as well press forward with figuring out how to deal with zombie cats and a reanimated severed arm. Sure, nobody would believe him, but if he could figure out what was going on, and what to do about it, maybe he could save the town from impending disaster. It'd be like comic book kids from *The Lost Boys*, hunting vampires: the unknown hero protecting the population from the forces of evil.

He opened a window to consult the great Google oracle and typed in ZOMBIE CATS. There was *Pet Sematary*, but he was pretty sure Oak Falls didn't have an ancient Indian burial ground hidden in its outskirts. He clicked the image search and scrolled a couple of pages of gruesome photos before (like usual) the results lapsed into bizarre, unrelated porn.

He decided to broaden the search to just ZOMBIES, this time avoiding the image search altogether. He brought up the Wikipedia page and started scanning. *Mind-control* — nope. *Voodoo slaves* — not unless there was a sorcerer in town who liked to get cats to do his bidding. *In Pop Culture: the reanimated dead* — bingo! *Typically the result of an unspecified virus or chemical outbreak, creating flesh-craving undead monsters.* That seemed to fit the picture, only with cats instead of people. Maybe the virus only affected cats?

He opened another search tab and typed in ZOMBIE VIRUS. Then he opened news articles, conspiracy theory forums, and paranormal investigation blogs. He read, then read some more, and it all started to become clear.

So this was how the world ended: You get a virus that turns ordinary people in mindless cannibals, the government tries to contain it, but societal collapse is inevitable. From here, you nod off and the next thing you know, you've woken up in a post-apocalyptic future where the name of the game is survival. It was outrageous, but it was everywhere. The irony was, society was so steeped in visions of the world post-apocalypse that nobody seemed to be wise to the signs it was actually happening.

An entire school in North Dakota, quarantined after students and teachers became infected with a rare bacterial skin infection; A man in Southern Ohio attacks and eats his dog; Some guy in Florida does a little drugs and eats another guy's face off. The warning signs were all there, but nobody wanted to believe it. Sure, the apocalypse was fun to *think* about — but it wasn't something to really take seriously. It was the kind of post-Regan Era paranoia that was more self-aware and fun than serious.

Wiz pulled away from the computer, his eyes burning, his head spinning.

"Nice ∂riving, ya ∂oomed fuck∂," he whispered. The dog on the highway had warned them, he just didn't see it then. Could he have stopped this if he hadn't hit the beast? Had the dog even been real, or had he imagined the whole thing? And if he had imagined it, then who could say he hadn't hallucinated the zombie cats and the severed arm too...

He needed someone to assure him he wasn't going completely bat-shit, but Noah had already left for work, the linebackers were out selling drugs, and Ava didn't want to speak with him. With his options exhausted, there was only one thing left to do: commune with Mr. Bong and try to calm himself. He headed to the living room, filled the bowl, sparked up a disposable lighter and took a huge rip off the bong.

He let the smoke crawl out of his mouth as he melted back into the couch, letting the cool tingling vibes comfort him as he tried to quiet his mind.

Knock, knock, knock.

With a huge amount of effort, Wiz pulled himself out of couch-lock. He shuffled over to the door, bong still in hand. He opened it, and found the sheriff waiting on the other side.

He couldn't remember the last time his brother made a house call. Then he noticed the man standing beside him, a sharp-dressed Hispanic with a nasty patch of bruises forming on his brow. Then he realized that this was probably the DEA agent Al had told him about.

"Hey guys," he chuckled, completely failing to hide the bong behind his back. "...What's up?"

Max Reyes took the bong out of his hands and his brother slapped a pair of handcuffs on his wrists. "Wiz Kowalski, you're under arrest."

Franz MacFee had spent the whole day telling himself *I am not a schmuck... I am not a schmuck*, over and over like a mantra to ward off self-loathing. It was also kind of true. Franz was not a bad guy. In fact, in his capacity as a doctor, Franz had even helped people. Setting broken hips, administering beta blockers and anti-diabetics to old timers; boosters, multivitamins and stitches to youngsters; condoms, birth-control, and antibiotics to teenagers and adults. He did good work — saved lives, even. But the one person he'd failed to help was himself.

The previous night, Pam, the thirty-one year old orderly he'd been seeing, caught him in drunken mid-grovel with Ava. Calling Pam unimpressed would be akin to calling the Inquisition a slight slip in taste for the Catholic Church. He tried to apologize. He tried explaining himself, but it was too late: the scalpel had slipped — the patient bled out.

Now, he was so deep in the dog house that he couldn't even muster a healthy rally for redemption. He was hungover, womanless, and it was all the little fuck in the top hat's fault. He'd been ready to move on, he really had. But when he learned about Ava going on a date, it was like a switch flipped. He didn't want to be with her, but he didn't like the idea of someone else filling his place. Now, the only place he had was full of beer bottles and pizza boxes. He didn't know how to care for himself. He didn't know what to do. He *was* a schmuck.

Self-loathing hit him like a dump-truck.

None of this would've happened if it weren't for the guy in the hat. Revenge was the only card left to play, and while he'd already witnessed the man vanish into thin air twice before him, he was sure there was a way to hurt him — and he'd find it. Oh, how he'd find it. There was hell to pay, and all he needed was to find the guy who called himself the guardian of the underworld to unleash his fury. He'd done his rounds, walking the red line along the corridors of the hospital looking for the Baron. He wasn't on the third floor, nor the second, and the secretary at the front desk hadn't seen anyone matching Franz's description — "You know, short, weaselly. Walking, talking fuckbag?" — that only left the basement to search.

It occurred to Franz that the man could have slipped out one of the fire escapes nurses used to sneak smoke breaks, but he couldn't give up without knowing for sure.

The basement of the hospital consisted of a loading bay

where the hospital's shipments were received; a records archive
Franz was pretty sure hadn't been opened since 1906, and the
long walk-in freezer that held the morgue. He rifled around
shipping containers, double-checked the lock on the archive's
door, poked inside the maintenance closet searching for a
weapon, grabbed a broom, and made his way to the morgue.

As he reached the great sliding door, the air began to chill.
The smell of cleaning solvents was thick on the air. The door
sat open a crack.

He grinned. This was it. No place left to hide for Mr. Peanut.
Moments away from unleashing his wrath. He grabbed the
handle, raising the broom over his head like a spear. He threw
open the door, gave his best warrior-cry and lunged inside. His
foot came down on something soft with a hideous squish and
he froze mid-lunge.

The room looked like a small cyclone had run through it;
overturning gurneys and ripping open the sliding compartments
where corpses were kept. They were all empty. Nausea crept
up Franz's throat as his gaze fell to reveal that he was standing
in what appeared to be the ribcage of Jerry, the coroner —
there wasn't really enough of him to tell.

"Fuck!" Franz yelped, leaping out of the wasted corpse,
ragged hunks of shoulder and spine connected to a pair of
stumps that had been his legs. Tatters of skin and chunks of
bone were strewn across the morgue. The floor was slathered
with huge slashes of blood. It was like someone had dunked
the coroner in a tank of piranhas and flopped him on the floor
when they were finished.

"Oh my god," Franz choked. Were those teethmarks on the
bone? "Oh my god. Jerry — who did this — oh Jesus Christ."

Another wave of nausea hit him and he wheeled around to
blow chunks into the wastebin by the door. Franz took great
gulps of air, trying to steady himself. Someone had snuck in
here and eaten the fucking coroner.

Dread crawled up his spine like a fourteen-inch centipede.
The guy in the top hat — had he done this? That meant this was

Franz's fault. What was he thinking? Knowingly dragging a crazy person with a samurai sword into the hospital and now poor, kind old Jerry was dead. And where were the bodies?

He steadied himself when a scuttling noise came from the other side of the room. Franz gripped the broom, holding it like a baseball bat. The scuttling continued, moving around behind the gurneys, coming closer. Franz peered around, feeling his heart beat faster as the noise grew louder. Then, the room's cooling fans whirred to life. Franz leaped about three feet in the air and spun when something caught him by the ankle.

It was a hand. It was a *severed* hand. There was a severed hand gripping him by the ankle...

Franz screeched, scrambling to get the thing off him, but he lost his balance on the gore-strewn floor. His feet slipped out from under him. The broom sailed through the air and he landed on his back—hard.

"Fuck!"

Franz kicked, sending a streamer of blood across the room. The hand held fast. He grabbed at an overturned gurney and heaved himself off the floor. He trudged over to the wastebin— the hand clamped to his ankle like a fleshy ball-and-chain— steadied himself against the door and started kicking it against the wall in mad panic.

With three good blows, the grip relinquished. The arm plopped into the wastebin with a dull thunk. Franz took a great gulp of air and sighed.

The bin started rocking back and forth, furiously.

The doctor scrambled for the lid sitting next to it and slammed it down until it clicked into place. Then, the bin stopped shaking.

"Take that, zombie arm," he said, ripping off his blood-soaked doctor's coat. He paused a moment, considering what he'd just said.

"...Oh, I'm gonna get a drink."

CHAPTER 18
NIGHT OF THE LIVING—WELL, YOU KNOW.

Noah Carpenter strolled along the gravel path of the cemetery, his flashlight fanning tombstones that littered the lot like cigarette butts in Death's ashtray. His nose ached. Every three steps, he encountered a shrieking pain in his side. He gritted his teeth and plodded on. He'd be damned if this absurd story got in the way of earning a paycheck.

He'd come to Oak Falls hoping to open a yoga studio, but along the way, his Honda Civic had broken down repeatedly. He limped the journey, stopping at every mechanic's on the highway, replacing part after part on the hatchback until he wound up in Oak Falls with what was essentially a new car and about three bucks to his name. He'd lucked out scoring an apartment with the Wizard after meeting him at the Pizza Shack, where he spent the last of his cash, but the bills kept rolling in. One day, skimming the classifieds of the Oak Falls Gazette, he'd discovered an ad for a job working nights patrolling the cemetery. He was hired on the spot. Slowly, his savings built, and with about a grand left before he could put down first and last month's rent on a studio space, he decided he needed a plan.

The plan was not working out like he'd imagined. Despite the fact that it was some of the most primo pot he'd ever sampled, it was selling worse than cheese at a vegan eatery. Even his new-age yogi friends didn't want any—citing a mass shift in cosmic energy that they didn't want to screw up their consciousness for. He was beaten, his plan was crap, so he walked.

Moonlight cast the cemetery in a sea of shadow. Crickets chirped in the distance, and the crunching of his footsteps echoed across the lot. Sure, it was a little creepy, but Noah did enjoy the graveyard for the quiet.

Up ahead, a strange sucking sound came from behind one of the trees. Deep moaning noises followed. Noah investigated, pointing the flashlight toward the source. He came around the corner, the light describing the shape of two people holding each other violently by the neck. He came closer, his eyes widening in surprise.

"Seriously, guys?" he said. "On a fucking tombstone?!"

On the fucking tombstone, Trav and Amy ripped away from each other as if someone had zapped them with a cattle-prod. The linebacker wiped his mouth as the warm rush of arousal fizzled from his mind.

"Noah! Dude, what's up?"

Noah panned the flashlight from Trav to Amy, who was furiously readjusting her bra underneath a tight black tank top. She primped her hair, cleared her throat.

"It would appear to be you, Travis."

The light panned down to the bulge wilting in the linebacker's jeans. He was, indeed, what was up. "Man, you scared the shit out of us."

"What happened to Hal? And who's us?"

"Dude," the linebacker beamed. "This is Amy. Amy, this is Noah."

"Hey," Amy said. "What happened to your nose?"

"High-speed collision with a guy's fist," Noah said, then to Trav: "How'd you do?"

The linebacker sighed. "Shitty. I sold like a quarter to Mr. Sneezebaker, but nobody else was looking. You?"

"Same." Noah plopped himself on the tombstone next to them and started playing with the flashlight. "Well, this sucks."

"So, let me get this straight," Amy said. "You guys are drug dealers?"

The two of them looked at each other and shrugged sheepishly.

"Not very good ones," Trav moped.

"Yeah, does it count if you suck at it?" said Noah.

"It does," Amy said. "How much are you guys holding?"

"Three pounds."

"That's nothing! You guys totally *do* suck at this." Amy chuckled. "Want some help?"

Noah wagged his head, even as Trav started nodding furiously. "I'm not sure that's a good idea—"

"Man, she's cool." Trav produced a joint from his jacket and lit it. "Do you know some people?"

Amy scoffed. "Only every college kid home for the summer." She flipped out her phone and started texting. "Three pounds... You guys will be cleaned out by tomorrow."

Noah wasn't sure. "Look—uh, Amy. It's real kind of you, but selling this stash has been nothing but clusterfuck since day one."

Blip-blip! Amy looked at her phone with a smirk growing on her face. "That's one..." *Blip-blip!* "Two..." *Blip-blip! Blip-blip! Blip-blip! Blip-blip!* She took the joint from Travis and toked smugly.

"Okay," Noah grumbled. "Trav, you need to find Hal and let him know ASAP. I'm going to wrap up here and get ahold of Wiz."

With that, he grabbed the joint from Amy, took three quick puffs, let off a long, rocky sigh and said, "This being in charge thing blows."

Then he was off down the path.

Blip-blip, blip-blip! went Amy's phone. She scrolled through the texts, ignoring the voicemail prompt dancing at the bottom of the screen. "He's not in charge," she said. "Looks like I'm your new boss, linebacker."

She passed Trav the joint. He sucked away at it, staring off into the night, his brow stitched in what appeared to be thought.

"Where *is* Hal?" he said.

A huge cloud of smoke climbed the air as "Roundabout" blared on a basement stereo. A figure slouched on a tattered corduroy couch, veiled in shadow beside a half-eaten bag of Doritos Nacho-Cheese. A disposable lighter sparked, a bong bubbled and Hal Pearson took another enormous hit of the skunky bud.

He'd been at it since sundown, figuring that if he couldn't sell the pot, he might as well smoke it—at least, he was pretty sure that was how he'd ended up here. He hadn't moved for over an hour, his limbs heavy, his body in a supreme state of couch-lock. He didn't mind, though. He had the Doritos, the music, three quarters of a bottle of Dr. Pepper. It was all good.

It was 8 P.M., and Hal Pearson was comfortably—deliriously—hopelessly stoned. He let his head sink back in the folds of the couch, and just before he broke into his fourteenth giggle-fit of the hour he said, "Where *am* I?"

"So, where were we?" said Amy.

"We were on a tombstone," Trav said.

Amy grinned, grabbed the linebacker by the collar, kissed him, and gave him a shove. Trav staggered back and landed between two of the tombstones with a thump.

"Ouch—hey!"

But before he could argue further, Amy pounced the linebacker with a vicious kiss that slammed his head against the grass. She pulled the joint out of his hands, reversed it, then put her mouth against his and started shotgunning the smoke into his lungs. Then, she pulled away, took another toke, and extinguished the joint on her tongue.

"What are you doing?"

"I'm starting my vacation," she said.

Sure, Mario was probably still waiting around at home, slowly coaxing a dimwitted explanation from his idiot brain — but Amy wasn't interested. This was her summer vacation. She didn't want to spend it dealing with lame drama from a guy who was such a nitwit he made a monkey look like it could out-math Einstein.

No, she wanted sex — lots of sex, a little bit of conversation consisting of more than drunken arguments over which Kardashian was the prettiest or rants about the merits of the parsley bush. She wanted hot, steamy romance. What was better than a little revenge-sex to get over the gardener?

The linebacker's hands moved from her hips to her bottom while their tongues did the spit-swap tango. Amy straddled him, pressing her breasts against him, her hand snaking into his jeans.

She would have her summer fling, even if it killed her.

Like most eighteen year-olds, Trav was completely obsessed with sex. He spent an inordinate amount of time making Kleenex deposits at the spank bank. But for all his marathon hours in front of the computer, shucking the monkey to a considerable amount of cosplay and fetish porn — doing it in a cemetery was really creeping him out.

For one thing, the ground was all cold and damp. It was probably the pot, but Trav was sure he could feel worms writhing in the dirt below... Not to mention there were a buttload of corpses down there, too. If that wasn't enough, he was facing a tombstone with an epitaph that said: THE LORD WATCHES OVER US, and although Amy was a total babe, and despite the fact that she was thumping up and down on top of him like a buxom rodeo queen, looking at somebody's grave while getting shagged just gave him the wiggins.

Amy brought him back to the ground with another kiss, biting his lip while her hips gyrated on his lap. Trav pressed up and started working his arms out of his jacket. Amy continued moving up and down, her breath coming in shorter and shorter bursts. He ripped himself free of the jacket and tossed it over the tombstone.

There, that was better. That was—oh, wow! That felt really good. His hands found her hips again. He guided her as she continued to move, and he fell back on the grass. He slid a hand up under her tank-top and started pinching at the clasp of her bra. After a moment's fumbling, the clasp popped open. He brought his hands up her abdomen, sliding the shirt and bra up...

And there they were. Trav felt a rising surge from his groin and he squeezed his butt cheeks to keep his tempo under control. Amy glistened with a film of sweat, a moan slipping from her lips. She moved her hips in a circular motion, and the thinking part of Travis's mind switched to full-bore meltdown. Before he gave into pure ecstasy, here's what he was thinking: *Boobs, dang! This is awesome. She's so hot. Oh my god... Don't come, don't come, don't come, don't come...*

Then Trav closed his eyes and went to that special place. He leaned back and Amy grabbed his hair, bucking her way to a screaming climax. Her other hand fell on his cheek. It was clammy, groping for his mouth. He adjusted, and let her finger slide between his lips. He went to give her a playful nibble when a smell filled his nostrils that was so putrid he gagged. Vomit rocketed up his throat, filling his mouth and nose, closing off his windpipe. He ripped open his eyes to find Amy still riding him, her eyes closed, leaning way back—her hands supporting from behind.

The hand in his mouth was coming out of the ground. It pulled away, slimy, blackened, and rotted to the bone. Another wave of vomit surged up. The hand holding him by the hair kept him in place. The acrid aroma was thick. He choked again, tears welling in his eyelids. He tried to scream, but it just came out as a gurgle.

He writhed, trying to free himself from the grip, and Amy mistook the movement for enthusiasm. She bucked harder, her hands coming down and pinning him by the shoulders. The putrid fingers found purchase on his brow. Pressure formed a white corona beneath his eyelid. Trav twisted, suffocating as the pressure reached such an excruciating crescendo that he let out a blood curdling scream, spraying vomit everywhere as breath reached his lungs. His eyeball gave with an sickening pop.

Teeth came up through the earth and clamped down on his shoulder. Hot, sticky blood spurted through his T-shirt.

"AAARRRRGGGHH!" he screeched. "AMY!!!"

"Travis!" Amy leaped off the linebacker as the rotting arms held him in a half-nelson. Blood poured down his face. A sickening tearing sound came from behind followed by a raspy groan. Amy got to her feet, her jeans still looped around her ankles. She grabbed him by the arm and pulled, but the arms held fast.

"Rrrrraaaarrrrghh!!!" Trav struggled, pulling on Amy's arm as every tendon in his body strained.

Amy planted her heels in the ground and yanked again. Travis came up as the sod tore loose from the grave. Amy bowled back, slamming the ground, cracking her head off the tombstone holding Trav's jacket.

The corpse of a woman with drooling eye sockets and wild straw-like hair clung to the linebacker, gnawing his shoulder. He cried out as the corpse dug into his flesh.

Amy hauled herself up, the back of her head screaming. Travis staggered under the weight of the corpse, struggling to keep his jeans from tripping him. Beside them, another grave ripped open and a man with great hunks of flesh hanging from his jaw sprouted from the ground. He heaved himself out, clawing toward them.

Amy pulled up her jeans and grabbed the corpse on Travis by the legs, coming back with handfuls of disgusting green goop that had once been skin. The corpse wheeled around, still clinging to the linebacker and hissed.

"Uuurruuuuugghhh," came a rattling voice from behind. Another corpse had freed himself and was lumbering toward them.

"Travis!"

The linebacker spun—the corpse's legs flying—and hit the lumbering corpse with a wild tackle, tripping over his jeans and sending them both flying into a tombstone with a crunch. The corpse on his back sailed through the air.

Amy panned around looking for a weapon—a shovel or a branch, anything—when a long, rattling chorus of undead moans came from the left. Another handful of corpses were lumbering toward them.

"Amy, go!" Travis called, struggling with the tackled corpse. "Run!"

But fear had Amy's legs glued in place. "Travis—"

"RUN!"

The corpses closed in on Travis and dog-piled him. Amy spun, grabbed his jacket off the tombstone and bolted up the cemetery path. She had to find Noah. He was a security guard right? Security guards had guns. She wasn't sure what the hell these things were, but she definitely needed a gun.

Back at the dog-pile, there was a hideous screech.

There was a hideous silence, followed by a groaning chorus.

Amy pressed on, pulling the jacket over her shoulders and yanking up the zipper. A layer of leather wasn't much, but it would at least protect her from teeth if the corpses caught up with her.

She rounded a bend and found the beam of Noah's flashlight, describing a bored figure-eight in the night.

"Noah!"

The light turned. Amy skidded to a halt next to Noah.

"Amy? What's—"

"Do you have a gun?"

"No, why?"

"We need a gun. We need large fucking guns!"

"What happened? Where's Travis?"

Amy took a gulp of air, tears welling in her eyes. "I don't
know. We were having sex and then all of a sudden this thing
rips out of the ground and starts biting him—Oh god, I think
they killed him."

"Woah, hold on. You mean like zombies?"

"What? No. That's ridiculous. There's no such thing as
zombies."

"Right," Noah chuckled, clearly not having any of it. "But
apparently there's such thing as corpses coming back from the
dead—"

"Right!"

"Well, reanimated corpses? It's pretty ridiculous *not* to call
them zombies."

Amy wound up and delivered a walloping slap upside his
head. "What we call them doesn't matter. Don't you get it? We
need to hide someplace."

"Oh," Noah scoffed. "I get it. Hilarious, Amy. Zombies—
ha! Do you have any idea how lame that is?"

"Noah—"

"I am up to my fucking ears with this zombie stuff. You,
Wiz… It's ridiculous."

"I'm serious!"

"So am I! Since when has our culture become so terminally
obsessed with the undead? It's not even that original."

"Noah!"

"And another thing," Noah said. "If Travis put you up to
this—"

Just then, a rustling noise came from the row of tombstones
to their right. Rotting hands started sprouting from the
ground.

"—Holy shit!"

Amy grabbed him by the arm. "Run."

The two sprinted up the path as more rustling sounds came
from every direction. Noah's flashlight danced off the
gravestones. They came up on a tool shed and Noah grabbed
for his keys, then paused.

"What the fuck?"

Amy looked back up the path. Shadows were beginning to stagger through the tombstones. "What the fuck, what?"

Noah held up the mangled padlock that kept the shed shut. "Someone's been in here."

Amy rolled her eyes. "Uh, bigger priorities here? We'll have to barricade it from the inside."

In they went. Noah slammed the door to the shed as every grave in the cemetery ripped open.

CHAPTER 19
HAIRY TALES

The cell door clanged shut behind Wiz. He pulled his hands through his great mane and sighed, slumping on the metal cot while his brother locked the gate. Reyes stood next to a desk, leafing through paperwork. Wiz's cell phone, wallet, his hobbit's pouch of weed, and his bong were lined up on the table, waiting to be tagged as evidence.

"This is bullshit, Al."

"It's for your own good," sighed the sheriff.

Wiz wagged his head. "Oh come on, a guy has a bong collection and a little pot and that's enough to lock him up and throw away the key?"

Al pocketed the key, just to make a point. "We've been over this. What we're booking you for is not why you're here."

"It's more the part where your criminal activities have lead a crazed Russian hitman to town," Reyes said.

"But I didn't—"

"It's over, Kowalski," said the agent. "You're a drug trafficker. We caught you. Sure, you don't have the product on you now, but I have a CI's testimony that cites you as the main point of contact with the Vloydeskvis. You should be thankful

I don't have you up in county taking butt stogies from a four-hundred pound Aryan named Shelly over a dropped bar of soap."

"Badger." Suddenly, this was all becoming very clear. When he hadn't delivered, Reyes had busted the wholesalers and Badger must've thought Wiz defected, called the Russians, and tipped the fateful row of dominos that lead him here. He chuckled, shaking his head. What was the saying? Paranoia was only paranoia if you were wrong, right?

"So, the perp finally comes clean," Reyes said with a satisfied grin.

Perp? Sure, he delivered a little pot to pay the bills. He wasn't a serious criminal. Hell, pot was practically legal in California, wasn't it? Where did this by-the-book, stick-up-his-butt doucher with the stupid goatee get off calling him a perp?

"Perp?" he said. "You guys are missing the bigger issue here. I'm telling you—"

"Oh, what? The dead rising? It's the end of the world?" Reyes chuckled. "Please. I've arrested a lot of idiots, but that is by far the most idiotic ploy I've ever heard."

"It's the truth!"

"Brother, I love you, but I have had it with all this zombie talk," said the sheriff.

"You're not supposed to call them that."

"Enough, Wiz. Now, there's a guy skulking around town who wants to kill you. The agent and I are going to go wait for him to come by your place again and arrest him. In the meantime, you're staying here."

Reyes sighed, setting the paperwork he was browsing back in its folder. "You ready?"

Al nodded. "Let's go."

With that, the lawmen made their way out of the station. Wiz cradled his head as a wave of hopelessness crashed over him. "But the dog said…"

"You've seen it too, huh?" Mack Gaffey said from the adjacent cell.

"Yeah," Wiz said. "I was driving and hit it. It got up and said 'Nice driving, ya doomed fucks.' It was the biggest dog I've ever seen and... Well, it's crazy, but its eyes were glowing red."

Mack nodded knowingly. "I gave the same creature a flea bath last night."

Wiz wagged his head as if—well, as if Mack had just said he'd given a giant evil talking dog a flea bath. "You're fucking kidding me?"

Mack chuckled, his eyes becoming twin pits of crazed desperation. "Last night, it came to my window asking for a flea bath. So I did. It told me to leave town, that something bad is on its way. It was pure evil, Wiz. I could sense it. Anyway, I came here first thing and told the sheriff and he locked me up. Thought I was high off my rocker."

Wiz, who'd spent most of his life high off his rocker, gave the kennel owner a nod in solidarity. "You mean a mysterious beast is in town, and you tried to warn the sheriff? Jeez, Mack you really might be nuts."

Still, this was a relief. The dog was real—sure, that was about where the relief ended and the impending doom started, but it was better than thinking you were going crazy, wasn't it?

"We need to do something," Mack said.

"Something what? Need I remind you we're locked inside the belly of the law beast? Unless you've got a nail file on you, we're not going anywhere."

Back on the table next to his bong, Wiz's phone started ringing. "Fuck!"

"Fuck indeed, Sorcerer," a voice came from down the hall. A small man—a little over five-foot, wearing a black suit with a top hat—marched in, his black cane clicking the floor.

"I'm not a sorcerer," Wiz said. "I'm the Wizard."

The little man scoffed. "You're the sorcerer."

"Yeah, well, whichever, man. I'm a little busy being imprisoned here."

The little man regarded the cage as if it were little more than a blathering drunk. "This prison is just a concept."

"Yeah, and the concept would appear to be *locked*."

The Baron grinned, sharp, pointed teeth gleaming. "Another concept. I need your help, Sorcerer. If you'll agree, I can free you."

Wiz sighed. "What, do you have a nail file under the top hat?"

The man frowned. "Not at all. I'm the Baron. I am Ghede, guardian of the underworld. Your bars are but a song to me."

"Well, sing away then, mister Ghede. Welcome to the crazy party."

The Baron walked over to the cage, placed a hand against the lock, and concentrated. Wiz was coming up with something clever to say, when the latch clicked and the door swung open.

"Okay. What can I do for you Mister Ghede?"

"There isn't time. We have to move. The beast's power grows. The dead rise, and your world hangs the balance. Come with me, and I shall regale you with the tale."

"I think my van's in the impound lot," said the Wizard.

The Baron snapped. "It is done. Your steed awaits in the front lot. Let us go."

Wiz blinked. "Uh… Okay?"

The Baron lead him down the hall of the Sheriff's office with fervent purpose.

"Hey," Mack Gaffey called after them. "Can you do that for me? Or… No?"

The van was waiting in front of the station, engine running, stereo blaring "Voodoo Child". The Baron strode over as Wiz fumbled with his bong and his hobbit's pouch, digging in his pocket for his keys. The Baron clapped twice, not breaking pace, and the van's doors flew open.

"Okay," Wiz said. "You have got to tell me how you do that."

"I told you, I am Ghede. The mortal world bends before my very presence."

With that, the little man shot into the air and landed in the passenger's seat of the ChevyVan. Wiz blinked, shaking his head in bemusement, then dumped his things in the back of the van and took the wheel.

"What exactly is a Ghede, anyway?"

The Baron adjusted his top hat as Wiz put the van in gear. "Fill your pipe and toke up, Sorcerer. It's a longish tale."

"Yeah, and why do you keep calling me that? I told you—"

"Are you going to let me tell the story? Or should I stitch your lips with spider legs?"

THE BARON'S STORY

The world you know was not always yours. In the beginning, it belonged to the Ancient Ones—beings bestowed by the Creator with the gift of creation. Their power was limitless. The Ghede were a race of Ancients who could create joy from a grain of dust; make a party out of a single tear; render orgasm from little more than a rock. We were the first. The eons passed as more Ancients came into being and started filling the world with legions of beasts more inventive and fearsome than even the Creator himself could imagine. It was pure creation, and of course, it was complete chaos.

In time, the Creator grew jealous of his creations. His world began to plunge into darkness as the Ancient's hunger for power grew. How could his children be such ingrates? How could they out-create the supreme power of all the universe? It could not go on. It was time to create a new concept: order.

He created a new species—a mortal one, blessed with his image, but powerless to change the laws of the cosmos. He gave them curiosity, joy, and one thing the Ancients, for all their powers, had never been able to savor: love. He locked the Ancient Ones away in the underworld, stripped of their powers, and forced to serve and protect the new creatures: man.

This, of course, put a thorn in the paw of many of the Ancients. To them, order was petty. They had been stripped of their abilities and relegated to the stinky netherworld where they could neither live nor die. The Creator betrayed them. Some of the old ones embraced their new duty to the realm of man, but for many, it was an insult. To serve mortals? To lose their purchase on the joy of creation? Mutiny brewed in the underworld. Man was inferior, and many thought them a waste of time — a crude joke made by the Creator.

From here, the underworld broke into sects: the ones who believed in the Creator's plan, who served and protected man from the darkness; the ones you'd recognize as the gods of your world's religions. The world was divided, and the gods were free to choose which part they would watch over. But the power-hungry Ancients and their legion of beasts were not so willing to take the change. They could only yearn for the world they once reigned. They remain locked away in the underworld, only able to affect the world through the subconscious of mankind — they are the things that make your nightmares. They feed on fear, and their strength returns when fear knows no bounds.

This is where your stories come from. Stories exist to curb the power of fear, to inspire hope. As long as there is hope, there is a chance to keep the evil at bay. But it's a delicate balance, and it only takes a kernel of corruption to bring down the wall that keeps us from them.

"Hang on," Wiz said, righting the van on the main drag, taking a huge toke from his stick-shift bong. "So mankind was created to piss off a bunch of evil gods?"

The Baron nodded. "The Creator is infinite in all things, even his douchebaggery."

"So, this is all mind-blowing and stuff, but I have to ask, mister Ghede... What's the point? I mean... Why tell me?"

"Buddha's joyful bunghole, man! Will you let me continue?"

THE BARON'S STORY, II

It starts in the Far East in the eighth century—the land that would eventually become China. In a tiny mountain village ruled by a powerful sorcerer named Gen Shai Gen. The sorcerer used his powers to have his village flourish. He was kind, considerate, and noble. His people were happy, well-fed, and revered his leadership.

The sorcerer was madly in love with a princess from a neighboring village named Ming Pi. He courted her. But on their wedding day, Ming Pi fell ill. Gen Shai Gen searched the world, consulting seers and witch doctors, poring over every ancient scroll and potion to find a way to save her. Try as he might, the great sorcerer couldn't find a cure. His princess died in his arms.

Madness consumed Gen Shai Gen. He devoted his life to find a way—no matter the cost—to resurrect Ming Pi. He travelled the world, searching every nook and cranny of the black arts. Nothing would stop his quest. In his travels, he came upon a very old invocation that would raise the Ancient Ones who guarded the passage to the underworld. He called up the old gods, against all better judgement. He called up me.

The sorcerer bound my will to his. "Ghede," he said. "Raise my beloved from the grave. Have her walk among us. Let her sleep no more."

"But Sorcerer," I implored, "you know that I cannot. Death is a sacred passage. Even if I brought her back, it would only be her body. Min Pi's soul has moved on to its next incarnation. You cannot interfere."

"I can and I will. Bring her back, Ghede. I command it."

Of course, being much smarter than the sorcerer, I refused. Once a mortal dies, their soul ascends to its next cycle. Even a god as cunning and powerful as I cannot interfere. To bring Ming Pi back would be to raise a corpse devoid of soul. To break the body's bond to earth is an offense so foul even immortals pay a price. I begged the sorcerer to relieve me of his bond, but he was unmovable.

What I didn't know was Gen Shai Gen had called up another creature. One of the darker Ancients — Seth, the dog you've met. Seth was a natural trickster, skilled at bending man's mind to his will. He agreed to raise the sorcerer's bride in exchange for unchecked freedom.

Despite my efforts to dissuade him, the sorcerer agreed to the dog's bargain. It was all a trick, of course. Seth raised the princess, and Gen Shai Gen relieved him of his bond. What the dog had failed to mention was that without her soul, the princess had gone... well, *bad*. That night, when the sorcerer and his bride reunited in their bed, Ming Pi began to bend to dark cravings worming through her mind. She killed the sorcerer, and ate him.

With the sorcerer dead, my bond was broken. I battled Seth, and locked him away in the underworld, where he was sentenced to twelve millennia of hellhound duty, only allowed to walk the mortal plane to collect the souls of people who make pacts with demons. So long as the princess and the sorcerer's souls continue to incarnate, so shall he be bound to the underworld.

Now, with the coming of the Cerulean Moon, the underworld's bonds have weakened, and Seth has found a way back to the land of mortals. Your town sits on top of a cosmic weak-point between the living world and the underworld. The beast seeks to open this portal and unleash the army of Ancients bent on destroying humanity and retaking the world as their own. He has raised the dead to help him open the gate at the peak of the moon's cycle — that's tonight.

"I tell you this, because your soul is the soul of the sorcerer," the Baron finished. "The fate of the world hangs in the balance, and it all comes down to you."

"So, you're telling me that I'm the reincarnated soul of an ancient sorcerer who effectively invented zombies?" Wiz said. "And that I've spent my whole life riding out the bad karma?"

"It's a stiff drink to swallow, but yes."

Wiz thought about it. "Actually, that kind of explains a lot." He took a great breath and shrugged. "Okay, fine. So what do I do?"

"You must return your soul to the underworld to break the dog's tie to earth."

"And I would do that, how?"

"You need to kill yourself."

"What?!"

"...In a sacrificial chamber. It's actually really complicated."

"Can we go back to the part about me killing myself?" Wiz said, gripping the wheel. "Because... No?!"

"It's your destiny."

"Well, screw destiny. And how does any of this make any kind of sense? Didn't you say the first time the sorc—I mean, *I* —died it broke the curse?"

The Baron shrugged. "I don't make the rules."

"Well I—what... What about the princess's soul? What happened to her?"

The Baron took a long breath, removing his top hat and rubbing his bald head.

Ava turned the tap and stepped out of the shower. The bathroom was sauna-thick with steam. She grabbed her bathrobe from the door and wrapped her hair in a towel turban, then wiped the fogged-up mirror with a sigh. Trying to steam out the frustration hadn't worked.

She'd given all the signals. She'd given him food, coffee; offered back rubs, flirted when appropriate—she'd even let him and his cronies hide out in her living room when a Russian gangster was after them.

And all of it flew right over his head. Was he seriously that much of a stoner?

You know, honey bean, I hate to say I told you so... But I did totally warn you so.

"Oh, enough of you. All I ever get is a backseat commentary."

Ava opened the door and padded to her bedroom. Steam crept down the hall.

Well, you drive like a maniac, passengers tend to talk. He's a textbook conspiracy theorist—a total burnout. What was all that crap about the zombie apocalypse? He's clearly a loon.

She walked over to her dresser and cracked open the underwear drawer.

"He's got potential," Ava said, selecting a bra and panties. "Besides, he's different than the other guys."

Potential my well-formed ass! He's stoned off his gourd 24/7.

Despite the criticism of her inner voice—or perhaps because of it—there was something about Wiz she really liked. He didn't have an agenda—and he clearly wasn't scrambling to get into her pants. Sure, he was a bit of a doofus, but he wanted to get to know her. He was sweet.

He's a loser!

Maybe a different approach. Why not just be straight up, call him, tell him how she felt and invite him over for dinner?

"I've had it with you," she said, slipping into a pair of jeans and a Supertramp T-shirt. "I'm just going to call him, go 'Wiz, I like you. Come over for dinner,' and there's nothing you can do to stop it!"

But—

"Nothing! You hear me? I'm taking charge here!"

"You go, girl," came a low, gravelly voice from the closet. A chill ran up Ava's spine. She turned. The closet door popped open. Floorboards groaned. A pair of red, glowing eyes appeared in the shadows. Adrenaline surged through her body, her heart thumping in her ears.

The door swung open with a creak, and a huge figure, hunching to fit through the frame, spidered out. Its head was doglike with a long, bloodied snout; its shaggy coat fringed around its neck, ears pointing like antennae. Its body was the shape of a human, only covered in greasy black fur. It panted heavily, the smell of blood filling the air as its claws raked the floor, leaving grooves in the wood.

Ava shrieked.

The beast shrieked.

They both stopped.

Ava wagged her head, trying to shake the vision from her eyes. "Wait, why are you screaming?"

"Hey, you're right!" The beast grinned. "So, here's the thing, toots. I've got bad news and bad news. Which do you want first?"

Ava started slowly backstepping toward the door, unable to break her gaze from the creature. "Uh —"

"Ha! Fooled you. Trick question. There is no news, but I'm gonna eat you now. Hold still, okay?"

The beast lumbered forward. Ava leaped and scampered down the hall. She reached the stairs and wheeled around as the beast roared, tossing the bed out of its way and advancing. Ava lost her balance and tumbled backward down the stairs, barking her head against the baseboard on the landing. She rolled the final set and came up in a low crouch.

She ran from the foyer through to the kitchen, taking a roundabout at the coffee table in the living room to grab her car keys.

The beast leaped down the stairs and landed between her and the doorway. It let out a deafening howl, spewing drool and bits of chewed flesh. "Come on!" it said. "I'm tired. I don't feel like doing this right now. Can't you just give up or something? Jeez, it's just never easy with you humans."

Ava scanned the room for a weapon. There, on the shelf a few feet to her left, a heavy stone Buddha. She lunged, grabbed the statue and wound back. The creature went up on its hind legs, claws slashing the wallpaper just an inch over Ava's head. She hurled the Buddha with all her might. It caught the dog at about hip-level. The beast staggered drunkenly, then steadied himself against the hallway.

"Ouch, fuck! I mean… Oooh! Oh no! Not the Buddha! Pudgy oriental guys, my only weakness!" Then the beast roared with laughter and clambered after her.

Ava lunged for the basement door to her right, grabbed the handle, flung it open, did a one-eighty and slammed the door just as the beast slammed against it.

Ava scrambled for the deadbolt as the door shuddered again.

"You're not making this any easier!" Seth snarled.

CHAPTER 20
UPPING THE AUNTIE

"This looked way easier in the movies," said Silas, the undead goth guy. He was helping a wiry corpse out of a grave with a shovel, grunting.

"This is the exactly the problem with youth," Dimitri the ex-teacher sighed. "No sense of patience. All those movies have made you lazy. If you spent a little more time with a good book—"

"Right, because *A Tale of Two Cities* is such a how-to on being a zombie," said Nancy, the shambling ad-exec. "Who has time to read anymore?"

The graveyard was a sea of movement. All the graves had opened, and corpses in various states of decay were working their way out of the ground. The undead hacked away at graves with tools they'd looted from the cemetery shed.

"Will you all just shut up?" Ash called across the cemetery. "Keep digging."

"I think I need a rest," said Andy, the pudgy one. "This is real work!"

"You've been saying that all night," said Carly, who was shoveling away at a ripe-looking man in gray pinstripe. "Cowboy up, Andy. A little exercise won't kill you."

"That's what my personal trainer said right before I died of a heart attack."

"Well, it's not gonna happen twice. Dig!"

Earl and Jerome were trying to help a guy in a moldy tweed jacket with a rusted pair of glasses pry his way out of the ground.

"Grab his arm, Jerome."

"Careful," said Rusty as they grabbed him by his free arm and pulled. They grunted. They heaved.

"Pull!" shouted Jerome.

"Careful!"

With a sickening pop, Earl and Jerome tumbled backward.

"Oh great," Earl said. "This guy's arm came off!"

"Are you idiots deaf?" said Armless. "I said be careful!"

"He's in better shape than this one," Ash called, standing next to a squirmy pile of rotted flesh making gurgling noises. "Focus on the fresh ones."

Earl sighed, wiping his brow and leaving a great slash of earth on his forehead. "Are we sure we're going about this the right way?"

Ash shrugged. "I'm open to suggestions. It's not like we've got a backhoe ready."

"I mean are we set on digging up the cemetery and killing the townspeople?"

"What do you mean?"

"I just seems—well… I dunno, *morbid*."

Asher sighed and planted his shovel in the earth. He leaned on it and said, "Haven't we been through this enough times? We're undead. We're here to eat brains and end the world."

"Braaaaiiiinnnnsss!" chanted the zombies.

Earl gave the zombie king a tired expression. "But what if we're not just undead?"

"Do you have a pulse?"

"No."

"Do you have uncontrollable cravings for human brains?"

"Braaaaaaiiiiinss!!"

"Braaaaaaaaaiiiiinns!!!"

"Fine!" Earl grumbled. "Forget it."

A half-hour later, the horde had grown to about fifty good zombies. They met in the middle of the cemetery around a huge grave where a team of four struggled to relive an enormous, pruned-looking woman in her sixties from the grave. The tombstone behind read: SUSAN CARPENTER.

As they lifted, she jolted awake, gasping. The zombies staggered under her weight.

"What in the—who are you?" she said. "What happened? Why am I covered in dirt?"

The exhumation crew struggled, but there's a three-hundred pound dead woman, and there's a three-hundred pound writhing undead woman. They toppled. Susan slammed the ground with a heavy *thunk!* Then, she surveyed the rotting troupe. "Oh… My! What's happening?"

Brenda took the lead, walking over and crouching by Susan's side. "It's Sue, right? I'm Brenda."

"Hi Brenda," Sue said in a stupor.

"Here's the dealio, Sue. It's the apocalypse, and you're a zombie now." Brenda motioned to the horde. "We're all zombies now. Welcome to the club."

"Oh…"

"So anyway, we're doing a sort of band-together thing before we have a meet-and-eat with the locals. What do you say?"

"Well, I do feel a little peckish."

Asher came to the front as Brenda helped the bloated zombie to her feet. He climbed up on the tombstone and raised his arms to call attention. "Now," he said. "I know there's been some question as to whether killing the whole town and eating their brains is a terrible atrocity—"

"Braaaaaaaiiiiiiiiins!!"

"—But we're zombies now. If there's one thing we know for certain, it's that people hate zombies. They'll try to kill us the first chance they get."

"Which is why we should eat their brains!!!" shouted Carly.

Ash nodded. "It's us or them, people!"

"So let's get some fucking braaaaaiiiins!"

"Braaaiiiins! Braaaaiiiinnnnss!! BRAAAAAAAIIIIIINS!!!"

"Then it's decided," the zombie king grinned. "BRAAIII—"

Then he slipped and thumped in the freshly turned earth.

"Smooth," Silas observed.

With that, the horde shambled out of the cemetery. They picked up branches and garden tools—a couple of the craftier ones started hot-wiring the cemetery lawnmower. They headed down the highway toward Oak Falls, chanting for brains all the way.

The basement door pounded, sending a spray of dust through the air. Ava crouched under the landing, holding a crowbar she'd found in a long-forgotten tool box.

Wham, wham, wham! The door began spitting splinters.

The basement had been her only option, but Ava was beginning to regret not making a break for the back door.

Wham! Wham! Crunch. Cracks started to appear in the frame.

Now she was trapped, with a four-hundred pound monster beating at the door. With every splinter sailing through the air, her crowbar looked more and more like a toothpick.

Wham! Crunch. Creeeaaaak. The door began sagging in the middle.

It was only a matter of time before the beast made it through. A bare bulb at the top of the stairs was all that lit the basement. It might be dark enough to make a break for it when the thing came down the stairs—that was assuming it couldn't see in the dark.

Wham! Creeeaaaak. Groan. Great spiderwebs formed as the door bulged inward. Bigger and bigger chunks of wood snapped across the basement.

Well, there wasn't any dodging it now. Ava gripped the crowbar with the flat end up. Let him come! Let the sonofabitch try and eat her! She wouldn't go down easily. Yeah, prepare for full-blown indigestion, beastie!

Wham. Groan. Creeeeaaaaak. Snap. The door exploded inward in a hail of splintered carpentry and the creature's hulking mass filled the stairs. He let out a furious roar and lumbered into the basement. Ava waited for him to recover, her heartbeat soaring as adrenaline surged through her veins. She waited, letting the creature poke around, sniffing, plodding toward her. When the beast was so close she could feel its breath, she wheeled around, leading with the crow bar, and drove it into the creature's chest with a sickening squelch.

"Ow!" the dog howled. "Ow! Ow! Ow! Where the shit did you get a crowbar? Dammit, that really hurts!"

The beast raked his claws across the concrete floor, sending a shower of sparks through the air. It caught Ava in the chest, flinging her across the basement. She slammed into a folded-up treadmill that she'd spent years meaning to revive and the wind knocked out of her. She landed, her knees slamming against the floor.

The beast rushed forward, jaws snapping, claws winding back. Ava dragged herself across the floor as the monster reared up and lunged. She ducked and the dog slammed into the treadmill, shattering it like candy glass.

"You are becoming a real pain my ass!" he snarled. "Just give up! I'm clearly going to eat you no matter what."

Ava rifled around, finding an out-of-date lamp and flinging it. The lamp caught the beast in the snout and he howled, furiously. "This is not how this is supposed to go!"

She snaked her way between a pair of dusty cabinets she'd been meaning to put in storage, and despite the situation, it occurred to Ava that she really needed to clean out this basement. She reached the foot of the stairs and started scrambling toward the doorway.

The beast tossed the cabinets aside, roaring. "Get back here!"

Then something caught her ankle, and Ava conked her head on the stairs. Stars spotted her vision. The creature yanked her back, jaws opening wide. Ava caught the gleam of the crowbar jutting out of the dog's chest. She grabbed it and twisted.

"Come ooooon!" he howled.

Ava ripped the crowbar out of his chest and started whacking the beast over the head, sliding her way back to the staircase.

"Ava!" Wiz's voice came from the top of the stairs. He was holding a baseball bat. The Baron stood beside him, removing his top hat.

"Sorcerer!" Seth growled gleefully. "Just the guy I was looking to kill next!"

"Seth!" The Baron howled, pulling the blade from his cane.

"Oh, great. A Ghede." The dog bounded toward the stairs and Ava scampered for the landing.

The Baron grinned, his blade flashing as he leaped through the air toward the beast.

Seth snarled and batted the Baron across the basement, sword skittering along the concrete. He took a claw and put it through Ava's side, skewering her to the wall. Pain shrieked up her ribs as the claw scraped bone. Hot blood stuck her T-shirt to her side and she gurgled. The beast withdrew the claw, and Ava's eyes rolled back as she slumped down the wall, a trail of red in her wake.

"Ava!" Wiz shouted, rushing the stairs.

"Hey!" the beast grumbled, but before he could turn, Wiz brought the bat in a screaming arc to the side of his head. It shattered with a gunshot snap.

The beast chuckled. "Is that the best you can do, Sorcerer? Really, I expected—"

Then suddenly, the shadow behind Seth reached out and yanked him by the hind leg into the depths of the basement with a thundering crash.

Wiz took Ava in his arms and rushed up the stairs as the Baron and Seth thrashed around the basement.

"Go, Sorcerer, I'll be fine!" shouted the Baron. "The beast is strong but—"

Another crash, a deafening roar, then silence. Wiz carried Ava down the hall. She was beginning to shiver. He grabbed her jacket by the entrance and rushed to the van, where he set her down in the back, gently. He wrapped her with the jacket and fished for his keys.

"Wiz," she groaned, reaching for his hand.

He took her hand in his, fighting down the panicked nausea crawling in his chest. "Hi."

"Well," she said with a shuddering breath. "I wasn't planning on dying tonight… But, for what it's worth… I was gonna call you—"

She took a wet gasp of air, the strength draining from her body. Blood blotted through her jacket.

Wiz noticed blood trickling from a gash in his temple. He wiped it, shaking his head. "No, hey. You're not dying Ava. Nobody's dying. We're going to get you to the hospital and they'll patch you up. Good as new."

He wanted to believe it—needed to believe it.

"Franz," she whispered.

"What?"

"Not the hospital."—another sharp breath—"You take me there and I'll die in the waiting room. Call Franz… He'll take care of me and then—"

Ava let out a long, wheezing cough. Blood trickled from the corner of her lips. Her head lolled back and she went limp.

"We are so dead," Noah said, his back to the pile of shelving that formed a barricade over the shed's door. For the past half hour, the cemetery had been alive with undead moans and a lot of bustling. The yogi had spend the time in the same position, his knees pulled up to his chest, rocking back and forth in a semi-catatonic state, chanting "We are so dead."

"Shhh," Amy shushed. "Listen."

Noah listened. "I don't hear anything."

"Exactly. I think they might be leaving." Amy peered out a hole in the door, sighing with relief.

"I'm sorry, how is that good?" Noah said, resuming the rocking.

"Because we can make a break for it, doofus."

"Make a break for it?"

Amy spun around, shooting Noah a look she thought would translate to, *are you a complete fucking nimrod?*

"As in run for my car and get out of here? Try to keep up, Noah."

Noah fidgeted. "You're sure you didn't... you know... wanna wait until morning or something?"

Jeez, this guy was a total sissy when it came to surviving the apocalypse. Weren't guys supposed to be obsessed with this stuff? Was *that* was this was? The apocalypse? It felt entirely too early for it to be the apocalypse. Sure, she'd never considered there actually being life after thirty—but she was only twenty-three. This was way too soon.

"No offense, but I'd rather not spend the night awaiting death in a musty shed with some guy who still wears baggy jeans. We're going."

Before he could argue, Amy snapped a leg off one of the shelves to use as a makeshift weapon. She repeated the process and handed one to Noah, who wagged his head.

"How did you even do that?"

"I dunno, plot-convenience. It's like a hundred years old. Ready?"

"Noooo," Noah whined.

Amy sighed, yanked him to his feet, and slapped him. "Get it together, Noah. Let's go."

They heaved the barricade away from the door and crept out into the cemetery. It was the site of a mass exhumation—the kind of thing you saw on primetime news reports after earthquakes or hurricanes. Everywhere came a sound like worms dancing in pasta—reanimated legs, arms, and chunks of flesh writhing around the graveyard.

Noah stood, makeshift club in hand, looking as if someone had just dumped hot coffee in his lap. "This was a baaaad idea."

"Shut up, wuss!" Amy hissed. "Move it."

They started up the path toward the parking lot, passing a

row graves where the grass was churning as if something not quite strong enough was trying to claw through. Amy hopped over a bench and made a beeline toward the funeral home. Noah groaned, bewildered, and followed.

She could see the Volvo sitting in the parking lot. They were only about a hundred yards away, when a shadow moved behind a tree.

"Uuuuhhhhhrrrrrrggggg" A man in rotted linen staggered out. Noah shrieked like a schoolgirl finding a spider in her lunchbox and leaped behind Amy, who swung her club into the side of the man's head. With a crunch, he toppled over.

Amy turned and grinned at Noah. "How awesome was that?"

Noah looked pale. They scampered down the slope toward the lot. Amy vaulted over a tombstone and landed in something soft and gooey.

"Aaaarrrrrrghhhh!" said what can only be described as a rotting puddle of flesh.

"Aaaaaarrrrrggggghhh!!!" screeched Noah. Amy sidestepped as the yogi brought his club up and slammed it over what could have been the man-puddle's head.

Thump. Thump. Thwack. Thuk. Thuk. Noah continued hacking until there were only squishing sounds. He turned, grinned at Amy and said, "Yeah!"

Then, a slimy hand wrapped around his ankle. He leaped in the air, shrieking, and continued hacking until the hand flopped off. Amy grabbed his the arm and dragged him to the Volvo.

As they climbed inside, the mashed puddle of man rolled its remaining eye and said, "What a sissy."

They pulled into town. As Amy pulled the Volvo onto a street overlooking the bay, Noah said, "So, if the zombies are coming to town, why exactly are we coming back here?"

"Don't call them that."

"But they are —"

"No, they're not. They're mutants or science gone awry or something. Anything but zombies."

"How would that be better?"

"I dunno. It just is, okay? Either way, I have to pick up the kid."

"Hey, we live on the same street. You have a kid?"

"I'm babysitting a kid."

They came up on the Wizard's log cabin, where Noah noticed a police cruiser parked in front. "Oh, fuck!"

"What?"

"Oh fuck, oh fuck, oh fuck. The cops are at my place. Oh, fuck! My car's missing too. I had like two pounds of weed in there. They must've impounded it or something. Oh fuck, fuck, fuck!!!"

CHAPTER 21
A LONG, DARK, HAPPY-HOUR OF THE SOUL

"Remind me why we didn't take your car?" Al said.

"You kidding?" scoffed Reyes. "Your car gets all shot up, the state pays for it. Whereas, if it's mine, I have to pay for the damage. Plus the insurance premium's a bitch."

They were sitting in the Wizard's living room, in front of a coffee table littered with ashtrays, joint roaches, two resin-caked pipes, an incense burner, a four-way bong that looked like a glass octopus, and a half-eaten box of Fudge-E-O's, each of them looking about as comfortable as if they'd sat on live eels.

Reyes sighed, rubbing his eyes. "Your brother's a pig."

"Well, technically…" Al grinned.

"You shouldn't talk about your work that way."

"Oh, I was making a joke. You should try it sometime."

Max frowned. "It's unprofessional."

"Right, and you're all about due-process, Mister Let's Park The Cruiser In The Front Yard." Al chuckled, leaning back on the musty couch. "Coming from you, I'll take it as a grain of salt."

"Coming from the guy who's spent the last six years *not* arresting his delinquent brother, I'll take that as a compliment."

Al sighed. The agent was really getting to him. He was—well, he was such a tight-ass. "You know, Max, doing what's right isn't always doing things by the book."

"Well, that's not up to us, Sheriff. Need I remind you you're the sheriff? It's our job to uphold the law, all the time. Not when it's convenient. You should have arrested him years ago."

"Oh, for what? A little pot? If we locked everyone up for their dirty laundry, there'd be no one left to police. Putting him away would only have ruined him."

"Putting him away is what you're paid to do. You do realize if you had, then none of this mess would be your problem, right?" Reyes sighed, shaking his head. "Stupid."

"He's my brother. It's my job to keep him out of trouble. And who are you calling me stupid? Aren't you the guy who's failed to arrest a cartel of Russian mobsters for how many years?"

Reyes grumbled something in Spanish, got up and started pacing. "You have no idea what the fuck you're talking about, *cabron*."

And now the sheriff stood, walking over and getting right up in the agent's stupidly-goateed face. "I know exactly what I'm talking about. I'm talking about morality, Agent."

"Due process!"

"Shove it! Your goatee is ridiculous!"

"I know!"

And here, either the two men realized they were behaving like nine-year-olds, or they just got tired from yelling at each other.

"I'm going to move the cruiser," Al pouted.

"Fine!" Reyes huffed. "It doesn't even matter. Vloydeskvi is obviously going to use the back door."

Al stormed over to the door and flung it open just in time for a neon orange Civic to pull up. The engine sputtered, the headlights shut off, and Boris Vlodeskvi climbed out. The sheriff turned back to Reyes, who was already drawing his Beretta M9.

"You were saying?" Al thumbed the snap on his holster and said, "Right there, Boris. Hands up, nice and slow—"

"It's over Vloydeskvi!" Reyes shouted, in no small attempt

to out-police the sheriff. "You're under arrest. Now… put your hands up and place them on the vehicle."

"I already said that," said Al.

The agent made a tired-looking expression, but before he could speak, a thundering gunshot ripped through the air. Al spun backward, a great geyser of blood erupting from his shoulder before he crumpled in the doorframe.

"Eat shit, pigs!" howled the Russian, firing another three rounds and advancing.

The house was dark. The TV droned in the living room as Amy hit the lights for the foyer. She tossed her keys on an expensive-looking ottoman.

"Nice place," Noah said.

"It's my aunt and uncle's place."

"That reminds me, aren't you a little old to be a babysitter?"

Amy shrugged. "It's good money and there's a plenty of time to get loaded. Why are you a graveyard security guard?"

Noah followed as she moved through the dining room into the kitchen. "Pretty much the same," he sighed. "Looks like nobody's home."

"Hello?" Amy called out.

Silence.

Amy walked back to the foyer. "Mario? Todd?"

No answer.

"Maybe they went out?"

"It's a little late for ice cream, don't you think?" Amy said. "Besides, they couldn't have. Mario's stupid muddy boots are right here."

She kicked Mario's stupid muddy boots.

"And Mario would be?"

Amy let out a long sigh. "He's a douche bag. I can't believe I let him look after the kid. He's sorta, kinda—well, he drinks a lot. And he's a douche. Have I mentioned he's a douche?"

Noah bounced an eyebrow. "Would that be why you were shagging the linebacker in the cemetery?"

"Hey, you don't see me jumping into your past and making judgements, do you?"

"Maybe he called. Have you checked your phone?"

"The last time I got a message from Mario—" and here she stopped herself, remembering Mr. Monkey. "Never mind."

She pulled out her phone and dialed for voicemail.

"*Welcome,*" said the automated voice. "*You have—three—new messages. To hear your newest message, press one once.*"

Amy keyed the button, putting the phone on speaker so Noah could hear.

"*First message.*"

"Amy? It's Mario. So, uh… Todd got in. He's acting—ah, well—he's acting pretty strange. He was all covered in dirt and stuff. And you know what? He cut his head on something. I cleaned it up and made him take a bath, but he's—well, just call me back, okay? Actually, just come home."

"*Next message.*"

"Amy, it's Mario again. Look, I know I'm a complete asshole. If you wanna break up, I totally get it… But you have to get back here. Todd is getting really weird. He tried biting me while I was watching TV, then chased me upstairs. I had to lock myself in the bedroom. There's something really wrong with the kid, Amy. Just get here. Soon."

"*Next message,*" continued the automated voice.

"Amy, you gotta pick up the phone. This is getting fucking crazy. He's smacking against the door. I'm trapped in here and the kid is going fucking psycho. He's got a really big knife, Amy. He tried to stab me. I called the Sheriff's Office but nobody's picking up… Where the fuck are you! Amy, I think Todd is—well, I think he's a zo—"

Then, there was hissing tumble as Mario's phone hit the floor, followed by a hideous shriek, the gardener's blood-curdling scream, and a sickening crunch. Then a gurgle. Then a gnawing sound.

"*End of messages. If you would like to save your messages, press one. To delete them, press seven.*"

"Gulp," Noah said, peering into the shadows of the upstairs hallway. It was the only place left to look. Knowing it was exactly the last thing he should do in this situation, he mounted the first step.

When he reached the upstairs, he froze. Mario's phone was next to the bedroom door, sitting in a puddle of congealing blood. He grimaced, pressed forward through the door, then doubled back, holding his mouth.

"Oh god—oh, holy mother of… Amy—"

But Amy had already trudged up the steps. "Mario?"

Well, it was really only what was left of him: a ribcage, half a shattered skull, and one brilliant blue eye staring blankly at the ceiling. The floor, the bed, the walls were all thick with blood.

"Oh my god… Oh no… Oh—" Amy nearly toppled down the stairs and collapsed by the entrance.

Noah came down beside her, putting a hand on her shoulder as she began to sob. "Amy, we need to get out of here. Sooner would be better."

Amy just continued to sob. Shuffling sounds came from the living room. Noah searched the entrance for a weapon and found the gardener's shovel leaning against the front wall. He grabbed it and peered into the shadows. The shuffling grew closer.

"Oh jeez, Amy—"

"Oh my god, Todd? Todd! Are you okay baby? We're gonna get out of here. We're—"

Todd moved forward. Amy shrieked. His entire front was caked with blood, his mouth ringed with a grotesque Kool-Aid ring of drying blood. It looked like he'd been chewing on his own tongue.

"What the fuck!?" Amy wailed. "What have they done to you?"

"Oh, Jesus," Noah moaned, raising the shovel over his shoulder. "His head's split open."

A flap of skin dangled from Todd's scalp. He grinned.

"Who did this to you!?" Amy screamed.

"Amy—"

Todd inched closer, making a guttural, inhuman snarl. He lunged for Amy, then knocked back with a gong sound as Noah brained the zombie kid with the shovel. Todd pendulummed up, then hit the floor with a *thunk*.

Amy was still kneeling on the floor, chugging with diesel engine sobs. Noah went to comfort her, when the undead nine-year-old sat back up and roared.

Noah smacked him over the head one more time, then caught movement from the top of the stairs—the remains of Mario were clawing toward them, the one eye glaring hungrily.

"Time to go." Noah grabbed Amy and dragged her out of the house. They ran back to the Volvo.

"Give me your keys."

"Huh?"

"Your keys, Amy. You're in shock."

He ushered her into the car, tumbled into the driver's side, and started the engine. "I also need your phone."

Amy blinked slowly and handed him the phone. Noah started furiously punching the numbers and put the Volvo in gear.

"Wiz? You're not gonna believe this—What? …You're at *the bar*?"

Ava was on a rock-face overlooking a village. It came in flashes: Farmers working fields. Blacksmiths hammering sooty anvils. Children running through the street, chanting music in a language she'd never heard but somehow recognized.

The sun eclipsed. Darkness. She found herself on the floor of an ancient tomb. A tall, tawny, Chinese man in dark robes crouched over her, next to the little man with the top hat named Saturday. In the background, the beast with glowing eyes trotted, wagging his tail.

She was her, but she wasn't her, tearing into the sorcerer's flesh, picking pieces of him from his bones—the relentless hunger twisting at her insides. She rose, discovering a mirror with the wear of centuries about its frame and the skull of a fanged bull on top. A chattering skull hung from one side; a pouch of magic powder on the other. Symbols smeared in blood—a triangle, a moon and an upside-down cross. She padded over to the mirror, staring into her reflection. She was a young, beautiful, and terribly dead woman with almond-shaped eyes, painted from head to toe in blood.

The reflection began to swirl like a tide pool. The mirror opened from its center, and the hungry faces of countless monsters—hungry-looking goblins wearing crude masks—the hands of a million rotting corpses, poured out of the portal. A river of blood flowed up from the depths and rushed toward her, exploding out of the mirror and swallowing her as the army of nightmares descended.

Ava shot straight up with a throat-tearing scream, awake, lying in the middle of the Gnarled Wood Tavern.

"She's awake!" Franz MacFee beamed, an empty syringe in hand. Wiz and the Baron flanked him. The patrons, who stood in a horseshoe around Ava, all cheered drunkenly.

"You think?" Wiz said.

"Well, crisis averted," Franz shrugged, tossing the syringe in the trash and heading to the bar. "Good old adrenaline. Never fails. Lanette? Whiskey, I think. Make it a quadruple."

"Whaa—?" Ava said.

The Baron leaned on his cane. To Wiz, "We've got to tell her."

"Shh, later!" Wiz crouched beside Ava, taking her hand. "Hi."

"Wiz? What happened?"

"The balance of the world in jeopardy and you fall on sentiment?" The Baron spat. "Mortals."

"Why are we in the bar?" Ava said, going to prop herself on her elbows. Pain shrieked up her ribs, where she found bandages wrapped around her midriff. "And I have no top— why do I have no top, people?"

"Yeah... We kinda had to cut your top off," Wiz said.

"For surgery," Franz added. A glass of whiskey sloshed down the bar.

"I really just enjoyed it," said the Baron.

"You passed out after the dog attacked you," Wiz continued. "I took you here, and Franz patched you up—"

"Because I'm a brilliant surgeon!"

The patrons cheered again.

Ava squeezed his hand and blinked, feeling a little loopy. "So I'm on drugs? Is that why you're all so melty?"

Wiz grinned. "I thought I'd lost you."

"Handful of Vicodin," Franz slurred over his glass. "Plus a bucket of antibiotics. You're lucky though, the wound missed all the important guts. You lost some blood, but you'll be fine."

"Tell her, Sorcerer!" the Baron said. "Bar-wench? Rum."

"Fuck yo-self," said Lanette. "Ain't no mothafuckah call me a wench. Bar, or otherwise!"

The Baron slapped his cane against the floor. His voice boomed. "I will not suffer this mortal fuckery! Get me my rum, and someone tell this woman what's going on!"

"Ava, there's more," Wiz said, taking a breath and preparing to tell the story about the souls and stuff when the door flung open, and Noah Carpenter strode in with a blonde in her twenties. They looked like they'd been rolling in mud.

"Zombie-fucking-apocalypse, people! Lanette? Pitchers."

The barkeep huffed, pulled her shotgun from behind the bar and fired off a round into the keg. "That's it! Next mothafuckah who barks an order at me gets a face-full of pain."

Wiz helped Ava into a chair at a free table.

Noah said, "Wiz, Ava, meet Amy. Amy, meet Ava and Wiz."

Wiz wagged his head "What happened to you guys?"

"You were right, Wiz. The dead are up and walking. And someone took all our pot. We're fucked." Noah grabbed the pitcher and four pints and started pouring.

"And doomed," Amy said.

"Fucked and doomed. What's up?"

"You lost the pot?" Wiz sighed and downed a pint. "The guy in the hat's a god, a giant evil talking dog attacked Ava, and Franz just saved her life."

"Because I'm a—"

"Can it, Franz! So you saw zombies too?"

Noah nodded. "The whole cemetery. We need to get the fuck out of here—"

"You fools," the Baron laughed. "You can't leave. The dead rise, the beast approaches, the world will end"—he pointed his cane at Wiz and Ava—"and the only way to stop it is for these two to sacrifice themselves. We have two hours. Now—"

"Excuse me?" Ava said. "I've already been clawed tonight. I'm not sacrificing anything."

"Woah, woah, woah," Noah said. "Explain?"

The Baron waved him off and guzzled half a bottle of rum. "Their souls are the key to return the beast to the underworld."

"Karma," Wiz explained.

"What a bitch," Noah said.

Ava took a slug of her pint. "Nope. Not doing it. There's got to be another way."

Wiz nodded. "A counter curse or something—"

"The only way to stop Seth is to send him back to hell before he opens the portal to the underworld. That needs you both dead. It's destiny."

"Well, screw destiny!" Wiz said. "If destiny revolves around something we didn't have control over, then fuck it. I mean, it's completely unfair—"

"Life isn't fair," A man said from the door to the Wood. The stench of rotted flesh wafted in. "You're here one minute, crossing the street and the next? Pow! Smoked by a speeding car. Is that fair? No."

Asher Cravington sauntered in. The patrons screamed as the floor cleared. The zombie grinned evilly, "Is existing fair to begin with? Did any of us ask to be here? No."

He spun, producing a bloodied pistol, and pointed it at Lanette before she could reach her shotgun.

"Wouldn't do that, precious," he said, then turned back to the patrons. "We're here tonight, folks, because we have roles to play. All of you, and me. For example"—he pointed the pistol at one of the truckers at the bar, squeezed the trigger, and the man's head exploded, spraying Lenny, Hunt, and Miles. The patrons screamed. Ash smiled menacingly, walking over to the corpse as it flopped off the stool.

He dug a finger in the exit wound, came back with a string of brains, and licked. "Monster," he said, pointing to himself, then he waved at the trucker. "Victim."

More screaming. Ash pointed at the ceiling and fired. "Here's another: Harbinger," he did the pointing/waving thing again, this time beholding the patrons. "Harbingees."

"That's... not even a word," Wiz said.

"Shut up!" Ash snapped. "Here's the message: apocalypse."

"Uh, yeah, we kinda figured."

Noah rolled his eyes. "That's seriously your speech, *Corpse Bride*?"

Asher panned the pistol to the yogi, eyes flashing gleefully. "I guess someone wants to be made an example of. No problem."

Then, the tip of a blade appeared in the zombie's chest and he let out a gurgling wheeze. Behind him, the Baron said, "Death is sacred. You are an abomination!"

He spun the zombie back toward the door, then kicked him off the sword into the street. "Enough! Humans, your world is collapsing. We need to—"

Then, a shadow licked in through the open door, wrapped around the Baron's ankle, and yanked him out of the bar. The door slammed shut.

"Take over?" Noah said.

"Yup," Wiz said. "Okay people! Let's get these windows boarded up. Grab a table, a chair, whatever. Lenny, Hunt, Miles? Help me with this."

"There were more of them" Noah said under his breath. "Way more than one. Where are they?"

CHAPTER 22
TWO HOURS TO MIDNIGHT

Jenny Kowalski was not dealing well with the tourist hell descending on Oak Falls. She bustled around tables, taking orders, reciting specials, and generally doing her best not to kill the load of self-entitled tourists who'd swarmed the Superior Bar and Grill. She was short-handed, with only the seventeen-year-old line cook/dishwasher and one extra waitress to help her. With so many plates spinning in the air, she was bound to make a mistake — she just wasn't expecting such an uproar from the guy she'd accidentally delivered liver and onions to.

"Don't you understand?" he said, nasally and condescending. "I'm a vegetarian. To see liver and onions is to witness the cruelty of the whole world taking the lives of innocent animals — are you a meat-eater?"

"No," Jenny said, trying to keep the peace. "I'm sorry, we're really busy tonight and I — "

"You're a meat-eater. I can tell. You have that look about you. The kind that says you're a cruel, heartless murderer. You know what? Forget the salad. I'm leaving."

"Sir — "

But the angry vegetarian was already storming out of the restaurant.

Jenny sighed, staring at the liver and onions, thinking: *traitor. Tasty traitor.* So she'd been lying about meat-eating to make tip—so what? All waitresses did it. It wasn't like she'd intentionally put the dish in front of a herbivore. This was single-handedly the worst night she'd had in years. Behind her, plates crashed.

"Dammit Carole!" she snapped. She couldn't help herself.

Suddenly, a huge crowd thundered down the street outside, all ragged-looking. Easily more than fifty, all marching in offbeat time down the main drag—a jazz marching band, perhaps—followed by a pair driving a lawnmower.

Before she could yell to clear all the free tables, a handful of them came over and started slamming the windows. Jenny noticed one, a guy in his early twenties, green skin sagging off his bones, who said, "You guys serve brains?"

"Braaaaaaaaiiiiiiinnnnns!" chanted the rest, grabbing the screaming vegetarian and throwing him under the lawnmower. Blood spattered against the diner's windows.

Lester Jones was sitting on a fold-out director's chair next to the ice machine in front of his Texaco station, smoking a cigarette, ruminating on the ways he could dupe tourists into replacement mufflers for a rattling transmission. It had been a busy day, with dozens of newcomers passing through, paying a tourist premium on the fuel pumps in front of the shop.

Much to his chagrin, the night had been quiet—most of the travelers parking and deciding to walk the main drag for the Palooza. He'd been expecting the usual surge in unexpected engine failures (mostly because he'd tampered with the fuel), and had spent most of the money he'd normally recuperate during the tourist season on a top-shelf bottle of Johnny Walker. It was waiting for him at home on ice, but he couldn't drink it with good conscience until his books were back in the black, so he sat, waiting.

He was just beginning to nod off when he heard the marching of dozens of feet down the main drag. He looked up and discovered a gang of ragged-looking tourists, shambling drunkenly down the main drag, chanting for what he was pretty sure were brains.

Three of them broke off from the group and came over.

"Hey," one of them said. "Got any gas?"

Lester eyed the glowing Texaco sign and nodded slowly.

"Great," said another. "We're gonna take some, that okay?"

"It's forty bucks a gallon."

The third of the group grinned, walking into the light. Skin hung in ragged strips from his cheeks. "Yeah, don't think so."

The three advanced on Lester. The mechanic was on his feet in seconds, running through the shop, as another handful of the undead broke off from the group.

"Oh fuck, oh fuck, oh fuck."

He hit a button in the back that controlled the fuel pumps, opening all the reservoirs. He came back through the front of the shop as the zombies heaved the ice machine and smashed the glass door. They climbed in and grabbed him.

"Eat shit, cocksuckers!" he screamed as they dragged him out toward the pumps. He pulled a Zippo from his overalls and flicked it twice. With a brilliant flash of light, Lester was gone, and the Texaco erupted in a huge ball of flame.

The Russian had them pinned behind the back of the cruiser. Three sprays of shotgun pellets spattered into the side of the car. Al cradled his shoulder, blood streaming between his fingers. When the shot had hit him, the only thing that crossed the sheriff's mind was Jenny—if the hit had been inches to the left; if it had slipped under his vest—if he'd died, how would she find out? How would she deal?

It didn't matter now. Another hail of pellets rained over the cruiser. Reyes was crouched by the hood, taking an over-calculated shot that ricocheted past Boris's head.

"Nice to have you back, Al."

The sheriff was at the back of the cruiser. He heaved the gun over the trunk—his arm screaming as he moved—and fired three shots that put holes in the hood of the Civic, just inches from Vloydeskvi's groin. The Russian gaped at the smoking holes, then rolled over to the other side of the car and opened fire.

Reyes waited for an opening, then fired again, this time shattering the hatchback of the orange car.

"Volydeskvi fucked up your shoulder pretty bad, Sheriff," he said. "You sure you're okay?"

Al heaved the pistol and squeezed the trigger. A gush of red exploded from the Russian's shoulder as he yelped and flopped to the ground.

"No, but I can do that."

Reyes peered over the hood of the cruiser. "Well, I'll take that as a big fat yes—"

Bang, bang, bang!!! Glass shattered by Reyes's shoulder. Holes appeared in the hood of the cruiser. Reyes let off another two shots at the Civic, clipping the rear-view mirror and putting a hole in the driver's side. Then, the chamber clicked, empty.

"Fuck!" the agent dropped his empty magazine. "Al, there's a duffel in the back seat. It should have a clip or two."

"Got it," the sheriff crab-walked along the cruiser and opened the back door. He slipped in as another blast from the Russian took out the rear windshield and rooted through the bag.

"Fuck!" he said.

"What?"

"You're out."

Boom! Boom!! Boom!!

"What?"

"The fucking bag is empty!!!"

"Damn," Reyes said. "I thought I had one more."

Al felt a strong urge to punt kittens. "And you just forgot?!"

The agent shrugged. "Do you know how many times I've been hit in the head today?"

Boom! The passenger's window shattered. Chunks of glass rained over the cruiser. Al slipped to the backside of the car, put the Russian in his sights, let his breath go and pulled the trigger. The bullet caught Boris at about hip-height, sending him in a backward spin as he yelped.

"Nice shot," Reyes said.

"Yeah, well it was my second-last one. Sorry, left my spares at the office."

The agent sighed, slumping behind the wheel-well. "Well, then it appears we're fucked, Sheriff."

Al put his finger in the air to mark the point as another spray of shotgun rained over the cruiser. "Not just yet. Go with me, okay? FUCK. THAT WAS MY LAST SHOT. YOU OUT?"

Reyes looked at him, confused, then realized what he was up to. "YEAH. YEAH, I'M DONE. YOU?"

"Yeah," Al continued, sounding as exasperated as he could. "You hit?"

"Multiples," Reyes gave a surprisingly convincing bloody cough. "You?"

Al channeled the pain coursing through his shoulder and said, "Yeah, think I'm…."

He lay down on the pavement, letting out a long, painful-sounding death rattle. He set his gaze at the top of the cruiser while Reyes lay down beside him.

They waited.

After a good minute, footsteps crackled over the shattered glass covering the driveway. Al waited until they reached the other side of the cruiser, then adjusted his gaze.

The Russian stood on the other side of the cruiser, his gun hanging to the side, a look of confusion blossoming on his forehead.

"Oh hey, Boris," Al said. He aimed the gun and fired.

With a great spurt of blood, the Russian shuddered backward, going cross-eyed. Then, he flopped behind the car in a bloody heap.

Al turned to the agent and said, "Bad guys always fall for that."

"Nice," Reyes said with a smirk.

The sheriff got to his feet, then gave Reyes a hand. "You owe me for the cruiser."

"State pays for it," grunted the agent.

Before Al could reply, a huge mushroom cloud of flame erupted on the main drag. The two lawmen looked at each other and said, "Car."

"Wait," Al said, motioning to the Russian's body. "What about him?"

Reyes sighed, eyeing the flames climbing into the night, then shrugged.

"Got a body bag?"

"Well, they're panicking and boarding up the place," Brenda said.

"Yeah, and that guy in the hat stabbed me," added Ash.

"All according to plan," Seth grinned. "Nice touch with the blowed-up gas station, though."

The king and queen looked at each other, shrugging. "That was improvised."

"What happened to the little guy?" said Ash.

Then, about three blocks over, something crashed into the roof of the Oak Falls library, shooting dust twenty feet into the air.

"He wanted to play fetch." The dog shrugged. "He lost."

The patrons were using tables and chairs to seal up the windows of the tavern as undead moans began to volley off around the perimeter. Fleshy thunking noises came from behind the barricades. A shockwave thundered through the tavern, rattling all the glassware as light filled up the north window.

"What was that?" Ava said.

"Sounded like something blowing up," Wiz replied.

"That would be the Texaco," Noah said, shoving the end of a barstool into a window. Glass shattered as a pair of rotted arms snaked through the opening and grabbed the yogi. "Oh fuck!"

"Noah!" Wiz shouted, rushing over to his friend as the yogi used the stool to bash the arms back through the gap.

"I'm fine," Noah said. "But these barricades won't hold forever."

Wiz nodded. They needed a plan. More pounding came from the door, which had been bolted shut and fortified with a stack of tables. They'd found a hammer and nails in the storeroom, and the patrons were all working in teams to get the openings sealed-off, but Noah was right. Wood and nails would only hold so long—and that was the way these things always went in the movies, wasn't it? You could try to stay holed-up, but the zombies always got through.

He scanned his mind for a solution when a blonde guy in his thirties who'd been drinking with his girlfriend spoke up. "Are we really sure we know what we're dealing with here? I mean, zombies? Really?"

"We've been through this," Amy said from a group working to overturn the pool table.

"They could be terrorists, though," the guy insisted. "Right?"

"Sure, if that makes you feel better," Wiz said.

"Uh, guys?" said Lenny from across the bar. He, Miles and Hunt were working to fix the *IT'S ALWAYS 5 O' CLOCK SOMEWHERE!* sign into a window. "Think we might have a problem."

Wiz, Ava, Noah, Amy and Franz all moved over and peered through the opening. A crowd was forming in the street. Easily thirty zombies circled the tavern. The pounding kept coming from all sides, and a withered, skeletal face appeared in the window, hissing.

Wiz grabbed an empty beer bottle from the bar, smashed the end of it, and rammed it into the zombie's face.

"Ouch! Motherfucker!" it said. "You jerk. You'll pay for that!"

Wiz looked at the gory end of the bottle and tossed it to the floor. "We need better weapons. Lanette?"

The barkeep gave a proud expression, pushing her wireframe glasses up her nose. "Thought y'all'd never ask."

She hauled her friend Betsy out from behind the pine. "Shotgun," she said. "Double barrel. Strong enough to mow two of those son-bitches down at a time if you work it right. Glock," she continued, setting a chrome-plated pistol next to Betsy. "Nine millimeters of nasty, oiled just this morning." She stooped over and produced a .38 snub-nosed from an ankle holster. "Revolver, because every gal ought to have one." Then she reached higher up within the depths of her skirt and produced a pistol about the size of a fist. "Derringer. Only got four shots, but you aim it right it'll do the trick," she said, almost gleefully, which may have been the scariest part.

The bar gaped at her. She smiled. Then, almost as an afterthought, "And since the sheriff ain't among y'all tonight..." She reached under the bar and produced a mean-looking sawed-off shotgun. "I call it Glenda, and I'll be claiming it as my own."

"Holy shit!" Wiz said.

"Holy shit!" Noah agreed.

"Holy flash-fried fuck!" said the doctor.

"Shotgun the shotgun," Ava said. Then, off the gang's worried expressions, "Oh, what? I can aim."

"Well that checks off weapons," said Amy. "What's the plan?"

"Right," Wiz said. "It's actually really simple. We're fortified, but those dead fucks will get in one way or another."

"Says who?" said the blonde guy, producing his own pistol from the back of his jeans.

Wiz waved him off. "Dude, have you never seen a zombie movie? They always get in. It's just how it goes."

"So what?" said Amy.

Wiz took the Glock off the bar and racked the slide. "We let 'em in."

"We *let* them in?" said the blonde guy. "You want to *let* them in? Are you fucking high?"

"Uh... Yeah?" Noah said.

"That's like totally irrelevant," Wiz added.

"Hey, do you guys smell something?" Ava said.

Wiz sniffed the air, then looked at his companions, hope draining from his expression like the air from a slashed tire. "Uh-oh."

"What?" said the blonde guy. "Uh-oh what?"

"It's gas."

CHAPTER 23
THE BIG VLOYDESKVI

Olaf Volydeskvi came to town a little after 11 P.M. The drive from Big Sur made his joints creaky, cramps were forming in his thighs, and he suspected (like usual) that he was growing far too old for this shit. But he hadn't heard from Boris since he'd given the order to kill the poopstick, and by the fifth missed call, Olaf was beginning to worry. Boris was tough, and useful in certain situations, but he wasn't exactly the smartest henchman—and he was his cousin. Family ties moved Olaf to action, and here he was, out, doing work, something he assumed a boss was not really supposed to do past the age of fifty.

He brought his Ford F150 toward the main drag, slowing to mess with the radio, when a bone-chilling bay at the moon came from a building on his left. It was a dog: big, black and shaggy, reminding him of the barn dogs his family kept back home—if, you know, their eyes glowed red. Olaf's mouth hung open as the beast trotted across the street, then looked at him.

"Nice," it chuckled. "You look good and ready to be lorded over."

"Mother Russia!"

The beast leaped into an alley behind the old stone mill, a towering building perched on the edge of the falls. On the lintel above the door were the carved symbols of a triangle, a moon, and an upside-down cross. Before he could get any more details, the boss floored the accelerator and brought the pickup straight toward the streets lining the bay on the other side of the falls.

He just didn't have a processor for the supernatural. It was too crazy to even try to think about, so Olaf decided to press forward with his mission. He brought the truck up the street and pulled in at poopstick Wizard's house. A battered Honda Civic sat akimbo on the driveway. Olaf killed the engine and climbed out, patting the service revolver he'd used since his run with the KGB.

When he noticed the shattered glass littering the lawn, the bullet holes peppering the hatchback's exterior, and the wide smear of blood across its hood, worry began to snake through his insides. He walked around the car, thinking.

"Boris, where are you now?"

"Right here, Boss."

Olaf spun to find his comrade slouching behind him, a police body bag pulled over his head like a mask.

"Boris! Why do you have body bag on head?"

"Well," Boris hesitated. "It got ugly, boss."

"If you are hurt, then you must show."

"I'd rather not—"

"Take fucking body bag off head now, Boris!"

Something was off. Boris wasn't the goofy type. Stupid, definitely. But goofy? Never. Olaf placed his hands on his hips as his cousin removed the body bag, then his eyes bulged in horror.

"Fuck! That's bad. Put bag back on."

When Olaf said "bad," he meant that Boris was missing a significant chunk of his cranium. It looked as if a freight train had clipped the top of his head clean off. Boris advanced on Olaf, curds of brain-matter spilling out of his skull.

"Boss, I am hungry."

"So we kill poopstick Wizard and get burgers," Olaf said, not really sure how to respond to a man who should by every standard be dead as the Cold War. "And vodka."

"No, Boss... I'm *hungry*." Boris gave his cousin a *how-are-you-not-getting-this?* kind of expression.

"Boris, you are zombie!"

"Yes boss. Hungry."

Olaf began to backpedal, his pulse quickening. "But... I am your cousin. Do you still want to eat me?"

Boris paused, considering. "Yes, boss."

With that, Olaf slipped the revolver out of his waistband and fired three rounds into his comrade. Boris staggered backward, his hands coming up to the holes appearing in his chest, then he slumped to the ground.

"You're fired," Olaf said.

It would be easier to accept the situation for what it was, have a very stiff drink, and forget about it. But the *how* of it all seized Olaf's mind. How could someone return from the dead? Could science do it? And if so, then why Boris? Why — of all people — would anyone want to bring back Boris? He was a useful idiot, but he was still an idiot.

Before he could go further, Boris started to get back up.

"You betray me, Olaf?"

"Boris, you are zombie. If I don't betray you, you eat me."

"Oh, that's good point," Boris said, then lunged at Olaf, who leaped into the open driver's side of the Civic. Boris went for his legs, but Olaf scampered in, slammed the door, found the bare wires by the ignition and started fiddling.

Boris reached through the shattered window, grabbed Olaf by the neck and chomped down on his skull. Olaf screeched as blood trickled down his forehead.

"You taste like cabbage," said the zombie.

"You reek of shit!" The engine revved and Olaf threw it in reverse, completely forgetting his truck was parked behind him.

The jukebox crackled "Stayin' Alive" while the patrons of the Gnarled Wood Tavern grouped around the corral of turned-over tables and chairs they'd piled in the entranceway. It funneled in from the door, all the legs pointing toward the five foot opening that described a path. The overturned pool table created a stop at the end of the funnel.

Wiz felt a little uneasy holding a firearm for the first time in his life. Noah, with the .38, looked like he was moments away from giving his best *Die Hard* impression. Lenny wielded the derringer, and Ava was propped up on the bar, pointing the shotgun at the entrance as the zombies pounded the door.

"Okay," Wiz shouted. "Showtime. Everybody in position."

Amy snapped the end off a pool cue and tossed it to the doctor, then repeated the process and handed a makeshift spear to Hunt, then Miles, then kept one for herself.

"But I'm a pacifist," Miles said, staring at the spear, mortified.

"And I'm a cheerleader," said Amy.

Wiz moved over to the edge of the barricade and reached for the bolt holding the door. "Now, everybody keep a safe distance from the barricade, watch where you're shooting, and remember. You need to shoot them in the brains."

"Are we sure about this?" said the blonde guy, pointing his gun at the entrance over the pool table. "Once we open that door there's no turning back.

"No," Wiz said. "But the deadies have this place covered in gasoline. We either let them in, or they roast us."

"But this building is made out of brick?"

"Hey fuckwad," Noah said from the other end of the table. "Do you even know how an oven works? Sure, we won't burn down, but the heat will cook us."

"Can we get on with this?" Ava said, pumping the shotgun. "I really wanna shoot some stuff."

Wiz fought back a wave of uncertainty. "Ava, are you sure—"

"Oh, blah, blah, surgery... Don't want to pop the stitches. Don't question me, stoner-boy. Pony the fuck up!"

"But..." said the blonde guy.

"Oh, shut up, ya big wussy Ken Doll. Let's party."

"I warned you not to mix those pills with alcohol," Franz said.

"Oh, coming from you that's hilarious."

Wiz felt the urge to try and calm her down—to protect her—but held it back. If he did that, she might shoot him instead of the zombies. He grabbed the bolt and turned. "Here we go, gang. One... Two... Three!"

He slid the bolt and the door snapped open. Wiz leaped to the pool table as a pudgy man whose jaw hung by a flap of skin and a green-looking guy in his twenties with a severe haircut lumbered into the bar holding garden spades.

"Someone say something about a party?" said Silas, the undead goth guy.

Heart-Attack Andy grinned. "Who feels like a snack?"

Ava panned the shotgun at Silas and pulled the trigger. The zombie goth shuddered backward, a huge ball of gore spewing out between his shoulders. He staggered, then looked down at the softball-sized hole in his chest.

Andy looked at his partner and started chuckling maniacally. "Now you can really feel empty inside!"

Silas frowned. "Shut up, man. That's not fu—" But before he could finish, his head exploded as Ava fired another shot.

Andy spun just in time to catch Amy's pool cue to the side of the head, skewering him like zombie shish-kabob. "Oooooowwwww"

Wiz lined up his gun with the pudgy zombie and pulled the trigger. Andy's body flopped on top of Silas's, just in time for another three wearing soiled hospital gowns to appear in the doorway.

"Can we make a public service announcement?" said Nancy, the ex-ad exec. "The committee of the apocalypse is in need of brains."

Noah leaped from behind the pool table and shot her through the head. Nancy crumpled to the ground. The two other zombies stared at her, then whipped back on Noah, furious. "You killed Silas? But he was such a sweetie."

They lunged at the pool table. Franz MacFee came at one of them swinging his pool cue and cracked the back of the zombie's head. "There's more!"

Wiz fired another three rounds at the growing wall of undead in the entranceway. Too many. They started clawing over the barricade.

"We're loosing ground here, Wiz," said Noah.

"Fuck!" Wiz shot again before the gun clicked empty. "Okay people, plan B!"

"What's plan B?" said Amy.

"Push!"

Amy pushed against the tavern door with Lenny, Hunt and Miles as four rotting arms came squirming through the gap. The undead roared angrily as they worked to find purchase.

"Sooner would be better with that pool table!" She took her cue and whacked at a zombie with a wax face.

"Ouch, you bitch! That was my eye." He grabbed a clump of Amy's hair and yanked toward the opening.

"Gross!" Amy struggled to free herself, but the door began to slide inward. Hands wrapped around her shoulders and started pulling her out of the bar.

"Miles, grab her!" Lenny shouted. Amy felt hands around her ankles and she was pulled into the air, stuck in a match of human tug-of-war between the zombie and the old guy.

"Fuck!" The zombie grunted. "Guys, a little help?"

Two more of the undead stopped shoving and grabbed her. They heaved. Miles's grip gave and Amy went toppling out of the bar, knocking over the zombies like bowling pins. She tried to recover, but the wax-faced one grabbed her by the hair.

"I don't mind a little fight for my dinner."

She lunged for the entrance, but the zombie's grip snapped her head back like a dog reaching the end of its leash. She screamed. The zombies she'd toppled lumbered over and grabbed her by the arms, holding her in place as the horrid breath of Dimitri the dead school teacher reached her neck.

Despite the circumstances, Amy realized the zombie was her twelfth-grade English teacher, and she'd skipped almost every single class.

Suddenly, two gunshots rang out and the skeletal hands released her. Miles was coming through the doorway, Lanette's derringer smoking. Through the ringing in her ears, Amy heard the old guy say, "Come on, Dimitri, it's definitely not protocol to eat the students."

The zombie roared, pulling her in by the hair.

"Get fucked, pacifist!" He bore down with blackened teeth, and Miles ran, leading with the tiny pistol. He shoved the derringer into Dimitri's mouth and the undead teacher's grip slackened. Amy ripped away as Dimitri chomped down. Miles shrieked and pulled the trigger, and Dimitri spurted a rancid streamer of black goop as he collapsed.

"Come on," Miles grunted, grabbing Amy by the arm. They tumbled through the entrance just in time for Wiz, Noah and Franz to heave the overturned pool table over the exit.

Without missing a beat, the fleshy thunking sounds came again. Amy flipped the deadbolt as Miles cradled his bitten hand, blood welling up in the toothmarks. "Sonofabitch."

"Franz?" Wiz said. "Now's your cue to play doctor."

"I'm fine," Miles sighed. "Just a little bitten. Anyone else hurt?"

When he looked up, half the bar was standing around him, all wearing grim expressions.

"He's bitten!" said the blonde guy. "That means he's gonna turn into one of them."

"Not necessarily," Wiz said.

"Oh, come on, Tommy Chong! Haven't you ever seen a zombie movie before? They bite you, you're one of them."

"It doesn't always work that way," Noah said.

"Bullshit. I know how these things work." He pointed his pistol at Miles, who whimpered and put his hands over his head.

"I thought you wanted them to be terrorists," Wiz said.

"I'm not — I mean... Am I the only one who saw those things? They're clearly not terrorists. It's some virus or something raising the dead. We know how to deal with that, right? Removing the head or destroying the brain, right?"

"Woah, woah, woah," Wiz said. "Can we hang on for one fucking second here? Yes, there's a horde of undead cannibals surrounding us. Obviously the dead are rising, but we don't know what's causing it. Can we not decapitate anyone for no good reason?" Then to Franz, "What do you think, doc?"

"How the shit should I know?" Franz said. "As far as I'm concerned it's the apocalypse."

"But, could it be a virus?"

The doc hung his head. "There are some viruses out there that induce zombie-esque symptoms — rage, psychosis... There are also parasites that kill the host and take over the nervous system... But that's all insects. Yes, there have been cases of blowfish toxin inducing a near-death state... But actually reanimating corpses?" He scoffed. "Forget it."

"Well, there you go," Wiz said, turning back to the blonde guy. "Now put the fucking gun down."

The blonde guy wagged his head, keeping the gun trained on Miles. Sweat beaded his brow. "He's infected!"

Wiz gave an exasperated sigh. "Dude, we just finished — "

"Shut up," the blonde guy shouted. "I'm not taking any more orders from a... fucking... stoner!!! Who else is bitten?"

"Me," Noah said, raising a hand wrapped in a bar towel.

The blonde guy wagged the gun. "Over there. Now!"

Noah shook his head wearily and walked over to Miles beside the pool table. "This is bullshit."

Blondie addressed the patrons, who were all standing off to one side of the bar, watching. "These people have been bitten by zombies. If we don't deal with them, they'll turn and let the rest of them in."

The patrons broke out in murmurs of uncertainty. Then Amy got up and stood between the blonde guy and the bitten.

"No."

"No? What do you mean *no*?!"

"Both of these guys have saved my life tonight. I'm not going to sit here like the rest of these mooks while you execute them. You're gonna have to go through me, discount-Ken."

"Way to flesh out a stereotype," Noah said.

"I know, right? I really need to get better at that."

Discount Ken wagged the gun. "Move."

"No."

"Move! Or I'll paint the walls with your brains."

"Brains! Braaiins!! Braaaiiins!!!" chanted the undead.

"Shut up," Ava shouted—and to everyone's astonishment, they did. She pointed her shotgun at the blonde guy. "Put it down. Nobody's shooting anybody, okay? Besides, the last thing we need is a guy with a flashy shirt and a cheap haircut calling the shots around here."

Ken's forehead went a shade of bright pink. "Have you people gone completely mental? I'm not—"

"Put it down," Ava pumped the gun. "Or it'll be you painting the walls."

Just then, Lanette Wilson, who'd steeled her approach to conflict resolution over the years, pointed her sawed-off into the empty keg and pulled the trigger. Everyone jumped—one man literally into his wife's arms. "That's enough outta y'all. Ain't no mothafuckah gonna paint these walls but me—now put all your fucking guns down before I put *you* down."

Without a beat, the guns went down and everybody stared at the floor like embarrassed teenagers. Lanette pushed her wireframe glasses up her nose with a smirk. "That's better."

Wiz sighed, the smell of gasoline strong on the air. "We're missing the bigger issue here."

On the roof of the Gnarled Wood Tavern, Brenda struck a match. *Thuppt*. The flame burst with a snarl of smoke, shimmering against her pale skin. She walked over to the edge of the building, looked back at Ash with a grin, and dropped the match.

"Oops," she said as it hit the side of the tavern and the whole place lit up.

The zombie king chuckled as he walked over to his queen and put an arm around her. "Barbecue."

As the flames licked up the bar, he kissed her, thinking *who says you can't be evil and romantic?*

"Oh, spare me!" Seth grumbled. "You two are disgusting."

Brenda pulled away, planting a seductive finger on Ash's chest. "Don't you need to get ready for the thing with the mayor?"

Ash sighed. "Can't we enjoy the moment?"

Brenda grabbed him by the collar and kissed him hard. "Sacrifices, oh king."

"Speaking of sacrifices," the beast said, his doggie nose probing the air. "I think I smell one. I'll be back. When I am, can you two make sure you've got a room to bang in? Jeez, you're grossing me out."

CHAPTER 24
UNDER PRESSURE

"Noah, fire extinguisher! Lenny, Hunt, Blonde Guy, quit trying to kill each other and get some pitchers of water," Wiz said, scrambling over to the bar where Lanette was using the tap to wet a bundle of rags. Smoke was rushing in from under the door. Burning gasoline dripped from the windowsills, creating flaming pools on the floorboards. The wood barricades began to smolder and crackle. Air whooshed out the windows as the fire roared.

"Everyone, grab a rag and get dousing. Go, go, go!"

Noah came back with the fire extinguisher and started dousing the barricade as flames snaked in around the table. He moved around the bar like a hummingbird, depositing great swaths of white goo that quenched the flames with a *thuppt*.

Franz, Amy and Ava all grabbed pitchers of water and ran toward the windows. Thick black smoke was beginning to swirl around the ceiling. Flames were crawled in the far side of the tavern. Franz tossed his pitcher and the flames hissed as a cloud of steam rose. The splash knocked up a spray of flame that caught the leg of his pants.

"Fuck!"

Ava came running, pointing the mouth of her pitcher at the doctor and drenching him. The flames around his ankles sizzled. Franz hung his head, dripping like a victim of a freshman initiation prank.

He spurted water from his mouth. "Thanks."

Ava grinned, brandishing the empty pitcher. "My pleasure."

At the next window, Amy reached above the flames and poured her pitcher, sidestepping the flaming splashes, looking at the soggy doctor with a chuckle. "Doofus."

Patrons gathered around the smoldering barricades, using the wet rags to blot out the fire while the rest huddled in the middle of the tavern. Lenny, Miles, Hunt and the blonde guy were all working to control a blaze by the bar. Noah made his way around the remaining windows, working the fire extinguisher until it sputtered empty.

In a few minutes, the fires were out. Outside, the roaring had stopped.

"We need to get out of here before they do that again," Noah said, wiping his brow.

Wiz nodded. "Noah's right. We split into five groups. Noah, Ava, Lanette, the old guys and I have guns, so we'll lead. We go out the back, one group at a time. Who's parked nearby?"

None of the patrons raised their hands. Wiz shrugged. "Okay, we'll go on foot. If those dead fucks come after us, the leader will mow them down and the rest of you run as fast as you can. Call for help as soon as you're far enough away."

Franz looked impressed. "You thought of all that stoned? Not bad."

"Are you crazy?" said the blonde guy. "The zombies are out there. The fire's under control. Why the hell would you want to risk going out in the open?"

"Those barricades were all burning. They might not be ash, but they're way weaker than when we started. We're sitting ducks in here."

"Well, I'd rather be a sitting duck than a dead duck!"

"More like a dead fuck," Noah said.

Blondie addressed the patrons in the middle of the bar. "Do you really want to listen to these people? Two of them have been bitten, one of them has been stabbed, this doctor is clearly a functioning alcoholic, the bartender's a nutjob and the leader is a fucking pothead."

The patrons all began to fan out as he walked to the center of the bar. "These people aren't leaders, they're idiots!"

"Oh right, says the guy whose only contribution was attempted decapitation because of a couple of fucking bite marks!" Wiz said. "And might I add, who the fuck *are* you?"

"Steve," he said.

"Well, Steve, do us all a favor and pull your head out of your ass. We can't stay locked up all night and —"

"Wiz," Ava said.

"—We're certainly not about to take your lead, Steve. No offense, but you're kind of a fuckwad."

"Wiz," Noah said.

"Noah—"

"*Wiz*," Ava repeated.

"What?!"

Ava raised an eyebrow, putting a finger to her lips to shush him. "Listen."

Outside, a tinny whirring sound was coming toward them.

"What is that?" said Steve.

It grew closer. Yes, that was definitely an engine revving.

Steve wagged his head. "Hello? People? I said, what is—"

At that exact second, the door exploded inward as a riding lawnmower piloted by two of the undead crashed into the bar. The pool table shot backward, plowing into Steve, sending him sailing across the bar.

"New plan!" Wiz said.

Three groups of the undead came out of the tavern dragging screaming patrons for a little mid-siege snack. Using their branches and pilfered garden implements, they started killing.

"No, no, noooooooooo!" a man screeched before the first group used a trowel to crack his skull like a coconut.

"Please," a woman's sobs. "Please don't. You don't have to do this, I have a fami—" the second group cut her off, slitting her throat with a saw.

"Wendy!" a man cried from the third group as he watched his wife sputter. He struggled, screaming his throat raw until Bernie, the ex-radio guy brought a great hunk of wood over his head and brained him to death, making two children sound asleep at the Rooms-R-Us orphans.

Sickening sucking sounds came as the undead feasted.

"What about ice cream," Earl said. "You sure you don't want to get ice cream instead?"

Carly chuckled, wiping a thick streamer of gore from her chin. "Yeah, maybe later, gramps."

Earl sighed, rising from the body of the woman. Guilty satisfaction warmed his belly like the last time he'd eaten a plate of bacon. "But this is all so horrible."

The zombie-ette raised a pointed brow, observing the slimy thread linking Earl to the woman's ragged skull. "I thought we've been through this?"

Earl wiped, shaking his head. "I know but—"

"You ate the brains, didn't you?"

"Yeah, but—"

She gave him a patient nod and said, "It's a little late for ice cream, Earl. It's time to get with the program. Eating brains is what we do."

"But..." try as he might, Earl couldn't escape the hunger as it clamped down on his insides again. He bowed his head, defeated, and belched.

"Come on," Carly said, affecting a pep-talk tone. "You know you want a little more. Come on, Earl... Brains?"

"Braaaiiins!!!" the undead chanted as they pooled around the tavern.

"Oh, fine," Earl said, getting up and joining Carly in the horde.

"This is frighteningly similar to our first plan," Ava said as another crunch of the undead poured through the entrance and grabbed more of the shrieking patrons. She pumped the shotgun and clipped two of the zombies as they scuttled toward the ragged hole where the door had been.

"We need to get that closed up," Wiz said, heading for the pool table. "Noah, Franz, give me a hand." Then to Ava, "When did you become such a good shot?"

Another throng of zombies came at the opening and Ava mowed them down with three shots. "My dad was a cop. Took me to the gun range until I was sixteen."

"Why'd he stop?" Wiz grunted, putting his shoulder into the table.

"He got worried I might shoot him."

Lenny, Miles, and Hunt were all using barstools to fend off the horde while Wiz, Noah and Franz worked to shove the pool table back the opening. After being bitten, Miles had given the derringer back to Lenny, who was currently reloading the tiny pistol. He didn't know the last bullet would be for a friend.

"Admit it, you were just doing it to impress her."

"No, I was doing it to save her."

"And get in her pants, right?"

"I'm an old man, Hunt. I wouldn't know what do if I even got in her pants."

"So you *were* trying."

"Oh, shut up, Lenny."

Just then, a set of heavy footfalls lumbered toward them. The undead began to fan out as an enormous woman, rotted like a month-old peach came waddling into the bar—wearing a remarkably pleasant expression for a member of the undead.

"Why, hello dearies!" she beamed. "Which of you munchkins would like to give me a snack?"

Back at the pool table, Noah's head bobbed up. "Oh for fuck's sake."

Wiz's head bobbed up beside. "Noah, is that…"

"It's my aunt Susan."

Noah's putrefied aunt took another heaving step. Bloody drool dribbled down her many chins. More zombies began wading in behind her. Amy grabbed a hunk of a splintered barstool and held it like a baseball bat.

"Er... Guys?" she said.

The old guys continued shoving the dead back through the entrance. Wiz took the Glock and handed it to Noah.

"I figure you'd rather be the one to... you know."

Noah took the gun as if it were a used diaper. His shoulders slumped. The responsibility was visibly crushing him.

"Guys," Ava said. A growing chorus of undead moans came from the horde. "Running out of time here..."

Wiz squeezed his friend's shoulder. "Brother, you gotta do it."

Noah wrapped his finger around the trigger and pointed the pistol at his aunt's head. He tried to steady himself, but the snout of the gun wavered.

"Christ, I can't," he said, his voice thick. "I can't do it. I just —I mean, it's..."

"Don't you want to give your auntie a kiss?!" zombie Susan howled as she lunged at the pool table.

All Wiz could hear was his own heart bleating in his eardrums. It happened in slow motion: his hand found the pistol and pulled it out of Noah's grasp. He spun toward Susan as she chugged like a jiggly locomotive toward them. Wiz aimed and squeezed the trigger. A red dot the size of a liberty coin appeared in Susan's forehead and she crumpled forward mid-stride, slamming into the floor, sending a small shockwave through the tavern.

The color drained from Noah's face as he slid down the back of the pool table and hugged his knees into his chest. Wiz felt like a bag of warm dog shit. He knew he'd done what had to be done—but he'd still shot his best friend's aunt in the face. Guilt perched on his shoulders like anvils. He wanted to sit down with his friend—to take a moment just to think...

That's when another wave of the dead came storming into the tavern, chanting for brains.

"Braaiins!! Braaaiiins!!!" Carly screeched as she came through the opening.

Somewhere between the brains and here, Earl had relinquished any of the nagging remnants of humanity holding him back. He was hungry for brains, he was evil, and he'd gotten with the fucking program. He shoved through the horde into the bar screaming "Braaaaaiiiiins!!!"

Then, Ava Elridge swung her shotgun on Carly and blew a chunk of the zombie-ette's skull off. Carly lurched backward, letting off a long gurgle as she slumped to the floor.

"Carly!"

"Earl?" a familiar voice beside him. It was Lenny Taltree and his ex-poker buddies. Lenny was pointing a tiny pistol at him. Miles and Hunt both had bloody barstools on their arms for zombie bashing.

"Lenny? Miles? Hunt?"

"Oh jeez," Miles said. "Earl, you're all zombified!"

Lenny kept the gun trained on him. "Well of course he is. He died two days ago—so, you wanna eat our brains, huh Earl?"

"Brains! Braaiins! Braaaaiiins!!!" chanted the undead.

"Well, I mean… That was the plan? I didn't know you guys would be here."

"We're always here," Hunt said, brandishing his barstool.

"Well, I'm sorry, okay? I'll stop. I can stop. Watch me stop."

The old guys did not look convinced. Hunt's chest was puffing up. Miles's arms were shaking. Lenny flicked the hammer on the derringer. "Sorry if we're not buying it, old buddy."

Earl wagged his head. Honestly, you play poker with these guys for fifteen years, then you wind up just a little undead and this was what you got? People.

"Guys," he chuckled. "Guys… It's me. You know, your old poker buddy?"

"Who wants to eat us," Miles said.

"No," Earl kept shaking his head. "No, I don't want to do that. Hey — "

"You *cheated* at cards," Lenny said.

"And you *have* eaten brains," Miles added.

"Honestly, I didn't like you to begin with," Hunt said.

"Well, whatever, Hunt. Just wait until you get what I left you in the will. Listen, guys. I promise, I'm not going to eat you — I was actually against the whole brain-eating thing to begin with. I'll even — "

Then Lenny pulled the trigger. With a surprised expression frozen on his face, the bullet tore through Earl Potvin's skull and he flopped to the floor.

"You always were a shitty bluff," Lenny said.

"Get those bodies out of the way!" Wiz called from behind the pool table as it slid toward the entrance.

The pool table came about three feet short when the next wave hit. Wiz pushed so hard he thought he'd pass out. His sneakers screeched against the floor. Noah, Franz, Amy, and the old guys all shoved until they reached the wall. The undead roared on the other side.

"Someone find the hammer and nails!" Wiz shouted. "Grab the chairs, free tables — whatever we've got to barricade it."

Amy came over and started securing the pool table to the floor. Furious pounding came from the other side as the zombies screamed.

"We can't just keep trying to hold them back," Noah said.

"We need to attack," Ava said.

"How?" Franz said. "We don't have a vantage point. They're all huddled by the door, we don't have any elevation. We can't even pick them off through the windows."

"Franz, we have to do something."

Ava was right. Wiz turned to Lanette. "How are we for ammo?"

The barkeep sighed. "Running dry."

"How much, Lanette?"

"We could take about half of them."

"We need to fight fire with fire," Noah said. "Can you mix up a couple of Molotov cocktails?"

"That's an idea," Wiz said. "But I have a feeling flaming zombies are worse than regular ones…"

"Well we can't just sit here!" Franz said.

All eyes were on Wiz for the answer. The patrons, his friends, everyone was looking to him, but his head was empty. The pressure to come up with a solution was too much. He couldn't think under the weight of it all… Wait a minute: pressure. That was the answer.

"Lanette," he said. "Your kegs run on CO2, right?"

The barkeep nodded. "Each with a dedicated tank. Why?"

"They wouldn't happen to run on timers, would they?"

Yes, this was definitely an idea.

"This is a helluva waste of beer," Lanette grumbled, dousing a bundle of rags with sambuca as Wiz and Noah rolled her fourth keg from the back room.

"I know, but we're out of options," Wiz said, heaving the keg upright. He stretched, catching his breath. "If anyone wants to get stoned, though… I still have some."

Five minutes later, the keg-bombs were ready. Each had a rag tied around its CO2 valve, lined up by the front of the bar. Ava and the old guys worked to free the barricade from the window.

"Okay," Wiz said. "So we open up the window, we open the tanks, light the rags and roll them out. Then, we take cover."

"The blast won't get them all," Ava added. "So find a weapon. When they blow, be ready."

Everyone shuffled around the bar looking for a blunt object. The people with guns grouped around the window, ready to take out any zombies who tried to use the opening. Amy found the blonde guy Steve's gun and got in position next to the window.

"Think we're all ready, chief," Lenny said.

"Okay, count of three," Wiz said, taking a disposable lighter and moving over to the kegs.

"One," he flicked the lighter.

"Two," The old guys and Ava slid the table away from the window. Everyone tensed up in a half-crouch, waiting.

"Three," Wiz twisted the valve on the first keg. The compressor hissed, pumping the tin drum full of gas. He touched rag with the flame, and it ignited. He repeated the process as the timers began ticking away the seconds.

Ava came over and helped him roll the kegs out of the bar, then the old guys jammed the table back in the window.

"Everybody, back of the bar!"

They scrambled for the hall by the jukebox as the kegs rattled into the street. The chanting moans of the zombies stopped right before the first keg exploded.

The floor shuddered with the blast. Wiz and Noah dove behind the short end of the bar as a hail of shrapnel sang through the tavern, pelting the supports on the windows.

The group huddled in the corridor, all holding their hands to their ears as the second keg blew and the tavern shook again with a spray of splintered wood, shards of metal, and a mist of beer.

A beat, and the third keg exploded — snapping the pool table in half. More chunks of metal sang viciously through the air. A long scrap of aluminum shot through the bar just inches above Noah's head. He turned to Wiz, eyes bulging.

"I think your keg-bomb invention works," he gulped.

Everyone tensed up, preparing for the final explosion. They waited.

Nothing happened.

"What happened to the fourth one?" Franz said.

"Fuse must've shot," Noah said. "Okay, people with guns, that's our cue."

No one moved.

Wiz looked at the group, a grin spreading across his face. "This, fellow patrons, is an excellent example of craftsmanship."

"Craftsmanship?" Franz said. "You friggin' idiot! The last one didn't even blow. How is that an example of—"

The fourth keg exploded.

"You were saying?" Noah grinned.

"What, our survival on the line—explosives, timers... And you thought I set them?" Wiz said. "Are you stoned, Franz? Ava set the timers."

Ava nodded. "And I set one to blow about a minute later than the others. I figured that would give the zombies time to come over to see what happened, and then..."

"*Boom*," Wiz said.

Slowly, the patrons recovered and collected their weapons. Everyone inched warily over to the entrance where the pool table had been blown in two. Chunks of tattered metal littered the walls, as if a million drunken knife-throwers had just finished practicing their throws at the bar. A thick cloud of beer mist hung like fog outside.

It was surprisingly quiet. No moans came from the street.

They grouped around the entrance, weapons raised, waiting.

"Guys," Amy said, peering out as the cloud settled.

Wiz and Ava came in behind, pointing their guns into the street. Ava was the first to let hers fall to her side. "Holy shit."

"Okay," Wiz said. "So... that worked?"

The street outside was a war-zone. The explosions had totally leveled the horde. They lay in a ragged, bloody, beer-soaked heap. Severed limbs and hunks of flesh peppered the street. It was quiet. Then, a great hunk of zombie leg fell from the nearest lamppost and commenced squirming pathetically on the sidewalk.

"Well, you don't see that everyday," Lenny said.

Above them, the zombie queen was hopping on one leg as she yanked a fourteen-inch piece of shrapnel from her thigh. She watched as the patrons edged out of the bar, inspecting the wreckage of Brenda's army. Keg bombs? She'd expected some resistance when the undead attacked—but fucking *keg bombs*? Things were not looking up for the apocalypse right now.

The survivors all looked at one another and cheered.

"Fuck!" Brenda hissed.

The survivors began collecting the worming bits of undead that had landed in the bar and got to work re-barricading the entrance. Terror had backfired on the zombies. Despite herself, Brenda began to worry. Asher was still out there, oblivious to the destruction. She needed to warn him, lest he be killed... again.

"Come on," she grumbled. "Why can't zombies be telepathic or something?"

Certain writer-types have often wondered the same thing.

CHAPTER 25
SACRIFICE

Shuffle. Thunk. Splat.

Seth was pleased when he discovered the undead Boris Volydeskvi missing part of his head. This was going to be easy. The Russian was by the side of the Wizard's log cabin, repeatedly walking into the side of it. Every time, he staggered back a few steps, recovered, then tried again. His head smacked the wall, leaving a gob of gore in its wake. It didn't look like he planned on stopping.

Shuffle. Thunk. Stumble.

Vloydeskvi let off a frustrated groan and tried again.

Shuffle. Thunk. Splat.

"Fucking walls," the Russian grumbled.

"Hey, hey, hey," the beast trotted over to Boris and head-butted him in the thigh. "Cut it out, slick. You'll hurt yourself."

"Boris doesn't care!"

Shuffle. Thunk. Splat.

"Oh, come on, buddy. What's the matter?"

"I am angry. First shit-eating pigs kill Boris, then he comes back, tries to eat boss—and then boss shoots Boris, too!"

"It might be on account of all this third-person talking," Seth observed.

"Oh," Boris sighed. "I am failure. I am angry. I am failure, and I am hungry." *Shuffle. Thunk. Splat.* "So hungry!"

"Aha, so you haven't had your daily dose of cranium yet? That's your problem."

Boris wheeled around, roaring in anger, then smacked his head against the house again. "I tried! Boss showed up to check on me and I tried to eat him, but he shoots me."

"Well, being undead will do that to you," Seth said. He was beginning to doubt he needed Boris to be missing half his skull to trick him—this dude was a total idiot. It was like talking to a cranky kid who needed brains, pronto.

"Oh, everyone hates Boris. Being zombie blows."

"Hey, don't knock it, amigo! It's better than dead, isn't it?"

"No!"

Seth woofed. "You are such a baby. You're a big, undead baby."

"Boris can't help it!"

"Again with the third-person stuff. You gotta cut that out, slick. People will think you're losing it."

But Boris wasn't hearing it. He reeled up and went for another smack against the side of the building when Seth lost his patience. He shifted into monster form and held the undead Russian back with a clawed arm.

"That's enough, slick."

"Ahhh!!!" Boris shrieked, cowering from the hulking creature.

"Chill, buddy. Chill. I'm trying to be a friend here. Friends don't let friends smack their ruined heads against walls."

"But there is no point!" Boris staggered backward as Seth's glowing eyes locked on his. Here the beast found purchase on the Russian's weakened mind. He let his thoughts snake into what was left of Boris's head.

"Death is the same thing as life, buck-oh. The meaning is what you make of it."

"But—"

"Now, you're angry, right?"

Boris considered. "Yes."

"And you're hungry, right?"

The Russian nodded slowly. Bits of brain spilled out of his ragged skull.

"Well, I'll make you a deal. You like deals don't you?" Years of experience making crossroads bargains hung on the dog's words. Boris tottered back and forth, hypnotized, or—well, you know... brain-dead. He nodded again.

"Swell. I need you to do me a favor. If you help me out, you'll get your revenge... And even better: you'll never be hungry again. How does that sound, amigo?"

A heinous grin spread across the Russian's face.

With the dead re-killed and the barricades repaired, the patrons of the Gnarled Wood Tavern grouped inside. Lanette served bottled beers and bar-rail mixers as all the survivors sat around the bar, quiet, rattled, and more than a little tired after the undead ordeal. The jukebox blared Supertramp.

It wasn't exactly a celebration—more of an outlet. They hadn't made it through the end of the world without losing a few people. Some of the patrons had lost a spouse or friends in battle. Moreover, surviving the undead attack had meant killing family, friends, and more than a few acquaintances who'd returned from the grave.

In short, it was a breather. Because the tables and stools were busy sealing off the windows, the patrons sat in circles, cross-legged on the floor. Some of them talked. Most just sat, nursing their drinks in silent contemplation—they'd survived, and survivors almost always feel guilty.

Lanette had returned to form, wiping down the bar and delivering sass, free-of-charge. In front of her, the gang with the guns sat on the few remaining stools. Wiz had Ava in his arms—and despite overcoming an entire troupe of undead brain-eaters, he still hadn't found the courage to kiss her. Contact of any kind was progress, so he held her.

Beside them, Noah Carpenter distributed a row of tequila shots. Amy was next to him, staring at a spot on the bar, deep in thought.

"Why do we even drink this stuff?" Wiz said. Because of the circumstances, Lanette had permitted him to roll a joint.

"To get drunk!" Noah said, raising his shot glass. "Cheers, everyone."

They slammed back the shots.

Franz MacFee clicked his empty against the bar and sighed. "Well, apocalypse averted. Lanette? How about another round for the heroes?"

The barkeep dropped her rag and collected the glasses. "Four shots then, Doctor Romeo. Coming right up."

"Aw, hey!" Franz pouted. "No fair."

"Come on, Lanette," Ava said. "Franz saved my life, remember? If I'm a hero, then that makes him like a hero's hero."

"Let's not give Franz too much credit," Wiz said, licking the rolling paper and christening the joint. The doctor's ego was already big enough to fill the tavern.

Lanette came back with five shots, all the same.

"Well, either way, cheers," Franz toasted. "To heroes."

"To fallen heroes," Noah said.

Franz tilted his head. "You mean douche bag Steve? Cause he was—well, a douche bag. Plus I'm pretty sure he'll be fine."

Across the bar, a battered douche bag Steve was nursing a beer next to his girlfriend.

"Travis," Noah said, ruefully.

With that, they all dumped their shots back and sat in silence. Amy put her glass on the bar and walked away.

Wiz sparked the joint and took a long drag. It had been hours since his last hit, but relief didn't come. His thoughts fell on his fallen linebacker buddy. Travis, his friend and brother in hoots was gone, just like that. It was exactly as the zombie king had said: one minute you were there, and then you weren't. The universe was a bummer.

He passed the joint around and everybody—including Lanette—smoked until it was roached. Silence filled the air with the smoke. Wiz stared at his shot glass and said, "I think I'm gonna need another one of these."

Noah was staring at a spot on the bar. "Wiz, you know we're not done yet, right?"

Wiz furrowed his brow. "What do you mean?"

"The Russians," Ava said.

Noah nodded. "We lost the pot, but they'll still want you dead."

Wiz looked at his drink and shrugged. "Well, if they come looking for us, I guess I'll just shoot them or something."

Noah bounced his brow. "Really?"

"Yeah," Wiz said. "I mean... Russians, pfft. We just defeated a horde of flesh-eating zombies. We can handle a couple of angry mobsters."

The old guys were sitting in the corner of the bar, all fiddling with the labels on their beer bottles. Lenny took a pull from his beer and shook his head. He was stuck under a heavy dose of guilt coupled with a good amount of disbelief. Killing a friend in battle was something he'd never thought he could do. He knew Earl had been a zombie, and more than definitely wanted to eat their brains, but he couldn't help wondering if he'd made the wrong decision.

Miles and Hunt seemed similarly troubled. Lenny had pulled the trigger, but Earl was a friend to all of them. A day ago they'd been arguing over where to play poker without their buddy. Now, it was fairly certain none of them would ever shuffle a deck of cards again.

Thank goodness for alcohol. After a few moments of staring at his bottle, Lenny raised it.

"To Earl," he said. "Who should never have had to go in such an awful way."

Miles nodded and lifted his bottle. "Yeah."

Hunt did the same, then said: "So what do you think was in the will?"

They continued drinking, and Lenny figured that they would continue for a very long time.

Amy sat in the hall next to the bathroom with her knees hugged to her chest. Her head was swimming with visions of the horror-show that had become her life: her undead nephew's inhuman shrieks; the flap of skin dangling from his head and the evil grin. Her ex-boyfriend's dismembered body, the bedroom painted with blood, the one brilliant blue eye staring as Mario's corpse dragged its way toward her. She worried about what she'd tell her aunt and uncle. Most of all, she thought of Travis. The one guy who seemed like he wasn't a complete idiot, and the undead dogpile—his bone chilling scream.

She hung her head as exhaustion muted the murmur of the bar. She was zonked, but sleep was something that could wait until her thirties. Sleep would mean nightmares. She wanted to run, to scream—anything but sleep. Her shoulders began to rattle as a lone tear ran down her cheek.

Noah appeared in the hallway with a bottle of whiskey. He slumped down beside her, put an arm around her and let her cry into his arms. He began to tell her a story. It's what we do when we're hurting.

"This one time, Wiz and I got his cat stoned."

"That's horrible," her nose was stuffed. It made the whiskey go down easier.

Noah went on. "The thing totally freaked. Travis was there, laughing that goofy way he does, and the fucking cat attacks him."

Amy passed him the bottle. Warmth began spreading from her chest. She sniffled. "Tell me he didn't punch the stoned cat."

"Not even. He was stoned, too, so he totally wigged out. Orphan—that's Wiz's cat—latched onto him, and Trav starts screaming like a girl with slugs in her pigtails. He spins around in this crazed figure eight, and the cat just won't let go. Dude was covered in scratches by the time we got it off of him. Lesson learned. He's been terrified of cats even since."

"He was really smart though, right?"

Noah nodded. "He had a full-service scholarship lined up. He was going to go to Stanford and not have to pay a dime because of his big brain. He was using his cut of the pot money to help get him out there, maybe get an apartment."

Amy shook her head and took another belt of whiskey. Her mouth came open, her mind finding the words. "I could have helped him," she said. "I could have slowed those things down and he might have gotten free—I could have—" Her voice broke. She buried her head in her arms. "It's all my fault."

Noah squeezed her shoulders. "Amy, he was attacked by zombies. It wasn't your fault."

"I was using him," she said.

"No, you weren't."

"Yeah, I was." She took a breath and looked at the ceiling, holding back the waterworks. "I was using him to get back at Mario. We were in that cemetery because I chose to take him there. If he hadn't lain down on that grave—If I hadn't forced him into it…"

"Actually, I'm pretty sure he did that willingly."

"I was on top of him. I had my eyes closed. If I'd been paying more attention… If I hadn't been so selfish—oh, god." She broke off, tears creating streamers of mascara on her cheeks. "I'm a terrible human being."

"No," Noah said. "You're not. Everybody is with everybody because they want something. There's nothing wrong with that. We fill our lives with the people we do because we've got needs. That doesn't make you a bad person. Some things happen because we choose for them to, and some things happen just because. You can't blame yourself for that."

Amy took a breath. "God, life really sucks sometimes."

Noah lit a cigarette. "Yeah," he said, breathing smoke. He handed it to Amy and she dragged. "You're pretty good at killing zombies, though."

Amy chuckled and looked at him. "You're not so bad yourself."

She stared at the wall, smoking, then said, "I'll miss him."

"Yeah," Noah sighed, taking the cigarette. "Me too."

"Survivors!" called one of the guys standing guard by the entrance. He came in carrying a woman in an apron covered with dried gore. A dazed-looking teenager with a huge gash in his forehead stumbled after them.

Franz, Ava and Wiz came over.

"Yeesh," Franz said to the teenager. "Let's have a look at that sucker. I'm a doctor."

"I know," said the teen. "You banged my mom a couple of times."

"Oh, really? How is she? You wanna drink?" Franz took the kid over to the bar and started cleaning the wound.

Lenny and the old guys helped the woman onto one of the remaining barstools. When she said, "I'm fine," Wiz realized it was his sister-in-law.

"Jenny?"

She snapped out of her daze, blinking. "Wiz?"

Wiz didn't know where to go from here. "Uh... Long time, no see? How have you been?"

Miles came back with a glass of water. Jenny drank, then said, "Have you heard anything from Al?"

Wiz shook his head. "We've been trying all night, but it's going straight to voice-mail."

"We need to find him. We need to get the National Guard or something."

"Hey," Franz said back by the wounded teenager. "Whatever happened to the little guy?"

"The Baron," Ava corrected.

"Yeah, Mr. Peanut. Whatever," Franz said. "Was he at the Soup?"

Jenny stared at the floor. "No, there's nobody at the Soup. They... Well, they *ate* everybody."

Wiz nodded, putting a hand on Jenny's shoulder.

"Typical," Franz said.

Wiz gave Franz a tired expression. "We all saw what happened to him. He got sucked out of the bar. The underworld probably took him back or something."

"Hang on," Franz said, moving to his tumbler of scotch on the bar and finishing it. "You mean that little fuck was actually a god?"

CHAPTER 26
MOONRISE

The Baron awoke in a man-shaped crater on the roof of the Oak Falls library. His head was stuck in the concrete, and while he didn't normally experience pain, his whole body throbbed with a stiff, creaky sensation. He needed a drink, immediately—but how far had the dog thrown him? How long had he enjoyed the slumber of gods?

He pulled himself out of the crater. His suit was coated in powdered concrete. Chunks of rubble lay all around. His top hat and cane were at the mouth of the dent in the roof. He stood, cracking his neck back into place and brushing the dust from his clothes. He padded over to his top hat, put it back on his head and looked out over the town.

Well, it was still here. That was a good sign. The stench of death was on the air—but not fresh death... And was that beer? He could just make out the ruined bodies of the beast's legion, scattered around the main drag, looking rather re-dead. He adjusted the hat and grinned at the work of the mortals.

Then, a purring chorus came from behind. The Ghede turned and found three cats closing in on him in a predatory triangle. A gray Siamese, a fat orange tabby, and a token black cat. The stench of death came from them, too.

The leader, the orange tabby, let off a rumbling meow and came forward with its ears pressed flat against its blood-crusted maw. The Baron craned his neck to find the others as they slunk closer, all joining in the growl. The tabby batted its paws against the ground and hissed.

"Ah crap," the Baron said. He reached for his sword.

Before he could pull the blade from the cane, the black cat flung itself at him with a vicious howl. He swung the cane in a wide underhand and caught the feline under the jaw, sending it spinning backward with a deadly snap. The cat flopped to the ground, recovered, and shook the daze from its head. It squinted at the Ghede and hissed.

The Baron grinned, removing the blade from its sheath. The cat leaped again, and he brought the sword in a quick upward motion. The cat split down the middle, entrails raining over the rooftop.

The Siamese snarled furiously. The Baron turned and held the blade at shoulder height, a darkened streak appearing where it had hewn the first cat. The Siamese faked left, then lurched forward, but the Ghede didn't flinch. He was amused a creature so small could think itself so terrifying. It reared up and leaped at him, and he moved the sword in a quick figure-eight. The feline's shoulders shuddered and its head bounced across the roof.

The great orange tabby roared. It glowered furiously at the Ghede. It hissed, swiping at the Baron, its claws catching the hem of his pants. It scuttled backward with a snarl, baring bloody teeth.

The Baron roared, flashing his own pointed teeth at the zombie cat.

"Come, you festering feline fuck!"

The tabby crouched, winding up, and leaped at the Baron. At the very last moment, the Ghede ducked, and the great tabby sailed through the air, right off the edge of the rooftop. Its screech dopplered off the surrounding buildings as it fell. Then there was a sickening *thump*, followed by silence.

The Baron re-sheathed his blade, strolling over to the edge of the roof to observe the mashed cat.

"Four-legged fucks," he mused, straightening his jacket and hat. He spat. Then caught his temper and cleared his throat.

"Now then," he said, examining the state of the town.

He laughed a great booming belly-laugh, and turned to shadow.

If there's anything in life that's an undisputed fact, it's this: Buildings with strange symbols carved in their lintels are bad news. You rarely find symbols leading to unicorns and fields of candy—and even that's bad news if you're diabetic. The old mill-turned-art-gallery at the end of the main drag in Oak Falls was no exception.

In 1903, the year Oak Falls became Oak Falls, a man named Edgar Crowley built the building. An ex-pat Englishman, his past was a mystery filled with rumors of black magic, unholy rituals, an unchecked promiscuous nature, animal maiming, murder, the whole deal. The rumors were all more-or-less true. Crowley was a real wizard. He worshipped the Ancient Ones, and was the founder of the Order of Cerulean—a cult with one motive: to return the earth to the gods of old.

The building itself was unremarkable. What lay beneath was the real reason he'd built it. The area had long been known as a mystical crossroads; a soft-point between the realm of man and the Ancients. Under the mill with the symbols on its lintel was a chamber, and under that chamber was a direct-access chute to the underworld. The order had died out long ago, and Edgar took the secrets of his mill to the grave. It was safe. That is, until now.

Seth lead Boris down a treacherous slope, snaking along the jaws of the waterfalls churning behind the building. At the foot of the falls, in the side of the mill, was a huge iron gate coated in decades of rust.

Boris moved over to the gate and grabbed the latch. He pulled, he yanked, he tugged furiously, but the old hunk of metal wouldn't budge. He sighed and gave the dog a bewildered expression. Seth shifted into monster-form, lumbered up to the gate, grabbed both sides, and tore the gate from its huge hinges like the lid of a can.

"What?" the beast shrugged. "God."

He set the gate against the building and they went inside. The tunnel was all burrowed stone, cavernous and dripping. The Russian found an old torch hanging on the wall, and lit it. Orange light painted the chamber as their footsteps echoed down the tunnel.

At the end of the corridor, they found an old door made of huge lengths of ancient, rotted-looking wood. There was no handle on it. The frame was cut from stone, much like the rest of the building, but this one held a lifelike aspect—it was almost as if the great archway was breathing. Carved at the top were the symbols again: a triangle, a moon, and an upside-down cross.

The Russian shoved at the heavy wood door with no effect. He pushed, he pounded, he body-checked, but the door wouldn't budge. "Fucking doors!"

He rounded up and delivered a kick to the middle. The wood flexed, then sprang back, sending the zombified Vloydeskvi tumbling across the slimy floor.

Seth chuckled, slipping his claws into the cracks where the wood met the stone. He grunted and ripped the heavy slab out of the frame, tossing it to the ground with an impact that shook the chamber. Stale air rushed out of the entrance. Boris held the torch into the shadows, revealing a stone staircase descending into blackness. Then, he turned back to the beast, uncertainty stitched on his brow.

Seth shrugged. "They're stairs. You know what to do."

"Okay," Boris sighed. "But being sacrifice is hungry work."

"Just a few more minutes, chief."

The stairs lead into a great circular chamber with a domed ceiling, easily over twenty feet high. Around the walls, torches sprang to life with dancing blue flames. The floor was shaped like a great stone funnel with a two-foot walkway around the perimeter. It was all unnaturally perfect brickwork. Great stone panels lined the slope toward a giant iron cap at the base. It was like a twelve-foot wide manhole. Heavy iron clasps held it in place. At the apex of the dome above, a nine-foot iron spike pointed downward. A coffin the size of a linen chest was welded to the middle of the great iron manhole.

Seth took the lead, finding a narrow set of stairs leading down the slope toward the platform. When they reached the bottom, the beast motioned for Boris to come forward.

"Okay chief, you're up."

Boris shuffled onto the platform and moved over to the coffin. He looked back at the beast, who nodded and grinned. "Open it."

The Russian heaved the lid off the coffin. Inside was lined with purple silk. In the middle was a large lever made of brass and polished oak.

Seth licked his teeth, red eyes gleaming. "Uhuh. Pull it."

Boris gave an exasperated sigh. He reached in, wrapped his hand around the lever and pulled. There was a great clanging noise that echoed through the chamber. Ancient gears began rattling to life as one-by-one, the latches around the platform sprang open.

Then the Russian looked up at the spike on the ceiling. "Uh-oh."

A clinking sound, then a long hiss. Then, the platform lurched upward—once, twice... Boris spun back to the dog, panic gripping his features. His mouth hung open as if to say *you tricked me!*

Then, the platform exploded upward with a great blast of air. The spike on the ceiling shot through the center of the great iron disc, skewering Boris as he was sandwiched between the plate and the ceiling.

Blood dripped from the end of the spike into the open shaft below. A narrow staircase corkscrewed into the darkness.

"Not bad!" Seth grinned. He padded over to the chasm and

looked in. The drips of blood seemed to echo for eternity. Then a soft rustling came from the depths.

Wings.

Seth's eyes lit up as the flapping grew closer, and a winged goblin-like creature burst out of the blackness. He was tar-black, oily, and wore a hideous mask stitched from some kind of skin. A great curved sword hung from his loincloth. He took a deep, satisfied breath.

"Smells different," he said.

"A lot's different," Seth said. "Welcome to the party, ugly!"

More creatures came from below. The ghoul licked his pointed teeth. "Thanks buddy. So, you've summoned us. What do you want?"

"Freedom," Seth said. "How long have we been trapped below? You're not too old to remember, I hope. This world used to be ours, amigo. It's time to take it back."

"Freedom, huh?" the old one said. "That's a very old word you're throwing around."

"Exactly! Out with the new, in with the old! This world has belonged to the humans long enough. I want chaos, destruction, and an enormous amount of bloodshed. You game?"

The goblin considered, playing with a stitch on his horrid mask. "Deal. I was gonna anyway. It's been ages since I had a manburger. Boys?" he called into the pit. "The word's apocalypse!"

Three more goblins soared out of the chamber. More wingless creatures began climbing the stairs from the underworld.

"Ouch, watch it! That's my sword."

"Sorry, just wanna get to the action."

"How often do we get to end the world? Oh, this'll be fun."

"S'cuse me. Giant spear coming through... Actually, giant in general."

There were hundreds of them, lumbering up to the world of the living.

The lead goblin turned back to Seth. "So then, where are we headed?"

Seth woofed with delight. "The village tavern."

"Swell," said the goblin. "I can't remember the last time I had a drink."

It had been years since Lenny Taltree had been this drunk. Douche bag Steve—recovered from his collision with the pool table—was being dragged around the bar by his girlfriend, an attractive woman in her late twenties, who everyone had been thinking of as Mrs. Douchebag. This, of course, was exactly why he was getting dragged around the bar. Her name was Tanya, and she was making Steve apologize to all the people he'd tried to shoot earlier.

Steve stuffed his hands in his pockets. His cheeks were bright pink.

"I wasn't myself," he said. "I can't begin to say how sorry I am."

"We could shoot you?" Lenny said. "That would show us how sorry you are."

Hunt slugged his beer and nodded in agreement.

"Not *that* sorry."

"Steve!" Tanya hissed.

"It's okay, Steve," Miles said, ever the pacifist. "I understand. You thought you were doing what's right."

"We could shoot you in the leg," Lenny continued. "Something superficial…"

Miles waved him off. "Lenny! Cut it out. Nobody's shooting anybody."

"What? It's only fair…"

"No, it's not. An eye for an eye makes everybody stupid."

"I think you mean *blind*, Miles."

"Well, I've been drinking, okay?" Then to the blonde guy, "Steve, I forgive you."

Steve sighed as if he'd just been informed his HIV test had come back negative. "Thanks."

With that, Steve and his girlfriend moved onto the next group of people he'd tried to kill.

"What a putz," Lenny said.

"Oh, he's just an idiot. You can't have a world without them."

"He tried to kill you," Hunt said, his face flushed.

Miles shook his head vehemently. "He was trying to do the right thing. He thought he knew what was happening and tried to act. Isn't that what makes people heroes? They *act*? Sure, you don't see it in the movies, but even heroes make mistakes. All he was doing was trying to be the good guy."

"I thought we were the good guys."

"We are!" Miles slurred. There were three empty beer bottles in front of him. Miles was usually the designated-driver of the group. "We had to shoot our friend in the face."

"*I* did that," Lenny said. Guilt squeezed him by the solar plexus.

"Did you see us trying to stop you? We were part of it. You think heroism is just having a strong jaw and a good attitude? Well, bullshit! Being a hero means making the tough call when you need to. We might be old, we might be messed up about it, but that's just the side of heroism nobody talks about."

Lenny sulked, staring into his bottle. "This is profound."

Miles nodded, standing. "We tried, guys. When the world threatened to end, we did something. We have to live with it, but—"

Before he could finish, Miles toppled over—not because he was drunk, but because something hit him. Lenny grabbed the derringer as Miles shrieked in pain. A body was on him, a boy of about nine, screeching and spewing chunks of flesh.

Blood spurted. A sickening cry filled the bar as the kid ripped into Miles's neck.

"STOP!!!"

The boy turned, flesh dangling from his maw. Thick gobs of blood pattered the floor. Lenny screamed, pulling the trigger. The kid somersaulted backward, landing in a gruesome pile.

"Oh my god," Amy shuddered by the jukebox. "Todd!"

"Arrrrrrrggghhh!" Todd squelched, blood streamed from the hole in his forehead. Lenny stood, pulling the trigger until the derringer clicked empty and Todd's body lay motionless on the floor.

Miles gurgled. His legs began convulsing.

"Miles!' Lenny said, slumping to his knees, cradling his friend in his lap.

"I wasn't expecting that," Miles gasped. Blood spurted from the ragged wound.

"No," Lenny wagged his head. "Miles, don't you die on me — you've got to fight…"

Blood trickled through his fingers. "Fight? But Lenny… I'm a pacifist…" — a vicious cough — "You know…"

And just like that, Miles was gone. Lenny fought back tears. "Help? Somebody help over here!"

Franz MacFee trundled over. He put a hand on Miles's neck, then slumped his shoulders. "He's gone."

Lenny began weeping, grabbing the gun and staggering over to the bar. "Lanette, I need more bullets… I — "

"Lenny," Wiz said, grabbing his shoulder. "I'm sorry — "

Before he could finish, the barricade at the front of the bar shuddered twice and exploded inward.

Everybody staggered back as a seven-foot tall goblin stalked into the bar.

"Hey, folks," it said. A grotesque mask sewn from skin covered its face. It removed it, revealing leathery, snakelike features. "Sorry. I know this is probably an emotional moment for you."

The ghoul produced an axe from its loincloth. "It's just, we have some things to cover. I'm Vince, and I'll be the one who flays your skin. Now, who wants to go first?"

"Arrraaaggggggghhhhh!!!!" Steve cried, rushing forward with his gun as he spattered the goblin Vince with bullets.

Vince cocked his head. "Hi. Good introduction. Like I said, I'm Vince. What's your name?"

The goblin extended a hand.

Steve froze in place, pistol wavering in front of the monster. "Uh…."

"Right," the creature grabbed Steve by the arm and swung his axe. Steve's head slipped sideways, his face frozen in a shocked expression as it fell into the old one's arms.

Twin spouts of blood spurted from his neck. Tanya shrieked as her boyfriend slumped to the floor.

The goblin grinned, teeth gleaming. "I guess this is yours."

He tossed the severed head and Tanya caught it like a football. She broke into a horrified howl. Before she could finish, the goblin leaped forward and tore into her neck.

"For fuck's sake!!!" Noah howled, lunging at the ancient god with his .38.

The goblin turned, grinning, and swung his blade at Noah.

Wiz lumbered forward. "No!!!'

But there was nothing he could do.

PART III
THE MONSTER MASH

CHAPTER 27
"YOU BROKE MY BAR!"

The goblin Vince swung at Noah as the Baron came bounding into the tavern, riding a shadow like a skateboard, his sword swiping viciously. The axe rattled to the floor. The old one's head sailed through the air. The body staggered, exploring the tarry stump of its neck, then toppled over.

"That was totally uncalled for!" the goblin's head said from the floor.

A long, protracted scream rang through all the patrons as they scuttled away from the animated head, which raised a pointed brow at the man in the top hat.

"Go tongue an unwashed taint, old one."

"Gee-whiz," Vince said. "You're a real grump, you know?"

"You're not supposed to be here, you unsightly fuckwad."

"Oh, language!" Vince sighed. "Don't be such a party pooper."

The Baron strode over, wiping black blood from the blade. "Your kind was driven out of this realm long ago. Your time is over, *fuckwad*. The creator —"

"Blah, blah, blah. Didn't you get the memo? We're getting the band back together."

"Not on my watch."

Vince's severed head chuckled. "Pish-posh. You think a sword will stop us? A sword and a bunch of talking meat?"

"Hey!" Wiz called from the crowd.

"I don't remember saying you could speak, *meat*," the creature snarled. To the Baron, "You're one of us. Join the soirée. We'll get you a fresh manburger."

The Baron grinned, planting a foot of the ghoul's face. "There's an order, old one. The Ghede are sworn to protect mortals."

The goblin sighed. "You are a real pain in the neck, you know that? Fine."

Then, the creature's body dragged itself off the floor, grabbing the axe.

Vince grinned. "Let's boogie."

The Baron and the headless goblin broke into a vicious clash of metal. Air sizzled with the slash of their blades as they connected with a spark. They moved so fast it was impossible to get a handle on who was doing better.

Wiz blinked, trying to follow the action. "...Manburger?"

Ava squeezed his hand.

"Pretty self-explanatory," Noah said. The yogi shook his head. "That would have been me."

More clanging.

"Pretty stupid of you," Amy observed.

"I didn't know what I was doing."

Another squeeze from Ava. "What do we do?"

Wiz turned back to the dueling gods, feeling completely helpless. "What *can* we do?"

"You know what I mean..." She looked him in the eye, and he immediately understood what she was thinking. He couldn't believe she was thinking it, but he knew.

"No. Ava—"

"We can't just let this happen, Wiz." Sadness in her voice. She shook her head. "We tried. We did pretty good, but none of it matters if we don't do what we both know we have to do."

Wiz wanted to argue. He wanted to have another plan. More than anything, he just didn't want to die. Not without telling her how he felt; without going on a real date; not without kissing her. If he only had a little more time… He sighed.

"You're right."

They turned just in time to see the Baron fling the body of the goblin Vince out of the tavern. He stooped, collecting the ghoul's head and punted it out the entrance like a football.

"Poiiintlessss…" it said, sailing through the air.

The Baron took the two halves of the pool table and slid them back over the entrance. He sheathed his blade and marched over to Wiz and Ava.

"Now you see," he said. "Now you understand. You have to understand, you fucking fools. There is no other way."

"We know," Ava said.

"That creature was only the first. If we don't move quickly, there'll be a swarm of them eating your friends in minutes."

"We get it," Wiz said. "We'll go."

"Not so fast," Noah said. "We've been through hell. Where were you, pint-sized? After all that, I'm not letting you take my friends away."

The Baron spat. "You cock garbling imbecile. This is the fate of the world we're talking about! This isn't a democracy."

"I don't get it," Franz said from the bar. "If you're a god, why can't you just change the rules?"

"It doesn't work that way."

"Why not?" Amy said.

"Because it doesn't."

"Gee, what's the point in being a god if you're so useless?" the Doctor grinned.

"I just saved your life, you sheep-shagging nitwit," shouted the Baron. "You want to put it to a vote? Fine! People of Oak Falls," he cried. "You've seen what the underworld has in store. Your friends are the key to stopping it, and if you don't give them to sacrifice, you will all surely die. Now, show of hands. Who wants to live?"

Everyone raised their hand except the heroes.

"And who wants to die?"

All the hands went down.

Wiz and Ava hung their heads. The Baron shot the doctor an indignant grin. "I believe that's what you'd call a consensus."

"If we go with you," Ava said. "We're not doing it for free."

"Yeah," Wiz added. "If we do this sacrifice thing, you've got to promise these people will be safe."

Ava nodded. "If you can't use your magic to save us, then you have to keep those uglies out."

The Baron clapped his hands. "It is done."

Everyone looked around. Nothing had changed. Wiz rubbed the back of his head. "Yeah, uh… We kinda need more than —"

Just then, a rumble tore through the tavern. Two of the great rafters running the ceiling splintered and collapsed, pinning the pool table's halves against the door. The windows all heaved, bricks crumpling into their frames. When the rumbling settled, all the weak points were sealed off.

"Okay," Wiz said. "Lead the way."

"AW HELL NO," Lanette Wilson screeched, tossing her sawed-off on the bar. "You mothafuckah… You broke my bar!"

Hand-in-hand, Wiz and Ava walked to the back door of the tavern. As he flipped the latch, Wiz felt another hand tug his arm. It was Noah Carpenter.

"Wiz…" Tears were welling in his eyes

"Here," Wiz rooted through his pockets, found the keys to the ChevyVan, and put them in Noah's hand. "You might need her."

"Dude, you don't need to do this."

Wiz sighed. "Actually, I really think I kinda do."

Noah shook his head. "We can just stay in here and get drunk. We could all go together…"

Wiz smiled, grabbing his roommate in a bear hug. "I'm sorry, dude."

"Yeah," the yogi sniffled. "Me too."

Goodbyes are never easy.

Agent Max Reyes stooped next to the sheriff at the edge of the smoldering hole that had once been the Texaco. They'd tried radioing the county fire department, but a stray bullet from the shootout had turned the CB into a crackling hunk of swiss cheese. They could only sit in the cruiser and watch as the station's wells of gasoline burned out.

"We're lucky he only had two pumps," the Sheriff said. "Otherwise we might be missing the whole block."

The heat was tremendous. Reyes surveyed the singed buildings around the blast zone. "What do you think happened?"

"It's obvious, isn't it? It blew the fuck up."

Max rolled his eyes. "Al, be serious."

The sheriff wiped beads of sweat from his brow. "Well, we'll have to get the fire investigator to look into it. But Lester's kind of an idiot. Wouldn't surprise me if—"

"Urrruuhrrrrughhhh!" came a raspy-sounding voice from the wreckage.

Al furrowed his brow. "What the hell?"

Something was moving down there. Before either of the two men could speak, three crispy-fried corpses came out of the rubble.

"We need to get to a radio," Reyes said. "How fast can we get some EMTs out here?"

"Let's get back to the office and find out."

They climbed in the cruiser and Al stepped on the accelerator. They sped up the main drag until they reached the carnage in front of the Gnarled Wood Tavern.

"What the hell?" Reyes said.

Bodies were strewn everywhere. The stench of beer and rotted flesh filled the air. Blood, guts and limbs painted the pavement. The whole front of the Wood was singed and it looked like the windows had caved in. The two lawmen climbed out of the cruiser, their jaws hanging open.

"Get back in the car!" a voice came from behind. They turned as a beefy guy in a football jacket came bounding up the street. "Get back in the fucking car!"

Al strode over as Hal Pearson trotted to a winded halt. He grabbed him by the shoulders. "Slow down. What happened? What's going on?"

"It's the fucking apocalypse," Hal gasped.

Reyes walked over to a writhing forearm clawing its way across the street. "Uh, Sheriff?"

"Just a second," Al shook the linebacker. "You need to tell me what happened, Hal."

The linebacker took another exasperated gulp of air when all of the undead started moving, picking themselves—and parts of themselves—back up.

"Now can we get back in the car?" Hal said.

Al spun as the corpses got to their feet and started lumbering toward them.

"Aarrr-guuh-ooouh!!"

"Barrhhuugggh!"

"Guuuuurrrgghh!!!"

"What the hell?!" he said.

Noah sat with his back to the door, playing with the keys to Wiz's ChevyVan, moping. Sure, the end of the world was a pretty ill-advised time to mope, but when the blues have got you down, you can't really help yourself. He'd just locked the door on his friend—his best friend—and he was feeling hopeless, shitty, and alone. He wanted to go back to the bar and get hammered.

Hands started furiously pounding against the door.

"Let us in!" a muffled voice said.

"Hurry!" said another.

"What the hell?" Noah stood and flipped the latch for the door. Before he could even grab the handle, it burst open and Hal Pearson, the sheriff, and a guy with a stupid looking goatee spilled into the entrance.

"Where's the Wizard?" said Reyes.

"Uh…"

"Where's Travis?" Hal said.

Noah rubbed the back of his neck. "Maybe you guys should come in."

That was when shrieks bounded in from the front of the tavern, and the recovered undead resumed pounding on the windows.

"Seriously?" Amy said. "Again?"

"I thought we dealt with this already," Franz said.

"We did," Noah said, walking over to the bar, grabbing Ava's shotgun and pumping a new shell into the chamber. "Apparently the beer wore off."

The sheriff and Reyes both reached for their holsters as the pounding continued.

"Al?" A voice from the crowd.

"Jenny!" The sheriff ran over to his wife and took her in his arms. "What's going on?"

"I told you," Hal Pearson said. "It's the end of the world." Then to Noah, "Where's Travis?

"Uh…" Noah said.

"He didn't make it," Amy said.

Hope withered from the linebacker's expression. "But he was supposed to be the sidekick."

"Which is exactly why we're going to kill those fuckers," Noah said, handing the linebacker the derringer. "I mean… Again… Or again-again."

"Don't be an idiot," Reyes said. "There's no way to fend them off from here. If you open those windows to shoot, we're all dead."

"Oh," Noah said. "So Mister I Have a Stupid Goatee decides to go all tactical when we're having an emotional moment."

Max shrugged. "I'm just saying. There's no advantage."

More pounding at the bricked-off windows.

"We can't just sit here," Hal said.

"Damn right," Lanette said.

"We're dead anyways," said Franz MacFee. "In case any of you missed the Cliff's notes, *Friday Night Lights* here has a point. It's the end of the world."

"Well, if you ask me," Amy said, grabbing the Glock from the bar. "If we go out, I say we do it with a bang."

"You're right." Noah's hand closed around Wiz's keys to the ChevyVan. "I need volunteers," he said. "We need to go to the hardware store. Agent Fuckwad is right, we have no advantage here, but if we can do what I think we can do, then we can mow these fuckers down."

A moment of silent contemplation.

"I'm in," Franz said.

"Me too," added Amy.

"Let's kick some undead ass," Hal said.

"I'll go," said Jenny.

"Jenny," Al grabbed her by the waist. "No. I can't let you. If something happened to you," he paused. It was too nasty to think about. "I'll go."

"No," Jenny said. "Somebody needs to stay behind to keep everybody safe. That's kind of your job, Sheriff."

Al wagged his head. "But—"

"But nothing. Someone has to stay, Al. And somebody has to go. You can't survive the end of the world if you worry about dying."

She took the sheriff in her arms. She kissed him.

"I love you," she said.

He kissed her again. The look on his face said he couldn't kiss her enough.

"I love you."

A moment later, she turned and met Amy, Franz, Hal and Noah. "So what's the plan?"

Everything was going according to plan. The asscrack of dawn was rising from the day's waistband while Ash and his gang of the undead hid behind curtains in the town hall. The Oak Falls town council grouped in the wide, darkened space with a carafe of coffee percolating on a buffet table next to steamer trays filled with complimentary breakfast, as advertised.

Mayor Larry Peters took the podium, striking his gavel like a grumpy carpenter. "Settle folks. Settle. Good morning."

"Good morning," the council answered.

"I hereby declare this meeting to order. Now, I know you've all seen the lovely table of snacks we have waiting for us. I've been told we're even getting crepes this time, so let's get down to brass-tacks."

The council chuckled.

Mayor Peters grinned. He shuffled through a stack of pages outlining the meeting's itinerary. "The first order of business is in regard to the rather hideous arrangement of plastic flamingos on Barbra Weissman's lawn."

A collective groan from the audience.

"They're hideous!"

"Such an eyesore."

"So 80s."

"The woman's got more tack-value than 3M."

"Nice one, Garreth."

The mayor slammed his gavel. "Order! Now, I suggest we make a formal request for her to remove the ugly plastic birds. Motion granted?"

More murmurs.

"Great. Now, the second order of business is—"

"Your untimely demise, I'm afraid," Ash said, coming from the shadows.

The council all wheeled around in their seats.

"Now—permission to kill the caterer?"

The mayor scrunched his brow. He was pretty sure that wasn't on the agenda.

"Permission granted," Ash said. He pointed his pistol at the guy tending the steaming trays on the buffet table and blew his head off. The mayor backed away from the podium, shocked. Then, Ash lined up the pistol and put a bullet through Larry Peters's head. The mayor slumped over the podium, and the zombie king walked over and sucked a gob of brains from the dead leader's skull.

"Now then," he continued. "Second order of business is... Well, forget it. Boys?"

Before the council could react, Asher's gang of undead goons fell upon them.

"Meeting adjourned," Ash grinned. "Time for breakfast."

"You better not expect us to jump," Wiz said. He was standing beside Ava at the mouth of the falls while the Baron surveyed the way down. The sun was rising on the horizon, washing everything in a soft red glow.

"You've never done that?" Ava said. "There's a spot over there where it's deep enough. It's wicked fun."

"We're not going for a swim," said the Baron. He pointed at the rusted gate beneath the old mill. "We're going in there."

"Ominous," said Wiz, staring into the depths of the tunnel. "Great."

The Baron slipped his cane into a hidden strap on his back and adjusted his hat. "Let's go."

They scaled the jagged rocks. After a couple of slips and stumbles, they stood, panting and sweaty, at the entrance to the tunnel. Wiz eyed the symbols over the rusted gate.

"What is this place?"

"The temple of the Order of Cerulean," the Baron said. "They were a cult that worshipped the old gods."

"Yeah, because you guys are so awesome."

Ava ran her fingers across the rusted gate. "This used to be attached. Someone ripped it off."

"Not someone," said the Baron.

"Something." Wiz gulped. "What are our chances we're not here alone?"

"Only one way to find out," the Baron said, heading into the tunnel. Wiz and Ava looked at each other uneasily, then followed.

A sour smell came from the darkness. The three padded

along the tunnel until they came up on the great wood slab sitting next to a shadowed staircase. The Baron took a heavy breath and held out a hand for their pause.

"I'll see that the way is clear. Wait for my signal."

With that, he descended the stairs, his top hat disappearing in the blackness.

Wiz turned to Ava, and the two exchanged expressions that said: *Well, we're totally gonna follow.*

They came up on the mouth of the chamber. The Baron peered in from the corner, then felt the two of them approach. "You were supposed to wait."

"Hey, we're sacrificing ourselves. You can't boss us around forever."

The Ghede sighed, his voice a whisper. "Fucking mortals."

The dog was sitting with his back to them, staring into the pit of doom. The Baron nodded and lead them back up the stairs to the tunnel.

"So," Wiz said. "That's a problem."

"Is it too late to start getting cold feet?" Ava said.

"I'm good with it," Wiz said. "I say we run and hide."

"How many more times do we have to have this discussion? You both know what must be done. We just need to find a way past the beast."

"Well, can you kill him?"

The Baron shook his head. "Seth is immortal. Even if we destroy him, he'd just come back."

Wiz was overcome with a sudden and desperate need to smoke copious amounts of cannabis. It would be so much easier to do this sacrifice thing if he were knocked out and— oh, wait a minute...

"I need a cell phone, right now."

Ava handed him her phone and Wiz started punching the numbers. The phone bleeped in his ear. "There's no reception down here."

"There's no time to be making personal calls," snapped the Baron. "We need to act."

"No," Wiz said, heading back toward the entrance. "We need to plan."

The phone caught a signal. Ava followed after him. "Who are you calling?"

"Mack?" Wiz said. "Tell me you're not still in jail."

"*Nope,*" Mack said. "*Released about an hour after you flew the coop. Thanks for helping by the way.*"

"I'm sorry, Mack. But I need a favor. If I wanted to tranquilize the giant evil talking dog, what would I need?"

"*A whole truckload of sedatives, if I had to guess,*" Mack sighed. "*I'm game. Where are you?*"

"Under the old art gallery. There's some ancient chamber leading to the underworld."

"*Get out! I always wondered what was in there.*"

"Well, you're about to get a close encounter. We're going to go find a place to hide. Call when you're here."

"*Will do.*"

"And Mack? Be careful."

"*Yahuh. Careful would be not helping you. See you in five.*"

Wiz hung up the phone. Ava gave him a smile. "Call the dog wrangler to deal with the evil dog. Pretty clever."

"Yeah, well... We don't know if it'll work yet."

"I seriously doubt it will," said the Baron.

Because three goblins were coming up the staircase, each brandishing a mean-looking sword.

"And it's a trap," Ava said. "Awesome."

CHAPTER 28
DEAD NEW WORLD

The ChevyVan was parked in front of Somerville's Hardware across from the exploded Texaco, ready for a speedy getaway. Noah led Amy, Franz, Jenny and Hal through the entrance. None of them noticed the bloody handprint on the bottom of the door.

"Okay," Noah said. "Let's do this quick. Jenny, you and I grab the batteries and wiring to make a fuse."

Hal grabbed a duffel bag from one of the stands near the register. "I'll get the propane."

"See if you can find some extra ammo, too. I don't know what kind of damage we can do with bullets, but more boomsticks never hurt."

The linebacker grunted cheerfully and headed off in the direction of things that go *boom*. He was born to sack explosives from hardware stores.

Noah went on. "Franz, Amy: sharp things. Find anything and everything that could chop a zombie down to stir-fry."

Amy racked the slide on her Glock, nodding. Franz sort of shrugged and they headed toward the carpentry aisle.

Jenny thumbed the hammer on her revolver. "Automotive department?"

"My thoughts exactly."

They headed down the aisle. Noah trotted toward a shelf of car batteries. "Bingo."

"What kind of wire do we need?" Jenny said, finding great spools of electrical cable.

"The longer the better," Noah nodded to one of the spools. "Might as well take the whole thing. I need a bigger battery."

"Kinda like this?" she said, kicking a battery the size of a small safe on the bottom shelf. There were another three behind it.

"If I take them all, we should be able to make the charge. Grab that cart."

Jenny turned and grabbed the empty shopping cart from the end of the aisle. She wheeled back, leaning on the handle. "Doesn't it strike you as odd that this was just sitting here, what with the place closed and all?"

Noah did find it odd, but they didn't have time to go busting ghosts with survivors waiting back at the Wood. "Yeah, well, this whole night has been chock-full of odd."

"It just seems a little too convenient, you know? Kind of like somebody *put* it there."

Noah hauled the batteries into the cart and sighed. "Hey, you're related to my roommate, right? Let's talk about that."

Jenny shrugged. "He's my husband's brother. Not much to talk about."

"Don't they ever talk to each other?"

Jenny stuffed her hands in her pockets. "Al doesn't want to get involved in Wiz's business. He figures the less he knows the better."

"Yeah, but they've got a deal going, right? Wouldn't it make sense for them to meet up? I thought the sheriff even got a cut of the profits."

Jenny bit her fingernail. "He puts all that money in the kids' savings accounts."

Noah blinked. "Aren't your kids both in their twenties?"

Another shrug from the sheriff's wife. "They're a couple of shits now. We're giving them the money after they hit thirty."

"Still," Noah said. "If they're working together, you'd think they'd get together, maybe share information from both sides? You know... shady cop/criminal stuff."

Jenny chuckled. "You watch too many movies."

Noah brandished his shotgun with a deadpan expression. "So?"

Amy and Franz were tossing boxes of saw blades, nails and exacto knives in a cart they'd found at the end of the aisle. The doctor pushed while Amy filled.

"You know," she said. "I'm a little offended you haven't hit on me yet."

"Huh?"

"Well, actually I'm relieved, but surprised."

Franz wagged his head. "What are you talking about?"

"You know," Amy said with a cheeky grin. "You've got a reputation."

"A reputation?" Franz chuckled. "Do tell, although I fear you plan to, anyway."

"Come on—everyone knows. Franz MacFee: genius surgeon, hapless horndog. It's all over the village. You're the dog, sticking your nose in everybody's butts just to say hello."

"What? I only did that the one time," Franz looked offended. "Jeez, you sniff *one* butt..."

They wheeled the cart over to the hunting aisle, hunting for big scary knives.

"I'm just saying," Amy continued. "You know... End of the world. Big scary monsters. It's frightening, Doc. I feel so very helpless. What with you, the hapless horndog, and me, the foxy temptress, a gal could use some comforting. I'm just surprised you didn't make a move."

"You definitely don't need any comforting," Franz said.

She tossed a whole rack of fourteen-inch blades into the cart. Franz sighed, although admittedly, he was pretty excited to find he had a reputation. "You're not wrong. I am indeed— as you say—a hapless horndog. I make no illusions about it. I know what I am. I like casual sex. There's nothing wrong with that—in fact, I'm pretty sure if we started unravelling your character we'd find something similar."

"Truth," she said.

"Point of fact," he went on. "You may be a foxy temptress, but you're also about a decade younger than where I draw the line for potential romance."

Amy gave him a bemused expression.

"What? You thought just because I'm a horndog I can't have principles?" He sighed, wistfully. "Youth."

"Please. The whole *I'm a doctor and save lives, therefore I can be morally inept the rest of the time* thing is tacky. I mean, it's really overdone these days."

Then she found what she was looking for: a box full of machetes on the bottom shelf.

Franz wasn't following. "What's your point?"

Amy grabbed the handle of one of the blades and pulled it out the case. It made the *shing!* sound for which machetes are so famous. She felt like a badass warrior woman—you know, in a baggy football jacket... A sort of John Hughes take on the warrior babe.

"My point,"—and here she used the machete to enumerate it—"is the doctor-by-day, playboy-by-night act is very passé"

"It's not an act. I really do like helping people."

"Really?" Everything she'd ever heard about the doctor was that he was a show-pony: a surgeon only to compensate for his being an egregious dick the rest of the time.

Franz shrugged. "People are usually more complicated than you think. Saving people is what I do, and I like it. Now, let's see if this place has any razor wire."

It was true, a lot of things had come to light that were making Hal Pearson have feelings. He'd lost his best friend. Presumably his drug dealer, too. Yes, the world was ending. There was really no question that linebacker was dealing with some serious feelings while he raided the gun department, stuffing shotguns, shells, .22s, 9mm rounds, and a considerable amount of beef jerky into his duffel bag.

Sure, he was having feelings. But then, the *Hulk* also had feelings while he was destroying stuff as an enormous green rage-monster. There is an unspoken correlation between the size of a guy and his ability to channel his emotions.

So, rather than wallowing, Hal was gleefully foraging for things that go *boom*. He moved to the front of the store, where a six foot steel shelving unit held a berth of propane tanks. It was caged off, and a padlock dangled from the front of it.

Well, this was smart thinking: he couldn't shoot at the lock without reducing himself and the front of the store to flaming chunks. He would have to get crafty. He found an axe hanging on the end of one of the aisle displays and decided he could risk making the spark. The lock broke easily.

"It's all good!" he hollered to the others. "Just me."

There were six tanks in the unit. He might be a tough guy, and even a moderately big guy, but he was not a total idiot. He wasn't going to manhandle all of the tanks from here to the van. He looked around for something to wheel them on.

And there, in the front display, was an oversized wheelbarrow that would do nicely. He grunted, grinned, and started loading.

Noah and Jenny pushed the cart toward the front. Hal was pushing the wheelbarrow filled with propane tanks to the door, and Franz and Amy were gathering sharp stuff in their cart when a ringing noise came from the back of the store.

Everyone spun. Light fanned in from the back door, which was swinging ajar. A little brass bell was jingling over the doorjamb. Noah squeezed Jenny's arm. "Stay here."

"But—"

Hal came over with a recently liberated shotgun and the two trotted toward the exit.

Jenny slumped her shoulders. "Great, now I'm alone."

Noah, Amy, Franz and Hal all stood around the open back door, their guns trained on the entrance.

"The wind must've blown it open," Noah said.

"Dude… When is that *ever* what happens?" Hal said.

"In real life?" Amy said. "I've had dozens of dorm-room doors do that."

"Slightly different circumstances," Franz said, looking like a complete doofus holding the derringer at the exit.

They crept toward the door. "Count of three," Noah said. "One.."

Amy flung the door open.

"Or, that…" Noah sighed.

They trained their guns on the opening. The only thing that came into the store was a beautiful, Californian summer morning.

"Huh," Franz said.

A long, blood-curdling shriek came from the front of the store.

"Jenny!" Noah broke into a sprint. Franz, Amy and Hal all followed.

Noah raced through the aisles, heading back to where he'd left Jenny, then looked left and skidded across the recently waxed floor. Amy toppled into him, followed by Hal, who toppled into her, and finally Franz, who caught himself before the crash.

Jenny was in the middle of the aisle, unconscious, dangling by the ankle in the grasp of one of the goblins. It tore the gruesome mask from its face and roared at them. The creature grinned, Jenny swinging in his grip like a pendulum. Franz stepped forward.

"No. Take me instead. Please."

The creature eyed him, curiously.

"Please. Just put her down. You can take me instead. You can eat me. Just put Jenny down —"

The goblin chuckled. Its voice rasping like grating steel. "Take you instead, huh?" It stroked its leathery, pointed chin. "You in exchange for the girl. That's your bargain?"

Amy grabbed Franz by the arm. Noah and Hal were behind him, guns trained on the creature. He didn't know what he was doing, and he really, really, really didn't want to die — but if that was what had to happen, then fine. This must be the doctor in him. He nodded.

"Yeah."

"Hmmm. Tell you what," the goblin produced an ugly blade from its loincloth and flipped it around, then thrust it straight into Jenny's chest.

Jenny howled, bolting awake. Her eyes fell on Franz, then glazed over and she went limp in the creature's talons.

"Here's my counter offer," it said. "She dies — rental fee for those carts I gave you. Then, *you* die. Then, everybody dies. That's my bargain — what'd'ya say?"

"No!" Franz pointed his tiny pistol at the goblin and emptied it into its chest. Hal, Amy and Noah all followed suit, sending the creature into a backward somersault as Jenny's lifeless body flung through the air. The creature shuddered and gasped, groaning on the floor.

"Time to go," Noah said. He grabbed Franz by the arm and they all scrambled toward the exit.

Noah and Amy grabbed the shopping carts by the front door. Franz was dazed. Years in ERs around the country had taught him to overcome this feeling, but still it came. He shook himself as Noah grabbed his hand and plopped the keys to the van in them.

"You sure?" Franz said. "I don't mind riding shotgun — "

"I need to ride in back with Amy to set this up," Noah said. "No offense, Franz, but I won't trust this to blow if I don't do it myself."

Franz chuckled, then realized he was the only person who related that to jerking off. Hal grabbed the door and ushered his friends with the shopping carts through. Franz followed and unlocked the van. Amy and Noah grabbed the supplies from the carts and climbed in.

Hal came bounding out of the store with the wheelbarrow filled with propane tanks. He dropped it by the van and started hauling the tanks out, passing them to Amy and Noah.

Franz climbed in and started the engine. Another tank was heaved into the van. "Is that it?"

"One more," Noah said, heaving the tanks up into the back of the van while Amy started spreading all the sharp stuff around the interior.

Hal shouldered the wheelbarrow into the van, then closed the side door.

"What?" he said. "Could be useful."

Franz hit the accelerator and the ChevyVan peeled off just in time for the front door of Somerville's to burst open, and the winged goblin lumbered after them.

Ava's inner-voice was seriously unhappy with her. *What is it tonight, Ava's fuggin' greatest hits of bad decisions? Holy steak-yielding cow, woman! Since you've been in charge, we've been gutted by a giant evil talking dog and nearly killed by a horde of zombies—all the while juggling this ridiculous crush you've got on the town pot-dealer. And to top it off, now we're about to be sacrificed by a bunch of fucking goblins!*

"This one's nuts," the goblin dragging her said to the other dragging Wiz by his beard.

"Ouch! Hey! Get the fuck off of me, will you?" Wiz said.

The creature scratched its head with his free arm. "Uh... no? That's not how this works."

"Yeah? Well *how this works* fucking blows!"

Brilliant. He whines to the evil monsters when they're rough with him. What a hero.

"Seriously, there's at least two voices in this one's skull," the goblin snickered. "What a fucking nutcase. She's arguing with herself. I can hear it."

"It's the soul," said the Baron, struggling against his goblin captor.

Ava didn't get it. Soul? What soul?

"Soul?" she said.

The Baron grinned. "You're the princess of this story, remember? There are two souls living within you."

What the what-the?

The goblin wrestling the Baron produced a blade and put it against the little god's throat.

"You'd try killing a Ghede, you cockmunching fuckweasel?"

"A Ghede?" the goblin keeled over, slapping its knee. "Ha! Oh, boy. That's just darling... You know? I really might."

Ava struggled against the goblin. "What do you mean, I have two friggin' souls?"

"What do you mean, what do I mean?" the Baron chuckled. "The voice in your head! It's not your own, mortal. It's the princess, arguing your beliefs. You're still you... You've just got—well—baggage."

"Everyone's got baggage," Wiz grunted. "You seriously mean for us to believe not only that we need to sacrifice ourselves to prevent the end of the world—but Ava also happens to have two fucking souls? Come on, that's crazy."

"Actually," Ava said. "It kind of explains a lot."

I'll say, honeybean. Uh... Nice to meet you? Please don't let us die.

Wiz wagged his head. "What are you talking about?"

"I always just thought it was my inner voice. You know, the one you talk to when you're alone or trying to figure something out."

Like not dying!

"How much crazier can this all get?" Wiz said. The answer, of course, was *much*.

The goblins dragged them into the great chamber and threw them on the stone floor. More of the creatures were milling around the edge of the pit, helping their comrades out of the chute to the underworld. They growled and slobbered, all hooting and brandishing crude weapons. There was a whole legion of them.

"Evil army," Wiz sighed. "Great."

"Great," Ava said.

"Great," said the Baron.

Great, said the princess.

"Right?" Seth chuckled, trotting around the edge of the pit. "This is awesome."

CHAPTER 29
A HELPING HAND

Noah lined the propane tanks against the back seat as Amy frayed the spool of copper wire and connected it to barbecue starters zip-tied to each tank. The van swerved back and forth as Franz mowed down a few of the straggling zombies heading to the tavern.

Hal was propped out the passenger's side window, firing the shotgun at the winged goblin flying after them. "He's chasing us right up the street."

Noah tore open the box of machetes and handed one to Amy.

"And what do we do about him?" she said.

Noah didn't know. "One step at a time. Let's mangle the zombies first. Wiz and Ava must still be alive. You heard the god. When they sacrifice themselves, the goblins will... die, or something."

"I'm still having trouble with counting on our friends killing themselves," Hal said, twisting in his seat, reloading the shotgun.

"I'm not crazy about it either," Noah said. "But we don't have a choice here, guys. Let's just do what we can."

The linebacker stared out the windshield with a troubled expression. Up ahead, the zombies swarmed around the tavern.

"There's too many of them," Amy said. "Once we get in the crowd, there's no way we'll be able to use the door."

Noah smiled and punched the keypad on the floor that he really enjoyed using. A digital beep, and a section of the shag carpet floor raised and slid open.

"This van has a secret compartment?" Amy said. "Now I really have seen everything."

"The shifter's a bong, too." Hal said.

"There's a trap door in the bottom of the compartment," Noah said. "We'll use it and just blow a path through those zombie fucks."

"Better get ready, folks!" Franz said, gripping the wheel as they sped toward the tavern. "Here we go."

The engine roared and the van slammed into the horde of undead. The windshield cracked, a spurt of blood raining over it. Angry moans came from all around as the van rocked to a stop.

"Showtime," Noah said. He and Amy opened all the valves on the propane tanks. Everybody piled around the trap door as the tanks hissed. Amy reached into the compartment and opened the latch. The trap fell away, clanging on the pavement. They slid under the van one at a time, each carrying a battery. Hal had the spool of wire in one hand, his battery wedged in the duffel filled with weapons.

Noah shimmied to the back of the van. The linebacker passed him and Amy each a shotgun and they climbed out from under the van. Most of the undead were grouped by the front of the van, trying to figure out what happened.

"Get around back! Run!"

Hal handed the spool to Franz and they all sprinted around the side of the bar, unravelling the cable as they went. Noah blew the heads off two of the dead who were coming to intercept them. They scrambled around the back of the tavern.

"End of the line," Franz said.

Noah and Amy set their batteries on the ground and started connecting them. Hal heaved his and Franz's batteries. When the wiring was complete, Noah said, "Okay. Let's do this."

Franz brandished the end of the wire. "Hey, could I do it?"

Noah shrugged—he didn't really care *who* did it. The doctor's eyes lit up gleefully as he stooped next to the batteries, frayed the end of the wire, and connected it. "Take cover!"

They lunged behind a flower box next to the bar.

Nothing happened.

Franz looked disappointed. "Really? After all —"

The van erupted in a huge fireball that swallowed the front of the tavern. The shockwave rattled through the pavement as great chunks of metal whizzed by them, peppering the surrounding buildings with shrapnel. Saw blades, nails, chunks of propane tank and ChevyVan pelted the undead as the twenty-foot flames swallowed them.

Then it all went very quiet—that is, except for the ringing in their ears. Noah rolled out from behind the flower box with the shotgun ready.

He couldn't believe the carnage. The whole army of undead were strewn across the street in pieces. Everything had been leveled. Lampposts and stop signs bent backward like trees caught in gale-force winds, rattling in the aftershock.

Hal and Amy stood, brushing themselves off, jaws hanging in disbelief.

"Woah," Hal said.

"So… That worked," said Amy.

Franz groaned, still leaning against the flower box. "Jesus. I think I pulled my *life*. Did we win?"

Noah nodded, unable to break his gaze from the war zone. "Creamed 'em."

"Great," Franz said. "Remind me later it sucks to be a hero."

He picked himself up as the shrub behind him started rustling. The four circled as the shrub wagged back and forth, and a severed hand leaped out of the brush and grabbed the doctor by the face.

"Rraaaaarrrghh! Gah!"

Franz struggled, ripping the hand away. It flopped on the ground and scurried at him.

"Oh no! Not again!" He grabbed Amy's machete and

started hacking the thing to bits. "Fucking zombie arms!"

Above them, a winged shadow circled. Noah pumped the shotgun. "Time to go, team."

They headed around the tavern to the alleyway leading to the back door when something knocked the gun out of Noah's grip.

"What the—"

"Brenda Menzrik?" Franz said.

Noah spun just in time to see Brenda wielding a hunting knife.

"Hiya, Doc."

She grinned and plunged the blade into Franz's stomach. He yelped and staggered backward, hands cradling the knife as red trickled through his fingers. He slumped to the pavement.

"Franz!"

"Now," Brenda said, the evil grin unbreaking. "As for the rest of you—"

That's when the oversized wheelbarrow—which had been airborne—came down and sliced the zombie queen clean in half. She didn't get back up.

From his growing pool of blood, it didn't look like Franz was getting up, either.

"This is nice, isn't it?" the beast said, pacing in monster-form in front of Wiz and Ava. "We're all together now. It's nice to be together for the end of times, right?"

The goblins had them on their knees at swordpoint while the Baron struggled in the grip of two more.

"Get bent, fleabag!" Wiz said.

"Heh, I actually had those taken care of," Seth chuckled. "And anyway, *I* think this is nice, and that's really all that matters."

"You do realize we're here to stop you, right?" Ava said, ignoring the sword poking her in the back. And yes, she was still a little miffed at Seth for putting a claw through her earlier.

"Really? You guys are doing such a swell job." Seth chuckled. "Serves you right for getting notes from this idiot. Baron, nice to see you again."

"Eat a bag of shit, you overgrown mutt!"

"Ah, behold!" Seth waved a claw while the goblins forced the top-hatted god to the floor. "The foul-mouthed Ghede! In his natural environment—at the hands of a more supreme being. What a *winner*."

"But he said if we die, you lose your power," Wiz said. "What are you gonna do if you can't kill us?"

Seth howled with laughter. He hunched over, holding himself against his gangly knees. "He told you that? That's rich."

"What do you mean? He said a sacrifice was the only way."

"It *is* the only way. The only way to get me back in the hole is if you both jump in first. But if you're dead? If I kill you, well, that's not exactly a sacrifice, is it?"

Wiz shook his head. "You're bluffing."

"Am I?" Seth said. He grinned, then grabbed Ava. She shrieked as claws dug into her ribs and blinding pain roared through her abdomen.

"Ooh, look at me," Seth said, affecting a mock-damsel-in-distress tone, wagging Ava like a sock puppet. "Oh, I'm such a sacrifice. The big scary dog is about to kill me, and if I die, then I do it in sacrifice. That's what you think, right? Say it!"

But Ava couldn't say it. The pain was so intense she was sure she would pass out.

"*Say it!*"

"I'm a sacrifice!" she wailed. "If you're gonna kill me, you better get it over with because I'm the fucking sacrifice!"

And here, Seth stopped wagging her. He rammed her into the floor and climbed over, his huge slobbering maw pumping fetid doggie breath in her face.

"There, was that so hard? Gosh, you people are so fucking dramatic."

"Ava, no!" Wiz cried, lunging toward them, but the goblin

grabbed him and slammed him back on his knees. "Stop it! Leave her alone."

Ava groaned. The claws dug further into her ribs. The dog snarled, squeezing so hard her breath wouldn't come.

"The woman has something that doesn't *belong* to her. I'm taking it back."

He raised his free claw over her chest and spread it wide, then slammed his palm into her chest. The last of Ava's wind knocked out of her, but the pain kept her from losing consciousness. She couldn't move. Couldn't squirm. She couldn't even twitch an eyelid. She was frozen there with the beast grinning over her.

Uh-oh, said the princess. *Mayday! Not good. Not —*

Seth pulled his palm back about six inches and a shadow fell from it, like ink falling through water. Smoky tendrils danced through the air and connected with Ava's chest. Everywhere they touched went cold — so wildly, so vividly, so blindingly cold that it burned.

Then, a brilliant white orb began to glow from the center of her chest. Seth's red eyes flickered, and he wrapped his claws around the orb.

Then a pain more concentrated and excruciating than Ava could ever have fathomed in even her wildest nightmare consumed her. It was the pain of the death of a soul.

Noah, Amy and Hal carried Franz through the back door of the tavern, leaving a smear of red in their wake. They set him carefully on the floor, which didn't seem to make a difference to the doctor, because he still moaned painfully. It looked like someone had dumped a bucket of red paint on his stomach.

"This is what I get for sleeping with patients," Franz groaned.

Noah gave him a half-hearted chuckle and tore the doctor's shirt open. He gaped at the wound, which gaped right back. Franz looked at his bleeding stomach with a sort of surprised frown.

"Guys, get the First Aid kit. We need gauze. Lots of gauze."

Amy and Hal rushed down the hall as the doc waved him off. "Don't bother. I'm three minutes from the big siesta here."

Noah squeezed his shoulder. "No, Franz. Don't talk like that."

"Of the two of us, which one's the doctor?"

"We'll stitch you up. You can walk us through it..."

"Forget it. It's over, pal. I'm... dead." The doc wagged his head, letting out a wet-sounding chuckle. "I'm dead."

Helplessness gnawed at Noah like an ulcer.

Franz nodded slowly, grim acceptance twisting his brow. He sighed. "Got any pot?"

Noah produced a joint from his cigarette pack. He placed it in the doctor's mouth, lit it, and slumped next to him. "I'm sorry, Franz."

"Why?"

Franz puffed the joint silently, staring off into a spot on the floor. They sat like that for a while, then Franz MacFee handed the joint to Noah. He closed his eyes, and he died.

Noah mashed the ember of the spliff against his sneaker, placed it next to Franz's body, and rose. He walked into the tavern where Amy and Hal were rifling through the first aid kit.

"Franz is dead."

The sheriff got off his stool next to Reyes. "What about Jenny? Where's Jenny?"

Noah rubbed the back of his neck. Not now. Not so soon after watching Franz die. He didn't have the stomach. "Al..."

"Where's Jenny?"

Amy signaled Lanette for drinks. "She's... I'm sorry, Al."

"Where is she?"

"She didn't make it," Hal said.

All the hope drained from the sheriff's face. It was replaced with a different look. His features hardened, his jaw tensed. This was rage. He sighed, pinching the bridge of his nose.

"What's next?"

Reyes got off his stool and went to pat Al on the shoulder. "Sheriff, before we do anything—"

"Shut up," Al snapped, wheeling around. "Try to touch me again and I'll break your fucking hand." Then to Noah, "What's next?"

Lanette came down the bar with the beer.

Noah grabbed a bottle and took a swig. "Well, I think we've proven that the zombies enjoy getting back up after we kill them again."

"But we blew them up," Lenny said. "Twice, in fact."

Hunt nodded. "How could they possibly get up from that?"

"We can't risk it," Noah said. "We need to go out there. I think... Well... I think we need to chop them up."

"Fine," Al said, heading over to the window by the bar and tossing bricks out of the frame. "Someone help get this open."

Amy squeezed Noah's arm. "What about the dead in here?"

"I'm really hoping they won't get up." He turned and addressed the patrons. "Okay people, there will be machetes and sharp stuff everywhere, so grab what works for you. Lenny, Hunt, come help us get this window clear."

CHAPTER 30
DO EVIL DOGS DREAM OF SATANIC SHEEP?

Ava's body fell to the floor as the beast stood, grinning, and plopped the glowing soul into his jaws. He gulped, and a second later belched a ball of steam. "Tasty."

"No!" Wiz cried. He lunged forward, and the goblins yanked him back.

"Oh, don't be such a wussy," Seth said. "You never get anywhere in life being a wussy."

"You fucking evil douche monster," Wiz said. "Baron? Baron! Help me out."

But the Baron was busy struggling with his own pair of goblins.

"Why would he help?" Seth chuckled. "You're a complete failure, buddy. You're officially one soul short on the sacrifice play, and it's not like you're going anywhere."

Wiz howled, writhing against the goblins. Too far. He'd come too far for it to end like this. He tried again to reach Ava. The goblin on his left slapped the back of his head with its sword. It didn't matter. Nothing mattered anymore. All he wanted was to be with her. All he wanted was for her to be okay. He took great gulps of air and tried again. He'd keep trying until they killed him.

"What's the matter, ya big wussy?" the beast said. "You running out of hope?"

"Avaaaaaa," Wiz planted an elbow in the right goblin's face and broke free, only to be ripped back by the one on the left.

"Oh, *this*?" Seth said. He snatched Ava's lifeless body off the ground and dangled it in front of him. "Is this what you want? Too bad."

With that, the beast flung her across the chamber as if she were a used candy wrapper. She smacked the side of the chamber next to the entrance and slid down the wall.

This was it. It was all over.

"Now then," Seth snarled, wheeling on Wiz as the goblins held him down. "Your turn."

He came at the Wizard, hungry maw gaping as it came over his head.

Oh fuck, oh fuck, oh fuck, fuck, fuck!

Blackness. Stench. Teeth clamped into his forehead. Drool slicked his hair. Then, a soft whooshing noise, followed by a *thunk*. The jaws loosened as the beast let out the whine of a wounded puppy and crumpled to the chamber floor, knocked completely-the-fuck-out.

"Bad doggie," Mack Gaffey said, brandishing his tranquilizer gun.

The goblins let go of Wiz, stunned. Everyone in the chamber turned to see what had happened, and the Baron used this slip to rip free of his bonds, grabbing his sword from the sheath hidden in his back.

"Finally!" he said, spinning and mowing down the two goblins with a slash of the blade.

The goblins who'd been holding Wiz—a red one and a green one—turned with their swords ready. The Baron grinned, holding his blade overhead, black blood dripping from its tip. He barreled forward, blocking the red goblin's swing, then kicking it in the stomach as he spun on the other.

The green goblin heaved its broadsword in a great golf-swing toward the Ghede, who sidestepped, parrying the blow as the goblin fell forward, crashing into the red one, who'd just recovered. The Baron leaped. Their blades sang as he slashed left, then right, then rammed the hilt of his sword into the face of the green one, swinging sideways and running the red goblin through the chest.

The goblin roared, flapping his leathery wings and pulling himself backward. He cleared the blade and came back hacking at the Baron. The green one swung angrily, clipping the Ghede's top hat as he ducked.

"Now, sorcerer! You've got to do it."

Wiz pulled himself off the floor, wiping his drool-slick hair from his eyes. He turned and found the stairs leading to the pit. *Don't do it! Don't fucking go down there, you idiot! Run. Fight. Puke. Whatever, just do anything but…*

Wiz blinked away the thoughts and shuffled toward the stairs.

The Baron whipped around, bringing the blade down over the head of the green goblin, splitting the creature all the way to the sternum. Great spurts of bug-like goo splattered the floor as the goblin fell. Behind him, the red one screeched, tearing off his crude mask. With his horrible snarling maw, he swung at the Baron, who blocked.

Their swords locked, sparks flying through the air. The goblin flapped its wings and brought itself over the Ghede in a whooshing somersault. The Baron parried, planting his foot between the goblin's legs. The creature stumbled backward, and the Baron slashed it clean in two.

Wiz stood at the mouth of the pit, staring into the hellish blackness. He knew what he had to do, but… *No! No, no, no, no, no!*

He took a deep breath, steadying himself for the jump.

"Wiz!" Mack said from the top of the stairs.

He couldn't do it. He let the breath go, hanging his head in humiliated humanity. He couldn't.

Then he felt the prick of a sword at his back.

"Do it, Sorcerer," the Baron said. "Or I'll do it for you."

The remains of the dead were stacked in a makeshift pyre next to the town square. The patrons had found machetes, sharp

hunks of metal, and even a couple of axes in the wreckage.
They all worked away, chopping up the dead before they could
rise again, looking like highway workers on that street paved
in blood that everyone talks about.

Max Reyes was using an exploded chunk of ChevyVan
door to hack up the groaning corpse of Carly the zombie-ette.
He slammed the metal down with a crunch. "We should be
wearing hazmat suits for this."

The old guys hauled bloody pieces of Silas past him.

"You really need to loosen up, agent," Lenny said.

The agent held out his arms in argument. "But—"

"Or a shave," Hunt said. "Seriously, it looks like there's a
beaver on your face. Now quit moping and get your limbs on
the pile!"

Noah chuckled and tossed the wriggling ribcage of zombie
Andy on the gory mound. He wiped his hands on bloodsoaked
jeans. "We need a cleanup crew for our cleanup crew."

Amy came up with an armful of—well, arms. She tossed
them on the pile and sighed. "I need a shower… And probably
a therapist."

Noah sighed, staring up at the brilliant sun as it climbed
behind picturesque clouds. He'd spent so long in action-mode,
doing what needed to be done he'd never really stopped to
think of how it all affected him. He looked across the scene,
which looked like a grotesque postcard advertising quaint
tourist adventures in Goreville (*Hack away your summer vacation
with the family!*) and reasoned that Amy was probably right: the
trauma would catch up with him later.

He thought of the friends he'd lost, of all the horrible things
the patrons went through—especially the sheriff. How would
any of them ever recover from such a nightmare?

"I don't think any of us will get out of this without—well—
damage."

Behind them, Hal Pearson planted an axe in the skull of
Dimitri, the zombified high school English teacher, looking
happier than a dog rolling in dead fish. "Speak for yourselves."

Noah rolled his eyes. "I was talking about the sheriff."

"Oh," Hal said, pausing in a fit of deep concentration. Then he shrugged and resumed hacking up the guy who'd flunked him in ninth grade.

Al Kowalski was across the street, standing over a zombie that can only be described as a squirming pile of flesh, wielding a chipped machete, chopping away like a drunken lumberjack. He hacked and hacked until the zombie was little more than a mushy puddle—then he moved onto the next ruined corpse and repeated the process.

"Someone should go talk to him," Amy said.

"Yeah," Hal agreed, resting for a moment on the hilt of his axe. "Someone should console him…"

Noah watched as the sheriff continued hacking, all the grief, all the anger and loss channeling through his arms as he swung.

"Well, don't all volunteer at once," he said. He shook his head and started over to the grieving lawman.

Thwack! Thwack! Thwack!

"Uh, Sheriff?"

He might have heard him, but Al didn't stop.

Thwack! Thwack! Thwack!

"Al, listen…" Noah wasn't really sure where to go from here. He bit his lip, willing the words from his rattled mind. "Look, I know you're hurting…"

Thwack! Thwack! Thwack!

"…But you need to chill out a bit."

Thwack! Thwack! Thwack!

"Sheriff? Al? Are you hearing me? Think of Jenny, Al. She wouldn't want you to—"

"She wouldn't want a lot of things." Al spat, wheeling around on Noah. "For instance, dying at the hands of these fucking monsters. I don't imagine she wanted that."

Clouds crept across the sunlight. Shadows scaled the buildings.

"Sheriff—"

"No, I don't need your help, thanks. I don't need any help. All I need is to make sure these fuckers never get back up. If I can't make them pay, I can at least do that, now fuck off!"

"Noah?" Amy called from behind. Noah turned to find her pointing toward the sky.

It wasn't clouds creeping the skyline—it was bodies. Winged shades were rising from the art gallery down the street like a cloud of bats. They crept across the sky with deathly silence: the goblin army.

"Now, Sorcerer," the Ghede said with his blade to Wiz's back. "I won't say it again."

Wiz stared into the chasm, his heart jackhammering in his eardrums. Every limb, every joint, every tendon in his body electrified with the realization he was staring his own death in the face. All the things he wished he could be—all the things he still wanted to do—everything left of life to savor... All flashing like a strobe in his mind.

There was so much left. Now that he was facing it, Wiz realized he hadn't slacked off in life for any good reason. All the things he thought he knew better than to pursue, all the opportunities he'd passed—and all because he was terrified of failure.

"No," he said, turning to face the Baron, grabbing the blade with his hands. It sliced into his skin. "No."

Blood trickled through his fingers.

"No? What part of you don't have a choice are you not getting here? You don't get to say *no*," the Baron's eyes were butane flames. "Jump, or I will run you through and shove you in. Sweet merciful fuck, you cannot be this stupid."

"I'm not being stupid," Wiz said. "I want to live. I have... things I wanna do with my life, and I'm not done living it yet. You want a sacrifice? Go find a cult and knock yourself out!"

"You selfish, idiotic, sheep-shagging bong for brains. If you don't do it, there will be no world left. This is your destiny!"

Behind him, a shadow rose from the chamber floor.

"Well, destiny can go suck an egg. And you can go fuck yourself, man."

The Baron sighed, staring off into the abyss. He gripped the sword, which sent waves of pain up the Wizard's arms, and said, "I have toiled with your mortal fuckery long enough. Here's your death—"

But before he could finish, a huge dog-shaped shadow caught him by the ankle and flung him across the chasm. The Baron crashed into the opposite wall as Seth stepped out of shadow and said, "You know, a smart god would've skipped the chit-chat."

Wiz staggered backward, clambering up the stairs as the beast lumbered toward the Ghede.

"P.S.," he growled. "That stuff is pretty fun, guys. Got any more? I'm catching a wicked buzz."

"Wiz!" Mack tossed Wiz a gun, which he completely failed to catch.

"Damn, I really need to work on my coordination," Wiz said.

The Baron pulled himself off the floor, grabbing his sword and shouting, "Seth!!!"

The dog grinned, and the two gods sprinted at each other, each turning to shadow and clashing like a great wave of darkness against the chamber wall. Wiz grabbed the gun, the tumbling mass of blackness whirling just over his head. He scampered back to where Mack was crouched over Ava.

Wiz got to his knees and took her in his arms.

"Ava," he said. "Wake up."

She didn't move.

Wiz blinked back tears as the Baron and Seth continued tumbling around the chamber in a tangle of shadow.

"Wake up, Ava. Please... Not like this... Not when... Please...Wake up."

He pressed his forehead against hers, and the tears came.

"Wake up!"

As the throng of goblins choked off the sunlight, Al Kowalski was nursing a brew of equal parts despair and self-destruction. He knew what was coming. So what? Let it! Let the winged death come. Who cared anymore? There was nothing left for him—nothing to live for. There was only darkness.

"Al? We need to go inside now," Noah said.

All the patrons stopped what they were doing to look as the beating of hundreds of wings filled the air.

"Everybody back in the bar!" Amy called out.

People scampered back toward the window. The old guys helped usher them inside. The sheriff, however, didn't even look up.

"Al… We gotta go."

"You go," the sheriff said. "I'm staying."

Noah grabbed him by the arm. "Al, it's suicide. I know you're in pain, but—"

"I said get back in the bar. Make sure everyone's safe. Seal off the window. I'm staying."

"No. I can't let you do that."

Finally, Al faced the yogi and chuckled. "What are you going to do?

Noah gave him a confused look, but before he could answer, a pair of goblins swooped in and landed on the roof of the bank across the street, looking like the nastiest gargoyles to ever have furnished a building.

"You're out of time," Al said. "Get inside."

"But—"

Heinous shrieks volleyed from around them. The batting of wings was so loud it shook in their chests. Clouds of dust and smoke whipped up from the street.

"Now, Noah. Let me go."

Noah made a pained expression, then let go of the sheriff's arm. He sprinted back to the tavern, where Amy, Hal and the old guys were waiting for him. Before he climbed in, he turned once more, as if hoping Al would get second thoughts.

The sheriff just nodded.

With that, they sealed up the opening. Al gripped the handle of his machete and looked up as the goblin army descended, their wings blotting out the sun.

There was no light when they fell upon him.

CHAPTER 31
DOOM AND GLOOM

Blackness greeted Ava Elridge. Something was different. She couldn't put her finger on it, but she could feel it. Everything was different. Even before her eyes fluttered open, she realized what it was: it was quiet inside. The voice—the constant nagging, the snarky commentary, the unwelcome narrator that had been with her for every step of her life—was gone.

It felt like there was a hole inside her.

She was on the floor of the chamber, cradled in Wiz's arms as he chanted "Wake up, wake up, wake up."

Snarls and shouting rattled around the chamber like the clatter of bowling balls. She wagged her head, a part of her still wishing this had all been some insane dream. Her body ached as she sat up.

"Well that sucked."

Big blue eyes, streaming with tears, greeted her. Wiz squeezed her hand and planted his forehead against hers, his shoulders slumping with relief. "I thought I lost you."

"Yeah," she blinked. "Me too."

Shadows whirled around the room. Ava tried to follow them, just making out the figure of the evil dog and the Baron as they fought.

"What happened?"

Behind her, Mack Gaffey brandished his tranq gun as a rumbling quake rocked the chamber. "Okay," he said. "That's our cue, time to go. We need—"

A huge purple tentacle came out of the pit, grabbing the vet by the ankle and pulling him up in the air. Mack shrieked as the tentacle dangled him back over the mouth of the pit and dropped him in. His cries were ended with the crunch of a massive set of jaws.

"Uh-oh," Ava said.

Another rumble shook stone from the ceiling as the tentacle retreated, and a long, phlegmy roar came from the chasm. Whatever it was—which was, in fact, a creature far more horrible and congested than any mortal can imagine—was too big to fit through the gap.

The shadows of the clashing gods continued spiraling around the chamber—with a great slam into the wall, the Baron's sword flung out of the darkness.

Wiz helped Ava to her feet, handing her the gun. "Here."

Ava blinked, still dazed. "What am I supposed to do with this?"

"You're a better shot than me."

"You want me to shoot the giant tentacle monster? How high are you?"

Before he could reply, a cluster of gnarled, slimy roots sprang from the pit. They snaked up the slope of the floor like sentient vines, spraying off in different directions looking for purchase. One wrapped itself around Wiz's ankle and yanked him off his feet.

Wiz conked the front of his head on the stone. Spots of light blotted his vision and he felt himself being dragged down the slope toward the pit.

"Wiz!" Ava shouted. She aimed the gun in an attempt to shoot the vine—but really, who was that great of a shot?

Wiz slid down the slope, clawing for anything to keep him

from the opening. He twisted, trying to find something to latch onto and found the Baron's blade.

He reached.

The vine yanked.

His fingers caught the edge of the sword's handle and he swung around, hacking at the horrible root. Black goo spattered out of the vine as a hideous shriek erupted from the pit. The rest of the vines climbed all the way to the ceiling, sprawling across the stone as they grew. Buds began forming at their ends, rapidly blossoming into brilliant blue flowers that resembled a Venus fly trap. Their jaws opened, spitting flame through the chamber.

Wiz scrambled to recover, but the momentum from the vine sent him tumbling directly into the grasp of a pair of leathery arms swathed in rotted linen. He was standing in the arms of a mummy—its features puckered and tawny like a deflated football. The mummy gnashed its jaws, going for the side of Wiz's neck.

Wiz shoved the creature backward, brandishing the sword. The mummy staggered, hissing. Wiz brought the sword overhead, having absolutely no idea if he was doing it right, and then a gunshot thundered through the chamber.

Twin holes appeared in the center of the mummy's chest, spraying dust as the creature shrieked and tottered.

"Ava, don't shoot the mummy! You'll just make him angry!"

The mummy snarled, knocking the sword away as it came at Wiz, who grabbed the creature by the shoulders and swung it over the edge of the pit.

The shadows of the Baron and Seth spilled off of the ceiling and landed beside him, turning solid for a minute, revealing the beast as he wrestled the Baron to the floor.

"Give it up, short-bus!" Seth growled. "It's pointless. The apocalypse has arrived."

As if on cue, the chamber rumbled again, and the mouth of the pit erupted like a volcano filled with nightmares.

The floor shook so hard Wiz lost his footing. Heavy chunks of stone fell from the ceiling. From the depths below, the shriek of thousands of tortured souls came barreling up like a freight train. A huge cloud burst from the pit—tendrils describing clawed arms, tattered robes and jagged jaws of spirits rising like steam and billowing out the entrance.

Ava shrieked, falling backward as another hunk of the ceiling fell beside her. Wiz went to run for her when the floor shook with a terrible groan, and an enormous river of blood spouted out of the pit, raining over the chamber, slicking the floor with red.

The Baron and Seth continued to struggle, the little god gripping the beast by the jaws and kicking furiously as Seth heaved him into the air, trying to chomp down on him. Before it could happen, the Ghede vanished in a cloud of smoke, which grabbed Seth by the legs and flung him into the floor.

A figure leaped out of the pit, sailing over Wiz's head and landing behind him. He turned to find a man in a tattered suit, his head the head of a frog. The frog-man observed the staggering Wizard with bulging black eyes, then opened his jowls and spurted a great streamer of green goo at him. Wiz toppled backward as the goo hit the floor and sizzled. The stone beneath the puddle began to smoke and burn away.

Wiz was hanging half-over the mouth of the pit. The chasm below was a writhing sea of goblins, millions of gnashing jaws of the whole spectrum of nightmare creatures, all scrambling over one and other to get to the surface. It was a brewing pot of apocalypse stew—and it was about to boil over.

The goblins slammed against the windows of the Gnarled Wood Tavern, chipping away at the barricades, sending bricks and wood splinters flying through the air. There was no longer any questioning it—the goblins would get in and kill everybody.

The patrons were huddled in a circle in the middle of the tavern, all holding onto each other, some crying, some screaming, and most just silently awaiting their deaths. Noah had his arms around Amy and Hal as the goblins tore through the walls. All the fight was drained from them.

For the third time in twenty minutes, the earth below them shook.

"It's okay," Noah said. "It's okay, guys."

"I'm fairly certain it's not," Amy said, burrowing her face into his arm.

"You know what I mean."

"This is some patent bullshit!" Lenny hollered from beside Hunt. "I don't want to die."

The first window gave way, and the goblins began fighting each other to get in.

Seth and the Baron did another rumble around the chamber, going in and out of shadow as they crashed at the mouth of the pit. The Baron flung another blow at the beast, but Seth grabbed his fist, then ran his claw through the little god's stomach.

The Baron howled.

Seth dangled him over the pit.

Wiz scrambled to his feet, snatching the Ghede's blade from the floor as the frog man spat another acid loogie. There was no time to think. There was no more room for indecision—for waiting for the situation to sort itself out. It was all on him, now.

Seth grinned at the Baron. "Enough of you, you annoying little gnat. Time to go home."

Wiz charged around the mouth of the chamber, gripping the hilt of the blade. He angled the sword and ran the beast right through the chest. The blade slipped through Seth and into the chest of the Baron, and both the gods gasped with surprise.

Seth howled, swiping at his back, knocking Wiz across the chamber. He smashed the steps leading back to the entrance and his head lit up with blinding pain.

The Baron looked down at the blade skewering him to his nemesis, then looked at the Wizard as a solution that hadn't occurred to him flashed through his mind.

He chuckled, gripped Seth by the shoulders, and flung

himself backward. The gods toppled over the edge of the chasm, falling into the blackness.

Wiz let out a sigh of relief, heaving himself up from the floor when an earth-shattering roar came from the pit. A thirty-foot, dragon-like creature — half raptor, half bat — burst out of the chasm, sending the bodies of the gods sailing through the air. The Baron and Seth crashed beside Wiz. The raptor bat licked its chops, flapping its wings. It let off another roar, then barreled out of the entrance to the chamber, roaring all the way.

Seth groaned, the Baron still pinned to his chest with the sword. Wiz scuttled over, and before the beast could get up, he kicked them both back into the pit.

This time, they really fell.

Wiz pulled himself to his feet, his whole body aching from the beating he'd sustained. The rumbling began to wane. Bits of stone and a cloud of dust settled around the floor of the chamber.

"Ava?" he said.

"I'm okay!" He could just make out her shape as she got to her feet.

Then, a sound like feedback began to come from the pit below. It grew louder, higher, stronger, until the whole chamber was vibrating.

"What now?" Wiz sighed.

It was deafening, shrill and unyielding, like the screeching of a blown-out amplifier dialed up to eleven. The noise brought both Wiz and Ava to their knees as it reached an unbearable crescendo.

Then a brilliant column of white light shot out of the pit. It reached a focus at the great spike on the ceiling, glowing and reverberating through the stone, so intense, so vivid and pure it would give Ghandi a boner.

Then, the light exploded outward, carrying a huge shockwave through the chamber and out into the world.

CHAPTER 32
EVIL GETS A SUCKERPUNCH

The light rocketed through the streets of Oak Falls, straight through the walls of the Gnarled Wood Tavern, blinding the patrons as the deafening screech knocked them all to the floor.

Noah, Amy and Hal all covered their ears as the shockwave followed, sending huge clouds of dust and debris through the air.

A moment later, the quiet that follows thunderstorms fell upon the bar. Slowly, timidly, the hands came down from the patrons ears and they began to rise.

"What the toilet-clogging shit was that?" Lenny said.

Amy gave the old guy a *what-the-fuck?* expression. "Gross."

Noah got up and surveyed the window. It looked like someone had slogged an enormous red paint bucket at the tavern. Bits of flesh dripped from the sill. A brilliant beam of sunlight fanned through the opening. Whatever had happened, the goblins were gone.

"Seriously, what was that?" Hal said, standing and brushing the dust from his shoulders.

"I don't know," Noah said. He started inching toward the window to investigate.

"My bet's a flash grenade," Reyes said, stroking his stupid-looking goatee. "The National Guard must be here. We should all stay put while they secure the area."

Lenny scoffed at the agent. "On a scale of one-to-realistic, where do you think that sits, Agent?"

"Uh," Reyes said.

"This is ridiculous," Noah said with a sigh. "I'm going to look."

"We don't know if those things are still out there or not. For all we know it was a trick or something," Reyes insisted. "We should stay put."

Noah blinked at him. "So which is it? National Guard or an evil trick? Do us all a favor, go shave that fucking beaver off your face."

Before Reyes could answer, Noah jumped out the window.

Behind the bar, Lanette Wilson poured herself a shot of Bushmills, tossed it back, and said, "Mothafuckah's got a point."

The street outside was slick with blood and bits of flesh. Every brick, every sidewalk panel and streetlamp; every store's window and awning was dripping red. Noah stepped out onto the sidewalk, his jaw hanging agape. A smoldering chunk of leathery wing sizzled by his feet.

In the middle of it all was Sheriff Al Kowalski, machete in hand, plastered from head to foot with gore.

"Holy shit!" Noah said. He trotted over to the sheriff, who dropped the machete and nearly collapsed. Noah put a steadying hand on Al's shoulder. "What happened?"

Al wagged his head. "They exploded."

"What the fuck?"

The sheriff nodded. "One minute they're all closing in — I even managed to chop the heads off a couple of them — and then they get me on the ground and I'm thinking it's all over. Then there's this crazy light and noise, and they all just kind of popped like water balloons filled with guts. I have no idea what happened."

"We won is what happened," Lenny Taltree said, climbing out onto the street.

"What do you mea—Holy fucknuggets," Amy said, staring open-mouthed at the carnage. "Yes, I'd say we definitely did."

The patrons began climbing out of the ruined tavern, all of them wearing the stupefied expressions of a band of Jehovas' Witnesses leaving their first strip club.

"I need a shower," said Al Kowalski, shaking his head.

"Yeah, join the club," Amy said. "I'm pretty sure there aren't enough showers in the world to clean this gunk."

The sheriff nodded at Noah. "You tried to save me back there. I'm sorry I didn't listen. But thanks, all the same."

Noah shrugged, too busy trying to wrap his mind around what had happened. If this is what the light had done to the goblins—then what had become of Ava and Wiz? The realization that he'd probably lost another friend—that he wouldn't be able to share this insane experience with his best friend—began to weigh on him.

"What now?" What now indeed. Clean the town? Have a drink? Get stoned? How do you deal with the fact that your friend has exploded in a huge ball of light? How do you move forward from that? It was the end of the end of the world, and Noah had no idea what should come next. This was the part they never showed in the movies, because—well—because it was hard. All he knew was, there was no way to go back to the way things were.

"Now, I'm going home," Al said. It was all he could do. He'd lost his wife and his brother he never talked to; he'd survived attack by hundreds of evil goblins and the end of the world. He'd survived, and Noah was beginning to realize that surviving was the most horrible thing of all.

The sheriff walked off. As he passed the agent, Reyes shook his head and affected a scolding tone. "That was wildly stupid of you, Sheriff. I know you're hurting, but you think that's an excuse? These people needed you and—"

And here, Al Kowalski coldcocked Max Reyes in the jaw.

The agent flopped to the ground like a dead fish with a stupid goatee.

The rest of the patrons just stood there.

Al cradled his fist and grinned. "Man, that felt good."

Asher Cravington, the zombie king, was not feeling so good. He'd left the old town hall feeling the secret blues that drove Mayor Peters to being such an intolerable asshole—and truthfully, he was beginning to feel like it was really *him* who was the intolerable asshole.

He walked toward the main drag, moping. He'd killed people. He'd eaten people. And for some reason, it was all beginning to feel crappy to him. Before it had been fun. It had been the razz that only the trick of power can give. Something had changed.

He didn't know how, but he knew his army was gone. The blood painting the buildings down the main drag confirmed his intuition, and now the zombie king felt like a week-old bag of dog shit. He needed comfort. He needed consolation. He needed love, and so he was looking for Brenda, his queen.

When he did find her, everything just got worse.

Brenda was lying in two halves behind the tavern: her legs tangled beneath a mass of gore that stretched across the pavement to her torso. Her lifeless eyes glinted gray under the bright blue sky. Her face was frozen in a surprised expression.

"Oh no," Asher's voice cracked as he slumped to his knees. "No, no, no."

He cradled his queen's head in his lap, rocking back and forth until the words would no longer come. He pressed his forehead against hers, and if it hadn't happened before, here the king's mind finally broke.

"I'm sorry," he said. "I'm so sorry."

Everything fell away: the defeat, the sadness, the pain, the hunger, the guilt—it all slipped through the cracks until all that was left was darkness. Ash sat there, letting blackness steep his heart, unable to let go of his love. There was nothing left—*he* was nothing. Then something glimmered in the darkness. Something burning white-hot, taking over every cranny of his sanity. His mind lit up like a New York Christmas with this new sensation.

Revenge.

He found a hammer lying in the wreckage and picked it up with a twisted grin.

Al Kowalski made it a block before the tears caught up with him. He trudged on, heading down an alleyway next to the bakery that lead to the riverwalk. In what seemed like another lifetime, Al had come here on lunch breaks to think, watching the water as it moved its ceaseless mass toward the falls. The world keeps turning: when he was having a bad day, remembering that one little fact—remembering how insanely tiny he was in the grand scheme of things—always helped get his perspective in check.

He didn't think it'd do the trick now, but he didn't care. He just needed to sit down and cry.

As he came out of the alley, Al couldn't help but noticed the bullet-ridden Honda Civic with a busted window parked behind the building. It was the same car Boris Volydeskvi had been driving before the gunfight. Inside the driver's seat, a figure slumped over the wheel, snoring violently into the dash. An empty bottle of vodka lay on the passenger's seat.

Al put his hand on his holster and edged over to the car. The figure snorted, puttered, and continued to doze. It was Olaf Vloydeskvi. The sheriff recognized the wiry old man from the case file Reyes had shown him.

He pulled out his revolver, reached in through the Civic's broken driver's side, and smacked the Russian in the back of the head with the gun.

"Mother Russia!"

"Well, howdy, Olaf," Al said.

CHAPTER 33
RETURN OF THE LIVING

Wiz's clothes clung to his body as he dragged himself up the stairs from the pit. The back of his head throbbed, somewhere along the way he'd bitten through his lower lip, and a row of deep gouges ran across his shoulder where the dog had slashed. His eyes were still adjusting: it was like he'd taken the world's biggest bong rip and stared directly into the sun for six hours.

He reached the top of the staircase and slumped on the floor beside Ava, who was sitting splay-legged, rubbing her eyes.

"Hi," he said.

"Wiz? Oh my god, your neck! Are you okay?"

"I think so... How can you even see anything right now?"

"But, the sacrifice? The dog, the Baron... What happened?"

Wiz shrugged, producing a ragged-looking joint from his shirt pocket and planting it between his lips. "I improvised."

There was a long pause as Ava surveyed the blood-covered chamber. "I think it kinda worked."

"Not bad for a slacker, right?" He chuckled and went to light the joint when Ava snatched it from his lips, shaking her head.

"Nuh-uh. No more joints, remember?" She gave a reproachful look, bouncing an eyebrow.

"But—"

"You *said*."

"I just stabbed two gods with a sword and averted the end of the world!"

"Nope," Ava chuckled. "You are a drug addict, and I will not be your enabler, do you hear me, mister?"

She gave him that look women in the movies always do right before they kiss somebody. By now, Wiz realized she was goofing him and was grinning too.

But she didn't kiss him. He didn't kiss her, either.

They took each other in their arms and kissed each other, and if there'd been a soundtrack, this is where it would have swooned.

"Ow. Ow. Ow." Wiz said, his split lip lighting up in agony.

"Sorry."

They kissed again.

What felt like a lifetime later, Ava broke away. "Hey, wait a second. What about the portal thingie?"

They both looked back at the pit. Wiz lit the joint. "There's gotta be a way to close it—"

With a rattling groan, the great metal plate slipped off the spike at the top of the chamber and slammed onto the open gate to the underworld. A cloud of dust erupted as the huge iron hinges all whirred to life and sealed it off. Then, the pancaked body of Boris Vloydeskvi flopped on top of it.

"Well, okay then," Ava said, putting her arm around Wiz's waist.

Wiz passed her the joint, exhaling a huge cloud of smoke. "You wanna get out of here?"

Noah Carpenter was hunched on a barstool next to the reopened entrance of the Gnarled Wood Tavern, watching the flaming pile of zombie parts cast a ribbon of black smoke into the air. It smelled like rotten barbecue, and for the first time in his life, the yogi was seriously considering going vegetarian.

"I'm hungry," Hal Pearson said, leaning on the doorframe with a bottle of beer.

The patrons were all inside the Wood, taking a break from

their hopeless attempts at playing cleanup crew for the apocalypse. Amy rested against the side of the bar with her arms crossed. She gave the linebacker a tired expression.

"You're disgusting."

Noah lit a cigarette. "Do either of you guys know anything about tofu? I don't know what it is, but I'm thinking about eating it for the rest of my life."

"*That's* disgusting," Hal said.

"I hear it's pretty good in stir-fry," Amy said.

"What about burgers," Hal said. "How about we go for burgers later?"

Despite himself, Noah's stomach grumbled. He shook his head. "No money, nothing's open."

"Come on guys," the linebacker said. "We're like town heroes or something. We don't need money. We'll eat for free!"

Amy chuckled. "You do realize that saving the world and changing it are different things, right?"

Down the main drag, two figures walked hand-in-hand up the middle of the street. Noah noticed, pitching his cigarette and leaping off his stool when he recognized them.

"I don't fucking believe it."

He broke out in a sprint down the main drag, meeting Wiz and Ava as they came up to the tavern.

"I don't fucking believe it," he repeated. "You're alive!"

"Yeah, barely," Wiz said. Ava had him slung over her shoulder. The two of them were covered in blood.

"We need the doctor," Ava said as Noah helped her carry Wiz. "He's hurt pretty bad."

"What happened?"

Wiz groaned as they brought him over to the tavern. "Oh, you know… It's complicated. Where's the Doc?"

Noah's grin faded. "He uh… He didn't make it."

Wiz blinked. "What?"

Ava bowed head with a long sigh.

"Jenny too," Noah continued, feeling like a bucket of ass-cheese. "The goblins… They got them."

Wiz took an exhausted breath. "Not Al?"

"No, the sheriff's still alive. He uh... He went kinda mental. He tried to take on the whole goblin army with a machete and a pistol."

"That's my brother," Wiz shook his head. "Where is he?"

"I honestly couldn't say," Noah shrugged. "He clobbered the agent and took off after this crazy light blasted the goblins."

"Yeah, we had that too," Wiz said. "Wait a sec... Where's my van?"

Shit. Noah had hoped to dodge breaking the news about Franz, Jenny *and* Wiz's van. "We uh... We kinda blew it up."

Wiz's eyes went wide. "You *what*?"

Noah hung his head, feeling strange that breaking the news of the van was harder than breaking the news about their friends. "The zombies were getting back up. We had to stop them so we rigged your van with propane tanks, a bunch of sharp things and blew them up."

Wiz thought about it. "That's actually kind of awesome," he said. "Except for the part where you *blew up my van*, Noah."

Noah threw his hands in the air. "I thought you were dead!"

"Exactly!" Wiz said. "And what's the first thing you do after that? You *blow up* my *van*? I mean... Who even does that?"

Noah wagged his head, totally unsure if his friend was just messing with him. "We were all out of options."

"I know," Wiz sighed, putting a hand on his roommate's bicep and squeezing. "I totally get it. It's just"—he shook his head woefully—"that van was my baby, man! Is anybody else dead?"

"Well, yeah. A whole army of zombies for starters. Hey— what happened to the little guy with the hat? The evil talking dog? The ritual?"

Wiz put his arm around Noah and said, "It's a long story, and I think we'll all have to get really blazed for it. Why don't you tell me about this big pile of burning zombie parts you've got going on?"

Ava squeezed Wiz's hand. "I'm going to go clean up and get some bandages. You're gonna need stitches."

Wiz nodded. "Noah and I are going to continue talking about this zombie bonfire."

"Don't let me stop you," she kissed him. "You kids have fun."

With that, she walked into the tavern.

Noah helped Wiz over to the burning pile of flesh. The two produced cigarettes. They smoked.

After a while, Wiz frowned. "It smells like burgers."

Noah chuckled. "That's what I said. Gross, right?"

"Whatever," Wiz sighed, flicking his cigarette into the smoldering heap. "I'm just glad it's over."

"It isn't," came a voice from behind them.

Asher Cravington brought the hammer in a brutal swing. With a meaty *thunk*, Wiz yelped and crumpled to the ground. Noah spun in full-blown attack mode, which was slightly understated by the fact that he didn't have a weapon.

"No!"

The zombie king stood over Wiz's prostrated body, frowning. He tilted his head, almost curiously.

"You killed her."

"Wiz!" Ava said, dropping the first aid kit when she reached the tavern's entrance.

Noah looked around for a weapon, but unless he planned to bludgeon the zombie to death with a charred arm, he was hopeless.

The zombie's face twisted with grief as his gaze moved to Noah.

"I loved her! You fucks cut her in two and just left her there... I loved her!"

He swung. Noah ducked, his arms coming up to block the blow. The hammer connected with a sickening crunch and blinding pain barked up to the yogi's shoulder. He shrieked, falling to his knees.

Ash brandished the hammer, an insane grin splitting his face.

"My turn." He brought the hammer overhead and lunged.

Then, there was a sound like snapping a banjo string, and the tip of an arrow appeared in the center of the zombie king's forehead with a great spurt of blood.

"I don't think so," said Travis Schwartz, appearing behind Asher, holding a crossbow—definitely *not* dead. He was wearing a grimy white T-shirt and jeans, and over the course of the night he'd apparently picked up a leather jacket and an eyepatch. He looked like a B-movie god.

"Moron," Ash chuckled as blood dribbled down his face. "You really haven't learned the *destroying the brain* thing doesn't work, have you?"

"Actually," Trav said cooly, pulling something out of his jacket. "I'm counting on it. I want you awake for this part, *Corpse Bride*."

Noah watched the zombie king prod the length of the arrow. Attached to the end of it was a twelve-inch length of black piping. The cap at the end had a little green light blinking next to an antenna. Ash's face widened in confused panic.

"Whaaa?"

What he didn't know, was the linebacker was headed to Stanford next year on full academic scholarship. His study of choice? Electrical Engineering.

"Pipe bomb, bitch." Trav grinned, holding a small box with a big red button. He pressed it. The light on the end of the pipe switched from green to red, and the device let out a high-pitched bleeping sound.

Asher struggled as the bleeps went faster and faster.

"Uh-oh."

The bomb exploded, splattering the zombie king's entire upper half across the street in a brilliant cloud of pink mist.

Trav tossed the detonator away and helped Noah to his feet.

"You're alive," Noah grunted as another wave of pain crashed over him. He was pretty sure his arm was broken.

"'Course I am. Check on Wiz."

Noah nodded and stumbled over to his friend. There was no blood. It didn't look like he'd been hit in the head. He rolled Wiz onto his back as Trav adjusted his eye patch and started messing with his hair.

"Uh... Is Amy — "

"Alive?" a voice came from the crumbled entrance of the tavern. "Yup, still here."

She came out smiling, and nearly knocked the linebacker off his feet with a tackling kiss. After a moment, she pulled away.

"You look like a pirate."

Trav frowned. "Really? I was going for sexy mercenary. But if it's a pirate she wants, then... Yarrrrgh! Avast!! and... stuff."

Hal Pearson came out of the bar and discovered his best friend not only alive and all the more badass from the apocalypse, but also tongue-deep in Amy's face.

"Dude, you're alive."

"Duh."

The big slab of muscle sniffled back a tear. "And you've got an eyepatch."

"I know."

Hal wagged his head. "That is like the most badass thing I have ever seen."

And here, the waterworks started flowing.

Wiz wasn't moving. Noah looked for a pulse while all the heartwarming going on in front of the bar seemed to suck away.

"Guys..." he said, "I don't think he's breathing."

CHAPTER 34
SO... THAT HAPPENED

The Wizard floated through blackness. Ava Elridge walked out of the shadows wearing a grin. She wrapped her arms around his neck and pressed her lips against his. There was no feeling, no sound, no existence beyond the kiss. Wiz closed his eyes. He slipped his tongue in her mouth, his hands reaching around the small of her waist. From somewhere above, light played across the surface of unseen water.

Ava pulled away, still smiling.

"Gross," she said in a man's voice.

Wiz bolted awake on the ground in front of the smouldering remains of the dead. Noah Carpenter stooped over him, wiping his mouth with a disgusted expression. Noah, Ava, Amy, Travis and Hal all stood around him in a horseshoe.

"What the hell?"

Everyone let out a relieved sigh. Noah flopped backward, wiping at his tongue as he furrowed his brow.

"Ack!" he said. "You know, just because somebody saves your life doesn't mean you're obligated to give them tongue action."

"What are you—" Wiz went to get up when blinding pain rocketed down the back of his neck. "Ow! Ow! Ow!"

"Ow-ow is right," Amy said with an amused expression.

"What happened?" Wiz wagged his head as Noah helped him to his feet.

"A zombie knocked you out with a hammer, I gave you CPR and you slipped me tongue is what happened," Noah said.

"You mean I?'

"Yup."

"But I—I mean you—I mean, I thought you were—" He looked at Noah, then at Ava, then back at Noah, a sense of panic rising in his gut. "...Oh."

"Yeah," Noah said. "So that happened."

Well, this was awkward. Wiz sighed as Ava came over and kissed his cheek.

"I thought I'd lost you."

"Yeah," Wiz furrowed his brow. "I thought he was you."

Everyone gave him a confused expression. Wiz went to explain, then let out a long sigh. "I require copious amounts of cannabis."

"I'll second that," Noah said.

"Food first," Hal said. "Pot later. I'm starved!"

Max Reyes awoke on the steering wheel of his BMW with a groan. His jaw felt like he'd fallen asleep on an angle grinder. His head throbbed, and he rose from the wheel, going to prod at his recently socked chin when something caught him by the wrist.

He was handcuffed to the wheel.

"Ugh," he moaned. His keys dangled under the steering column. His gaze met itself in the rear view. The word DOUCHE had been scrawled on his forehead in Sharpie. Something moved in the backseat. He twisted and found Olaf Vloydeskvi, lying like a stuffed pig in the back seat with his arms zip-tied behind his back.

"I want to make phone call," said the Russian.

"You have the right to remain silent," Reyes said, reaching over and twisting the key in the ignition. "And I seriously advise you use it."

The Russian groaned.

Max put the car in gear and pointed it at the exit for the highway. He could almost taste the vacation. As he peeled off down the road, he imagined the smell of shaving cream, and a grin spread across his face.

They walked out of Pizza Shack, Wiz and Ava wrapped in each other's arms; Trav and Amy hand-in-hand, Noah and Hal on either side. Wiz filled his pipe with what was left of his personal stash and they passed it back and forth, walking down the main drag toward the river.

Wiz passed the pipe to Ava.

"I'm sorry I kissed him."

"Hey!" Noah said. "Don't blame yourself. It's my yogi charm."

Wiz laughed and squeezed his roommate's shoulder. "Dude… I'm sorry I shot your zombie aunt in the face earlier."

Noah waved him off, taking the pipe from Ava. "Sorry I blew up your van."

Wiz sighed. "You did what you had to do. We all did."

"Come on," Noah said. "I know a shortcut."

They took a left at the alley leading to the riverwalk. When Noah reached the other side of the alleyway, he froze.

"Holy shit!"

"What?" Wiz said.

"Holy shit!"

"What?!"

"Dude, it's my fucking car! I don't believe it."

Wiz looked at Ava, confused. She shrugged and they all came out into the opening behind the buildings. There was Noah's car, riddled with bullet holes. An empty bottle of vodka lay on the passenger's seat. The yogi went over and popped the hatchback.

"Yes! It's still here."

"What's still here?" Wiz said.

"The pot, you tool. We got our two pounds back." Noah howled in victory, pulling the two bricks of Red Leopard out of the trunk.

Wiz chuckled, putting his arm around Ava. "Remember the Russians?"

"Problem solved," she grinned and leaned over for a kiss when a man's voice came from behind.

"Uh, excuse me?"

Wiz nearly jumped out of his skin—a sensation he was getting seriously sick of.

"Woah! God. Jeez, Lenny. Please never sneak up on me again."

Lenny and Hunt both shuffled awkwardly over to the gang.

"Sorry," the old guy said, his forehead turning a bright shade of pink. "Well, this is awkward…"

"What," Noah said. "The fact that you made him scream like a girl? Or the fact that the two of them can't stop sucking face now that the crisis is over?"

"Uh, I'm going with *both*," Hunt said.

"Yeah, ditto," Lenny said. "Look, Scoobies. I hate to bother you right now, and—well—this is my first time ever doing this… But do you think we could score some pot off you?"

Hunt nodded, crossing his arms.

Wiz panned back and forth between the old guys, wagging his head. "Really?"

"We have money," Hunt said.

Lenny nodded. "Just waiting for the bank to open."

Wiz stroked his beard. "How much?"

Lenny sighed, sheepishly. He rubbed the back of his neck. "We uh… Kinda wanted all of it."

Noah blinked. "*Seriously*?"

"Guys," Wiz said. "That's not exactly ATM withdrawal kinda money you're looking at."

"We just inherited ten-thousand dollars from a zombie," Lenny said.

"Deal."

Noah sighed and handed the bricks over to the old guys. "I guess it kinda goes without saying that if you don't pay us in the next two days, your knees are broken… Or something."

"We know," Lenny said.

Wiz felt like the old guys were getting the wrong impression of how he liked to do business.

"He's just kidding about the knee-breaking. You guys are all-good. Just call me when you have the cash. But I gotta say, man... That's a *lot* of weed for two newbies. I'm kind of an expert."

"We know." And here Wiz could see the sadness in the old dude's eyes.

Hunt put a hand on his buddy's shoulder. "We've been through a lot."

Wiz nodded. "I think we all have."

"Mind if we take a pinch off the top?" Noah said. "We just ran out."

Ava leaned on the hatch of the Civic, shaking her head as the old guys broke off a half-pound of the weed and handed it to the yogi. Wiz walked over and shrugged.

"What?"

"You guys never change."

Noah walked the old guys back to the main drag with his arm around Lenny, making friendly but startlingly not subtle threats about the consequences of failed payment to drug dealers.

"Hey," Wiz said. "That's not entirely true."

Ava gave him a quizzical eyebrow.

"I mean... We *never* forward the product before payment on a deal like this."

She kissed him, then walked off, shaking her head. This time, she didn't need an inner-voice to question exactly what she'd gotten herself into.

After several showers, a pot of coffee, and a bottle of Pepto Bismol, Sheriff Al Kowalski returned to the office. He wasn't sure why he'd come. All he knew was, being in the house he'd shared with Jenny was too painful. Everything looked the same. Nothing about the place had changed, and that was what killed him: everywhere he looked, tiny reminders of the love he'd lost.

It was all too new—too raw—for him to suffer. The office was his hideaway. His mountain of paperwork was there waiting for him. The sun fanned in through the blinds. It was exactly as he'd left it, just like the house. Everything the same, but different.

Grief hung around the sheriff like a cowl.

The reasoning part of his head told him it would be this way for a long time, but like everything in life, time would make it better. How long was anyone's guess. He'd survived. A new day had broken, and here he was. There was no going back. There was no undoing of the things that had happened. Things, generally speaking, move forward. There's nothing any of us can do about that.

So, like many widowers before him, Al poured another cup of coffee and poured his grief into his work. He'd keep at it until the mountain became a molehill. He'd slog paperwork until there was nothing left to file—and by then, there would surely be more.

Jenny wouldn't want to see him hit bottom. If her death drove him there, then evil really had won. She wouldn't want his life to wind up that way. So, either out of obligation or choice, he went on, because that's just what people do.

EPILOGUE
LIFE UNLEASHED

Life isn't easy. Would that every story ended happily, every crisis be averted, everything get a pretty shiny bow, but that's not the world we live in. Life is harsh. Things go wrong, People get hurt, and some even die. That's just the way it goes.

Life moves forward. There's really no avoiding it. For better or for worse, the big wheel of time keeps turning. Through happiness, through pain, through bumps and scrapes and all the windfalls, life continues relentlessly.

Where it leads? That's anyone's guess. Life is a mystery, an enigma. The second it seems to be all figured out, it changes course, dancing and occasionally tripping up our expectations. It goes on. People rebuild. It's just what we do.

The people of Oak Falls came together again to put their town back together after the Almost-pocalypse. They cleaned. They comforted. They shared. In the wake of an enormous catastrophe, they did what is all that any of us can do: they moved forward, headlong into the unknown.

Still, since we all would gaze the crystal ball a spell, a taste of future to whet your pallet.

LINEBACKERS

Trav left Oak Falls as soon as the summer was up. He went on to grab a degree in electrical engineering, making things blow up in newer and better ways than he'd ever imagined. He moved to Stanford with his girlfriend, Amy Savage in the fall, using the money from his endeavors with the Wizard to pay the way.

About a year later, his buddy Hal Pearson joined them, and years later the two would be responsible for creating the first Artificial Intelligence that didn't shut itself off after reading Hemmingway.

AMY

After the ordeal with the zombies, Amy returned to school where she was pre-med. She and Trav would spend long nights drinking, dancing, talking, having sex, arguing, arguing while having sex, dancing while arguing about having sex—and generally doing all the things young couples do. Her aunt and uncle would return, and give Amy her first ever one-star-rating as a babysitter, citing "letting the child be murdered by undead cannibals" as the prime reason for no one to ever trust her with a kid again.

After a few months of struggling, Amy would eventually find a well-paying job as a stripper and her college bills would pay themselves after three months of objectifying herself to the hungry gaze of middle-aged men in need of a pick-me-up. She'd never admit it to Travis, but it was the most fun she'd ever had involving a pole.

That is, aside from the antics the two got into behind closed doors, and what happened there… Well, that's none of your business.

LANETTE

In the years that followed the Oak Falls massacre, life moved on as it always had for the barkeep. Every year, tourists would pour in. She'd pour them overpriced cocktails, and they'd leave with the vague recollection of being an idiot.

Eventually, word spread of Oak Falls in the way the strange happenings of Roswell, New Mexico had years before. From all around, people would come looking for a snapshot of the supernatural, and when they found none, they'd find the Gnarled Wood Tavern and have a few drinks.

She retired Betsy to a display behind the bar, but the sawed-off Glenda would remain a prominent fixture: the empty keg filled up with bullets, and Lanette kept making threats at passers-by.

She kept an extra three kegs in the back, along with enough ammunition to mow down a small country, because you never knew when crisis would strike—or better yet, more tourists.

NOAH

Noah Carpenter eventually retired from the yoga industry to pursue the martial arts. He spent eleven years traveling the Far East to learn the craft, and after earning a black belt in every fighting sport you could shake an angry stick at, he returned to Oak Falls, opened his own dojo on the main drag, and has been servicing the skin-tight lycra crowd looking to kick ass ever since.

He never fully understood his clients' enthusiasm for defending themselves against yoga teachers, but only a finite amount of people ever really learn.

THE COUNCIL

Shortly after the cleanup, the townspeople discovered the remaining zombies hanging out in the old town hall. After a weeklong standoff, the townsfolk and undead reached a truce. In exchange for quitting cannibalism, the zombies would request the duty of running the town.

They switched to cow, and after a few uneasy months as the new council members settled into their roles, the people of Oak Falls discovered that even with a bunch of zombified ex-cannibals running the show, not much changed.

AL KOWALSKI

After another three years of sheriffing Oak Falls, Al retired. He moved to Hollywood and acted as a screenwriting consultant on a bunch of cop movies people would never go to watch. Two years after that, he started dating a makeup artist named Ashley, and the two settled down after five years of working together.

Before he left Oak Falls, he placed a motion with the town council to elect Noah Carpenter as the next Sheriff of the county, and after a good amount of deliberation, they agreed.

He now lives in a cottage with Ashley, and to this day, Al has never watched a zombie movie.

THE OLD GUYS

Hunt and Lenny eventually smoked their way through the stash the Wizard sold them. Both of them went on to being successful novelists: Lenny being a romance writer and Hunt a renowned author of Cold War espionage stories. Both would go on to having at least two of their works turned to film — and both would refuse offers to write horror screenplays, citing the tastelessness of the genre as their main reason.

Neither would play poker again.

REYES

Retirement ran from Max Reyes's scope like a rabbit who knows it's being hunted. Olaf Vloydeskvi had earned him the confidence of the agency, and his very next mission, tracking down the Italian mob's coke distributors in Boston, would end with him nursing three bullet holes in a hospital ward while his superiors figured out a way to fire him.

He would find himself in a Las Vegas casino years later, divorced, drunk, and wondering how he got there. The only time he thought about the things he'd seen in Oak Falls was when he had nightmares — which is to say, every night for the rest of his life.

He still chain-smoked himself to sleep, and he still dreamed of burning alive. But even today, the agent hasn't figured it out.

THE COVEN

For the three who had seen what was coming, very little changed in the lives of Margy, Suzanne, and Ellie. After a three-month retreat to Hawaii to better find themselves, the only change any of them had to adjust to was when a crew of muscly workmen changed the sign above Ava's Bakery and Cafe to Ignatio's Gourmet Desserts and Coffee.

They went on reading *The Abridged Encyclopedia of Dreams for Divas, Vol. II*. The fact that everything they dreamed was for someone else in town never dawned on them.

BADGER

Badger went on to have a successful career as a consultant working for the DEA. In three years time, he'd replace Max Reyes as the chief in undercover work for most of California.

After ten years of service, the agency would grant him early retirement based off his extensive catch record. By age thirty-seven, he'd quit smoking pot entirely, although by age fifty he'd developed a rather nasty drinking problem to cope with the stress of the job.

WIZ AND AVA

Wiz and Ava spent the autumn taking over the Russians' abandoned camp in an unknown corner of the Big Sur wilderness area. After a healthy harvest, they used the profits to migrate to San Francisco, where they married trades, establishing the state's most successful medical marijuana dispensary: Wiz procuring the strains of weed while Ava made the shop's supply of buzzing treats.

They lived well. The honeymoon period would eventually wear off, but there was no denying the two had potential to make it work — hell, once upon a time, it had been their destiny to be together. What was certain was they loved each other, and when you've got that you can pretty much trump whatever else comes your way.

It would take a good amount of work, a considerable amount of patience, and an unfathomable amount of foot rubs, but in the end — at least for a while — they lived happily.

What happened to the raptor bat is another story altogether.

ACKNOWLEDGEMENTS

I must tip hats, severs, and cows to the following peeps. To my beta-readers: Terry McMillan, Stephanie Kilbank, Vanessa Ricci-Thode, and Ian Wienert, thanks for the thoughtful reads and comments. You've been lovely.

To my superstar-ninja editor, Aidan Cullis, for making me look significantly smarter—I owe you an uncountable amount of deep-fried pickles.

Jacob Leonard, thanks for all your patience: the long and often boozy nights hearing my ideas and ramblings. Skot Lachance, my rogue illustrator, friend, and general swell dude. To my trusty encouragers, Carla Voellmecke, Ben van Duyvendyk, Andy Joy—thanks.

To Christopher Moore, for the line that opens this passage, the ace advice on penmonkeying, and the countless good reads over the years. I hope it probably honors you as much as you wished. Muchos, gracias.

Haley Wolk; my sister Melanie; my parents, Alastair, Denise, and Manal Younger—well, let's be honest. You can only blame yourselves.

And ultimately, this is for you, reader. If you got this far, I owe you a debt beyond acknowledgement. You're the reason I did it—so, I mean… If you hated it? Totally your fault. There's really no one else you can hold responsible.

ABOUT THE AUTHOR

DANIEL YOUNGER is Amazon's least-known bestselling author of *Delirious: A Collection of Stories*. He lives in Canada (Eh?), where he mushes a pack of wild huskies next to a river of maple syrup every morning. He enjoys spicy food, gourmet coffee, beaver-racing, and acid jazz. You can e-mail him at danieljyounger@icloud.com, or find him causing a ruckus on Twitter @youngerdaniel.